# NO MAN'S LAND

Matt shimmied up the tallest pine he could see. Higher and higher he climbed, until the top swayed with his weight. Then he shaded his eyes and looked around.

Natchez lay behind him, just on the horizon. Beyond it lay the Mississippi. But the great river was far away—much, much farther than Matt had hoped. He craned his neck to see the other way. The wood stretched as far as he could see. Wilderness, all of it. Full of snakes, alligators, bear and wildcat, as well as beasts of the two-legged variety. And him with no rifle, and a woman to protect. And the biggest problem lay in finding a safe and sure way through the five hundred miles of wild country between Natchez and Nashville. Matt groaned out loud with the hopelessness of it.

Then, somehow, his eyes began to make out something in the trees. It was a trail, he realized, his heart leaping. He knew what that trail was, and the thought of what might lie ahead made the skin prickle on the back of his neck. This was the infamous trail, the one he'd heard blessed and cursed by so many tongues. This was the Natchez Trace.

# WHITEWATER DYNASTY
# THE MISSISSIPPI!

## BY HELEN LEE POOLE

**ZEBRA BOOKS**
**KENSINGTON PUBLISHING CORP.**

ZEBRA BOOKS

are published by

Kensington Publishing Corp.
475 Park Avenue South
New York, N.Y. 10016

First printing: August, 1984

Printed in the United States of America

# I

Matthew Forny Cooper cursed under his breath. One big hand reached down and groped at the stout bramble twig that had embedded itself in the seat of his breeches. He jerked it sharply away, a bead of crimson blood appearing on the tip of his finger.

It was all Slocum's fault, he thought, dabbing at his pricked finger with the end of his tongue. If that blasted dog hadn't run off into the woods after a squirrel, and if Matt hadn't gone after him, they'd have been halfway home by now. As it was, they'd be late for supper, and Matt, as usual, was hungry. Worse, if he walked in the door with another rip in his pants, his mother would give him the devil.

Gingerly he strained at the bramble. It was firmly caught. He could not pull loose without ripping his trousers. Matt cursed again. If only he hadn't dropped his knife in the river while he was cleaning the fish he'd caught. At least he'd have a chance of cutting himself free. But here he was, snared like a possum in a trap and feeling like a total fool.

He thought about his mother and father.

They'd warned him before about getting home on time to eat with the rest of the family. They'd be annoyed all right. It wasn't fair, Matt thought grumpily. He was nineteen years old and he could outrace and outfight any boy in Louisville. At least he ought to be able to come and go as he liked.

"Slocum! Come on, boy!" Matt whistled softly. "Come on, you good for nothin'—" but the dog was nowhere in sight. Probably all the way to the riverbank now, Matt thought forlornly. He'd named Slocum after the trader who'd given him the puppy four years ago. The name, however, had proved to be an apt joke. "Slow-come," Matt's younger brothers and sisters called the big yellow mutt. You could whistle for him all day and he wouldn't pay any heed. Then, just when you were about to give up, he'd come loping around the corner of the house, his mean little eyes bright with mischief, his long, pink tongue slathering happily.

"Slocum!" Matt strained his ears. He could hear nothing but the twitter of birds and the distant sound of the falls. Well, let the damned dog go, he thought. Slocum always came home by nightfall anyway. He had problems of his own right now, and the most urgent was getting loose.

The brambles surrounded him on three sides now, high as his head, and deceptively pretty with their froth of white spring blossoms. But they had wicked thorns that could grab onto a body like claws, ripping and tearing when they were pulled loose. And Matt's breeches were new. Why, they'd only been washed twice. Cautiously he reached back and inspected the place where the prickly branch was caught. He couldn't see it, not even when he twisted backward and craned his neck. But he was caught fast, all right. He sighed. There was only one thing to do: step out of his pants so that he could see what he was doing, then work the stickers loose as best he could.

Matt lowered his head and began to push the thin wooden buttons through their holes. He'd finished the right side and was starting on the left when the sound of a twig snapping somewhere beyond the screen of the brambles froze him like a statue.

Someone—or something—was coming, moving slowly in Matt's direction.

Indians? That was the first thought that flashed through Matt's mind. He'd spent enough of his boyhood years in a state of constant watchfulness for those red devils. The old fears died slowly. But there hadn't been any Indian trouble along the Ohio for five years, not since 1794, when Mad Anthony Wayne smashed them once and for all at Fallen Timbers. No, it couldn't be Indians, Matt decided, and it didn't move like Slocum. Slocum would be all over him by now, tail thrashing, tongue slobbering in his face—

Voices. Matt tensed as he heard them. A boy's voice and a girl's, and both of them sounded familiar. Ever so cautiously, Matt leaned forward, peering through the tall screen of brambles. There was a little clearing on the other side, sun-filled, and lined with young, green grass.

"See, 'told ye, there ain't nobody knows 'bout this place, 'ceptin' me!" The boy spoke as they came into sight. Matt swallowed hard as he recognized him. It was Aaron Weir, a good friend of his. And the girl was Elvina Hastings, who lived up the road from the Cooper house. Matt had heard stories about Elvina, but he'd never known if they were true.

"We be alone, all right." Elvina glanced around. She was a stocky girl with carrot-red hair, green eyes and a freckle-spattered face. She wasn't really pretty, though she wasn't bad. Her breasts, however, were objects of awe among the young men of the settlement—twin mounds that thrust out ahead of her, filling the bodice of her dress to the bursting point. "Ye see Elviny's tits go past and ye know the rest of 'er'll be along in a minute or two," Matt had heard one young buck remark with a leering grin, and he'd laughed along with the others. There'd been a good deal of speculation about what Elvina would look like without her clothes, and one or two of the boys claimed to have seen her. They weren't the kind of fellows you could believe one way or the other, though.

Matt winced as the needle-sharp tip of the bramble dug into the tender flesh of his rump. Damnation! Here he was, caught like a fool, his pants half unhitched, and they were coming right

8

toward him. If he so much as moved a muscle they'd see him. What would he do then? Aaron and Elvina stopped just a few paces from the spot where Matt was standing. No, they couldn't see him, he decided. The brambles were thick, and he was standing in the shadows, while they were in the sunlight. But he could see them well enough, all right. A fly landed on Matt's nose. He wiggled it away, and it came buzzing back again.

"You gonna show me like you promised?" Aaron demanded.

Elvina wagged her head reproachfully. "Don't ye know nothin'? Ye don't jest stand up to a girl and say, 'Well, let's see 'em.' Ye got to get her in the mood, so she'll want to let ye. Ain't you ever been with a girl afore?"

Matt, watching, drew in his breath. His palms felt damp. He'd heard Aaron brag about how he was going to figure out a way to get a look at Elvina. Maybe he'd bribed her with a length of calico from his father's store. That sounded like something Aaron Weir might do. Aaron wasn't very handsome, with his long, bony face and wire-thin frame, but at least he knew how to get what he wanted.

"Well?" Elvina stood facing him, hands on her broad hips. Without a word, Aaron jerked her hard against his chest. His open mouth found hers in a long, grinding kiss that bent her backward over his arm. Matt, watching, licked his lips nervously. Damnation! What he wouldn't give to be someplace else.

Aaron and Elvina broke apart at last; both of them were breathing hard. "Glory be, but ye know how to set a body a'tingle!" she exclaimed. "I'll take another o' those, Master Aaron Weir!" She melted against him this time, her arms slithering up around Aaron's neck, her big, round rump twitching as Aaron's thin arms ranged up and down her back, groping for buttons, fumbling them loose one by one. Matt could almost feel the heat coming from them. He could hear Elvina moaning softly as Aaron worked her dress down off her shoulders and slipped off the straps of her camisole. Elvina's breasts tumbled out like two quivering, white melons, the nipples brown and shriveled and plump as raisins.

"Oh, Lordy!" Aaron gasped. His hands hefted the twin globes, feeling the soft, warm weight of them. Matt could almost feel them himself. His face was hot. His breath rattled in his ears. The fly was crawling along his nose now, but he was scarcely aware of it. He had never seen a girl naked like that before, not unless you counted occasional flashing glimpses of his sisters, and they were no match for Elvina.

She reached for Aaron's head and pulled it down to her bosom. "Suck me," she moaned. "Oh, lordy, Aaron, suck me!" The left nipple and most of the soft, mauve circle around it slid into Aaron's mouth, and Matt heard licking, smacking noises. A trickle of sweat ran down his face. He caught it with his tongue. He was faintly aware of a growing ache somewhere down between his legs, but the sharpest sensation of all was the prick of the brambles in his butt. He breathed a little curse and blew at the tickling fly.

Elvina's hips were pitching and rolling like a bullboat shooting the rapids. "Oooh!" she breathed. "Oh, Aaron, the other one, too. Oh Lord, don't stop! Don't—" Her voice rose in a gasp as Aaron's hand slid up her skirt and clasped the curve of her rump, but that fascinating, undulating motion of her hips went right on.

"The whole damned bolt if you'll let me do it!" Aaron rasped, the nipple popping wetly out of his mouth. But he needn't have even asked, because Elvina's fingers were already tugging at the buttons on his pants. Matt swallowed hard. She knew what she was about, all right, that Elvina. Probably done it a few times before. But he'd known Aaron for years, and he'd bet a good string of perch that for Aaron it was the first time.

Matt closed his eyes and tried not to look at them. It wasn't even decent, standing here like this and watching them. Damn it, if *he* was in Aaron's place, he wouldn't want anybody looking. But he just couldn't help it. What was happening on the other side of those bushes held him just as fast as the brambles in the seat of his pants.

She had Aaron's trouser flap open now. Aaron groaned loudly and fumbled with the waist of her dress. Matt's face reddened as he felt the tight strain against the crotch of his own trousers. He licked his lips in embarrassment—and in envy.

"Here—" Elvina, impatient, reached back

11

and unhooked the dress with one hand. It fell around her in a circle. With a little tug at a bow-tied string and a little shimmy of those ample hips, she dropped her pantalets as well. Matt caught his breath. The bush between her plump white thighs was as red as her hair.

Aaron muttered something that Matt could not understand as he pulled Elvina down into the grass and rolled awkwardly on top of her, making odd little grunts. Matt clenched his fists. His body felt as taut as a Shawnee bowstring. So this was what it looked like, the thing that all the boys talked about, joked about, wondered about, bragged about. This was what was supposed to make you into a man. But, Lord's mercy, it was torture on a body to see it like this. Like watching somebody bite into a haunch of juicy beef when you were starving.

Matt didn't want to think of Winifred, not now, of all times, when he was in enough torment already, but she had crept into his mind and now she wouldn't go away. Winifred had been his sweetheart for nigh onto six months now. And if he said he'd never thought about doing this with her, well, he'd be lying. Winifred was a pretty girl, with yellow curls and round, blue eyes, a little bit plump, maybe, although she wasn't in a class with Elvina. In some things, nobody was. But Winifred was prettier.

Matt had kissed her plenty of times, down by the river in the afternoon shade, and at night in the shadow of the big sycamore that grew along-

12

side her fence. Once he'd laid a hand on her breast, both of them quivering like frightened rabbits until he took it away. The feel of her had sent a sweet, hot current shooting up his legs and through his body. And the last time—Matt ground his teeth, the tightness in his crotch almost unbearable. The last time he'd been with Winifred, she'd pushed up against his body so tight that he could feel every little line and curve of her through her dress, the soft places and the hard ones too. He'd reached down and pulled her hips tight against his, pressing her into the throbbing hardness of his erection. He thought she'd fight, but she hadn't. She had stood there, letting him press her that way, her breath coming in tiny, quick gasps. Then, suddenly, with a nervous giggle, she'd broken away from him and raced up the walk to her front porch. Matt had stood there by the old sycamore, his loins aching so badly he could hardly walk home. He'd felt pretty daring about the whole thing. Until now.

He blinked away the fly where it had settled just below his eyebrow. The grass was long, and he couldn't really see Elvina any more, except for her arms and a little of her hair. He couldn't see too much of Aaron either, except for the twin pink lumps of his buttocks, bobbing up and down over the top of the grass. He had her all right. Aaron was doing it, Damnation! Matt dared to lift a hand and wipe away the sweat that was pouring down his forehead. It was hot for spring. Damned hot, and he was hurting. His pants were so tight he was afraid he'd split a seam, and his heart was pounding like an Indian tom-tom. It wasn't decent, getting all worked up like this over something that was happening to somebody else. Matt swore a steady stream of curses under his breath. It only helped a little. He was in agony, and the way Aaron and Elvina were going at it, they could be here all night.

Matt had forgotten about Slocum. Even when the bushes on the opposite side of the glade began to quiver and rustle, Matt didn't realize what was happening until the big, ugly yellow head thrust into sight. Slocum squeezed out of the underbrush, trotted into the glade, and stopped a scant two paces from the heaving forms of Elvina and Aaron.

Slocum sat down on his haunches and cocked his head. What's this? his manner seemed to say. Slowly he got up, strolled over and sniffed at Aaron's leg. Aaron didn't seem to feel it. Maybe he thought it was the grass, or maybe he wasn't paying much attention.

Matt swore. He had to get that dog out of there! He puckered up his lips and gave a low, very soft, coaxing whistle. "Slocum!" he whispered. "Here, boy! Come on, you dumb dog!"

Slocum heard his master. His ears went up. His tail went up, and he came, galloping right over the top of Aaron and Elvina. They sat up. Elvina shrieked.

Slocum plunged into the brambles and headed straight for Matt, his tail wagging ecstatically.

Aaron was on his feet, struggling with his breeches. Elvina was streaking for the trees, her dress clutched around her. Matt didn't see what happened next. Slocum's hurtling weight knocked him off balance, ripping him free of the bramble and leaving a healthy-sized shred of his pants attached to the stickers. He toppled backward, and ended up flat on his back in the leaves, Slocum's muddy paws planted in the middle of his chest. Matt groaned. The big dog sneezed and licked his face adoringly.

Aaron was lurching about the clearing, still fumbling with his buttons. "Matthew Cooper," he bawled at the top of his lungs. "If ye be within hearin' I want ye t'know that I'll get ye for this! I'll have your hide nailed up 'longside the barn like a coon's! Y' hear me, Matt Cooper?"

Matt heard him, but he did not answer. He was crawling away through the underbrush, inching along like a snake. Most days he could take Aaron Weir with one hand tied behind his back. But today, he suspected, wasn't one of those days. Aaron was sore, and he had a right to be. Not in a thousand years would Matt be able to convince him that he hadn't been spying on purpose. And as for Elvina, a riled female was more dangerous than a wounded catamount. If there was a way to get him, she'd find it, Matt warned himself. It wouldn't be safe for him to show his face in town for the next six weeks!

Matt stopped crawling long enough to listen to the sounds of the woods behind him. He could hear Slocum snuffling around in the dead leaves, and the breathy, far-off roar of the falls, but that was all. Aaron didn't seem to be coming after him. He was probably too embarrassed, But Aaron would get him later, Matt knew, probably sometime when he least expected it. Aaron was like that.

Little by little Matt got to his feet. He looked down at himself and sighed. His stockings were full of burrs, and the knees of his breeches were caked with mud. There were big, muddy paw prints all over the front of his light brown linsey shirt, and one small section of his backside felt unreasonably cool. He remembered his mother and groaned out loud. Likely as not he wouldn't get any supper at all, and he was starving.

Slocum sidled up to Matt and nuzzled his hand. His hide was full of foxtails, and one ear was turned inside-out. Matt rubbed his head. "You old son of a yellow devil," he muttered. "You lop-eared, good-for-nothing old trouble-maker, it's all your fault." But the anger was gone from his voice. Slocum thumped his tail against Matt's leg and drooled on his shoe.

They moved out of the woods and onto the road. Matt glanced anxiously up and down the length of it for any sign of Aaron or Elvina, but he saw no one. They must have cut through the woods and gone home, he decided.

Somewhere back the other way was the string of fish he'd hung in a tree when he'd left the road to go after Slocum. Well, he'd never find them

16

now; and some critter would have them for sure before morning. All in all, the afternoon had been a total loss. He should have stayed in town and helped his father in the warehouse instead of taking off to go fishing, Matt scolded himself. Well, his father had plenty of hired help, and Matt wasn't sure he was cut out to be a merchant anyway, even if Forny & Cooper *was* one of the biggest trading companies on the Ohio, and even if he *was* the oldest grandson of its founder, Edward Forny. He remembered his Grandpa Forny's stories about the old days, how he'd opened up the trade routes in his canoe, exploring new territory and outwitting Indians all the way. That was the kind of trader Matt would have chosen to be— not the owner of a whole block of warehouses like his father, Ned Cooper, was. Matt had no love for the warehouses, with their endless shelves and piled-up crates filled with everything from calico to whiskey. He hated the sight of ledgers and invoices, the crabbed, little figures in red and black ink. There was a whole world upriver and down, and Matt wanted to see it all.

Still—he walked along, swinging one arm and feeling a little better. They *had* looked pretty funny, Aaron and Elvina, bumping up and down in the grass like that. And the expressions on their faces when Slocum had gone romping over the top of them—Matt chuckled as the full impact of the memory came back to him. Aaron jumping for his breeches, Elvina shrieking . . . himself, caught in the brambles, falling over backwards and then crawling off into the bushes so that Aaron wouldn't catch him. Lord! Matt's chuckle turned into an open-mouthed guffaw, and the next thing he knew he was laughing so hard that he had to sit down on a rock at the side of the road. He laughed till his ribs ached, and Slocum had to lick away the salty tears that rolled down his cheeks.

When he had recovered, he looked down the road toward town and saw a small, dancing figure coming toward him. He recognized it as his twelve-year-old sister, Cecilia.

"Matt!" she called out, breaking into a run when she recognized him. She was slim and dark and lively, and would be a pretty girl in a few years. "Matt! Hurry! They're waitin' sup for you, and Grandpa Forny's here! Down all the way from Vincennes!" She stopped short as she got a look at him. Her mouth dropped open. "What happened to ye, Matt?" she whispered.

He tugged at her ponytail, pleased by the news that his grandfather had come for a visit. Grandpa Forny was the only person who seemed to understand him these days.

"Nuthin' for you to know," he said teasingly. Then he let her take his hand and swing it back and forth all the way home, Slocum frisking along behind him.

# II

Edward Forny leaned back in his chair and surveyed his daughter's family with a sense of warm satisfaction. He'd always nursed the secret hope that Marie would give him a whole pack of grandsons, a hope that evidently was not to be, but he couldn't complain. Not when her three daughters were pretty enough to bring tears to his eyes. Not when Matt, her eldest and the only son, was a strapping, gentle boy, a lad to burst his grandfather's heart with pride. *Sur ma parole*, he thought as he gazed around the table. Such a crop of children! Edward was sixty-four years old, and the fruits of his life were sweet.

His dark eyes, still bright and flashing, rested on Matt for a lingering moment. Matt's face was damp from scrubbing, his hair hastily slicked back and tied with a strand of brown leather. *Mon Dieu*, but he'd been a sight when he'd walked in the back door a short while ago. His poor mother had almost dropped the pan of biscuits she was taking out of the oven. Matt's hair had been mussed and tangled with foxtails, his shirt muddied and his breeches torn. "Oh, no!

Not again, Matt!" Marie had gasped in dismay. She would have said a good deal more, Edward suspected, if her father had not been visiting. "Go and wash up," she snapped. "I'll be having a word with you later, Matthew Cooper."

Matt sat around the corner of the table from his grandfather now, carefully cutting his ham and spearing the pieces on his fork. It seemed to be a trial for him to eat slowly, Edward observed. In fact, it seemed hard for Matt to do anything slowly. He was all impulse, all impatience. *Oui*, Edward thought with a twinge of pleasure, the boy is very much like me when I was young and full of fire. He's got the Brewster height and coloring, with those thick brown curls; and the Cooper shoulders . . . but inside he's all Forny!

Ned Cooper had relinquished his seat at the head of the table to his father-in-law. A good man, Ned, Edward mused, studying him. A good husband to Marie, a good father to my wonderful grandchildren. Ah, but he has too much common sense for his own good! No imagination. No sense of adventure, and my own son Henry's just the same. Too blasted careful, both of them. Forny & Cooper's not what it used to be. We've grown, we've prospered. But, *sacre bleu*, we're getting as staid and fat as an old setting hen!

"Mind your manners, Cecilia. No elbows on the table," Ned Cooper admonished his youngest daughter sternly. The earnest young man who had won Marie's heart and married her in Vincennes was now one of the most prominent businessmen in Louisville. It had been Ned's idea to set up the general headquarters of Forny & Cooper here, in the settlement that had grown up alongside the falls of the Ohio. Since most of the goods bound for the towns downriver had to be taken ashore for portage around the rapids, there was much opportunity for buying and profitable reselling. The decision to build warehouses and offices here had been a wise one, but the nature of Forny & Cooper had changed over the years because of it. Edward's dream for the trading company had always been to keep ahead of the frontier, to bring his trade goods to places where they were scarce and would be prized. But times had changed. Ned, and Edward's son, Henry, who ran the Nashville branch of the business, were more interested in profits than in adventure. More warehouses, they said. More offices, clerks. That was the way to grow. And they were right, of course, Edward mused. Business was excellent. But where were the new rivers? Where was the frontier? It had left them far behind.

Edward glanced knowingly from his son-in-law to his grandson. Well, that, he told himself, is about to be changed. And I know just the young man to change it! Ned's kept the boy too long at home. A lad needs stretching room. He needs to learn about the world, like I did. Edward smiled to himself, anticipating the moment when he would break the news about his plan. He was still the head of the company, and he would not be ready for pasture for a good many years. He had the power to put his plan into action; in fact, he had already taken the first steps.

Marie Forny Cooper leaned over the table with a plate of fresh biscuits. Her pretty face was flushed from the heat of the kitchen. Little tendrils of sweat-dampened hair curled around her cheeks and forehead. Edward watched her affectionately. She was still blooming, his little Marie. After four children, she was still a beauty. Even the plumpness that had rounded her face and body over the years was becoming. Edward liked to see a little meat on a woman. Wistfully he thought of his Abby, back in Vincennes, in the comfortable stone house he had built for her. What a shame he hadn't been able to bring her with him this trip. She'd have enjoyed this visit with her daughter, and with Henry's family in Nashville as well. But he'd wanted to make a swift journey this time, and Abby was no longer up to the rigors of that kind of travel. Perhaps, he mused, it was time they sold the house in Vincennes and moved to Louisville, so that she could enjoy having her family around her as she grew older. He would have to give the matter some thought.

The table almost sagged with the bounty of Marie's kitchen. There was sliced ham from the smokehouse and potatoes from the cellar, peas and white beans, fresh biscuits and hoe-cake, with apple pie for dessert, and even real coffee for the grown-ups. Edward, who had long since learned the wisdom of tempering his own appe-

22

tite, watched in amused wonder as Matt put away helping after helping. The boy was big as a bear, and still growing!

"I thought you were going to bring us some fish, Matthew," Edward said with a smile. "Your mother said that's where you'd gone today."

Matt's eyes rounded and the color rose just slightly in his cheeks. "Lost 'em," he said between bites. "Hung 'em in a tree while I went to look for Slocum, s'pose some critter got 'em." He went back to the serious business of eating, Edward suspected that there was more to the story than what Matt had told him, but decided it might be wise not to ask.

"Really, Matt," Marie bustled about the table, laying out saucers for the pie, "the store you set by that dog is enough to make a body laugh. Ye didn't have to go lookin' for him an' lose the fish. That rascally mutt can take care of himself if anybody ever could!"

Matt shrugged, reddened a bit more, and took another slice of hoe-cake.

"Your mother's right, Matt," Ned Cooper admonished his son. "Ye waste the whole afternoon at a time when I could've used ye in the warehouse. Ye lose the one worthwhile thing that come of it, an' ye come home lookin' like a ragamuffin, all muddy an' tore up. Ye be nineteen years old, boy. That's plenty old enough t' be takin' on a man's duties."

"*Oui!*" Edward put his fork down beside his plate. "You're right, Ned, Matt is old enough to take his place in the company. And I have just the job for him. That's one of the reasons I came."

An expectant hush had crept into the room. Every eye was instantly focused on Edward. He smiled and cleared his throat. He had not really expected to break the news so soon. But *c'est la vie*. He gave a little mental shrug. One time was as good as another. "*Dites moi*," he said, "what do you know about the Mississippi?"

Matt's eyes had rounded like saucers, but he did not speak. Ned merely shook his head. "It ain't our territory," he said. "It was closed to Yankee traffic for years."

"But it's open now!" Edward leaned forward in his chair. "It's been open for some time, all the way to New Orleans. There's a treaty with the Spanish. It guarantees us the right of deposition—"

"And what might that be?"

"That means, Ned, that they've promised us the right to unload our cargo at New Orleans and store it there, duty free, until a seagoing American ship can pick it up." Edward's eyes sparkled intently.

Ned was not impressed. "Well, now, we got all the business we can handle right here, 'twixt the Ohio, the Wabash, the Cumberland, and the Tennessee. An' I heard about the Mississippi. They say the river pirates is worse than the Indians ever was. I know what ye be thinkin', but it be a risky business, traffickin' on the Mississippi."

"Risky? *Tonnerre!*" Edward exploded. "This

24

trading company was born and suckled and weaned on risk! How do you think *I* got started, eh? By sticking to the forts and towns? When this country's filled with people, the Mississippi will be the most important river in America! Plenty of traders are going down it already. We wouldn't be the first, by any means. You know that, Ned. You're no fool. But if we don't join them now, if we don't set up our route all the way to New Orleans, the day will come when Forny & Cooper won't be able to compete with the companies who've done it. We won't survive."

Ned chewed thoughtfully on a buttered biscuit. "You talk a mighty good argument, Papa Forny. Got to give you that."

"If I do, Ned, it's because I'm *right*! It's the only thing to do. We're already falling behind. We've got to move down the Mississippi, and we can't delay! Not another season! Or we'll be lost!'"

Edward had been watching Matt out of the corner of his eyes. The boy had put down his fork and was listening intently. He hadn't spoken. That was not his place in such a discussion. But Matt was excited. That much showed in his eyes.

"I still say it's a risky business," Ned said slowly. Yes, Edward reflected, Ned was a cautious man, even more cautious than Henry. That caution had saved Forny & Cooper from some costly blunders in the past. But now was not the time for caution.

"The pirates? We've been fighting off pirates

25

on the Ohio for years, as well as Indians. And if it's financial risk you're talking about, Ned, there wouldn't be much of that. We'd start out slowly at first. Say, one small shipment to begin with. Just to test the water. What do you say?" Edward glanced at Matt again.

Ned scratched his head, wrinkled his brow, and finally smiled—a slow and easy smile that took years off his face. It was that smile that Marie Forny had fallen in love with more than twenty years ago, Edward reminded himself.

"Well, Papa Forny, I'd say you've already made up your mind. And ye ain't askin' me. Ye be tellin' me. Knowin' you, I figured ye got it all planned out."

"*Oui, mon fils.*" Edward laughed out loud now that the ice had been broken and he knew that he would win. "Not only planned out, but already set in motion." He moved his plate aside and leaned forward on the table, resting his arms. "I was given the name of a certain Spanish gentleman in Natchez, a freight broker by the name of Don Esteban Montoya. I have contacted him by letter, and received a reply only two weeks ago. Don Esteban will be more than happy to arrange for the disposal of a small cargo of mixed goods in New Orleans for us. We have only to get it there." Edward glanced around the table with a feeling of satisfaction. Here, he had said it. All faces were turned in his direction, waiting to hear more.

"And who's to take the shipment? It's got to be

a man we can trust, and I can't spare one. Neither can Henry." Ned spoke his lines so perfectly that Edward almost had to laugh. Yes, it was going just as he'd hoped it would.

"*C'est facile*," he answered with a smile. "Matt."

Ned's jaw dropped slightly, and Marie gave a little cry of protest. Matt made a noise that sounded as if he were stifling a Kickapoo war whoop. Edward silenced them all with a motion of his hand. 'Now, Ned, you were not even seventeen when you left your family in Pitt to go trading with me. Matt's a grown young man, and he's very capable. As for you, Marie, if you're worried about your son, there's no need. I'll be hiring an experienced flatboat crew in Nashville—in fact, I've already written to Henry about it. They'll handle the boat and the cargo. Matt would only be going along to see to the interests of the company, to deal with Don Esteban in Natchez, and to see that things are wrapped up good and proper in New Orleans." Edward glanced from Marie to Ned. "But he's your son. I can't order you to send him. What do you say?"

"Papa . . . Mama . . . please—" Matt blurted out in spite of himself.

"Hush, Matt." Ned frowned at him. "I got only one question, Papa Forny. Looks to me you've had this cookin' for a long time. You even wrote to Henry 'bout it. How come you just now got around to tellin' me?"

Edward gazed down at his hands. It was not an

27

easy question to answer, but he would answer it truthfully. "*Vraiment* . . ." he began slowly, "it was Matt I wanted for this job. And I wanted the job for Matt as well . . . *compris*? It would be a fine thing for him." He glanced from his grandson to his son-in-law. "Ned, I know you and Marie set a great store by the boy. I—" Edward spread his hands and smiled weakly. "To be honest, I was afraid that if I asked you before it was all arranged, you might say no. That would have ruined everything."

Silence hung in the air when Edward finished speaking. He saw Marie's eyes, and Ned's, meeting across the table, speaking a language that defied words. At last, almost imperceptibly, Marie nodded.

Ned cleared his throat. "We be willin' to let him go. The final say's up to Matt. What think ye, son?"

All eyes were on Matt. He swallowed hard. Then his face broke into an eager grin. "I be thinkin' I'd like to go!"

"*Bien!* Then it's settled!" Edward spoke with relief. "Finish your dinner, Matt. We'll talk more about it in the morning, eh?"

"I be finished," Matt said hastily. "Will ye excuse me, please? There . . ." He reddened slightly. "There be somebody I got to go see."

"Go on then. Till tomorrow." Edward smiled as Matt slipped out of the room.

"He's sparkin' a girl," Marie said. "Probably couldn't wait to tell her the news."

"A girl, eh? Well, it's about time." Edward listened as Matt whistled his way through the kitchen and out the back door. The door banged shut. Then, unexpectedly, the silence of the whole outdoors was shattered by Matt's ear-splitting, joyous whoop.

The moon was almost full. It hung in the sky, silhouetting the top of a gnarled and ancient pine tree. Its light silvered the new leaves of the big sycamore, and outlined the pale and pretty features of Winifred Van Cleve's face.

"Will your Pa be waitin' up again?" Matt asked uneasily. The hour was uncommonly late, half past nine at least. The last time he'd kept Winifred out that late, her father'd been waiting on the porch, his nightshirt tucked into his breeches.

"Not t'night. He had his jug on the table when I left the house." She giggled. "I know what that means. Pa'll be sleepin' like a bear in December. Ma, now, she be different. She remembers what it were like t' be a girl." Winifred's blonde hair was mussed, and her mouth was damp from kissing. She nestled her head against Matt's shoulder. "But I wish ye weren't goin'. I'll be right lonely till ye come back."

"By thunder, ye'd better be!" Matt nuzzled the warm hollow behind her ear and Winifred giggled again. Slocum whined and nudged Matt's foot with his paw.

"Don't see why ye have t' bring that old dog every time ye come," Winifred complained. "He's always right there, sniffin' and pawin' and gettin' in the way."

"I locked him in the shed before I come," Matt said. "But he dug out under the door. By the time I was halfway here, he'd caught up with me. Slocum, he goes where I do."

"Now, that be a powerful shame." Winifred glanced down at Slocum's sleek yellow back. "A right powerful shame."

"Why d'ye say that?"

"Cause . . ." Winifred tilted her head roguishly. "Cause there be things that can't happen twixt a certain boy an' girl when a certain ol' hound dog keeps gettin' in the way."

Matt blinked, sudden, swift visions of what he had seen that afternoon between Aaron and Elvina flashing through his mind. What else could Winifred mean? Lord, they'd done about everything else. His heart began to pick up speed. Was it really that easy?

"What kind of things?" Matt's voice was strangely hoarse.

Winifred laughed. "Oh . . . things. Just things. Do ye like it when ye kiss me, Matt?"

"Aye . . ." he whispered.

"An' do ye like it when I do this?" She slipped into his arms and pressed the length of her body against his, tight and hard and quivering. It was only for the space of a breath or two, but the feel of her was enough to send hot arrows shooting

30

through Matt's body. He felt the familiar straining. He wondered if she knew about it, that warm, uncontrollable swelling that surged up whenever she got close to him. How much did girls know, anyway? Elvina hadn't seemed too surprised when it happened to Aaron. But Winifred was different—at least he hoped she was.

"An' this?" She took his hand and slid it up to her breast. Matt's trembling fingers felt the softness of her, the hard little knob of her nipple through the thin muslin.

"Aye. . ." she whispered, "I can tell ye like that." Then she snatched his hand away, leaving him breathless and hungry for more of the feel of her. "There be more things you'd like, Matthew Cooper. But I can't show ye less'n ye get rid of that dog. Don't want his old wet nose sniffin' and pokin' around, do we now?"

Matt drew in his breath sharply. He was already aching for her. Was it that simple? Was it really just a matter of getting rid of Slocum? "Here, boy!" Matt whistled softly to the dog. He bent down and spoke in Slocum's cocked ear. "You git for home, boy! Git!"

Slocum took a few reluctant steps, then stopped, whined, and looked questioningly back at Matt.

"Git! Git for home, Slocum!" Matt picked up a chestnut-sized rock. Impatiently he flung it at the dog. It whizzed through the air and bounced off Slocum's right haunch. It must have stung a little, because the dog yelped.

31

"Git! Git! Slocum!" Matt hissed as loud as he dared. The last thing he wanted to do was wake Winifred's father.

But the rock had done the trick. With one final, accusing glance in Matt's direction, Slocum curled his tail between his legs and trotted forlornly back up the road toward the Cooper house.

Matt turned back to Winifred. She was smiling demurely. "Now—" He pulled her close, the sound of his own heart filling his head. He kissed her, felt the thrust of her tongue, delicate as the jab of a kitten's paw, darting in and out of his mouth. Slightly dizzy, he kissed her again, hotly and forcefully. He felt her gasp as his hands fumbled wildly for buttons, tiny, tightly caught buttons that slipped away from his big, blunt fingers. Frustrated, his hands moved downward and began to lift her skirt.

"No!" she panted. "No, Matt, not here!"

"Where?"

"There!" Winifred jerked her head toward the half-open door of the barn. "There be clean straw in there—"

"Come on!" He jerked her arm, wild with impatience. She followed him, stumbling over rocks and tufts of grass, until they swung around the barn door and stood in the darkness of its shadow.

Again he tried her buttons. They were small and close together, hooked into tiny loops. It was hopeless. Well, the devil with buttons. He kissed her again, a furious, awkward kiss that jammed

32

his mouth on hers, hurting. One hand began to bunch up her skirt again. She stood still and let him, but he found that she was wearing pantalets underneath, and the waist was cinched tight. Damnation! Even poor Aaron had had an easier time of it than this! Matt's erection was threatening to burst the seams of his pants. "Help me!" he muttered.

When Winifred hesitated, he seized her hand and guided it to the buttons of his trouser flap. He remembered how Elvina had touched Aaron, and he wanted Winifred to touch him like that. Still holding her, he ripped the flap open and thrust her hand inside.

"Oh!" she squealed. "Oh!" She jerked her hand away as if she'd just touched a red hot poker. Inexplicably, she began to giggle again.

"Winifred—"

"Oh! Oh, Matthew Cooper! You naughty boy!"

"Winifred, I thought—"

"Ye thought I'd be the kind o' girl to do such a thing. Why, I'd never do *that* with a boy . . . less'n he marries me."

"But you said—"

"Never mind that." She looked down at the straw-covered floor. "I was only funnin'. Just wanted to see what ye'd do." She giggled again nervously. "Reckon I found out. But if you want me, Matt Cooper, there be only one way to git me!"

Fuming, and feeling like a fool, Matt turned

away from her and buttoned his trouser flap. He was still painfully erect, and his hands trembled so hard that he could scarcely find the button-holes. But the blow to his pride hurt worst of all. He had let Winifred bait him, had lost all control of himself, and in the end had come out looking like a bigger fool than poor Aaron Weir.

"Matt—" Winifred's voice was like a little girl's now, sweet and timid and quavering. "Matt, you ain't mad at me! I was only funnin' with ye. Ye know ye can have it all, Matt, if ye just—" She laid a hand on his arm. "I'll be waitin' when ye come back. Ye know there ain't nobody else. Matt . . . look at me!"

She reached up, caught his chin with her fingers, and turned his face toward her. Matt's eyes blazed at her, filled with hurt, frustration and rage. "Oh!" She took a little step backward, moving out of the shadow of the barn door and into the moonlight. "Oh, Matthew Cooper, ye be n't fair. I couldn't help it. Ye ain't got no right t' be mad like that!"

Matthew wanted to speak to her. He wanted to explain calmly that if a girl didn't plan to go all the way with a fellow, it wasn't fair to act like she would. But the blood was still pounding in his head. He could only glare at her in mute fury.

"Oh!" she cried again, half afraid of him. Then she picked up her skirts and fled, across the yard and onto the front porch of her house. He heard her feet cross the planks and the light, swift slamming of the door.

"Winifred—" He took a step forward, his tongue freed at last. But she was gone. Still hurting, Matt closed the door of the barn and made his way out the front gate. Even the moon seemed to be laughing at him.

Damnation! It hurt to walk! He kicked at a rock that hurt worse as he walked up the road toward home. He'd never been very good at figuring out girls, especially Winifred, he told himself. Yet, somehow, the more he walked and the more he thought about it, the clearer his understanding became. Winifred wanted to marry him, and was trying every trick she knew. Getting a fellow all fired up, and then pulling away the bait. Aye, that stunt had good reason to work. Maybe that's how Winifred's mother'd caught a husband. For all Matt knew, the good lady could have passed on the same trick to her daughter. Things were making more sense now.

Well, he wouldn't mind marrying Winifred. She was pretty, and a good cook to boot. Last week she'd made a gooseberry pie just for him. Matt had eaten every bite, except for one little piece that he gave to Slocum. No, Winifred wouldn't make such a bad wife, and maybe one day he really would marry her. But not yet. Matt wasn't ready to marry anybody. There were too many things he hadn't done, and too many places he hadn't seen.

He was feeling better now. After all, how could a fellow be mad at a girl, when she wanted to marry him so much that she'd go and try a low-down trick like that? He began to whistle. Maybe Slocum would hear him. Poor old Slocum.

The road wound past freshly planted corn-fields, and through a stand of oak and blackberry bushes. The night was quiet, except for the chirping of crickets in the underbrush. Matt was beginning to wonder where Slocum had gone. Slocum had a way about him. If you hurt his feelings, he'd sulk for days sometimes.

Matt scarcely had time to hear the rustling in the bushes before something hit him from behind. The sudden force of the blow knocked him forward onto his knees, into the mud. Wild, furious fists pummelled his head and shoulders. Kicking and grunting, Matt worked his way over onto his back. His arms went up to defend his face while he tried to see his assailant.

"Take that, damn ye, Matt Cooper. Ye don't deserve t' live!"

It was Aaron, as he should have known it would be. Matt groaned. Aaron wasn't very big, but he was quick, and feisty as a banty rooster. "You an' that pesky mutt! Gonna shoot 'im next chance I get! an' I oughta shoot you too. Sneakin' and spyin' around—"

"Blast it, Aaron, it weren't my fault—" Matt fended off the blows with his hands. Aaron was too mad to do much damage. Most of the blows glanced off Matt's shoulders and arms, stinging but not really hurting.

"Get up, damn ye! Stop hunkerin' up like that an' fight me like a man, Matt Cooper! I'm gonna pound you into bloody dust! I'm gonna pin yer hide t' the barn for the crows t' peck at! Fight me, damn it!''

Matt groaned. The last thing he felt like was fighting Aaron Weir. Aaron didn't deserve the licking that Matt was capable of giving him. He had every right and reason to be mad. Besides, Matt didn't feel like fighting anybody tonight. He was too deflated from his experience with Winifred, and too excited about tomorrow. But just to humor Aaron he struggled to his feet. "Fight me, then," he muttered. "Go ahead."

He found himself wishing that Slocum would show up. Slocum could be downright ferocious when he was defending his master. That would have taken the wind out of Aaron's sails in a hurry and the fight would have been over. But Slocum didn't come. Most likely he was off sulking somewhere, feeling sorry for himself.

"Come on," Aaron taunted, dancing back and forth in front of Matt. "Put your dukes up, Cooper!"

Matt sighed and raised his fists. "Now, Aaron—" He didn't have time to finish. Aaron hurled his full weight into one flying blow that caught Matt on the jaw. Matt staggered backward, his head spinning. What the hell, he thought. Aaron deserved to win this one anyway. Matt's ears were ringing. He let his legs buckle and slipped down in the cool dampness of the mud. It felt almost good. He closed his eyes, leaving just enough of a slit to see Aaron standing above him in the moonlight, still quivering with rage.

"There, I showed ye!" Aaron stared down at his fallen foe for a long moment. Then he went stomping off down the road toward town.

Matt sighed with relief and opened his eyes fully. The stars spread above him in the inky sky, farflung and glorious. He lay there for a while, just looking at them, before he finally got up and went home. He didn't hurt anywhere anymore.

# III

Edward Forny dipped his paddle into the sparkling ripples of the Ohio. His muscles responded automatically, their rhythm as natural as breathing. Edward had spent forty years on the rivers, and the canoe was almost a part of his body. Paddling came as easily to him as walking.

The day was filled with sunshine, the leaves of the oak and sycamore pale green in their newness. Pussy willows hung over the river's edge, their supple branches trailing in the current. The winter had been long, and Edward was grateful for the spring. He was grateful for the sunshine, for the sleek beauty of the canoe, and the presence of his grandson behind him.

"*Comment ca va?*" He glanced affectionately back at the laboring Matt. "How are you doing? Is it getting any easier?"

Matt grinned. "A little. I try t' move with you. That helps some. But I'll be sore tonight, I can tell that already."

"*Oui*, that you will. It's always like that the first day. I brought some of your grandmother's liniment to rub on your shoulders tonight. It burns like fire, but it helps." Edward guided the canoe skillfully around a floating log. "It's a good thing we've got a few days of going downstream on the Ohio before we hit the Cumberland. It's upstream all the way to Nashville from there. But you'll be in good condition by then. By the time we get to your Uncle Henry's you'll be paddling like you were born in a canoe." He laughed. "I tried to make a river man out of your father, but it didn't work. Once he'd married your mother, Ned Cooper decided he'd rather push a pen than a paddle. But *c'est la vie*. With Forny & Cooper so big, it takes more than one kind of man to run her, *non*? I only wish I'd had more chance to take you out on the rivers myself."

"Aye . . . so do I." Matt leaned into his paddle. "But I still can't see why we didn't just go by horse. Closer that way, 'specially now that there ben't no Indian trouble to worry 'bout. I been that way afore, with Pa."

"*Ca ne fait rien*," Edward responded. "I know. But I wanted you to get the feel of the river and in a canoe. A fishboat's one thing. It's big and clumsy, and a man steering it can only do so much in the way of controlling it. He's at the mercy of the river—especially if he's a stranger to the water. Ah, but a canoe—it's as delicate as the bow of a fiddle. You feel every ripple. A man in a canoe is the master of the water. He uses the currents, he plays on them, he goes fast or slow, back or forth, as he likes, because he understands the river. He feels her mood beneath him . . . calm, playful, angry . . . and he knows how to take advantage of it." Edward flashed a smile back at his grandson. "The river . . . she is not so very different from a woman, *eh bien?*"

Matt reddened slightly. "Grandpa Forny, if I don't get t' understand the river any better'n I understand women, ye might as well toss me overboard right here, 'cause I won't never amount to nothin' as a river man!"

"What? A handsome fellow like you, with woman troubles?" Edward shook his head. "Your mother said you were sparking a girl. So it's not going so well, eh?"

Matt let out his breath in a long, whistling sigh. "It . . . it's just that I can't figure out what she really wants. One minute it's all hot breathin', and pressin' up to me, an' wigglin' her fanny like a cat in season. Why, the other night she even took hold of my hand an' put it—" He broke off, struggling in an agony of embarrassment.

"*Vraiment*, Matt. I was a young man once myself, I remember it well."

"One minute she's like that," Matt said, "and the next minute she's pullin' my hands away an' gigglin' and callin' me a naughty boy. It's that, or she gets mad and runs in the house."

"And what do you make of it?"

"I figure maybe she be wantin' to marry me. She almost said so herself the other night. Said if I wanted it all, there be only one way t' get it. What do you think?"

"I think you understand a lot more about women than you give yourself credit for, Matt. The young lady's no fool. You're probably the best catch in Louisville, whether you know it or not. Your father's got money, and you'll be head of Forny & Cooper one day. And you're a right handsome lad to boot. I'd say she wants to trap you while she's got the chance, and she's using the oldest trick since Eve to do it. *Dites-moi*, Matt, is her trick working? Do you want to marry her?"

"Maybe. Some day. If she don't drive me crazy first."

"You love her?"

Matt was silent for a long moment, his paddle dragging in the water. "Don't rightly know. Guess I never really asked myself that question. Sure can get all fired up about her. If that be love, then I reckon I love her."

"She's pretty?"

"Aye . . . Yellow hair, like ripe corn. Big, round blue eyes. An' she ain't skinny. Ain't really plump, just sort of . . . soft. Like a woman."

"*Oui* . . . I know the kind," Edward smiled wistfully. "Your grandmother was a bit like that. Still is."

"Grandpa Forny—" Matt drew in his breath. "You ever been with any other woman 'sides Grandma?"

Edward missed a stroke of the paddle. The question came as a total surprise. He pondered the answer for a moment. Should he lie, and leave the boy with his illusions—illusions that would surely be shattered one day—or should he tell the truth? He stared down into the rippling water and decided on the truth.

"*Oui*," he answered softly. "A few. I left

42

France because of a woman, you know. The very young wife of a doddering old duke. He put a price on my head, and I had to run for it. Then there was a girl in Canada, an Indian girl. She was killed just before I met your grandmother."

Edward remembered Spotted Doe, her dark eyes and her eager, supple body. It had been years since he'd thought of her.

"And afterwards? After you married Grandma?"

Edward sucked in his breath. He'd hoped the boy would be satisfied with his exploits *before* his marriage. "A few," he admitted reluctantly. "But only a few, and none at all for a long, long time." *Non*, Edward reflected uneasily, his little sins had not been many compared to those of some men who traveled the rivers. In most cases, the women had thrown themselves at him, and he had been no more than human. Some he remembered well, like the lust-maddened Pearl Jonas, who'd practically raped him in her husband's barn. And then there was black-haired, blue-eyed Mathilde Rodare, the most beautiful woman Edward had ever seen, and one of the wickedest. Edward had met her on his first visit to Vincennes, and had been fascinated by her for a time. But when that fascination had nearly destroyed his marriage, he had promised himself that he would never be unfaithful to Abby again. It was a promise he had kept. "I always loved your grandmother," he said to Matt. "The others were nothing. I hardly ever think of them now."

Matt was silent for a time, and Edward was beginning to wonder if perhaps he'd told the boy too much, when Matt spoke.

"I ain't never had a woman. Nineteen years old, and I ain't never even come close to havin' one. Reckon I just don't know how to go about gettin' one."

"There's time," Edward smiled back at him. "There's time. Don't worry. It'll happen when you're ready. Maybe it won't be till you're married. There's no harm in that, you know. Waiting a bit never hurt a fellow." Edward paused, expecting some kind of response from Matt, but the boy did not answer. "*Regardez*, Matt," he said. "Listen to me. Some women come cheap. They're easy to get, and when you get them you don't have much. The best thing you can do is enjoy them and pass them on to somebody else with your blessing when you're finished. Other women, like your Winifred, put a price on themselves and demand that you pay it. They're smarter than the first kind, but you have to decide whether the price is worth it. Sometimes it isn't, but you don't find out until it's too late."

"Then what's the best kind of woman?" Matt asked his grandfather.

"The best kind . . . " Edward thought of Abby and the years they'd had together. "The best kind of woman is the one who only gives herself for love. Remember that and you won't go far wrong."

They paddled until it was nearly dusk, talking from time to time of the Ohio, *La Belle Riviere*, its history, its geography, and all the small secrets

44

of navigating its waters. Matt was an apt pupil, avidly taking in all that Edward told him, repeating names, asking questions.

At the edge of a small glade they beached the canoe and made camp. Supper was cold roast duck from Marie's kitchen, corn dodgers and hot chicory coffee. "Eatin' makes me miss old Slocum," Matt glanced around the camp, one of the little corn biscuits in his hand. "Slocum, he sure likes these. Catches 'em in the air, like ye'd catch a ball. Wonder if he's lonesome?"

"Slocum? *Ne vous en faites pas!* He'll be all right." Edward inspected his rifle, which he always kept loaded and ready. "Your little sisters will take good care of him."

"But I ain't never gone off and left him like that. He looked so sad, tied up to Ma's clothesline pole like that. Wish we coulda taken him along." Matt munched wistfully on the corn dodger.

"A dog that size in the canoe? *Mon Dieu!*" Edward whistled, grateful that he'd managed to dissuade his grandson from taking the big mongrel along. Not that he didn't like dogs, but they had their place, and that place wasn't in a canoe.

"I know what happens with a man and a woman. Even saw it once," Matt said slowly. "But I don't know what ye do t' make a girl want it. Don't know what pretty words to say. Don't know the right way to touch a girl so's she'll like it and not get mad." He sighed wearily. "I got a lot to learn, Grandpa Forny."

"Matt—" Edward tossed a twig into the fire. "You worry too much. When it's right, it will happen, and nothing will go wrong. Nature intended those things to work. She made it easy. You'll see."

"But, when?"

"*A temps.* All in good time, *mon fils.*" Edward smiled and rose to his feet. "Would you like to take the first watch? Or should I?"

"Watch? But what for? There be just two of us, and there ain't no more Indians to worry about. We ain't got nothin' much to steal."

Edward raised an eyebrow. "On the river you can't be too careful, Matt. You never know what might come along. Last month a tale came up the river about some preacher who'd just washed ashore on the Tennessee. The poor fellow'd been stabbed in the back. Then his belly'd been sliced open and filled up with sand to make the body sink. But who'd want to kill a preacher? Doesn't make any more sense than killing us would. That's why we keep watch. There's no way of telling what's out there in the bushes, or around the next bend of the river. Remember that."

Matt's mind was still on the murdered preacher. "They got any suspicions about who killed him?"

"*Oui.* But doing something about it's another matter. There's a pair of brothers, the Harpes, who've been robbing and murdering travelers. They started out along the wilderness road, over by Knoxville, but it's looking like they've moved their deviltry west, to these parts. Sometimes they kill for money and supplies. Sometimes they kill . . . just for the love of killing, like blood-maddened wolves." Edward shuddered. "It figures they killed the poor preacher for that reason. He certainly didn't have much to rob. . ." Edward let his words hang in the air, while their full impact sank into Matt's mind. He didn't like to scare the boy, but it was a good lesson. An extra measure of watchfulness could save his life one day.

"I'll watch first," Matt said swiftly. "Ye can go to sleep, Grandpa. When the moon's at the peak of the sky I'll wake ye."

"*Tres bien*. Do you want some liniment first?"

Matt shook his head. "My shoulders ain't as sore as I feared at first. I'll be fine." He settled his tall, muscular frame on a log by the fire, his rifle propped across his knees. The boy wouldn't go to sleep, Edward reflected with a smile. Not after what he'd just heard. And Matt was a crack shot with a Kentucky rifle. Edward had seen him drop a squirrel at a good fifty paces.

With a contented sigh Edward settled into his blanket beside the fire, and closed his eyes. He was not as young as he used to be, and long days like this one made him weary. Still, there was no sleep sweeter than the rest at the end of a day on the river, with the stars shining overhead and the embers of the campfire glowing warmly beside you. Edward began to drift almost as soon as his head touched his pack. Strange dreams wound themselves like smoke in and out of his consciousness. Mathilde Rodare . . . her long, black hair twining around him . . . her blue eyes engulfing him like some vast, deep sea. He had not

47

dreamed of her like this for years. Maybe the mention of her to Matt had triggered something in his mind. But he still could not understand it, for he had never loved her. When he had ended his liaison with her, she had taken revenge on his wife and daughter. In the end, when he thought Mathilde had destroyed them, Edward had almost killed her with his bare hands. She had fled Vincennes after that, half-crazed with fear and guilt. Edward had never seen her again. But this dream . . . Mathilde's satiny legs spreading wide the thick, dark woman's plumage between them and the glimpse of an opening, a warm, red flame, waiting, beckoning. He felt himself, grown huge, plunging into her again and again, in and out, until he burst in her like a rocket. He fell back, drained and exhausted, and began to drift again. . .

"Grandpa—" Matt was shaking his shoulder. Edward opened his eyes. The moon hung high at the sky's dark peak, and Matt was yawning.

"*Qu'est-ce que c'est?*" Edward muttered. What is it? Then his brain began to clear and he knew that it was time to take his turn at watch. *Ouf!* Sleep had been more exhausting than staying awake. "Go to sleep, *mon fils*," he said to Matt. "You've let me rest too long. Dawn will be here before you know it."

Matt needed no prodding. He rolled himself into the blanket and was snoring softly in minutes. Edward leaned on his gun and poked at the coals of the fire. His mouth felt dry. A clump of birches at the clearing's edge shimmered like long, thin bones in the darkness. It was cold. Edward drew his blanket around his shoulders and sat down on the log, his rifle beside him.

The dream had shaken him. Maybe he was getting too old for this kind of travel after all. Henry's oldest daughter in Nashville had married last year and was already big with child. The baby would make Edward a great-grandfather. And here he was, dreaming like a youth. A damp stickiness down the inside of his leg told him that it had been more than a dream. Why couldn't a man stay young forever?

He must have dozed, because when he next noticed the moon it had moved some distance across the sky. Edward sat up with a start. Had he heard a sound, or was it only his own uneasiness that had awakened him? He listened carefully. Yes, there it was again, the faint crackle of something moving through the dry bushes. Something big. And it was coming closer.

The hair rose on the back of Edward's neck as he lifted his rifle. It wasn't Indians, he told himself. A whole tribe of them wouldn't make as much noise sneaking through the brush. But a white man would. A stray horse or cow would. A bear might, if it wasn't stalking something. Edward wondered if he should wake Matt.

Just then the bushes quivered, and a massive yellow head thrust into sight. Edward had raised his rifle before he realized what it was. *"Mon Dieu—"* he muttered in wonder and exasperation as the hulking form broke cover and made straight for Matt, yelping with joy, tail thrashing,

49

sides heaving, tongue slathering.

"Slocum!" Matt sat up, rubbing his eyes and fending off the assault of wet kisses. "Slocum, you old devil! You old yellow bastard!" He put his arms around the dog and hugged him gleefully.

"*Parbleu!*" Edward muttered, lowering his rifle. "Now all we have to do is figure out how we're going to get that *elephant* to sit still in the canoe!"


By the time they had left the Ohio and turned up the meandering Cumberland, Matt felt as though he had been paddling a canoe all his life. His muscles were hardening to the monotonous stroke and rest, stroke and rest. The rhythm was becoming a part of him.

He was getting the feel of the river, as well, as Edward had said he would. He knew how to spot a submerged tree, whose sharp limbs and roots could entangle and wreck a canoe. He knew how to navigate rapids, when to forge ahead, when to turn aside, when to cross the current. He was learning the ways of the river, and he could not have had a better teacher.

Slocum, too, was getting used to river travel, though he'd been nothing but trouble for the first few days. Twice he'd almost overturned the canoe when he'd spotted animals on shore and jumped up to bark at them. The second time it happened, a sputtering Edward had threatened to leave him behind on the bank, to fend for himself or find his way home. But Matt's pleas had won out, and after a time Slocum had learned. Now he sat proudly in the middle of the canoe, nothing moving but his head—though he did have a way of inching forward sometimes until his massive chin rested almost on Edward's shoulder. There he would stay, panting wetly, his great pink tongue just brushing Edward's ear.

"*Sacre bleu!* Such a traveling companion!" Edward muttered. "No more of this! A woman breathing down my neck I don't mind, but a dog—" He glanced back over his shoulder, his nose almost touching Slocum's. "Matt, call him back—softly, now. *Soigneu.* If he licks my ear one more time I will jump out of the canoe."

"Slocum—" Matt whispered the name. His whistle was little more than a breath, but Slocum turned around. The canoe rocked violently as he stood up and came padding back toward Matt. "No—sit, boy! Right there, boy. Sit!"

The canoe teetered precariously in the water as Slocum leaned to one side and scratched his ear. Matt flung his weight to the opposite side of the canoe to balance the little craft until Slocum had settled down. "Well, at least we can both sleep nights since we got Slocum with us," he said cheerfully. "He be a fine watch dog!"

"*Oui,*" Edward gave his grandson a feeble smile. "Last night he woke me up twice barking at an owl." He leaned into his paddle. "But no sleeping in the open for us tonight. I've got some friends that live just around that next bend. Jess and Angie Carter. Fine young folks. They'll be glad to put us up for the night."

51

"Good. I been hankerin' for a real home-cooked meal." The canoe surged ahead as Matt dug his paddle into the rippling water of the Cumberland. The river current was slow here, and moving upstream was not difficult. The day was warm, the sun pleasant. Matt was totally happy. He did not even miss Winifred as much as he'd thought he would. He was too caught up in this great adventure, this epic journey that would take him all the way to New Orleans and back before he saw his home—and Winifred—again. "How much longer 'fore we see Nashville?" he asked his grandfather.

"Not long. A few days. Henry should have the flatboat built by the time we get there, and most of the cargo arranged for. Then, it will be yours. I'll stay in Nashville for a good long visit, and you'll take her back down the Cumberland, onto the Ohio, and from there onto the Mississippi. Ever see the Mississippi, Matt?"

"Never have. Only heard of it."

"It's like nothing you ever saw in your life! Wide as a lake, and muddy as sin, and it goes on and on, forever almost—*Tiens!* Up there ahead! That would be the smoke from the Carters' cabin! *Allons!*" Edward broke into a little song in French, something he often did when he was in high spirits. His paddle flashed in the water. His shoulder muscles rippled with the joyous effort.

Matt's eyes followed the thin, gray trail of smoke upward against the afternoon sky. A flock of crows circled above it, flapping and cawing. The sight and sound of them sent a little shiver up

Matt's spine. A vague uneasiness stole over him, though he did not know why. Surely Edward felt none of it. He was still singing and paddling enthusiastically.

They beached the canoe at the small landing. The house could not be seen from the river. Edward had explained that it was set back in the trees, a few hundred yards from the water. "Angie Carter was expecting a little one when I saw them more than a year ago," Edward said. "They were hoping for a boy. Now we'll see if they got their wish!"

Matt followed his grandfather along the narrow path, one finger looped lightly through Slocum's collar. The big dog pressed close to Matt's legs. That was strange, because he usually wanted to bound ahead whenever they went ashore. Maybe it was the crows, Matt thought, glancing up at the sky again. Slocum had never liked crows.

Through the trees they could catch glimpses of the cabin. It was large and well built, the logs carefully chinked with mud. "The place seems a little quiet," Edward said. "You can usually hear Jess's axe all the way to the river. Maybe they're not—"

He was interrupted by a rumbling growl from Slocum's throat. Matt felt the hackles rise on the back of the dog's neck. Edward stopped in his tracks, stiffened, and raised his rifle. "Something's wrong," he said quietly. "Hold onto the dog, Matt. Don't let him run ahead."

Cautiously they moved into the clearing. Nothing seemed amiss at first. The axe lay alongside the chopping block, as if someone had dropped it. A lone chicken pecked in the grass. A plow rested against a corner post of the porch. "I don't see the horse," Edward said, his voice tense. Slocum growled again, his black lips curling back to show long, white fangs.

The front door was closed. Cautiously Matt and Edward mounted the porch. Edward knocked on the door. There was no answer, but it swung open when he pushed on it. Carefully he stepped inside. Matt waited on the porch, holding fast to the straining, growling Slocum.

"*Mon Dieu!*" Edward made a small strangling sound in his throat and stumbled backward over the threshold. "They're dead in there. All of them!" His face was pale with shock. Matt pushed past him, into the cabin.

A man lay face-up on the split-log floor, a young man, handsome even in death, except for the gaping, red hole that had been blasted through his chest by a shotgun at close range. Flies were already buzzing around that hole, and around the limp, bloodied form of a baby, flung like a discarded rag at the base of the north wall, its small skull shattered by the blow. The woman—yes, she'd been pretty—was sprawled on the bed in the corner, a rawhide strap twisted about her neck. It wasn't hard to guess that she'd died last. Her clothes had been ripped away. Her white legs had been forced wide apart, and it was plain to see that she had been brutally and repeatedly raped. Her face was bruised and swollen, her

54

nails torn and caked with drying flesh. Matt backed out of the doorway and leaned against the outside of the cabin for support, one hand convulsively gripping Slocum's collar. His knees felt watery. His stomach churned. Slocum was whining, growling, straining against his collar.

". . .Indians?" Matt choked out the word.

Edward shook his head. "Look at the yard. Boot tracks, and the prints of shod horses. This was done by white men."

# IV

They tied Slocum to the porch and went back inside to begin the grim task of readying the three bodies for burial. The corpses were fresh, the blood still red on their wounds. Not more than an hour or two could have passed, Edward calculated, since Jess and Angie Carter and their child had been living, breathing human beings.

"God, if only we'd come along sooner," Matt muttered in a choked voice. "Maybe we could've run the bastards off."

"You learn not to say those things after a while." Edward's throat ached when he spoke. "It only makes you feel worse, Matt. Who knows what we could have done? It happened, that's all. And asking why only hurts." He took the knitted shawl from the empty cradle and bent over the body of the baby—a boy. His eyes blurred as he scooped up the small form. It lay across his hands, soft and limp as a dead rabbit. He placed it on the shawl, folded the fringed ends over the battered head and tiny feet, and rolled the corners around it, shrouding the baby in a gray, woolen cocoon.

"Look—" Matt spoke through clenched teeth. "Damn it to hell, look at this!"

Edward turned around to find his grandson staring at the split-log table.

"Four trenchers," Matt said. "One for him, one for her, and two for them. And they still got food on 'em. The dirty bastards had lunch 'fore they done their butcherin'!" He kicked one leg of the table. The tin cups and forks jumped and clattered.

"Two of them." Edward studied the four places. "That matches the tracks in the yard."

"The Harpe brothers?"

"*Qui sait?* Whoever it was, they were murdering swine!" Edward shuddered. "Let's do what we have to. You take care of Jess. There's an extra blanket on the floor by the bed." Edward's eyes stung as he gazed down on what was left of Angie Carter, averting his eyes from her bare breasts and loins. Angie'd been a pretty woman, warm, merry and brave, not unlike his own Abby in her youth. Now Angie's brown hair was tangled and matted with blood. A lock of it was stuck to a big welt at the corner of her mouth. Edward brushed away the flies that had clustered on her bloodied face. He closed her parted legs, biting back the wild rage that boiled up in him at the sight of the murderers' seed, smeared and flaking on her thighs.

It didn't seem fitting, somehow, to bury her naked like that. Her dress was nowhere to be found. Maybe the devils had stolen it. Edward felt around in the bedclothes until he found her long muslin nightgown, still folded and tucked under one of the pillows. Gently he slipped it over her head and pulled it down over her body and legs. Then he bundled Angie Carter in the patchwork quilt she had made herself.

Matt had managed to wrap the heavy body of Jess Carter in the blanket. He stood over him now, pale-faced and breathing loudly, the sound filling the dead stillness of the cabin.

"Jess kept a pick and shovel in the shed," Edward said wearily. "*Venir*. We'll bury the three of them together, alongside the house."

They spent the night on the riverbank, five miles upstream from the Carter house with its three crude wooden crosses thrust into the fresh earth. They had paddled like madmen, both of them driven by the need to leave the horror of the afternoon behind them. Neither Edward or Matt had wanted supper. They had tethered Slocum between them and rolled up in their blankets without even bothering to build a fire.

"Sure be some God-awful things happen in this world," Matt spoke softly, as much to himself as to his grandfather.

"*Oui* . . . they happen. Even to good people."

"Think they'll ever catch the murderin' bastards?"

"Sooner or later, *peut-etre*. I'll go to the authorities in Nashville, but they'll be long gone by then. This country can swallow up a man like he never existed. It's full of men hiding from the

59

law. Sometimes the only justice is that of *le bon Dieu*. But fate has a way of catching up with men like that. *Qui sait?* Maybe we will catch up with them ourselves, *eh bien?*"

"Lord, I hope so. I'd like to get a bead on 'em with a rifle someday—" Matt yawned with the simple weariness of youth. In the next moment he was asleep. But Edward lay awake all night, staring into the darkness.

Matt always liked to come to Nashville. It was the biggest town he had ever seen—a thousand people at least; maybe two. It was hard to say, since the place was growing so fast and had so many travelers passing through it. Carts and wagons rumbled up and down its muddy streets. Horses nickered and whinnied, their harnesses jingling. There was a fair-sized inn and two taverns, as well as a real post office, and a general store run by Lardner Clark, Esq., that was the wonder of the whole frontier. It had *everything*, that store. Anvils and millstones, saddles and harnesses, shovels, axes, hammers and picks. There were Kentucky rifles, their stocks and barrels gleaming with newness; tin plates and cups, iron skillets, candles, gunpowder and lead rifle balls, leather boots in all sizes, calico in twenty different patterns. Matt liked to wander through the place, slack-jawed with amazement. The awareness that his family had a part in this bounty gave him a nice sense of smugness as well. Forny & Cooper was one of Mr. Clark's major suppliers.

The landing, too, was an exciting place. Since Nashville marked the end of the Wilderness Road, a good many westward-bound travelers loaded their worldly possessions on rafts and flatboats, and set off down the Cumberland for the Ohio and Mississippi valleys. An abundance of trees furnished lumber for boatbuilding.

Matt stood on the landing now, his thumbs in the waistband of his trousers, his chest puffing with pride as he surveyed the newly-finished flatboat that would carry him all the way to New Orleans. Excitedly, he paced off the length of it—a good forty feet, and half that distance in width. Slocum bounded after him, barking excitedly and sniffing at the new wood. "Come on, boy!" Matt strode back over to where his grandfather, Uncle Henry, and his cousin, Slade, stood looking at the boat. "Come on, Slocum!" He whistled insistently.

But Slocum took his time. He sniffed at the boat until he found a corner that smelled just right. Then he lifted his leg and marked it his.

Henry Forny roared with laughter. "Well, we can call it christened, now. It's been done proper, Matt." Henry was about the same age as Matt's own father, dark like Edward, but a bit huskier, his features less sharp. "What think ye, boy?"

"It's big." Matt cocked his head at the boat where it sat at the water's edge, its planks the lovely pink and gold of brand new pine. "It be bigger'n I ever imagined."

"They call it a broadhorn," Henry said. "It's

61

got a place for three big steering oars, one on each side o' the front—that's the horns—and another in the rear. Think ye can handle it?"

Matt's eyes widened in puzzled alarm. Was he supposed to steer the thing by himself? Then he looked at the grin on his uncle's face and realized that he was joking.

"Don't ye worry, now," Henry laughed. "The crew's been hired already! Five o' the best men on the rivers! Just came up the Trace together last week. Ye'll be meetin' 'em when ye cast off."

"Course, if ye be need' any more help, I'll be glad to come along with ye." Slade Forny spoke up. "What d' ye say, Pa?"

"Not yet, Slade," Henry frowned. "Ye be almost two years younger 'n Matt here. Next year, maybe. Or the year after that. There be time, boy."

"Ye weren't but seventeen when Grandpa sent ye out from Fort Pitt to open up trade in these parts," Slade argued.

"Now, that'll do, Slade. Ye ain't goin' and that's that!" Henry cut him off gruffly.

Slade thrust his hands into his pockets and gazed longingly at the flatboat. He was a slim, wiry youth, who was growing day by day into a bronze-cast image of his grandfather, Edward Forny. He had the same fine-chiseled features, the same lithe, sinewy grace. He stood like Edward, walked like Edward. There was only one striking difference between Slade and his grandfather. Unlike the dark-haired, dark-eyed Edward, Slade was as fair as his mother. His hair

62

was like thick-spun gold that gleamed in the sun; his eyes a sharp, penetrating blue, and there wasn't a girl whose gaze didn't follow him when he rode past. "Matt wouldn't mind. He'd take me," Slade said.

"Less'n half the cargo'll be ours." Henry ignored his son for the moment. "I contracted out the rest. There be plenty folk wantin' their goods freighted." He scratched his chin as he studied the flatboat. "After I thought about it for a while, I figured you had the right idea. Forny & Cooper won't stay afloat less'n we take on the Mississippi, an' Matt's the one to open it up, just like I opened up the Cumberland twenty years ago." He grinned at Matt. "What say ye, boy? Rarin' to go?"

Matt let his eyes trace the line and bulk of the flatboat. He was as excited as he'd ever been in his life. But he did feel sorry for Slade. He knew what it was like to be tied to a town, to want to go so badly that the desire was like a gripping, gnawing hunger. "I truly wouldn't mind takin' Slade," he said slowly. "We could have a good time, him and me."

Henry frowned. "Ye ain't goin' for no good time, Matthew Cooper; an' Slade stays here. A year, maybe two, when he's growed up a mite, then it'll be all right. But Slade's different from the way I was at his age. He's got a wild streak in 'im, and he ain't goin' nowhere till he outgrows it." He glared at Slade. "Now not another word, neither one of ye!"

Slade scowled and kicked a rock into the river,

but when his blue eyes met Matt's in a flickering glance they were filled with warmth and gratitude. At least Matt understood. That was better than nothing. "Pa, can I show Matt the new filly?"

"Now, Slade, d'ye think Matt's got time for such foolishness? There's the boat to be readied—"

"*Il y a temps*," said Edward. "let them go, Henry. There'll be time for the boat. Let them have a few hours together. After all, they'll likely be partners in the business someday when we're gone. At least they ought to have a chance to be friends, *eh bien?*"

Henry shrugged his shoulders in resignation. "All right then, but don't ye run her too hard, Slade. An' the both of ye, be back in time for the party tonight."

"Party?" Matt's eyes widened questioningly.

Henry nodded vigorously. "Just a little get-together for Andy Jackson. He's come home from the statehouse in Knoxville for a spell, him and his wife."

"Jackson?" Matt gaped in amazement. "Ye mean Senator Andrew Jackson?"

"It be Judge Jackson now that he's back from Washington," Slade said. "He's an old friend of my pa's." He nudged Matt's arm. "Want to see how our new filly can run?"

"Aye. That I do."

"Come on, then!" Slade was off in a streak, in the direction of the Forny house. Matt hurried after him, Slocum loping at his side, half tangling

64

himself in Matt's feet.

The Forny cabin lay on the fringe of the town, and had been expanded from its modest original size to a grand place, with a long covered porch and a new section with a second story. The shed, long, and sturdily built, sat forty paces behind it, with a stable on one end.

"See, what'd ye think of her?" Slade stroked the neck of the fine-boned little roan. "She be fast as a deer and twice as pretty, eh? Fanny, that's her name, after the first girl I ever kissed." Slade grinned. "She had red hair, too."

"Your pa let ye name her?"

"Aye. Pa don't care much what a horse be called. Want to ride? We could go down the Trace for a piece and be back afore sundown." Slade glanced at Matt's stocky frame. "Best I ride Fanny here. She's a bit skittish and not used to weight. Broke her myself, I did, and she behaves herself for me. Ye can take Pa's buckskin. Saddle's over there."

In no time they'd saddled the horses and set out at a trot down the road, toward the point where the road narrowed and swung south. This, then, was the beginning of the Natchez Trace, the well-beaten trail that cut through five hundred miles of forest, swamp and canebrake to emerge finally at Natchez, far to the south on the banks of the Mississippi.

"Ever been down the Trace?" Matt asked his cousin casually.

"No more'n a few miles. Too dangerous after that. But for sure ye'll get to know it afore the summer's out. Pa says ye'll be comin' back that way from New Orleans.''

"Aye.'' Matt shaded his eyes in the bright spring sunshine and gazed down the Trace to where it vanished into the trees. Edward Forny had explained it all. The flatboat would make only one trip down the Mississippi. Since it could not return upstream, it would be sold for lumber in New Orleans, and Matt would return by land, following the Mississippi's bank as far as Natchez, then cutting inland, up the Trace, to Nashville.

"The devil's backbone, they call it,'' Slade said, reining in the dancing little roan. "Hell's name, I wish I was goin' with ye!''

"Aye. Me too.'' Matt leaned on the saddle horn and studied the trail, while Slocum investigated a rabbit hole.

"Just crawlin' with snakes an' painters an' quicksand an' bandits!'' Slade sighed. "Ye won't be goin' it alone, naturally. Nobody in his right mind goes up the Trace alone, 'ceptin' maybe John Swaney.''

"Swaney?'' Matt was intrigued.

"The mail carrier. Been ridin' the Trace for years. Makes it the whole way in ten days, half the time it takes most folk.'' Slade scratched the roan's ears. He sat his horse with the easy grace of an Indian. "They knew 'im. Injuns, varmints, bad men and all, and they leave 'im be. Rides like the devil, the man does, at full gallop most all the way.'' Slade's voice had taken on a dreamy quality, but n ow he sat up straight in his saddle.

"He'll be at the party tonight. Maybe ye'll get a chance to visit with im! Come on, let's go!" He nudged the roan forward.

Matt hesitated, and Slade laughed. "Don't let me skeer ye! It be safe as far as the first creek, an' we'll be turnin' back there. Let's go!" He dug his heels into the roan's flanks and the filly took off like a shot. "Yeeehaw!" Slade whooped, leaning forward in the saddle, his yellow hair whipping in the wind. Matt kicked the buckskin into action, but Slade kept well ahead of him. The buckskin was bigger, older, and slower than the roan filly, and Slade rode like he was part of her. They flew down the trail, Matt pounding on the buckskin and Slocum streaking behind them.

Slade reined up hard at the creek, letting the filly rear high. Then he sat back in the saddle and grinned while Matt caught up to him. "This be as fur as we go. T'other end of the trail comes out at Natchez. Golly damn, what I wouldn't give t'see Natchez, now. They say there be men there rich as King Solomon and women as wicked as Jezebel!" Slade whistled. They let the horses and the dog take a long, cool drink from the stream.

Matt stared down the trail, his spine prickling at the memory of what he and his grandfather had found back on the river. "Y' ever hear of two brothers named Harpe in these parts?"

"Hear of 'em? Aye. But there ain't nobody what claims t' have seen 'em. Nobody that lived t' tell 'bout it, that be." Slade ran a hand through his sun-gold hair. "One day there'll be signs o' the two of 'em up 'round Knoxville. Then the very next day ye'll hear they been doin' their deviltry all the way down in the Chickasaw country. They be like ghosts, comin' an' goin' . . . I heered Grandpa Forny tellin' my pa what ye found at the cabin back on the river. Coulda been the Harpes, all right." Slade spat expertly into the grass.

"It was awful," Matt said, looking down. "That poor woman, all beat and bloodied up like that. An' she'd been a pretty one, too." He dug his heels into the buckskin. "C'mon!"

"Race?" Slade leaned forward expectantly in the saddle. "Naw. Don't feel like it. Besides, ye'll only beat me."

They walked the two horses through the sun-dappled wood, Slocum ambling behind, pausing to sniff the grass and leave his mark on an occasional tree. For a time they were silent, Matt's memory reliving the horrible scene at the Carter cabin. His mind dwelt on it until it threatened to overcome the fun, the happiness, the excitement of the day. "There gonna be any girls at the party?" he asked, desperately trying to clear the blackness from his mind.

"Plenty!" Slade grinned.

"Any of 'em yours?"

"All of 'em! But I'll lend ye one for the evening. Take your pick!" Slade studied Matt, his blue eyes narrowed. "Ye got a girl back in Louisville?"

"Aye . . . ye might say that. But we ain't promised or nothin'."

Matt stared down at the buckskin's dark mane. "Slade . . . Ye ever been with a girl? Ye

68

know what I mean . . ."

"Aye, I know." Slade patted the roan's neck. "Maybe . . . an' maybe not." He grinned. "A real gentleman never tells, they say. An' Slade Forny's a real gentleman. You?"

Matt felt the color rise in his cheek. He envied Slade's coolness. It had been a perfect answer. "I . . . I be a gentleman, too," he said, though the words didn't sound quite the way they did when Slade said them. He looked up and caught Slade's eyes studying him. They looked at each other for a long time. Then both of them burst out laughing.

"All right!" Slade was holding his sides. "All right, I ain't never done it! An' I reckon you ain't never done it either! We square?"

"Aye . . ."

Matt let out his breath.

"Touched a girl once," said Slade. "She squealed like a caught possum and run off."

"Aye . . . me too," Matt admitted.

"Reckon you won't get past Natchez without doin' it, though. I heard tales from the river men what come up the Trace. Heard tell there be a street in Natchez that don't have nothin' on it but whorehouses. Cheap ones, fancy ones, Spanish girls, French girls, Indian girls, Yankee girls . . . Ye pay your money an take your pick! Oh, damn it, but I wish I was goin' along!"

"I'll tell you all 'bout it when I get back." Matt chuckled.

"They say it puts hair on your chest."

"I'll show ye my chest when I get back to Louisville!'' Matt teased. "Ye'll need t' comb the hair with a garden rake!''

"Haw!" Slade brought the flat of his palm down hard on the roan filly's rump. The horse erupted like a rocket under him, shooting straight for home. A whooping Slade leaned over the smooth neck, one with the surging motion of the powerful body. Matt followed him as best he could until the Trace broke free of the woods and opened up onto the main road. Then he reined in the buckskin and sat watching while Slade and the roan flew up the road and across the open pasture as if the devil himself was chasing them.

# V

The girl in Matt's arms had a bewitching little brown mole in the corner of her mouth. Never mind that she was too short and squat for real beauty, or that her jaw was unbecomingly square. That tiny dot of flesh held Matt's eyes like a magnet, and when he looked down at her he could think of nothing but kissing it.

Her name was Carrie, and she had eyes like small, bright, black beads. She also had wild-looking dark brown curls and a bosom that was almost as big as Elvina Hastings'. It brushed the lower part of Matt's rib cage when he whirled her in the fleeting contact of the reel. But that was not what held Matt fascinated. No, it was the soft, pink lips, the flashing teeth, and most of all, the mole.

She spun in his arms and then she was gone again, bobbing gracefully in the intricacies of the dance. Matt followed her with his eyes, stumbling over his feet a bit as he lost sight of her. Lanterns hung around the yard, casting a yellow glow on the party. A long plank table, covered with a cloth, was spread with hot cake and custard, johnny cake, pickled peaches, waffle cakes, preserved cucumbers, ham, turkey and apple sauce.

The single fiddle whined merrily, as well it should have, since the fiddler, an old man named Gambel, was the best in the state of Tennessee. And he could play anything. You only had to whistle a few notes for him, and in a twinkling the fiddle would be following the sound, like a mockingbird. He could imitate the wind, the rain, the river, the sounds of chickens, ducks and geese. He could make you cry with that fiddle.

The reel ended with whooping and clapping. Matt bowed over Carrie's hand with a perspiring "Thank-ee!" and then she spun away from him again, whisked off by another partner. But he would dance with her again, Matt resolved, if he had to lick every swain in Nashville to do it. And before the night was out, he would have a taste of that little mole.

He glanced around for Slade. There he was—in the middle of that cluster of girls. Slade seemed to attract them like fresh meat attracts flies. He knew just what to say to make them blush and giggle and come back for more. And he danced the way he rode, with an ease that was all natural grace. That afternoon when he'd declared that all the girls were his, he hadn't been joking. Matt wondered enviously how many times Slade had tasted Carrie's mole.

Edward was standing alongside the table with the older folk. He must have cut quite a figure himself in his younger days, Matt mused, as he studied his grandfather. Edward was still slim and elegant, his black hair silvered only at his temples. He was stronger than men half his age, and a devil when it came to pretty words.

Matt sighed. Words had never been his own strong point. When he got around a girl he liked, his tongue seemed to tie itself in agonized knots. What he did on a dance floor was more like stumbling than dancing, and his hands always perspired at the wrong times. Even Winifred, he lashed himself, probably wanted him only because his father had money that would be his one day. If she'd *really* loved him, she wouldn't have gone running back into the house that last night. What was it Edward had said? The best kind of woman only gives herself for love. Well, if that was so, then Winifred didn't love him. The price she'd put on herself was money and respectability. It was a high price, but it was a price all the same.

"Matt!" Edward beckoned his grandson over to where he stood with Henry Forny and a tall, rawboned stranger, "*Venez ici*, Matt. I want you to meet someone!"

"How d'ye do!" Matt found himself gazing up into a rugged, long-jawed face. Steel gray eyes drilled into him. The stranger was lean and hard as whip leather, but when he smiled there was a gentleness about his mouth.

"Andy, this be my nephew, Matthew Cooper," Henry Forny said. "Matt, I be pleased t' present Senator Andrew Jackson!"

Matt shook the long, bony hand, amazed at its strength. "Pleased t' meet you, Senator," he stammered. He'd been hearing stories about Andrew Jackson from the Forny family since he was a little boy. Meeting the man in person was like meeting the hero of a familiar fairy tale.

"Senator? Not any more." Jackson's voice still carried the twang of the frontier, but he put his words together like a man who'd had his share of book learning. "I'm through with Washington for good. Never did like the place much. It's got nothing to compare with Tennessee!"

"That's right." A striking, dark-haired, black-eyed woman had come up to slip her arm through Jackson's. Matt bowed slightly, as his grandfather had taught him. "Andrew's through with Washington. He promised me himself. He's going to stay with me on the farm for a change, 'cept when court's in session in Knoxville. I declare, I won't know what to do with havin' a husband at home all the time. Will I, Andrew?"

He smiled down at her tenderly. "Oh, I reckon you'll find some use for me after a spell, Rachel."

She smiled back at him. Rachel Donelson Robards Jackson was almost as much a legend in these parts as her husband. The daughter of one of Nashville's founders, she had fought Indians from a raft in her youth, and her beauty had made her the belle of the frontier. Her marriage to Andrew Jackson had been tainted with scandal, for she had wed him in Natchez, mistakenly believing that the Tennessee legislature had granted her first husband a divorce. When the truth came out, it set tongues to wagging all over the territory. The gossip had hurt her, but Rachel Jackson

74

was among friends in Nashville. Here she could smile and be as gay as she wished.

"Dance with me, Andrew!" She tossed her black head as a polka began. "Oh, I can't listen to old Gambel without wanting to move my feet! Come on!" She tugged her husband's arm, and he caught her up by the waist. They whirled onto the floor, a stunning couple. Jackson's russet hair gleamed in the light. Rachel's yellow dimity gown, the envy of every woman there, swirled out around her ankles.

Matt felt a light touch at his elbow. He turned his head. Carrie was standing there, smiling up at him. "I told Orville Dickinson I'd promised this dance t' you," she said saucily. "Ye don't want to make me out a liar, do ye?"

Matt grinned, suddenly feeling seven feet tall. His arm circled her waist as he swung her out onto the dance floor. His clumsy feet seemed to have wings. Slade danced by, a rosy-cheeked, brown-haired girl in his arms. He gave Matt a sly wink over his shoulder. Aye, thought Matt, some moments in a fellow's life were worth living. The hanging lanterns were a blur around him as he danced. Carrie laughed up at him, the light flickering on her pert face. Closer and closer they moved to the edge of the dancing circle, closer to the shadows outside the ring of lanterns and gay cotton streamers. Matt could feel her willingness in the way she let him steer her out of the crowd. Yes, he told himself, his heart pounding wildly, she knew what he wanted. She wanted it too.

They escaped in a few bounding steps, out of

the light and into the shadows. The next instant they were running up the dark road between the houses and under the trees. They were laughing, and breathing hard when Matt finally pulled her to a stop behind a clump of willows. She giggled as he pulled her against him, and then she wasn't giggling any more, because they were kissing and kissing. Matt nibbled at that little brown mole. It was as sweet as he had dreamed it would be. Her mouth was soft and wet and open. Her small, plump body molded itself to his. She made little squeaking sounds as he pulled her tight, murmuring something against his lips that sounded like 'L . . . More . . . oh, Lordy, more . . . Yes! Yes!''

Matt's lips moved down to her throat, her shoulders. She gasped and moaned in his arms. He wasn't even sure quite how it happened, but suddenly the front of her dress was open. He found himself slipping the straps of her camisole off her shoulders. Her breasts were as soft and white and warm as fresh bread dough, and salty to the taste. She lifted them and pushed them up against his mouth. One brown nipple popped out of the camisole. She pulled his head down to it. It puckered fascinatingly in his mouth as he drew it in, deeper and deeper. She urged him on with moans. Her hips had begun to twitch against him. She could feel the pressure of her body against his aching loins. It was heaven and hell all rolled into one.

"Carrie . . . I want ye," he whispered, his voice trembling.

"Aye . . ." she whispered, pushing herself

against him. "And I wanted ye from the first time I saw ye tonight." Her fingers tugged Matt's trouser flap open.

Matt felt dizzy. He wanted her, all right, so bad he could taste it, but he hadn't expected things to happen so fast. He thought he'd be doing well to kiss her. Not in his wildest imaginings had he expected this.

"Touch me—" She shoved a wad of her skirt into his hand, "Come on—hurry! Oh, ye gotta touch me." Carrie wriggled excitedly as Matt's hand lifted her skirt and slid up her legs. She was wearing nothing underneath her petticoat. Her flesh was cool from the night air. Matt hesitated. She seized his hand and guided it. "Here . . . Aye . . . here!" He caught his breath as he felt the soft prickle of hair, the moistness beneath—

"Carrie!" The harsh, angry voice split the air like a thunderclap. "Carrie Mae Buchanan, where be ye?"

Carrie sucked in her breath. "Oh, Lordy, it's my pa!"

Matt heard the scrape of heavy footsteps on the road, a few yards away.

"Carrie Mae! I seed ye go off, you an' that young feller! I told ye now, I'll not have ye turnin' out like your sister, with a brat that ain't got no father! Ye get out here, now! If ye ain't right here by the time I counts t' ten, by gad, I'll horsewhip ye!"

Carrie had pulled down her skirt. Her fingers flew up the front of her blouse without missing a

77

single button. "Don't ye move," she whispered to Matt. "I'll head 'im off!"

She ran on into the trees. Matt stood frozen in his tracks as he heard the rustle of leaves grow fainter.

"One . . ." Carrie's father had begun to count, muttering under his breath between the numbers. "Two . . . three . . . gonna kill that girl when I find her. Four . . . five . . . six . . . seven, eight . . . nine . . . damn it all to—"

"Pa? You out there?" Carrie had circled around her father and come out onto the road well up in the direction of the party. "Pa, ye be lookin' for me?"

"Aye, I be lookin' for ye, girl! Where the devil ye been?"

"There be things a girl got t' do by herself, Pa. Went t' the bushes 'longside Dolly Martin's house. That be all."

"An' that young whelp I seed ye dancing' with?"

"Lawse, Pa, ye think I'd go and do a thing like *that* with a boy around?" Carrie's voice was indignant. "I ain't seen 'im! Not since the polka finished! Far as I know he be with some other girl!"

The man sighed. It was easy to guess that he'd argued with his daughter plenty of times before, and long since found that there was no way to win. "It be gettin' late," he said gruffly. "Time we was goin' home. Go find your ma, while I get the wagon."

"No," Carrie wailed. "The dance just got

78

started. Won't be over for a long time yet!"

"There be plowin' and milkin' to do in the mornin', girl. Come on. Get ye goin'!" He ambled wearily up the road toward her. With a little huff of anger, Carrie fled back toward the dance.

Matt let out his breath. He was shaking now that it was over. There'd have been big trouble if Carrie's father had caught them together.

His trouser flap was still hanging half open. Seething with frustration, he jerked it shut and pulled the buttons through. He was hurting even worse than he had that night after Winifred had left him. He squeezed his eyes and a tear trickled down his cheek. The whole experience had shaken him—the fun, the surprise, the wild, raging desire, the fear, and now the aching, throbbing frustration. Would he be any happier if he'd had Carrie? Was it what he'd really wanted?

He didn't know. He only knew that he hurt. He was too old to cry, so Matt doubled up his fist and slammed it into a tree.

Slade was waiting for him when he finally reappeared at the party. His lean, handsome face wore an impish grin. "So ye be in one piece, eh?"

Matt only scowled at him.

"I shoulda warned ye 'bout Carrie. She be a wild one, but her pa don't let her out o' his sight. Ye be lucky, Matt. Most times he packs a rifle just for runnin' the boys off. Ye be right lucky ye didn't get your britches shot off." Slade's chuckle was the devil's own.

"If she be so full o' juice an' ginger, how come ye ain't had 'er yourself?" Matt demanded.

79

Slade only grinned, shrugged in that annoyingly mysterious way he had about him, and helped himself to a swallow of peach brandy from a jug on the table. The reflections of the lanterns made yellow dots in his blue eyes. "I was hopin' John Swaney'd be here." He scanned the crowd. "I knowed ye wanted t'meet him. Just came in off the Trace this afternoon, somebody says. He can tell ye all about it."

Slade gave a little whoop. "Aye, there he be. Come on—" He grabbed Matt's arm.

The mail-rider stood at the other end of the table, munching on a slice of preserved cucumber. Matt could see why Slade had had trouble spotting him. He wasn't the kind of man who'd stand out in a crowd. There was nothing impressive about his size. The top of his head wouldn't have come any higher than the tip of Matt's nose, and he was as thin as a wire.

"Mister Swaney!" Slade spoke his name and he turned at the sound of it. He had a homely face with a narrow, expressionless mouth. His skin was burnished dark brown by sun and weather, up to the line of his hat. Above that point it was as white as a frog's belly.

"Mister Swaney, this here be my cousin, Matt Cooper, down from Nashville," Slade announced, presenting Matt with a flourish.

"How do." Swaney extended a hand. The strength of his handclasp was so astounding that Matt winced, not in pain but in surprise. He looked Swaney up and down. The little man's body was all muscle, sinew and bone. There was

80

not an ounce of extra flesh on him. Matt thought of the feat John Swaney had performed twice every month for years, riding through more than five hundred miles of danger-infested wilderness in ten days—when it took most folks three weeks to make the same trip. For all Swaney's small size, Matt mused, the little man was made out of nothing but strength, courage and stamina. An admiration began to grow in him, so strong that it almost amounted to reverence. "Pleased to meet ye, Mister Swaney . . . right honored in fact," Matt replied, stumbling a bit over his own tongue.

"Matt'll be goin' downriver soon," Slade said. "He'll be comin' back by way of the Trace."

Swaney took another bite of preserved cucumber and chewed on it thoughtfully. Slocum emerged from under the table where he had been sleeping. He stretched his front legs and yawned. Then he raised up enough to see what was on the table. Casually he eyed the platter of corn dodgers, stretched his neck, took one in his mouth and disappeared under the table again.

"Yer dog?" Swaney chewed some more.

"Aye." Matt flushed.

"Good dog. Ye ought t' be teachin' him better manners."

At the words, *good dog*, Slocum sidled out from under the table, wagged his tail and leaned against Swaney's legs.

"He likes ye," Matt said. "He don't like many strangers."

Swaney glanced down as Slocum sat on his

boot, but he didn't say anything.

"I been wantin' to ask ye about the Trace, being's I'll be comin' back that way," Matt said hesitantly. "What can ye tell me about it?"

"Ye don't go it alone," Swaney said, spitting out a seed. "Ye find somebody what's done it afore an' ye go with 'em. That be the only safe way, boy."

"Ye ride it alone all the time."

"That be different." Swaney turned back to the table and took a swallow from the jug of peach brandy.

"Ever hear o' the Harpe brothers?"

"Aye."

"Ever seen 'em?"

"Ain't. But I seen what they done."

"So did I," Matt said eagerly. "On our way up here, comin' up the Cumberland. They killed three people, a man, a woman and a baby. Lord, it was awful."

"Did ye see the Harpes?"

Matt shook his head. "They was gone afore we come."

"Then it coulda been anybody. Maybe Mason an' his bunch. Ain't been much sign o' the Harpes up that way." Swaney took another swallow of the brandy.

"What do they look like?" Matt asked. "How would I know if I saw 'em?"

Swaney shrugged. "Ain't a few what sees 'em an' lives. But there be a big one an' a little one—Big Harpe an' Little Harpe, they call 'em along the Trace and the Wilderness Road. But ye needn't have no fear of 'em if ye be travelin' in a fair-sized company." Swaney glanced up at the moon and then turned away and wandered off, the conversation finished as far as he was concerned. Slocum followed him for a few yards, sniffing at his heels. Then the big yellow dog sneezed and trotted back to Matt.

"He be a strange one," Matt said to Slade as the mail carrier disappeared into the crowd.

"Aye. Takes a strange man to do what he does. But Swaney's tougher 'n old rawhide. Can't help but look up to a man like that."

"Aye." Matt patted Slocum's head.

"Say—there be Susanna Perkins! Ain't danced with her yet—"

Slade was off on a new pursuit, leaving Matt alone at the table.

He picked up another corn dodger, broke it in two, and gave the biggest half to Slocum. Somewhere off behind him in the night he could hear Carrie, still arguing with her faster. "No, Pa! I'd rather walk home than go now! Lemme stay!"

Then the sound of her voice faded as the wagon rolled away.

# VI

The new flatboat had been rolled into the river on round logs. Now it floated beside the landing, tugging gently at the rope that had held it prisoner while the cargo was being loaded. The two big millstones had rolled aboard first, and stowed in the bottom, flat on their sides. Between and around them had gone the casks of cider and Monongahela whiskey that had come down over the Wilderness Road and through the Cumberland Gap by wagon. Over these had been laid the main cargo, hundreds of prime pelts, trapped that winter in the North—otter, mink and beaver, fox and wildcat, along with fifty buffalo skins.

The decking had been laid over these, and the living quarters for the crew set up in a small cabin placed at the boat's rear. Edward Forny inspected the whole structure carefully. The future of Forny & Cooper could well depend on the boat's safe arrival in New Orleans. And it was not just the trade goods Edward was thinking of. He was entrusting the life of his precious grandson to this boat. He wanted to make sure it was as sound as possible.

He had met the crew earlier that morning. They were a good lot, he reflected, tough, competent and merry. *Bonhommes*, he told himself. Matt would learn a good deal from these men before the long voyage was over.

He watched them stow their gear in the cabin. There were five of them—LeClerc, a bandy-legged little French Creole from New Orleans; Kovalenko, a gigantic, easygoing Pole; Maddox, who had a round white scar on the crown of his head where a Shawnee had scalped him. There was pug-nosed Oscar Sutton, clearly the joker of the crew; and then there was the boss.

He stood on the deck now, cocky as a rooster, in his red flannel shirt and loose, blue coat, a mangy looking coonskin hat with a turkey feather in it perched on his head. His name was Mike Fink.

The original man who'd been signed as crew boss had taken sick with the fever two days before the planned departure, leaving Edward and Henry with the problem of choosing a replacement for him. It was John Swaney who'd mentioned that Fink just happened to be in town. "Ye won't get nobody better," Swaney had told them, "if ye can get him at all. He be a keelboat man, an' a real keelboat man won't even spit on a flatboat. But there ben't no keelboats going out o' here, and I heerd tell he's a bit down on his luck of late. Ask 'em. Worst he'll do is tell ye no."

Edward and Henry had found Fink in one of the taverns, staring grumpily into an empty mug. "Fill her up with whiskey for me! Then we'll talk," he'd said.

"To the top?" Edward had asked cautiously. The mug was a big one, of the kind usually reserved for cider or ale. *Ma foi*, that much whiskey would be enough to stupefy a buffalo bull!

Fink raised one bushy eyebrow. "Aye, old man, to the top. And stop askin' questions."

When the tavern keeper brought the brimming mug back to the table, Fink lifted it and took a long swig. "Aye, that's better," he said, lowering the jug to the table and wiping his mouth on his sleeve. "Now ye can tell me your business!"

Henry had told him what they needed, a crew boss on a flatboat, to leave in two days. Fink had scowled and taken another long swallow of the whiskey. "I'm a keelboat man," he'd replied at last, his big, square jaw set stubbornly. "If'n ye want me to boss your damned flatboat, ye'll have to pay me twice again whatever the rest of the crew's gettin'."

"*Tonnerre*, no man's worth that much!" Edward had exclaimed disgustedly. "*Mon ami*, we pay our crews a fair wage. The boss gets more than the others. But twice as much! Finish your whiskey, *Monsieur* Fink. Drink it in good health, but we'll do our looking elsewhere."

They had spent the next two hours prowling the town, looking among the river-toughened boatmen who'd come in after three weeks on the Trace. Most of them had planned on enjoying at least a week or two of rest before setting out again. None of them wanted work on a boat that would be leaving day after tomorrow. So cautiously Edward and Henry had begun to ask

87

questions about Mike Fink.

"Won't find a better man on the whole damned river!" one grizzled veteran had told them.

"Aye, Mike's the best," his companion agreed. "But Lordy, how that man can drink. Once I seen 'im down a gallon of Monongahela in less'n an hour. Then he got out his rifle and plinked off a muskrat on the bank, so blasted far away that the rest of us could barely see it. I asked him if he could shoot any better when he was sober. He just laughed."

"Double wages he wants, be it?" Another man put in. "By hell, ye be damned lucky. Fink'd be worth triple at least. Ain't a man on the river what can out-bully him! He runs a crew like they was 'is own arms and legs!"

So Henry and Edward had gone back to the tavern, filled Fink's mug once more, and offered him double salary. Even after the second mug was gone, he was still sober enough to sign his name to the contract.

And Fink looked sober enough this morning, Edward reflected, gazing at him from the landing, though you never could tell. "Ye cut Mike's finger," someone said, "and what runs out o' it won't even be red. It'd be pure Monongahela whiskey! Ye could bleed 'im into a glass and drink it!"

Matt had yet to meet Fink, though he'd been introduced to the rest of the crew. The boy had been busy packing his things, and then re-packing them. Edward was sure that Matt hadn't slept a wink the night before, he was so excited about the departure. But where was he now? Edward glanced anxiously up the road that led from the landing to the town. He'd just left Matt finishing a huge breakfast that his Aunt Sara had cooked for him. The boy'd told him he'd finish eating, round up Slocum, and be down on the landing ready to go in a few minutes. What could have delayed him? Fink and the others were getting restless.

Just then Matt came into sight around the bend. He was carrying his clothes and bedding in a roll on one shoulder. His other hand held a long rope, and that rope was attached to Slocum's neck. Slocum was slinking along close to the ground, his tail tucked tight between his legs.

"*Quelle diable?*" Edward muttered, puzzled. But as soon as the two of them got a little closer he knew what had happened. He groaned out loud as the hideously pungent odor reached his nostrils.

The smell had reached the boat as well. Fink sniffed the air and began to curse. Oscar Sutton began to laugh.

"Skunk," Matt said sheepishly as soon as he was within speaking range. "Right after you left this morning. Aunt Sara didn't have nothin' that worked on it. Thought maybe if we throwed 'im in the river—"

"Throw him in?" Fink roared. "Hot holy hell, we ought to drown the mangy mutt! And the boy too!"

"Won't do no good," Maddox rumbled in his deep voice. "Won't come off in water. We had a

89

hound do that once. Had t' bury 'im in the ground up to his neck for three days. Died afore we got 'im out. Dumb dog."

"That be true," Oscar Sutton agreed. "That smell, it stick like bear grease. Water won't do it. Ye got t' roll 'im in fresh cow manure. Don't do much for the skunk stink, but at least it makes it so's ye don't know what yer smellin'!" He chuckled. "Well, ye can't bring that dog on the boat, boy. No two ways 'bout it!"

"No—" Matt's eyes darted from the boat to Slocum to his grandfather. "Ye know Slocum, Grandpa. He won't stay behind. He'll chase the boat first chance, and Lord knows what'll happen to 'im!"

Edward groped for a way to resolve the situation. Matt was almost in tears. Slocum cowered on the ground, a far cry from his usual cocky self. The air all around him reeked horribly. It was a smell to make the eyes water and the stomach turn over. Edward had long considered himself the master of almost any situation. But this time he was at a loss.

"Well, I ain't gettin' on no flatboat with no dog what smells like that!" snapped Mike Fink. He folded his arms across his broad chest and stood on the deck like a statue.

Kovalenko, the big Pole, stepped forward at last, pushing his knit cap back from his homely face and clearing his throat. "If it works to put the dog in the ground, then maybe it work to put the ground on the dog," he said in his strangely gentle voice. "We could put the mud all over him

90

and let it dry all day, eh? Then at night we wash it off and put on more. Soon the mud, she soak up all the smell, eh? A few days, no more. We could tie him up outside the shack. What you say, eh Mike?"

Fink pursed his lips and wrinkled his nose in distaste. "Might try it," he said slowly. "But you listen t' me, boy! If'n that mutt gets within ten paces o' Mike Fink, there'll be hell t' pay! I'll use 'im fer target practice, I will!"

"Yessir," Matt muttered, tugging the reluctant Slocum toward the water. The big dog dug his feet into the muddy grass and braced himself against the rope. It took all Matt's strength to inch him forward. Fink and the crew roared with laughter. Even Edward had to chuckle as Matt kicked off his shoes and waded knee-deep into the water. Slocum had always hated water. He was as bad as a cat that way. Matt jerked him into the current. He yelped as he lost his footing, then thrashed the water into malodorous foam. But the smell remained.

"We try the mud, then," said big Kovalenko. "Here, boy, I help you." He came splashing off the side of the flatboat, pulled his thick-bladed knife, and began to scrape away at the dark mud along the bank. "Hold him, now. You just hold him, boy, an' I throw on the mud, eh?"

Matt dragged Slocum up onto the bank and the big Pole began to throw mud onto him. Mike Fink squatted on his haunches and watched them, a devilish grin splitting his pug-nosed, Irish face. "I got jest one question!" he yelled when the mudding of Slocum was finished. "Which one of you be the dog? Ye'll be so covered with muck that I can't tell one of ye from the other. We'll have t' tie all three of ye behind the shack!"

By the time Matt and Kovalenko had wrestled Slocum onto the boat and washed the mud off themselves, the rest of the Forny family had come down to the landing to see the boat off. Henry still had the dust of the warehouse on his breeches. His Sara stood beside him, slim and golden-haired as Edward remembered her from the first days of their marriage. Slade was there, almost chewing his lip with envy. The two little girls, giggling towheads, played tag among the grownups.

Matt stood before them now, his clothes and hair drying rapidly in the warm morning sun. Edward clasped his grandson's broad shoulders. "*Au revoir.*" His eyes stung. "Take care of yourself Matt. Here—I've got something for you."

Edward bent down and opened up the pack he had laid on the ground. Out of it he lifted a shining-new long-barreled Kentucky rifle. "It's yours," he said, handing it to Matt. "I'll be giving you powder and wadding and shot to go with it. Use it well. By the time you get back to Louisville I want you to be the best shot on the whole Mississippi!"

Matt took the gun and gleefully sighted it along the barrel. "T'won't be hard with a shootin' piece like this!" he exclaimed. "Thank ye, Grandpa."

Edward happened to glance at the boat just then. His eye caught Mike Fink gazing at Matt and the new gun. The look on his coarse, pugnacious face was disturbing. Was it envy? Greed? Malice? Edward could not be sure, but suddenly he was worried.

"No foolish chances with this bunch, eh?" he cautioned Matt. "They're not bad boys, now, but they're wild. You're a cut above all of them. Learn from them, but don't let them teach you too much, *eh bien?*"

"All right, Grandpa." Matt was almost dancing up and down in his eagerness to be off. "Goodbye, Uncle Henry and Aunt Sara. Goodbye, Slade."

Slade nodded a grudging farewell. He looked more downcast than ever, since Edward had given Matt the rifle.

Matt bounded up the gangplank and pulled the plank up behind him. Slocum hunkered on the back end of the flatboat, a great lump of misery and drying mud. The air still reeked with the odor of the skunk.

Maddox and LeClerc poled away from the bank. The boat caught the current and began to drift downstream.

"*Bonne chance!*" Edward shouted, waving his arms. The others waved, too, all except Slade. He just stood with his arms hanging at his sides and watched the flatboat until it disappeared around the first bend.

Henry was already headed back to the warehouse, Sara to her washing and baking. Except for a few passers-by, Edward and Slade stood alone on the landing. Edward put a hand on his grandson's shoulder. Something tugged at his heart. This boy—looking at him was like looking into a mirror of his own youth. "You wanted very much to go, *vraiment?*"

"Aye."

"Well, another time. Right now you can help me carry that pack back to the warehouse. I'd carry it myself, but it's . . . a bit heavy." Edward's eyes twinkled. "Go on, pick it up."

"But it's—" Slade picked up the loose pack. "It ain't empty, Grandpa."

"*Oui.* And whatever's inside is yours, I suppose." Edward smiled. "Go ahead. Open it, *mon fils.*"

Slade's eager fingers tugged at the remaining laces. "It . . . it's . . . Oh!" He pulled out a brand new rifle, identical to the one Edward had given Matt. He hefted it ecstatically, grinning.

"*Allons-y!*" Edward patted his shoulder. "Let's go see what we can bring home for dinner, eh?"


Slocum was gone. Matt's heart plummeted as he saw the chewed broken rope, and the smeared mud on the end of the deck. They'd been on the river no more than half a day, and Matt had checked on the dog from time to time. Slocum had been there the last time he'd looked, not an hour ago. He'd been sitting there with his head drooping and his tail between his legs, a stinking lump of sun-hardened mud. Now he was gone. Matt had not even heard a splash.

Matt swallowed hard. Maybe Slocum had made it to the shore. Maybe he'd find his way back to Nashville, or else maybe that night when they made camp, he'd come bounding through the brush to cover Matt's face with big, sloppy kisses. Or maybe he wouldn't come back at all.

Matt walked back around the shack. His eyes stung, blurring the bright sunlight. Mike Fink glanced back at him from his position at the right hand steering oar. "Your turn next, Master Cooper! Come on over here! I'll show ye how t'work this steerin' oar, so's ye can take your turn with the rest o' us. Ain't got no room for laggards on this trip, no sir! Not even if they be the owner's own boy grandbaby!"

"Aye. In a minute." Matt's eyes were so full of tears he could hardly see. Slocum or no Slocum, he couldn't let Mike Fink see him like that. Fink would give him no mercy.

He fumbled in the pocket of his breeches for a handkerchief to wipe his eyes and blow his nose. As usual, he'd forgotten to put one in. But his Aunt Sara had tucked a handful of them in the bag with his clothes. The bag was in the cabin.

"Master Cooper!" Fink's voice had a nasty edge to it. "I got your grandpappy's permission t' teach ye how t' run a flatboat. An' the first thing ye learns is who the boss is!"

"Just a minute," Matt said, ducking into the door of the cabin. "I be right there!"

The cabin seemed dim after the glaring sunlight. Matt could make out only the silhouette of LeClerc where he sat at the rear window, handling the long sweep that controlled the stern. Le-Clerc was staring out the window at the river, his attention on the oar and the current. He had not seen Mike come in, and it was clear that he had noticed what else was in the cabin.

Slocum, muddy and stinking, lay sprawled contentedly on Mike Fink's bed.

Fink, unfortunately, picked that moment to enter the cabin. "Look, ye young whelp, I'm the boss on this boat—and when I say for ye to come runnin'—" he went white around the mouth as he spotted Slocum on his bed. His jaw dropped in sputtering silence.

"Slocum!" Matt hissed frantically. "Out! Out with ye! Go on, boy!"

Slocum yawned and turned over on his back for a belly-rub.

"Get him out o' here!" Mike Fink roared. "Get him out *now*, or so help me, I shoot the mutt right here!"

Slocum turned back over, sat up and scratched his ear with his hind foot, throwing flakes of dried mud all over the cabin.

With a muffled curse, Fink reached for the pack where he kept his rifle. Matt made a dive for Slocum and grabbed him by the scruff of the neck. "Out! Out with ye, ye fool dog!" His relief at seeing Slocum alive and safe was blotted out by a surge of panic. Fink was mad enough to kill the dog, and he looked like he was capable of doing it.

Matt shoved Slocum out onto the deck. Mike Fink had his rifle out now and was ramming the barrel. He paused long enough to kick angrily at his befouled bedding. "We be a' tradin' beds, Master Cooper! This be your bed now, and I'll be takin' your clean one if ye'd be so kind."

"Aye!" Matt braced himself between Fink and Slocum. "Anything ye say, Mr. Fink! Just as long as ye let the dog be."

"I had enough of that mangy cur to last me the whole damned trip!" Fink growled. "Either he goes, Master Cooper, or I go, an' I takes the whole crew with me! Ye and the mutt can take this stinkin' flatboat to New Orleans all by yourselves! One side!"

Matt stood his ground, his jaw set, his knees braced against their shaking. "Ye'll have to shoot me first," he said, trying to keep his voice calm. Slocum sneezed and laid down on the deck.

For a moment the two of them glared at one another. Matt felt the sweat popping out on his forehead as he met Fink's hot green eyes. Then, with a slow, lopsided grin, Fink lowered the gun.

"I'll tell ye what, Master Cooper. Ye look like a sportin' man, an' a good man in a fight, too, I'll wager. If ye can ship old Mike Fink in a fair fight, I'll do whatever you like. The mutt can sleep wherever he wants. I won't pay him no mind. An' I'll even let ye have your own clean bed back."

The back of Matt's neck prickled with wariness. "And if I lose?" he asked slowly.

"If ye lose, the dog goes. Either I shoot him or we put him ashore and leave him. An' I'll take that new shootin' piece your grandpappy gave ye this mornin'. We got a bargain, Master Cooper?"

97

Matt weighed the offer in his mind. It did seem a bit one-sided in Fink's favor. "Your own rifle ought'a stand in the wager t'make it even if I win," he said.

"All right then. The dog and the rifle if ye be wantin' it that way. We got a bargain, eh, Master Cooper?" Fink's eyes squinted at him.

Matt looked the man up and down. He wasn't all that big, though he had a chest like a bull and a quick, nervous way of moving that made Matt's spine prickle with caution. But did he have a choice?"

Matt took a deep breath. "Aye," he said slowly. "We got a fight."

# VII

Matt followed Fink out onto the deck. There was no need to announce the fight to the crew. They'd heard every word of Fink's challenge, and they waited eagerly, like wolves licking their chops. Only Kovalenko, who had taken the right hand sweep, had a kind word of caution for Matt.

"He be a tricky one, that Fink," he said softly as Matt moved past him. "He don't wear that turkey feather in his hat for nothing, eh? You'll be lucky to take 'im, boy."

"Tie up the mutt," Fink ordered. "Don't want no stinkin' dog jumpin' me when I go for ye, Cooper."

"Aye." Matt tied Slocum to the cabin door. Fink motioned to Sutton to check the knot's tightness, and Sutton made a great show of readjusting it. "Had to see ye didn't tie no slip knot!" He grinned, showing two missing front teeth below his full upper lip.

Matt felt himself sweating in the warm afternoon sun. How had he ever gotten himself into this? Fink was a man in his prime—tough, experienced, and meaner than salt on a burn. Most

99

likely licked men all up and down the river. He could probably make sausage out of a nineteen-year-old boy. Matt glanced over at Slocum. The dog was tugging at his rope, a puzzled expression on his muddy face. Matt straightened up and forced himself to look Mike Fink straight in the eye. "Let's be gettin' it over with," He said.

"All right, Master Cooper!" Fink slipped out of his coat, then began to unbutton his red flannel shirt. His chest was muscled like a stallion's. His arms bulged and rippled with naked power. Matt swallowed hard as he stripped off his own shirt. He'd never been ashamed of the way he was built, but compared to Mike Fink he looked like a skinny youngster.

"Well—" Matt faced him, trying to keep his knees from shaking.

"Not till I warm up!" Fink declared, taking a deep breath and flexing his arms.

"An' how long's it take ye to do that?" Matt was getting impatient. Waiting wouldn't make it any easier, especially when he was getting more scared by the minute. He'd be all right once the fight started, he knew. But much more of this damned waiting and he'd wet his pants. "How long?" he demanded.

Fink didn't answer. Instead he crouched low and drew in his arms like some animal about to spring. Then he leaped straight up in the air. "Heee-haw!" he whooped. "Will ye look at me? I be half horse, half alligator, and half Tennessee mule! I was sired by a hurricane, an' whelped by the Allegheny Mountains!" He whooped, leaped

100

up into the air again, and came down with his nose a hand's breadth from Matt's face.

"Listen t' me, boy! I am a man! I am a team! I can out-run, out-hop, out-jump, throw down, drag out, and lick any man in the country. When I snore, the wind blows the trees over. When I belch, the earth shakes. I'm a Salt River roarer. I love the women and I be chuck full of fight! Be ye ready, boy?"

"Aye," Matt's throat was dry. He'd never seen such a display in his whole life.

Fink backed away, lowered his head, and pawed the deck with his feet like a bull. Matt raised his fists. If Fink came in swinging, he'd be ready for him. He knew how to punch.

But Fink, when he came, charged head first. His rock-hard skull slammed into Matt's stomach, knocking the wind out of him. He staggered backward, gasping. The punch he'd been set to land glanced harmlessly off Fink's back. Before he could regain his footing, a deft kick from Fink chopped the backs of his knees. He fell over backward.

The impact of his rump on the deck stunned Matt. It was also enough to make him mad. He flung himself over, grabbed Fink's ankles, and jerked hard. Fink went over, but as he fell his boots crunched into Matt's face. Matt tasted blood. Then the two of them were rolling on the deck, punching, kicking and wrestling.

Slocum had set up an awful din, growling, barking and lunging at the rope that held him fast. The men were hooting and cheering. Matt pounded Fink's ribs with his fist. It was like pounding an oaken barrel, and it must have hurt his hand more than it hurt Fink. Matt gasped and doubled up with helpless pain as he caught a well-aimed knee to the groin. "You dirty—" he muttered.

"Had enough?" Fink leaned back and chuckled as Matt writhed in agony.

"No, damn you!" Matt muttered through clenched teeth. "You ain't give me a chance t' lick ye yet, but I'm gonna do it!" He struggled to his knees, then to his feet. He still felt sick inside, but one glance at Slocum was enough to keep him going. By damn, Fink would have to kill him to take that yellow mutt.

He lunged at Fink, his fists flying. Matt could lick any boy his age in Louisville. At least, by hell, he'd do some damage before he was through with Fink.

Fink's kick, aimed right for the bottom of his rib cage, knocked the wind out of him again, but the force of his lunge sent them both rolling to the deck again. Matt was learning. He kept himself clear of Fink's jabbing knees. His fists assaulted Fink's ironhard gut. His body dodged and twisted, avoiding the worst of Fink's vicious jabs. But just when he thought he was doing all right, he felt something clamp onto his ear. He yelped with pain, surprise and rage. He'd thought they fought mean in Louisville, but by hot, holy thunder, they didn't *bite!*

Fink ground his teeth on Matt's ear and twisted hard. It hurt. It hurt like hell. Matt clamped his jaws together to keep from crying out again.

"Hey, boy!" Maddox leaned over them. "Ye'd better say 'enough'. Fink'll bite yer ear clean off. I seen him do it afore, down in New Orleans. Ye be too young t' go lookin' like that feller did after ol' Mike got through with 'im."

Matt just grunted. Fink could damn well bite his ear off. He wasn't giving up. His hand groped for Fink's chin. He clasped the grinding jaws and tried to pry them open. His thumb went deep, digging into the flesh under Fink's jaw, thrusting hard. It worked. Fink let go, spitting out Matt's blood. "Ye young whelp! Why ye ain't even lost your milk teeth yet! I'll show ye!" Fink shoved Matt away from him and leaped to his feet.

Matt struggled to his knees. He could feel the warm blood trickling down the side of his neck. He didn't dare feel his ear. He'd almost gained his feet when Fink leaped for him, boots-first. Like a cannonball he flew through the air. His feet caught Matt's midsection. The air whooshed out of Matt's lungs. He stumbled backward. Then Fink's fist slammed into his jaw. He saw stars. His knees weakened. The sound of Slocum's frantic barking faded in his mind as he felt himself swaying. "Had enough?" Fink grinned. He didn't even sound winded.

Matt blinked and spread his legs to steady his footing. "No," he muttered. "No, ye bloody bastard. I ain't had enough. I ain't givin' up! I'm gonna whup ye till ye squeal like a stuck pig!"

Fink's fist crashed into him again. Matt felt the

bones of his face yield to the blow. He tasted blood. A good lot of it, and he knew Fink had smashed his nose. He raised his fists and swung them wildly. Fink parried the blows like an expert, then ducked low and sent a vicious chop that hit Matt right at the belt line. Matt felt a sense of nausea rising in him. He stumbled forward, then backward, and finally fell on his side.

Mike Fink kicked him over onto his back. "Now, by hell, I reckon ye've learned a lesson, Master Cooper. D' ye give up?"

"N . . . No," Matt whispered. "Never . . ." He could hear Slocum's anxious whining somewhere beyond his head.

"Mike, that's enough." It was big Kovalenko's voice. "You have already hurt the boy. Do you want to kill him eh? Let him be."

"Enough?" Fink glared down into Matt's face.

"No. I ain't licked. Ye want t' call it a draw, an' I'll go along with that. But I ain't licked. Ye ain't touchin' my dog, ye bastard."

"Ye give up right now, or by Gawd I'll stomp ye right into the deck."

Matt set his jaw stubbornly and said nothing. If he was going to die in the next minute or two, by heaven he'd die like a man. He glared back up and Fink shook his head.

With a blood-curdling whoop, Mike Fink shot up into the air and came straight down, his vicious boots aimed for Matt's chest. This time, Matt's instincts took over. He shifted slightly and grabbed Fink's legs as he landed. Then, with an excruciating twist of his body, he jerked Fink's legs and sent Fink's body slamming into the deck. Fink grunted as he hit.

Fink was stunned. He was also mad. He scrambled to his feet, his face beet red.

Matt had struggled to his feet. He stood there, swaying dizzily. Mike Fink's image doubled for a moment, then returned to normal.

"By hell, I be tired o' playin' games with ye!" Fink muttered. "It's time I put ye away proper." He was swaying a little himself. The fall onto the deck had left him breathless, and at least stung a bit. He drew back his arm, poised his body, and threw his full weight into a whopping punch that struck Matt squarely on the chin.

Something seemed to explode in Matt's head. He saw sparks of light; then there was nothing but blackness as he buckled like an empty sock and collapsed full length on the deck.

Matt felt something warm and damp on his face. It was Slocum, licking his cheeks and making worried little whining noises. When Matt opened his eyes, the big, yellow dog went into a fit of joy. He wagged and yipped and shook skunk-flavored mud all over the deck. Matt put his arm around Slocum, mud, skunk, and all. "Stupid old dog," he whispered. "Don't ye know I lost? Don't ye know I didn't save ye?" Tears began to fill his eyes.

Slowly he became aware that the other men on the boat were standing in a circle around him.

Mike Fink stood at his feet. He was wearing his blue jacket again, and his red flannel shirt and the ratty coonskin hat with the turkey feather stuck in it. His face had been washed, and his hair slicked back. He was grinning. "Ye was out quite a spell, boy," he said.

Matt sat up slowly, leaning on his elbow. His ears were ringing, and his brain still seemed befuddled. He opened his mouth to speak. No words came out, but the movement of his jaw sent waves of pain radiating all over his face. With one trembling hand he felt for his ear. Yes it was still attached to his head, and still more or less in one piece. But he could feel the raw marks of Mike Fink's teeth on it, and his fingers were tipped with blood when he took them away.

With even greater dread he felt his face. His nose was decidedly smashed, and already beginning to swell. There was a long, excruciatingly tender bruise all along one cheek. He wriggled his jaw cautiously. It didn't seem to be broken, but it hurt like blazes.

"Ye'll live," Fink exclaimed with a good-humored chuckle.

"And when ye be an old man, ye can tell your grandbabies how the great Mike Fink gave ye your first lickin' on the river!"

Matt was feeling with his tongue for loose teeth. "Who says I be licked?" he muttered, every syllable hurting.

Fink roared with laughter then. "I declare, Cooper, ye be the toughest young whelp I ever fit in my life. But ye lost all right. Them's the rules.

Once a man's out colder 'n a dead fish on ice, that be the end o' the fight, and the one what's still standin' wins it."

Matt glared at him, trying at least to hang onto some dignity. That in itself wasn't easy, with Slocum drooling all over the front of his shirt.

"Tell ye what," said Fink. "I be a powerful sore loser, but by gawd, no man can say Mike Fink ain't a good winner. Ye wagered the dog and the rifle agin me. Tell ye what, boy. Since ye fit such a good fight, I'll be satisfied with one or the other. An I'll let ye take your pick. The rifle or the mutt. Which is it ye'll be choosin' to keep boy?"

Matt's arm went around Slocum's neck. "The rifle's in my pack," he said slowly. "Take it. Ye won it."

Slocum seemed to understand. He sneezed wetly. His muddy tail beat a joyous tattoo on the deck.

Fink strolled off to take a long swig of whiskey from the jug that Sutton offered him. Then he went into the cabin, and Matt heard the sound of rummaging as he found his prize—Matt's new rifle, the one his grandfather had just given him. It hadn't even been fired.

Kovalenko handed Matt a tin dipper filled with water. He watched as Matt took a few swallows, then poured the rest of it over his head. The stinging shock of the cold water cleared Matt's mind at least. He could think now, though he was more aware of the pain that throbbed in his smashed face, his bruised ribs, and his mangled ear.

"You all right, boy?" Kovalenko leaned over him. He had a thick neck, like an ox, and small, bright, kind eyes. "You all right?" he asked again.

"Aye." Matt spat over the edge of the boat into the water. "It was the rifle Fink wanted all along, wasn't it?"

Kovalenko nodded. "It's a right pretty shooting piece. I saw Mike Fink's eyes when your grandfather gave it to you. He had already made up his mind that he wanted it. And that man, he always finds a way to get what he wants, no matter what it is. A gun, a woman. A jug of whiskey. What he wants, he takes. Hold still, boy." Kovalenko dabbed at Matt's ear. "It is not so bad. There will be a scar yes, but I do not think the ear will lose its shape, the way some do. Yes . . . turn your head. I was with him once, on a keelboat. We saw some fine sheep along the shore. Mike Fink, he ordered us to stop. Then he caught two of the fattest rams and rubbed snuff in their noses. Made them sneeze and paw at their faces. 'Look,' Mike Fink told the owner. 'They got black murrain. If I don't kill them for you, all the rest will get it. For a price, I will take them off your hands.' "

Gently the big Pole wiped the blood from Matt's nose. "I don't need to tell you what a fine mutton supper we had that night, eh? But Mike Fink, he is not a bad man. Only wild, and tough with a bit of the devil in him. I know him. He would never have hurt your dog. That was only . . . how you say it? a bluff. That is the word. A bluff, to scare you. It was the gun he wanted. That's all. But you know better than to fight him again, eh?"

Matt avoided Fink for the next few days. He didn't have much to do with the rest of the crew either, except for Kovalenko, who helped him with Slocum every night. The mud seemed to be working. Every night they washed it off in the river, and put on a fresh pack. By the end of the third day they decided to leave the mud off altogether. Slocum still smelled, but the odor was faint now, just a pungent memory of what it had been before. No one complained about it but Mike Fink. "By hell, they'll be able to smell us comin' a mile down the river!" he groused between swigs from his ever-present jug. But he said nothing worse, and Matt even saw him slip a leftover biscuit to Slocum one night after supper.

Matt could almost have forgiven Fink for the licking he'd given him, if it hadn't been for the rifle. Fink flaunted the gun, always cleaning and sighting it when he knew Matt could see him. On long afternoons, when it wasn't his turn at the oar, Fink would take the shiny, new rifle, load it, and plink away at objects along the shore. Matt had always considered himself a fair shot, but Mike Fink was downright amazing. He could hit targets that most people couldn't even see. Even when he was drunk he could hit a rabbit between the eyes at ninety paces.

Matt would watch him and seethe. Fink had

baited him into giving up the gun. He knew that now, and he came near to hating Fink for it. Still he said nothing about it. Fink was boss on the flatboat, and you didn't make trouble with him if you knew what was good for you. Matt had learned his lesson. He bided his time. But one day his chance would come, he vowed. And then he'd get even with Mike Fink.

They had left the Cumberland by now, and were floating down the waters of the Ohio, *La Belle Riviere*, as Matt's grandfather had always called it. The spring days were getting warmer, and the journey was pleasant, but they were in dangerous territory now. This section of the Ohio crawled with river pirates. Now, when they tied up for the night, not one man but two kept watch, rifles loaded and ready.

At last, Slocum began to prove his worth. At night he slept with one ear cocked, growling at the slightest strange noise in the darkness. Once his deep-throated bark was answered by a frantic rustling and crashing in the bushes as whatever had been sneaking up on the boat—man or beast—made a hasty retreat.

Near the joining of the Ohio and the Tennessee they tied up for the night alongside one of the strangest looking boats Matt had ever seen. It was a flatboat, more or less, but it was smaller than a cargo boat, and the cabin covered most of the deck. One end of the cabin had a platform built onto it, with a rough curtain behind it, and places on the deck for people to sit. A crudely lettered sign nailed above the place where the curtain hung down proclaimed: *Doctor Martingale's Kickapoo Medicine Show.*

Edward had warned Matt about strangers on the river. You could never tell which friendly faces hid the greedy, ruthless souls of river pirates, and so Matt was cautious. But Fink and the others had traveled the river a good many times. They'd seen shows like this before, they said. And there was no harm in them.

Doctor Martingale himself appeared a few moments later, popping out from between the curtains. "What a pleasure!" He was short and balding, with thick spectacles perched on his nose. His clothes looked as though they had once been expensive; but now they were faded and patched. "Come on over after sup," he called out cheerfully. "We'll put on a show for you! That's our business. We entertain folks on the river for free, and maybe sell a little Kickapoo oil and Indian herb remedies! My wife makes them up. She's a full-blooded Kickapoo Indian. A mistress of the art of healing! Ah, these red brethren of ours—they could teach our fine Eastern physicians a thing or two, eh? They've got remedies for everything from gout to consumption! And we've got the bark as well, if any of you suffer from swamp fevers!"

"I don't like him. He talks too much," Matt muttered to Kovalenko.

Mike Fink overheard him. "Horsefeathers!" he snorted. "He be a harmless old jaybird. Let him chatter. Ain't much to do 'tween here and the Mississippi. If'n he wants to give us a show and

111

sell a little snake oil, I say well an' good! Anybody what wants t' argue with me—" He looked at the faces of the crew. There were no challenges, not even from Matt.

That night, after a supper of ash cakes and fried venison—from a deer that Fink had shot with the new rifle—they tromped across the gangplank to the traveling medicine show.

Slocum was tied on the deck of the flatboat to guard it for the evening. He whimpered discontentedly as Matt patted him and gave him a leg bone from the deer to gnaw on. "You watch 'em, boy," Matt admonished. "We won't be long, I promise ye!"

Lanterns hung on pegs at the rear end of the small boat, casting yellow circles on the rippling, black water. Martingale motioned Matt and the others to the low barrels that had been placed as seats for them. Then he leaped up onto the platform and began the show.

"Gentlemen—there bein' no ladies present—I bring you the miracle of real Indian medicine!" He leaned closer to them. "Yes, brothers, the red men had the answer. How many Indians have you seen with gout, eh? Or palsies, or ague, or constipation? How many Indian men, I ask you, fail to carry a full, thick head of hair to the grave?"

"What happened t' *yer* hair, Martingale?" Oscar Sutton hooted from the audience.

"Alas—" Martingale rolled his eyes upward. The lantern light gleamed on his own balding head. "Alas, I discovered the miracle remedy too

112

late. But it's not too late for you, brothers! A few drops of genuine Kickapoo oil each day on the head of a young man like you—why you'll never in your life lose another hair!"

"Ye said ye had the bark. I heerd of it. Let's see it." The deep voice was Maddox's.

"The bark. Ah, yes!" Mr. Martingale whisked a beaded deerskin bag into sight from somewhere behind him. He took something out of it that looked like dried, shredded wood. "This, my friends, comes all the way from South America! It's more precious than gold. Boiled in water and drunk, it will cure all manner of swamp fevers, even the malaria! It can save your life, brothers, and it was discovered not by white men, but by Indians." Martingale made a sweeping gesture toward the curtain. "I want to introduce my wife, the daughter of a Kickapoo medicine man! Brothers, she knows all the secrets! And her secrets are yours for the price!"

The curtains parted and a dumpy-looking Indian woman in a deerskin dress shuffled out, looking down at her feet. "Here she is," Martingale announced. "The keeper of mysteries! The brewer of secrets! Only she knows how to make this miracle oil! Why, she won't even share the recipe with me, her husband!"

He reached behind the curtain and pulled out a small clay jug with a corncob stopper. "Gentlemen, here it is! Brewed in the light of the full moon, by the daughter of the Kickapoo medicine man!"

"Where be the entertainment?" Mike Fink

113

growled impatiently. "Ye promised me, ye little blighter!" He took a deep swig from the whiskey cask he'd brought along with him.

"The entertainment?" Martindale chuckled. "Oh, yes! It's coming, gentlemen! A sight to make your eyeballs spin! With a genuine Indian medicine show, we must have genuine Indian entertainment, no? Very well, then, without further ado, I present my lovely daughter, Eva, doing a genuine Kickapoo love dance!"

He snatched up a rawhide drum and pounded it with a flourish. The ragged curtain parted slightly, to admit the tall figure of a young woman. The watching men sucked in their breath as the light fell on her. She had warm, golden skin, braids like thick black ropes, and a voluptuous figure that was revealed to its fullest in the clinging doeskin dress she wore.

Martingale's wife had taken the drum. With a little round-tipped stick she began to beat out a slow, compelling rhythm. With the grace of an uncoiling snake, the girl began to move. An arm, a leg, an arching back, a swaying head, until her entire body was rippling with a subtle, sinuous movement.

"Well, I ain't never seen no Injun dance like that!" Oscar Sutton whispered out loud, his voice harsh.

The rhythm of the drum grew, picking up speed and intensity. The girl's hips began to twitch like twin, flowing circles. The meaning of the dance was clear now. Matt felt the familiar rising and tightening of his body, and he had the feeling that every man who watched was experiencing the same sensation. He could hear them breathing around him, smell the lusty sweat of their bodies. The drumbeat grew stronger, faster; the girl's movements freer and more savage as the men watched, and waited.

III

# VIII

Suddenly the drumbeats were interrupted by the sound of loud, frantic barking from the flatboat. Matt sprang to his feet. Something was riling Slocum, all right. He wouldn't bark like that at an owl or a fox along the bank.

Suddenly it all made sense. The medicine show, the girl's dance, calculated to hold all the men mesmerized—

"Get 'em!" howled Mike Fink. He pulled a pistol out of his belt and fired a single shot that struck Martingale between the eyes. Martingale fell backward, dead by the time he hit the water. The rest of the men raced for the flatboat, pounding across the gangplank, drawing knives, grabbing axes. There were shouts and splashes on the far side of the boat as the would-be thieves hit the water.

"Get the women!" somebody yelled. Matt had been the last man off the medicine boat. He leaped back across the gap between the two boats and caught the girl by the wrist just as she was about to jump over the side. He yanked her close, twisting her arms behind her back to hold her.

She struggled, but only half-heartedly. Matt had the distinct feeling that she didn't really mind being caught.

The squaw was nowhere to be seen. Either she'd gone into the water, slipped off into the woods, or been hit by one of the stray bullets that seemed to be suddenly singing through the air. But the girl wasn't going anywhere. She hung over Matt's arm, breathing jerkily.

From the flatboat, Mike Fink whooped like a Shawnee and fired the rifle at something in the river. There was a splash, then silence. "Got that one," yelled Fink, and Matt wondered if it was the squaw. "That be all of 'em. Bring the girl over here, Cooper, and let's see what we caught ourselves!"

The plank was put back between the two boats, and Matt led the girl across. She came without a struggle, though she was trembling. "Here, bring 'er into the light!" Fink beckoned with the lantern. He took the girl's wrist from Matt, swung her around and flung her half-lying onto a heap of barrels. She landed with a little cry, her legs apart, her braids flung back.

Fink held the lantern close. By its light the men could see the girl well. She wasn't so pretty as she'd appeared to be during the dance. Her features were somewhat coarse, and lightly scarred by smallpox. And she didn't really look Indian at all, though she did have dark hair and dark eyes. Those eyes gazed up at Matt now, frightened and pleading as a trapped animal's.

The silence was awkward, and oppressively

heavy. Matt cleared his throat. "I— I be right sorry 'bout your ma and pa," he said, and realized at once that the remark sounded a bit silly under the circumstances.

The girl took a deep breath. "He weren't my pa. And she weren't my ma. And I be damn well glad to be rid of 'em. Ain't nothin' ye could do to me short of hangin' that'd be worse'n what they done to me on that boat!"

"And so maybe we'll be hangin' ye, then!" Fink stood looking down at her, his legs planted apart, his hands on his hips. "Less'n ye can convince us that we ought to keep ye, that is." He rubbed his chin. "That was a right entertainin' dance you done for us this evenin'. What d'ye say ye finish it for us, eh?" He glanced around at the men. They grinned wickedly and nodded their heads. LeClerc, the little Frenchman, got the drum and the small rawhide beater from the medicine boat. "Play it," ordered Fink.

LeClerc began to beat the drum, a bit unevenly at first, but he soon got the feel of it, and the cadence settled into something that at least resembled what the Indian woman had played. Fink pulled the girl to her feet. "Dance," he said.

Slowly she began to move. This time she seemed shy and self-conscious. She kept her eyes lowered, her mouth sullen. Her feet shifted on the deck. Her arms lifted awkwardly, and at last her hips began to twitch.

"That's better," said Fink. "Faster, LeClerc. Louder!"

Little by little, the rhythm caught the girl. Her

grace returned. Her sinuous body began to curve and ripple the way it had before. She threw back her head. Yes, Matt admitted wonderingly, she was pretty again. She was almost beautiful.

The fascination grew, and the spell of the drum and the girl returned. Matt felt his blood begin to race. He felt the warm rising of his body again. The excitement in the air could almost be touched and smelled. The men were beginning to breathe faster as the primitive lusts stirred in them. The tension grew. It became painful, almost unbearable.

It was Mike Fink who sprang forward and jerked the girl into his arms. His mouth found hers in a hot, hungry kiss that arched her backward and molded the lower part of her body against his. She struggled for a brief moment. Then her arms flung themselves around his neck. Her fingers taloned into his hair.

Without a word of a look at the men, he swept her into the cabin and slammed the door behind them. The men stood in awkward silence, looking at one another. "For the love of hell, stop playing the damned drum, LeClerc!" Maddox growled. He snatched the drum from the little Frenchman and threw it far out into the river. It landed with a small, distant splash. Then he strode to the edge of the flatboat and stood staring down into the water.

The sounds of panting and moaning floated through an open window of the cabin. Matt stared down at the boards of the deck in the moonlight, his eyes uneasily tracing the grain of the wood. The others did much the same. They could not raise their eyes to look at one another. Those looks would reveal too much.

Slocum edged up to Matt and thrust a wet nose into his hand. Matt remembered how the big mutt's barking had saved them all from robbery, or maybe even death. "Good dog," he murmured, stroking the massive head. "Good Slocum. Good boy."

Mike Fink kept the girl, and he bristled with rage if anyone else so much as looked at her. He curtained off one side of the cabin for them, though that didn't make much difference. The sounds that came through that curtain at night were enough to drive any man out onto the deck with his bedroll.

She washed his clothes, and cooked his food— no one else's. When Oscar Sutton had the gall to suggest that she cook for the whole crew, Matt thought Fink was going to punch him. Nobody mentioned the idea again.

Her name wasn't really Eva, Matt learned, and she wasn't really half Indian. She was really an Irish girl named Mary Kate Flannery, an indentured servant who'd run away from her masters in Philadelphia. Somewhere along the way she'd fallen in with Martingale and his bunch, who were quick to see her potential as an asset to their trade. They'd threatened to kill her if she didn't help them. She'd performed that devilish dance of hers dozens of times, usually with exactly the hoped-for result. The men on the boats were so taken by the sight of her that they forgot everything, including their precious cargoes, until it was too late.

Matt couldn't help wondering if she loved Fink. She was faithful enough to him, but then she didn't really have much choice in the matter. Love him or not, however, Mary Kate seemed content to be Fink's woman, to wash, scrub and cook for him and to warm his bed at night. With the other men on the boat she was discreet and demure, never giving them so much as an improper glance. But for some reason, she seemed especially drawn to Matt. Maybe it was because he was so close to her own age; or because he was younger and gentler than the others. Whatever the reason, she often found a place near him when she was mending or had potatoes to peel. She would talk to him then, not in a flirting, boy-girl way, but as one friend talks to another.

Matt enjoyed the talks, and he liked Mary Kate. The earnest girl with her plain, pock-marked face and disheveled black hair bore little resemblance to the siren who had made his blood race with her dancing. She never aroused him. Still, sometimes he felt Mike Fink watching them from his place at the sweep, his eyes like hot, green flames. At such times, Matt would feel a shiver of foreboding pass over him, like a shadow of what was to come.

Spring ripened into lush early summer. They were on the Mississippi now, its coffee-brown expanse so wide that it staggered Matt's imagination every time he looked at it. It was like a great, moving lake, so broad that the trees, houses, animals and people they saw along the shore were small and far away.

Mike Fink still flaunted the shiny new rifle, when he wasn't flaunting Mary Kate. It was an even greater challenge to shoot targets on the shore when the shore was not too far away. And Fink delighted in showing off for anyone who'd watch him shoot. He loved to wager as well, and was always challenging the crew to shoot against him. But they all knew him too well for that. Nobody accepted. Not until one sultry day in early June, the first really hot day of the summer.

Mike Fink was seated on a barrel, half-leaning against the wall of the cabin, the rifle in one hand, the whiskey jug in the other. He'd been drinking all day, even more than usual, for some reason known only to his own soul. Maybe it was because he'd argued with Mary Kate over breakfast that morning when she'd scorched the bacon. Whatever the reason, he'd been surly all day, and pulling at the jug even more than he generally did.

When a flock of ducks passed high overhead, he took a casual shot at them. He often shot birds with the rifle, so it was nothing new. But today, perhaps because he hadn't really aimed, he missed. He sat up straighter, blinking in surprise as the flock flew on, untouched.

Maddox, manning the left-hand sweep, chuckled. Fink frowned sourly. "Well, you couldn't a done it either. None of ye! Don't look so damned smart. Tell ye what. This rifle goes to the man what can bring down a flying duck in one shot and have it in the pot tonight."

"*Oui*. And if he fires and loses?" LeClerc asked suspiciously. He was wise to Mike Fink's tricks.

"He takes my shift for the rest of the trip!"

"No thank-ee!" Maddox laughed, and the others shook their heads.

Matt came out of the cabin just then. "Here," he said impulsively, grabbing the gun, and loading it so fast that his fingers were a blur. Maybe he was crazy, but something was pushing him to try. Another flock of ducks was going over, so high that the birds were little more than dark specks against the sky. Matt fired the rifle. Like magic, one of the ducks dropped out of the sky, toward the river. The men cheered.

"I said ye had to put it in the pot tonight," Fink said, though his voice quivered with surprise. "Ye'll not be findin' that bird. Not in a dozen years!"

"Wait—" Matt was trembling. The shot had been a lucky one. He was good, but he wasn't that good. He couldn't have made it a second time in a thousand years. His eyes scanned the river frantically. "There it is!" He spotted the floating form ahead.

"Ye still got t' get it out," Fink said warily.

"Slocum—" Matt coaxed his dog toward the edge of the boat. "Look, Slocum! Go fetch it! Go fetch, boy!" He pointed toward the floating duck. Slocum did not budge.

"Slocum! Fetch!" Matt got behind the big mutt and tried to shove him toward the water. Slocum dug his toenails into the deck. The watching crew howled with laughter.

The duck had caught an eddy and was drifting around and around, toward the center. It looked perilously close to sinking. With a muttered curse, Matt kicked off his boots and dived headlong into the swirling brown water. He was an average swimmer, no better, but he had to get that duck. He struck out determinedly. The duck was somewhere up ahead. The water was getting in his eyes. His breath was coming in gasps. There—there it was. He seized the still warm ball of feathers and struggled to hang onto it while he swam. "Put it in yer mouth, Cooper!" Oscar Sutton yelled. "Come on, like a good duck dog!" He hooted with laughter.

Panting with the effort, Matt reached the edge of the boat. Kovalenko, his homely face split in two by his grin, reached down and pulled him up onto the deck. "A duck for the pot!" he chuckled.

"No thanks to ye!" Matt glared at Slocum. The dog's big tail thumped happily on the deck.

"Can't be sure it's the same duck," Mike Fink said sullenly. Maddox inspected the dripping bird. "Got a rifle ball clean through the breast, I'd reckon it be the same duck."

"*Vraiment*, the boy beat you, Mike," LeClerc agreed. "A man of honor would not dispute it."

Mike Fink took a long swig from the whiskey jug and stood up. He flung the gun at Matt. Then he stalked into the cabin and slammed the door shut behind him.

"Here, Matt." Mary Kate took the duck from him. "I'll pluck and clean it for ye. I'll cook it too."

"Thank ye, Mary Kate." Matt gazed down at the rifle in his hands. It was even more precious now than it had been the day his grandfather had given it to him. Never again would he risk such a prize in a foolish wager.

"What a shot, boy!" Oscar Sutton clapped Matt on the shoulders as he passed him on the deck. The other crewmen beamed their approval. Matt felt ten feet tall. These tough, lusty rivermen had never quite accepted him. Except for the tender-hearted Kovalenko, they had held back their friendship, waiting for Matt to prove himself their equal. Today, at least, he had come close. He felt the warmth that radiated from their homely, sunburned faces, and he realized for the first time how much he liked them. Mary Kate was singing softly as she cleaned the duck, kneeling at the edge of the boat to wash it in the river. The weight of the rifle was gold in Matt's hands. Slocum leaned against his legs and whuffed contentedly.

Some moments in life are almost perfect, and for Matt this was one of them. Even the sight of the ominously closed cabin door, Mike Fink brooding sullenly behind it, could not spoil it. Matt scratched his dog's ears, hefted the rifle to his shoulder and grinned into the sun.

\* \* \*

Fink's anger hung in the air for days, like black smoke. It was even worse once he'd sobered up enough to realize what he'd done. He was annoyed with Matt, but he was angriest of all at himself. He groused and grumbled and nursed the whiskey jug constantly. When LeClerc lost a pole in the river, Fink growled at him like an enraged bear and shoved him overboard to get it. The little Frenchman caught an undertow and would have drowned if Maddox had not thrown him a line.

But most of his ire was taken out on poor Mary Kate. He snarled at her if his breakfast was slow, and once, when she'd burned the biscuits, he'd slapped her face. From the sound of what came through the curtains at night, even his lovemaking was brutal. Mary Kate would appear in the morning with her face bruised, her eyes red and swollen from crying.

Matt was fishing off the stern when she came to him one day after lunch. She sat down next to him, her long, thin toes trailing the water. "Ye got t' get me away from him," she said through her teeth. "I can't stand it no more, Matt. He's jealous, accusin' me o' carryin' on with the whole crew, from you t' big Kovalenko." She chuckled bitterly. "As if I'd have the chance, him not lettin' me outa his sight from morning till bedtime!"

"Where's Fink now?" Matt asked cautiously.

"At the sweep up front. He won't trouble us none." She sighed wearily.

"Lord, Mary Kate, I wish I could help ye, but

127

I don't know how," Matt said. "Reckon I could ask Mr. Montoya in Natchez if he'd have a place for ye. But Natchez is still a way off. We won't be there for two weeks or more. LeClerc told me that this morning."

"I could go," said Mary Kate. "When we tie up for the night, I could just disappear. Wouldn't care much what happened to me."

"Well, I do," said Matt, "and it ain't safe. I'll talk to the others. We won't let 'im hurt ye."

She tossed a chip of wood into the water. "Oh, it ain't that he hurts me so much. It's the way he makes me feel. Like he owns me. I don't like bein' owned. That's why I run away from Philadelphia in the first place."

Matt reached over and patted her hand. He felt a brotherly sort of tenderness toward her, nothing more. "Don't worry," he reassured her. "We'll find a way for ye—" He caught his breath in mid-sentence, stunned by what he saw. "Lordy, Mary Kate, will ye look at that!"

Off to the right, between the boat and the river-bank, a strange craft was moving up on them. From the shape of it, it looked to be half flatboat and half canoe. A huge, square sail was hoisted above the cabin. Strangest of all, the boat was moving upstream, propelled both by the slight breeze and by the stream of men who walked around the edge of the deck, pushing long poles against the bottom. Yet another team of men moved along the shore, pulling on a long rope at-tached to the mast. "Damnation, if it ain't a keel-boat!" Matt had heard talk of the contraptions

128

for years, but he had never seen one before. They were the only craft that went up the Mississippi. The passage was grueling at best, slow at fifteen miles a day, and expensive. That, Matt's grandfather had explained to him, was why almost everybody went north by way of the Natchez Trace.

One of the men on the keelboat had evidently recognized Mike Fink. "Hey, old horse!" he shouted across the distance between the two boats. "What the devil ye doin' on a flatboat, Fink? You're a keelboat man! Ye come down in the world or somethin'?"

Fink shouted back from his place at the sweep. His words sounded something like "None of your gawd-damned business!" but Matt could not make them out for sure.

"Hey, Fink! Sam Bowditch up front here says he can lick ye easy! Says he can outshoot, outfight an' out woman-love ye! What d'ye say to that, eh?"

"You just tell that son-of-a-whore to come over here an' prove it!" Fink yelled back, letting go of the sweep and walking backward to keep even with the keelboat. "He wouldn't dare say that if he was over here, by damn!"

Fink was moving back toward the stern, his eyes on the keelboat. So it was that he almost stumbled over Matt and Mary Kate, sitting together behind the cabin. When he set eyes on them, he forgot all about the keelboat.

"Sneakin', lyin' bitch!" He jerked Mary Kate to her feet, ripping the sleeve of the light cotton

129

dress she'd brought with her from the medicine boat. "The minute I turns me back, here ye be, pantin' after some other man! An' this one—why, he ain't even weaned yet!" He swung her around and began to drag her forward.

The keelboat had stopped moving. The men on the deck and on the shore had slacked the rope and raised the poles to watch the spectacle of Mike Fink putting a woman in her place. Both boats were drifting with the current, even, more or less, on the river.

"I'll teach ye!" Fink roared. "I'll teach ye once and for all!" He swung her around the corner of the cabin, to the place where a pot of beans simmered on the small stone hearth. Seizing a long, thin stick of kindling, he thrust it into the coals until it began to blaze. "Now, ye sneakin' bitch, I'll be puttin' my brand on ye, so's ye'll not get any more notions about whose woman ye be!"

Mary Kate was struggling. She screamed as the stick of kindling burst into flame. Matt, who was closer than the other men, sprang forward to save her, but it was too late. Mary Kate clawed Fink's arm. He dropped the brand and it landed on her skirt. In an instant the dress was ablaze. She began to scream.

Matt's forward momentum knocked her into the river. For a long moment she disappeared beneath the swirling brown water. Then she burst into sight, coughing, spitting, but apparently all right. She hung in the water for a few seconds, staring up at Mike Fink, pure hatred burning in her dark eyes.

Matt bent down and held out his arms. "Here, I'll pull ye out, Mary Kate."

But Mary Kate shook her head bitterly. She gave Mike Fink one long, last, glaring look. Then she turned and set out swimming—in the direction of the keelboat!

The keelboat crew watched, stunned. Then, as soon as they realized what was happening, they began to cheer her on. "Come on, girl! Aye, this'll be paradise after Mike Fink, an' ye can have us all!" "Swim, girl! Swim for it!" They hooted with laughter as Fink fumed and raged from the deck of the flatboat.

Mary Kate was a fair swimmer, but the distance was long, the current of the river deceptively powerful, and her trailing dress cumbersome. She was a little over halfway to the keelboat when she began to falter and struggle.

A man from the keelboat, young, tall and broad-shouldered, dove like a flash into the river. With powerful strokes he reached Mary Kate just as she was going down. Yes—he had her. The keelboat crew cheered and whooped wildly as he towed his prize home.

"After them!" Fink roared. "Steer for them, damn ye all! I'll show the lot of 'em!"

But the keelboat had already started to move upstream again, and the flatboat was drifting down, with the pull of the current.

As for the men, some of them looked at the sky. Some of them whistled. Fink, for once, was as invisible as if he had not been there. He stood with

131

his legs planted wide apart on the deck, cursing the keelboat, cursing the sky, cursing all women in general, and cursing the river as it carried them irresistibly, irrevocably away.

# IX

They rounded one last bend and Natchez came into sight, shining on the bluff like a white crown. The crew broke into cheers when they saw it. Matt cheered with them, throwing his hat into the air with the others. For more than three months they'd lived on the river. They would sleep on shore tonight, and for the next four nights as well. Oh, where they would sleep— what they would eat and drink! No city on the river could match Natchez when it came to having a good time!

Even Mike Fink cheered up a bit at the sight. He'd been as cranky as a wounded bear since the loss of Mary Kate, driving and goading the crew without mercy. Matt had lost count of the whiskey jugs Fink had emptied and tossed over the side of the boat. The size of the shipment that Forny & Cooper had loaded in Nashville for sale in New Orleans had shrunk considerably, and Matt could only hope that his grandfather and his Uncle Henry wouldn't be mad. The sacrifice of the whiskey had been a near-necessity. The only thing

133

worse than Mike Fink when he was drunk, it seemed, was Mike Fink when he was sober.

Still, in spite of everything, Matt had to admit, Mike Fink was a superb river man. He could steer a flatboat over the worst rapids as slick as grease, and he knew the Mississippi the way a man knows a woman's body, every curve, curl and shadow of her. For all his boastfulness, all his drunken cantankerousness, Mike Fink was worth every penny of the outlandish wage Forny & Cooper was paying him.

Matt stood at the right-hand sweep and watched as Fink strode up and down the deck of the boat, growling orders—orders that were swiftly and skillfully obeyed. He felt a swelling of pride in his chest. The flatboat had made it all the way from Nashville to Natchez, and he, Matt Cooper, had been a part of it all. He'd grown strong and sunburned at the sweeps, learned to steer through the roughest current, learned to fight and curse with the best men on the river.

Slocum leaned against Matt's leg and thumped his big tail on the deck. Matt reached down with one hand and scratched the dog's ears. It had been a grueling trip. And, by hell, it wasn't over. There was still plenty to be learned, and Matt Cooper intended to learn it all.

He squinted into the bright sunlight at the city that shimmered like a dream on the distant, green-topped bluff. Natchez. Four days in Natchez. He thought fleetingly of his cousin Slade. What a shame Slade wasn't here to be taking it in with him. And what a tale Matt would have to tell when he saw Slade Forny again!

"Quite the town, boy!" Oscar Sutton grinned at him from his place at the left-hand sweep. "But what ye see ain't the half of it. That's the hoity-toity part ye be lookin' at from here, the part o' town where the rich folk live. An' there be rich folk a' plenty in Natchez. Spanish gents, brand new rich cotton planters—houses an' carriages ye think ye'd only see in heaven!"

"Aye." Matt remembered his Spanish business connection, Don Esteban Montoya. Likely he'd live up there on the bluff, in one of those houses. In any case, Matt reminded himself, he'd know soon enough. He had instructions to call upon Don Esteban the morning after his arrival in Natchez. But as to the night before—

"Far's we be concerned, the real town's the one below the bluff, down on the flat." Sutton continued. "That's where a man off the river can have his fun for a night. Why there be women that—" Sutton chuckled. "But I reckon ye be too young for that yet, eh?"

Matt returned his grin. "Not as young as ye think!" he said, trying to sound natural and easy, like the other men would. But his spine tingled and his knees turned watery when he thought of what this night—his first in

Natchez—might bring.

They landed an hour later and tied up the boat at the wharf. Matt stepped ashore amid the sights, sounds and smells of Natchez. It was late afternoon by then, fast ripening into evening. The scent of magnolias drifted down over the bluff, but here on the flat the strongest smell was the smell of the river, of mud and catfish, of tobacco and whiskey and human sweat. The streets, what few there were, ran parallel with the river. They were lined with a bewildering array of cheap inns and rum shops. Matt looked around for the women, but the only ones in sight were two plump, middle-aged negresses with baskets of fish balanced on their kerchiefed heads. But the streets teemed with men from the river. The wharf was thick with flatboats, keelboats and pirogues whose crews had stopped off for a few hours of fun. They were a rough lot, these rivermen, with their sunburned hides, their rakish clothes, their wild manner. Voices echoed from the taverns, boasting, brawling. A woman's high-pitched giggle ended in a shriek.

Slocum sniffed at a dead rat in the mud. Matt wondered briefly if he should have tied the dog up and left him on the flatboat. But when he thought about it he realized it wouldn't have done any good. Either Slocum would have raised an infernal ruckus, or he would have chewed himself loose. Either way there might have been trouble.

The men had already disappeared, each to

his own business. Kovalenko, Matt had learned, had a wife and family here in Natchez. LeClerc had a sweetheart. Sutton and Maddox promptly went off to their favorite gambling house, and Mike Fink vanished without saying a word. Matt paid a guard to watch the boat, and set out to see the town on his own.

He passed by an inn and a grog shop, wondering when all this fun he'd planned on having was supposed to begin. None of the places looked that inviting from the outside. They were just rough, wooden buildings, not so different from the ones in Louisville or Nashville. But they were lively, all right, full of singing, shouting, drinking men. Matt picked one that looked as good as any, walked uneasily in through the open door, and sat down at a table. Slocum curled up at his feet.

"Yer pleasure, sir?" The man waiting on the tables was bald as an egg with huge, hairy arms. There wasn't a woman in the place. Matt cleared his throat. His father had kept him out of taverns. He had never actually gone into one and ordered a drink before. He cleared his throat again. "I—I'll have—"

"He'll have whiskey, and be sure ye fill it high!" a gruff voice spoke up from the bar. Mike Fink swung around on his stool. Matt's jaw dropped slightly.

"Well, now, why not?" Fink grinned. "Ye've become a real river man, Cooper. Even beat me some at me own games. The least old Mike

137

Fink can do is buy ye a drink!" He rolled off the stool and ambled over to where Matt was sitting, his own brimming mug in his fist. "So ye be ready to have a fine time, eh? Well, ye can't have it alone, and there ain't nobody can show ye around like ol' Fink here! Drink up, boy! The evenin's just gettin' started!"

Matt took a deep swallow of whiskey from the glass that had been set before him. It burned all the way down to his insides, like sweet, hot fire.

"That's it," Mike urged him, grinning like Satan. "Drink up, and when your innards are warmed up good, I know a place where the ladies are willin' for a fair price. I'll take ye there myself!"

By the time Matt had finished the second glass, the world had taken on a rosy haze. He felt warm and loose inside, ready to bear-wrestle the whole town and enjoy it. Mike Fink had begun to sing, in a rich, lusty tenor, Matt joining in on the chorus.

> "Mush-a-ring-a-ring-a-rah!
> Whack fol'd the dady O!
> Whack fol'd the dady O!
> That's whiskey in the jug!"

They swaggered out into the street, arm in arm, still singing. Men who recognized Mike Fink laughed and waved at him. "This way, Cooper!" Fink pointed up the hill. "This way to heaven, eh?"

The house was bigger than most of the buildings on the waterfront, but it was tucked away in a side street. Matt hadn't seen it earlier. He'd have remembered it if he had, because it was built of stone, and its windows were opulently curtained in red velvet.

They mounted the stoop, and Mike Fink rapped loudly on the heavy door with his doubled-up fist.

The door inched open until it revealed a small, skinny Spaniard in garish red livery. "Yes, *Senores?*"

Fink chuckled. "Miguel, you pompous little ass! Never change, do ye? Well, tell Madame Rodare that Mike Fink is here, and he's brought a friend!"

The fellow actually bowed. "Step in, *por favor.* I will tell Madame that you are here." He showed them into a red and gold room, motioned to a settee, and glided off through a curtained doorway.

Fink laughed. "Good old Miguel! Never forgets that he used to work up on the bluff, for Madame's former husband, no less! Now that's what I'd call coming down in the world!" He leaned closer to Matt's ear. "They say Madame in there had a daughter by this highfalutin' Spaniard. Purty little thing—well, Madame musta been a looker 'erself in 'er day. Anyway, the little girl, she lives up on the bluff with 'er pa, an' they say she don't ever get t' see—" He broke off as the ridiculous little butler came back through the curtains.

139

"Madame will see you now, *senores*." He glanced down and noticed Slocum for the first time. The big dog was sniffing suspiciously at the edge of a red velvet ottoman. "*Senor*, this is not a kennel."

Mike Fink swung his hand and gave the fellow a hearty slap across the seat of his britches. "'I'll thank ye not t' talk that way to me mate here. An' that hound's a damn sight better'n some of the women, too! Leave 'im be, I say, or ye'll answer t' Mike Fink!'"

"Whatever you say, *Senor* Fink." The little man scuttled back through the curtains. Fink motioned for Matt to follow him. Matt pulled Slocum away from the ottoman and hurried after the two of them.

They passed down a narrow hallway, lit by a single small lamp, then through a heavy double curtain, into the biggest room Matt had ever seen.

The walls were covered with paper in a shade of pale gold. Red rugs were scattered here and there on the floor. The light came from candles in crystal brackets that were attached to the walls. Matt could not see well until his eyes had adjusted to the dim light, but now he began to notice that there were other people in the room—sprawled on many couches and big, soft chairs. And some of them were women.

"*Monsieur* Fink! Mike!" The woman who glided out of the shadows was tall, with a figure that appeared at first glance to be slim and youthful. But when she emerged into full light, Matt saw that the flesh hung almost loosely on her frame. Her face was painted, the cheeks and mouth artificially rosy, but there were deep shadows about her eyes. Even to Matt's unpracticed gaze she looked ill. Still, when she flashed a smile, traces of what had once been a dazzling beauty flickered through. She looked to be about fifty, though the hair that was coiled and piled on her head was still black as a raven's wing. Her eyes were a startling blue, and her throat was circled by a showy garnet necklace.

She extended her hand, a sweeping gesture. Mike Fink bent low and kissed it with an audible smack. "Madame Rodare—"

She giggled, a hoarse and lusty sound. "Ah, Mike . . . *mon ami*, it has been too long. Have you eaten?"

"Eatin' can wait!" Fink snarled good-naturedly. "But there be some things what can't wait! I got me a friend here what's been waitin' nigh onto twenty years for a bit o' the sweet life, an' by hell, he can't wait much longer, else he's gonna bust his britches!"

Madame Rodare's blue eyes looked Matt up and down. She seemed to like what she saw. "*Magnifique!* But first we have a drink eh?" She clapped her hands and the little Spanish butler scuttled over with a bottle of claret and two glasses on a silver tray. "Wine, *mon cher* Mike. Not that rotten whiskey you're always steeping yourself in, *eh bien?* This is a place of

141

some refinement, you know." She poured the wine herself. Her eyes flicked thoughtfully over Fink's well-muscled body. "Now tell me what brings you here this time, eh, Mike? Were you with one of the keelboats that came upriver today?"

"Not this time. This time it be a flatboat for a change. But don't ye fear. I'll catch me a keelboat back upriver from New Orleans an' be here again in no time."

"A flatboat?" Madame Rodare raised her brows.

"Aye, Signed on in Nashville for one trip downriver. Workin' for an outfit called Forny & Cooper."

"Forny & Cooper?" Madame Rodare's brows shot straight up. "Who was it hired you, *cherie?*"

"Why the head of the company himself! Fellow name of Edward Forny. This here's his grandson, matter of fact. Matthew Cooper. Matt, boy, I'd like you to meet Madame Rodare!" He hiccuped and clapped Matt on the shoulder.

Madame Rodare was staring at Matt, her eyes huge. "You! The grandson of Edward Forny! *Mon Dieu*, let me look at you, young man!" Her red lips parted. "*Oui . . . oui*, I see it now! In the eyes, the chin, . . . the shoulders. Edward's grandson! Ah, *mon cher—*" She clapped her hands with delight. "Cooper . . . but of course. Your mother would be that plump, pretty little Marie—and your father

142

that handsome young lad of hers—*Tonnerere!* How time passes. One is young—then not so young—" Her fingers fluttered down Matt's arm, their touch went through his sleeve.

"How do ye know my grandpa, Ma'am?" Matt asked politely, then realized, looking at her, that it was a foolish question. Edward Forny was no saint. He'd even admitted to casual involvements with women from time to time. It was easy to guess that the once-beautiful Madame Rodare had been one of those women.

That beauty still flashed through in rare moments, though her features were ravaged by that illness whose nature Matt could not guess. Her coloring, with that black hair, blue eyes, and fair, fair skin, must have been lovely in years past. Now Matt saw her through coatings of powder and rouge. Her movements, naturally flowing and graceful, seemed cramped by spells of pain every few moments, and her throaty voice betrayed some hurtful difficulty in speaking.

"Edward Forny's grandson!" She shook her head in disbelief. Laughter made her quiver through the light blue silk of her gown. "We were . . . friends. Long ago, in Vincennes. Mention me to your grandfather when you see him, *cherie*. Ah, but to your grandmother and your mother—*non!* Silence, I think, would be best."

She refilled the wine glasses. Matt liked the wine better than the fiery Monongahela whiskey he'd had earlier. It was sweet, and just slightly heady. He tried not to drain his glass too quickly.

He glanced around the room. The furniture was arranged in intimate groupings, plush couches around small tables. Some of the men sat alone, drinking or smoking. On other couches there were couples, some of them just talking, some of them twined passionately in each other's arms. From time to time, a couple would get up and drift arm in arm toward the curving stairway.

Madame Rodare cocked her head gracefully. "And who is your choice for the night, *Monsieur* Fink? The twins again? They seemed to please you last time, eh?"

Fink scratched his head. "I was thinking maybe the Duchess—"

"Ah, so sorry, but the Duchess is engaged for the night. Lucinda's still free. And one of the twins—the gentleman, alas, didn't want both of them this time. He took Violet—that means Pansy's still available—"

"No." Fink drained the wine glass, then took a deep swig from the bottle itself. "Not Pansy. I be a bit wearied of dark-haired women. But Lucinda—she'll do, I reckon. Fat and blond and not too smart. That's just what ol' Fink's in the mood for tonight." He glanced at Matt. "But what about my mate here? The first time ought t' be a time to remember! Right, mate?" He punched Matt in the arm.

"*Vraiment*," Madame agreed heartily.

"Why if I were younger, I would initiate this one myself!" She looked at Matt, a glint in her eye, "But, *non*. Mathilde Rodare is no fool. You need a young girl—but not too young. We have a new one—just up from New Orleans. She's French—like me. Her name's Yvonne. She's a pretty child and . . . most accomplished." Madame Rodare's eyes glittered. "You, Mike Fink, may pay me before I bring Lucinda. You know the rules of the house, *non*?"

"Aye. Ye be a hard one." Mike grinned and fumbled for his money.

Madame Rodare turned a radiant smile on Matt. "But for you, *cherie*, for the grandson of my dear Edouard, the first time will be my gift to you." She clapped her hands. Miguel emerged from the shadow next to the wall. She spoke a few words to him, and he glided away, silent as a lizard.

He returned a moment later, a woman following him. She was soft and delicately rounded, with tousled yellow curls. Her purple silk wrap clung to the curves of her body, so tightly that it was plain to see she had nothing on underneath. Her bland eyes lit up when she saw Mike Fink.

"Lucinda!" He gave her a mocking bow. Then his hand snaked around her waist and slid down to give her rounded behind a none-too-subtle pinch. She squealed and giggled, and rubbed up against him.

Madame eyed them with satisfaction. "You

wish the wine here, or in your room?"

"Hell, leave it outside the door," said Fink. We'll drink it atween times." He gave Matt a lewd wink. "See ye in the mornin' Master Cooper!" Then he swung Lucinda around and swaggered off toward the stairs.

Matt glanced down at Slocum, who had curled up next to his feet. In the past few minutes he'd totally forgotten about the dog. Now he wondered what he was going to do with him.

"Tie him in the back yard," Madame Rodare read his thoughts. "I'll have the cook give him some bones from the kitchen. He'll be all right." She beckoned to Miguel.

Wrinkling his nose in distaste, the little Spaniard took Slocum's collar and began to lead him out of the room. Once or twice the big dog looked forlornly back at Matt, but when Matt did not call him, he allowed himself to be led out the back door.

"Ah, here she is," Madame exclaimed.

Matt turned around, his knees suddenly water. The girl who stood before him was not really beautiful. But she was pretty. Very pretty. If her features were slightly coarse, they were nonetheless pleasing. She had full, warm-looking lips, olive skin, and brown hair that fell in unruly little curls all around her face. Her gown, of a style that Matt had never seen before, floated loosely about her lush body, without petticoats or stays. It was pale yellow, so sheer that he could see the nipples of her breasts and the soft swell of her belly. He looked down at his feet. The blood rushed to his face as he cursed his own awkwardness. Why couldn't he just laugh and grab her somewhere the way Mike Fink would?

"*Cherie*, this is Yvonne," Madame said with a smile. "She likes you, I can tell that already. Unfortunately—" Madame Rodare shrugged. "She will not be able to tell you herself. She speaks not a word of English. Only French and Spanish. Ah, but words are no barrier between a man and a woman. Sometimes they only get in the way, *vraiment?*"

"Aye," Matt whispered, gazing at Yvonne through the smoky haze of the room. His head was spinning from the whiskey and the wine. He felt light, as if his feet were floating off the floor.

Yvonne touched his arm and murmured something in French.

"Ay, yes . . . She likes you," Madame smirked. "She says you are very handsome, and she asks if you would like to stay down here and have a drink or if you wish to go right upstairs."

Matt swallowed a small belch. He felt himself swaying slightly. "I . . . I think . . . upstairs."

He felt Yvonne tugging at his arm, her little hands warm and insistent. He flowed after her, barely conscious of the movement of his arms and legs. She led him upstairs to a long hallway lined with doors. From out of her dress she drew a key (Matt found himself wondering where she could conceal anything in a dress like that) and opened one of them.

The room was small, and simply furnished. In fact the only piece of furniture Matt really noticed was the bed. His knees weakened at the sight of it.

Yvonne closed the door and locked it with the key. Her smile was sly and knowing, like a fox's, but her touch was gentle as she moved into Matt's arms and began to unbutton his shirt. Her fingers were light and quick. They tickled his bare chest. He laughed nervously.

"*Maintenant?*" her pert little face gazed up at him amused and questioning.

Matt groped for something to say. He knew a few words of French, but they had flown from his muddled mind. He couldn't even think of anything to say in English. To cover the awkwardness of the moment, he kissed her. It was a hurried, clumsy kiss, but her response saved it. With a little purr she moved close to him, warm and silken and fragrant. His arms went around her. His hands felt the full, rounded curves of her body through the thin fabric of her gown.

She had begun to breathe harder, her lips moving under his, her little tongue thrusting into his mouth and out again. Her hands snaked up and down his body, stirring his blood. Matt felt his senses catch fire. His heart began to pound. A pulsing heat surged downward through his body, filling and swelling his loins. Her hands fluttered down to the buttons of his trousers. Expertly she loosened them. The flap fell free. He felt her clasping him. The tiny, stroking motion of her fingers sent waves of maddening desire shooting through his body. She moaned and guided him to the bed.

A simple tug on a string loosened her gown, and it fell in a circle around her feet. She turned and pulled down the covers of the bed. Then they fell into it together.

She was naked in his arms, her whole body twisting with desire. Matt's head was spinning. His mind was filled with nothing but the feel and scent and taste of her, the silkiness of her bare flesh in his arms, the curves, points and hollows of her.

Her legs parted, drawing him in until he felt her warmth close around him, soft, moist and clinging. He could not keep still. Before he knew it he was on top of her, thrusting and plunging, faster, harder until the force that had built up in him burst like a rocket. He heard her cry out beneath him. Then the fireworks died into warm, delicious darkness. He rolled to one side and collapsed in her arms.

# X

Scrubbed, combed, and dressed in his new brown suit, Matt climbed up the steep roadway that led up onto the bluff. His head ached. His eyes smarted in the glare of the morning sun. His arms and legs felt like lead.

The last thing he had wanted to do this morning was get up, bathe and dress, and tend to his grandfather's business with Senor Montoya. The warm bed, and Yvonne's arms, had held him back so deliciously that it had been torture to leave. The blood crept into Matt's face as he remembered the night that had passed. The whole of it had been one long, passionate tumble beneath the quilts. Yvonne had taught him things he'd never even imagined a man could do to a woman. There was nothing, Matt reckoned, his face warm, that they hadn't tried. Once she had even taken him in her mouth and—Matt forced himself to break off the thought. The way he was going on, he'd be in no fit condition to face Don Esteban Montoya by the time he got to the top of the bluff. He took a deep gulp of fresh morning air, and tried to think of the business ahead. He wanted to do a good job. His grandfather had faith in him. Still, it was hard to keep his mind from drifting back to Yvonne and last night. He'd done it, all right. He'd done the thing he'd talked about, joked about, dreamed about for so many years. The experience had been exciting beyond his wildest hopes. And yet, he sensed that something was missing. Yvonne was a delightful girl, and maybe she had really liked him. But she was still a professional, doing her job. He'd have to remember that.

The road was narrow, steep, and muddy from spring rain. Matt picked his way around wagon ruts, trying hard not to get mud on his shoes and stockings. He felt painfully aware of his own body. Each movement, each ache and twinge, each slight pressure of his clothing brought back a memory of something he had felt last night.

The road was crowded by the time he reached the top of the bluff. Sellers were hauling their wares up to the markets—fish, vegetables, live, squawking chickens, tin pots, rope, whiskey, in an endless procession of creaking carts and strong shoulders. Someone drove a herd of young pigs almost between Matt's legs. They squealed and snorted and yanked at the strings that held each of them prisoner by one hind foot.

The fragrance of magnolia and orange blossoms grew stronger as Matt reached the top of the bluff. He caught his breath at the grandness of the city that spread out before him.

Natchez stretched almost as far as Matt could see. Why, there must have been close to three hundred houses in it, and some of them were mansions. They were of frame construction, most of them, airy and open, with balconies, windows and louvered doors. Much of the town was built in the Spanish style (Natchez had just recently passed from the hands of Spain to the United States), with arched colonnades fronting the street and lacy grillwork edging porches and balconies. The spire of some grand church rose in the distance, above the cool summer green of the trees.

The main street of Natchez lay ahead of him, running east from the bluff. It was lined with a dizzying variety of shops, their goods moved out of doors for the day and spread along the sidewalks. Matt picked his way among them, his eyes round with awe. There were soaps and laces, bolts of cloth, candles in all shapes and sizes, fine bridles and harnesses, cabbages, potatoes and yams, even flowers. The street was already crowded with carriages—not the rough wagons that Matt was used to seeing up North, but real carriages, gleaming black and drawn by prancing horses that must have been groomed and brushed for hours.

Ladies rode in most of the carriages, twirling dainty parasols to shield themselves from the hot morning sun. The gentlemen, most of them, rode alongside, on their own splendid mounts, dressed in white coats and white hats, their riding crops delicately balanced in gloved hands.

Matt glanced down at his own brown coat and breeches, which he had thought were quite elegant once, and realized he looked like a country bumpkin. His shoes were of the older style, low cut, with heavy brass buckles. Worse, they were caked with gray mud from the long climb up the cliff. The gentlemen on the fine horses wore shiny leather riding boots, without a speck of mud on them. Matt took one step, and another. His feet felt like big, ugly lumps of mud. His eyes darted down the street. In the next block he saw the sign of a cobbler's shop. He felt the weight of the money in his pocket. Yes, he had enough.

Twenty minutes later, Matt stepped back out into the street, wearing a pair of gleaming brown boots. They pinched a little. The cobbler hadn't quite had his size, but they looked absolutely elegant. He stepped carefully ahead, pausing every few steps to look down at them. He felt better now. The boots seemed to make a difference. But he promised himself that tomorrow he would buy himself a white suit and hat to go with them.

The boots were already speckled with mud by the time Matt had reached the street where his grandfather had told him Don Esteban Montoya lived. He scowled down at the boots. Gentlemen, it seemed, did not walk in the mud. They rode, and did not dismount to buy things from the shops. Well, he shrugged, he could hardly be expected to go so far as buying a horse and saddle. Not when he'd be back on the flatboat in a day or two. But, he resolved, when the cargo was sold in New Orleans, he'd buy himself the finest piece of horseflesh to be had for the trip back to Natchez and over the Trace. Then he'd be as much a gentleman as any of them, by damn!

Matt checked the address on the letter of introduction that his grandfather had given him. Was this where Senor Montoya lived? He stood outside the gate, staring in amazement. This was the grandest house he had ever seen in his life.

The house was set back in a grove of tall cypress, fronted by a rolling green lawn as big as a meadow. White pillars supported a broad balcony that overhung a massive front porch. The roof was tiled, its earthy red tone a charming contrast to the glistening whitewash that covered the rest of the house. The whole effect was stunning, and very Spanish.

The iron gate stood open. A broad, smooth roadway led up to the house. Matt followed it with his eyes, glad, now that he had not brought Slocum along. It was Madame Rodare who'd talked him out of taking him. Slocum would be just fine with her, the kind lady had argued. Besides, it would never do to take such a mischievous and undisciplined dog visiting up on the bluff. Not if one wanted to make a good impression, at least.

He'd not seen Mike Fink that morning. The familiar sound of Mike's heavy snoring had echoed through the door of his room. Well and good, Matt thought. He'd been half-afraid Fink would want to go up to the Montoya house with him. And if a mischievous, ill-mannered dog was guaranteed to make a bad impression, Matt shuddered to imagine what a man like Senor Montoya would think of Mike Fink.

Quivering with anticipation, he stepped through the gateway and began to walk up the path. His boots were hurting more by now. He'd have blisters before the day was over, but at least he looked like a proper gentleman. Funny, but that had never mattered to him before today. He'd been content with old shoes and patched breeches. But that was back in a frontier town like Louisville. That was before he'd seen the world in all its magnificence and realized what a shabby creature he was. No more, Matthew Cooper resolved. He was a man of the world now.

His boots were hurting right sorely by the time he'd reached the front porch and mounted the steps. The knocker was a heavy iron ring, molded in the shape of a lion's head. Matt was not even sure what to do with it. Nobody had such things back in Louisville. But when his knuckles produced no better than a faint rap on the thick hardwood door, he lifted the ring and let it fall three times. The letter of introduction crackled importantly in his hand.

Slowly the door swung open. A small, balding, elegantly dressed man stood there looking up at him

Matt thrust the letter forward. "*Senor* Montoya, my grandpa give me this letter—" he began awkwardly.

The small man shook his head, a disdainful expression on his face. "*No, Senor. Yo no soy Don Esteban. Pase, por favor. Espere aqui.*"

Matt could not understand a word the man said, but the man's motions were understandable enough. He was to come in and wait. The little man bobbed his head, and Matt suddenly realized that he was nothing but a servant.

"*La carta, por favor.*" He held out his hand until Matt gave him the letter. "*Espere—*" he motioned to a marble bench. Matt sat down uneasily as the man scurried off. He could only hope that he would return with *Senor* Montoya, and that *Senor* Montoya would speak at least a little English.

Matt waited, his eyes roaming around a room so big that an entire frontier cabin could have been placed in it. Yet this elegant room seemed to be nothing more than an entry hall for the rest of the house. There were no tables, no chairs of any comfort, only these benches of polished stone. They were beautiful, but they were cold and hard against his buttocks. Matt gazed in awe at the floor of polished wood, the blue velvet curtains, the massive chandelier that hung from the ceiling like a great wrought iron flower, its petals holding a hundred little white candles. Never had he imagined such a house could exist, except maybe in heaven.

He waited until he began to get fidgety, and still no one came back. He felt vaguely like a little boy who had been told to sit on a stool as punishment, as if someone might come and scold him if he got up. But the time ticked by on the tall clock that stood across from him. It seemed to be the only thing in that huge quiet house that had life and movement. Tick-tock . . . tick-tock . . . Matt was getting restless. The house began

157

to call to him. He had an uncontrollable urge to peer down hallways and through half-open doors.

When he could stand it no longer he got up and began to walk in small circles, whistling softly under his breath. The circles grew wider. He found himself wandering down a wide hallway toward a frosted glass door. Sunlight shone through its panes, as if perhaps there might be a garden on the other side. Cautiously he opened it.

Yes, it *was* a garden—an enchanted garden filled with vines and flowers. An ancient-looking fountain gurgled away at the end of a path, sending a delicate stream of water from a pitcher held by the carved stone figure of a little girl. Matt stood blinking in the sunlight, dazzled by the colors of the flowers. A purple vine spilled over the wall in one corner, a pink one in another. Red and yellow flowers blossomed around the base of the fountain, interspersed with sprays of a flower that looked like white lace. The fragrance was soft and warm, like the air.

As he moved down the brick path, he became aware of another presence in the garden. It was not so much the sight or sound of another person as the vague sense that he was not alone. He glanced about him. At first he saw no one. Then, as he turned down a new branch of the path, he almost stumbled over a girl, seated on a low stool in the shade of an oleander.

She turned. Her hand went to her mouth and she uttered a delicate little gasp. Her eyes were round with surprise. They were also dark as black-eyed susans, and fringed with thick lashes of amazing length. Her small head sat like a flower on the graceful stem of her neck, and her hair was pulled simply back, falling in a cascade of black ringlets from the crown of her head. Her skin, in contrast, was so white it was almost translucent, the cheeks an exquisite pink.

Matt swallowed hard. It was almost as if his heart had leaped up into his throat. "Good . . . Good mornin', Miss," he muttered awkwardly. He bobbed from the waist in a frontier-style bow.

She laughed, a totally unexpected reaction. The sound was like the bubbling of the fountain in the corner of the garden. "Oh," she said, in a voice that had not lost its little-girl quality, "you bow just like a puppet in a puppet show!"

Matt would have been insulted, but the delight in her voice was so genuine, the humor so naive, that he could not take offense. He opened his mouth to reply, but no words would come. He could only gape at her like a fool. She was the most beautiful thing he had ever seen in his whole life.

"Did you come to see my father?" Her voice was bell-like, its accent slightly foreign. Yet it was obvious that she'd either been taught English or had considerable chance to learn it.

"Aye. . ."Matt managed to stammer. "I—I been waitin' for him—in there." He gestured toward the house. "When he didn't come right away I got wantin' to explore the place a mite. Hope ye'll excuse me, Miss. I didn't mean t' barge in on ye like this. Beggin' your pardon."

She laughed again. "Oh, I like the way you sound. I don't get to meet many Americans—though Papa says that *we're* Americans, now that Natchez doesn't belong to Spain any more. It's . . . how do you say it? It's very confusing."

Matt drank her in with his eyes. She was wearing a white dress, made of cotton lace and simple as a child's. The cut of it was something Matt had never seen before—tight about the square-necked bodice, then flowing softly out in lines that began well above the waist. The petticoat seemed to be very light, for it did not hold the skirt stiffly outward. Her slender body did not even appear to be laced. He wondered if the style was peculiarly Spanish, or if it was some late fashion that had not quite reached all the way to Louisville.

"My father would still be at breakfast," she said. "He was working late last night. Old Juan would have told you that, I suppose, if he could make you understand." She frowned—an expression almost as adorable as her smile. "I've told Papa a dozen times that he ought to get an English-speaking butler. Now that we're part of America, we'll be having many American visitors. Don't you think so?"

"Aye," Matt whispered, gazing down at her. He was hardly aware of his own speech, or even his own breathing. He could hear nothing but the birds, and the sound of his own heart drumming in his ears. He was not even aware that he was not alone with the lovely little creature until the sound of a masculine throat clearing just a few yards away made him jump.

"If you please. *Dona* Amalia, I must capture you before the light changes. With all respect, would you please look back this way?" The voice was thin and reedy, the voice of an older man. Matt looked down the path. A gray-haired gentleman, plump, and with an oddly twisted back, stood before an easel, a brush in his hand. "If you please, sir, I've been painting the young lady's portrait, and I want to capture the effect of the light on her hair before it changes." He frowned. "If you would be so kind, *Dona* Amalia—"

"*Si*," she murmured, turning her beautiful head away from Matt and freezing into the position. "Is this all right, *Senor* Rushton?"

"Raise the head a bit. Aye, that's fine. Don't let me tire you, now." The artist spoke like a man of breeding, but he was ugly to the point of grotesqueness. A gray, powdered wig sat on a head that looked bald underneath. His clothes were quaintly old-fashioned, with big silver buckles at the knees of his gray satin breeches, and a coat that was well-made, but twenty years out of style.

"I'll warn you, young man," Rushton addressed Matt as he painted, his eyes twinkling slightly, "It's a good thing I was here. Don Esteban's most particular about seeing that the young lady is well chaperoned at all times. I'm only allowed to paint her because I'm too old and ugly to cause any kind of scandal. But if you, on the other hand, had been caught in this garden alone with her—" He shook his head.

"But I—I just—" Matt stammered. He was used to the girls in Louisville and Nashville, girls

161

like Winifred and Carrie. He'd never met a real lady before—especially a Spanish lady. He gazed down at her, still awed by her beauty. She looked so pure, like a small white flower growing on the peak of a mountain. And if it was really a scandal for a young man to be caught alone with her, she must be totally untouched. Matt found himself wondering if she'd ever been kissed, or had her hand held under a full moon. No, he decided. You could tell that by looking at her. She was as innocent as a child.

"Beggin' your pardon," he said to her softly, "I wouldn't never have wanted to cause ye no trouble. If ye'll excuse me, I'll go back in the house and wait for your Pa."

She glanced up at him without moving her head. Her dark eyes flashed "Stay. Papa keeps me locked up like a nun! I get so tired of not seeing anybody but my duenna, and the maids and the butler and the gardener!" The tip of her foot, clad in a dainty, cream-colored kidskin, drummed impatiently on the flagstone. "I don't even get to go to the balls! Oh, me!" Her lower lip thrust out charmingly.

"Now that will all change tomorrow, and you know it," Rushton humored her gently as he wielded the brush. "You'll be sixteen years old, young lady, and you'll be having a ball right here in your own house. That's why I'm in such a hurry to finish your portrait. It's to be unveiled tomorrow night, and the paint won't even be dry. Hold still, please. Painting you is like painting a hummingbird, *Dona* Amalia."

162

Matt leaned against the tree and watched her. Aye, he thought, Rushton was right. She *was* like a hummingbird, a small, iridescent beauty, full of life and movement. His eyes could not get enough of her. He found himself wishing that time would stand still, that he could spend the rest of his life right here, in this garden, with this girl.

"*Senor* Cooper?" A deep, cultured voice spoke Matt's name from the doorway. The man who walked toward him was in his fifties, small and quick, like Amalia, with sharp, handsome features. His eyes, too, were like Amalia's, intense, darting, like a bird's.

"*Senor* Montoya," Matt stepped forward and extended his hand, wondering why the gentleman would look so annoyed when they'd only just met.

"I see you've found my daughter," he said, looking from Matt to the girl. Then he scowled at her and said something in Spanish. The words were stern, even angry. The girl lowered her eyes, then lifted them defiantly, the pupils darkly blazing.

"I apologize for this little scene, *Senor* Cooper," said *Don* Esteban. "But you see, Amalia knows better than to let herself be found alone with a young man. In our culture, such a situation is an open door to scandal and disgrace. Please understand."

"Papa!" she pouted indignantly. "You're being silly! We weren't alone. *Senor* Rushton was here the whole time! Why do you always act as if I'll do something terrible if you turn your back on me for more than a moment?" Her lower lip quivered, and Matt was almost afraid she was going to cry. She dabbed at her eyes with a tiny lace handkerchief. "Why, Pape, I don't even know his name!"

*Don* Esteban sighed. "Very well. This is Matthew Cooper, the grandson of my business associate, *Senor* Forny." He glanced from Matt to his daughter, then back again. "*Senor* Cooper, may I present my very strong-willed daughter, Amalia Maria Teresa Montoya."

Amalia inclined her graceful head. "I am now pleased to meet you, Matthew Cooper," she said, a note of sauciness in her musical voice. Matt bowed again, enchanted.

"And now, *Senor* Cooper, it might be best if we went upstairs to my study to discuss our business. Then *Senor* Rushton can get on with his portrait in time to finish it for my daughter's birthday. If you'll be so kind—" He turned toward the house, motioning Matt to follow him.

In his study, which was lined with books and paintings, *Don* Esteban seemed to relax a bit. He leaned back in his chair and lit his pipe. Then he actually smiled at Matt, who had taken the chair across from his desk. "Yes, the disposal of your cargo has already been arranged. You need wait here only a few days while I send word downriver by horse that you have come this far. The buyer will send word back that he is ready to receive you and make an offer on your cargo, which you may accept or decline—ah, but he is a fair man. There will be no trouble. It sounds bothersome, I know, for one who is not accustomed to this way of business, but I tell you it is a hundred times better than docking in New Orleans with no one to buy your cargo. I have known boatmen who arrived with no place to tie up, and no buyers. One of them was robbed as he waited. Another lost his cargo to a fire before it could be sold. This way, you know exactly where to go and who to see. You even know how much money you will get for your goods."

"I see the good sense of that, thank ye," Matt said politely. "My grandpa said you knowed your business, and I reckon he be right."

"Thank you." *Don* Esteban blew out a cloud of tobacco smoke. "And where are you staying, my young friend?"

"I—" Matt started to answer the question truthfully, then realized a true answer would not exactly make a good impression on *Don* Esteban. "In an inn, sir. Down by the river." Well, that was mostly true.

"Ah— that will never do. Please accept my invitation to be my guest for the few days that you are here. I can send a wagon for your things, if you like."

"No—" Matt felt a surge of sudden panic. "I ain't got much. Reckon I can bring it up myself. And thank ye kindly, sir."

"You are invited to my daughter's birthday ball tomorrow night, of course. But allow me to give you a word of caution."

Matt waited. *Don* Esteban's eyes had grown hard and severe once more.

"I see you have taken an interest in my daugh-

165

ter," he said. "That is natural enough. Amalia is a beautiful girl. But take care that you do not pursue that interest, my friend. Amalia is betrothed. Her engagement will be announced tomorrow night at the ball. In the meantime, you are not to be alone with her. We must not have one breath of scandal, *Senor* Cooper. *Entiende?* Not one breath of scandal."

"Aye." Matt looked down at his boots, which were hurting mightily now. He thought of the place where he had spent last night, of Yvonne and the notorious Madame Rodare. Would *Don* Esteban Montoya have offered him lodging in his house if he had known? "Aye," he murmured again, "I understand sir." But when he thought of Amalia's face he knew that nothing could keep him from seeing her, in any way he could.

# XI

Madame Rodare smiled over her wineglass—a sly, knowing smile. "So you have been invited to stay on the bluff, *eh bien?* You are leaving my humble roof for a mansion on high!" She chuckled, deep in her throat. The light in the big room was dim, the shades tightly drawn.

"Aye," Matt said. "You've been right kind to me. Don't think I ain't obliged, Ma'am, but I figured that since *Senor* Montoya's doin' business with my family, I'd best get to know him for a spell."

Madame's eyebrows shot upward. Had her ravaged face paled under its paint? "Montoya? Do you mean *Don* Esteban Montoya?" She put her wineglass down on the table.

"Aye, the very same. Spanish gentleman. Big house." Matt sipped on his own wine. He had come in to tell her he was leaving, but she had insisted he sit down and have a drink with her. "Do ye know him, Ma'am?" Matt asked after a long pause.

"*Oui.*" Her voice was strangely hushed. "I know him, *mon cher.* I know him well." She lifted

167

her wineglass and drained it in one painful swallow. "Tell me, *cheri*, did you meet anyone else there today?"

"Ay. The butler. And an old man name of Rushton who's some kind of painter."

"Ah, yes. *Monsieur* Rushton has been a customer from time to time. He doesn't come often, but he pays well." The casualness of her voice was hiding something, Matt sensed. "And did you meet anyone else? A young girl, perhaps?"

"Aye." Matt felt his face redden, and knew that she had noticed. Not many things about a man escaped a woman like Madame Rodare.

*"Dites-moi!"* her whisper and deep and intense. "What did she look like. What was she doing? Forgive a curious old woman, *cheri.*"

"Rushton was painting a picture of her." Matt felt the redness deepen. "They were in the garden, him and her. She was sittin' on a stool, pretty as a little bird. She's got black hair like yours, and skin as white as a daisy petal, and—" Matt suddenly stopped speaking. He stared at Madame Rodare, the story Mike Fink had told him flashing through his mind. He could not speak.

Madame Rodare's fingertips were white where they gripped the stem of her empty wineglass. *"Oui, mon fils.* Somehow I think you have guessed. She is my daughter."

Matt's jaw dropped. Aye, it all fit together, especially with what Mike Fink had told him about Madame having a daughter on the bluff that she wasn't allowed to see. He would have guessed it the first time he looked at Amalia if he had not been so stupefied by her beauty.

"It'll be her birthday tomorrow," Matt said. "She'll be sixteen years old."

Madame Rodare looked down at her hands where they cradled the stem of the wineglass. When she looked up, something glistened in her eyes. "You think I don't know it, *cheri?*" she whispered. "I remember that day well. Sixteen years ago . . ."

"You an' Don Esteban . . . ?"

"*Oui.*" Madame sighed and refilled her glass. "I left Vincennes—with a sick mind. For days, weeks—I wandered in the woods, not remembering where I was or even *who* I was. Why I did not die I cannot imagine, Matt, *mon cher.* Indians . . . wild animals . . . I don't even know how I kept from starving to death!" Her hand reached over and clasped Matt's. In spite of her illness there was amazing strength in her fingers. Here, Matt sensed, was a tough, resilient woman, a survivor.

"At last I collapsed on the bank of the Wabash, far downriver from Vincennes," Madame said. "I lay there, until a young Spanish trader in a canoe came along and found me. He nursed me back to health. By the time we reached Natchez, where he lived, he had asked me to marry him."

Madame Rodare quaffed the wine in one hard, bitter gulp and poured the few remaining drops from the bottle into the glass. "It wasn't so bad *d'abord.* Not until after Amalia was born. We were even happy for a while. Then he started getting . . . jealous. For no reason at all! If I said

169

good morning to a man on the street—*pouf!* A jealous rage! That's a Spaniard for you! He was growing rich by then. I'd had property in Vincennes, you see. He'd arranged to have it sold, and invested the profits in his business. It was paying . . . handsomely. But a life with that man was growing *terrible!* One night he went completely insane. He threw me out! Me, the mother of his child! I tell you—" Her voice shook with bitterness. "From that day to this, I have not been allowed even to speak with my daughter. I . . . I have only caught glimpses of her from the street."

"But don't she want to see you?" Matt asked gently.

Madame Rodare shook her head. "I don't know. I don't know what he has told her, the pig! *Le cochon!*" Her fist clenched on the table.

"And . . . this place?" Matt glanced at the room around him. It was richly furnished. It must have cost a good deal of money.

Madame Rodare laughed. "Ah, yes. Esteban gave me some money. Oh, not much. Only enough to leave Natchez and buy a cabin and some land in another town. That was what he expected me to do, I know. But I fooled him! I stayed here! I did the only thing I knew to survive—*compris?* You understand?" She finished the wine. "And that, *cheri,* is my revenge, you might say. The revenge of Mathilde. I stay here, to embarrass him, to worry him—the pig—and to be near my daughter."

170

***

Matt did not see Amalia again until the ball the next evening. *Don* Esteban, he suspected, had made certain of that. Though the Spaniard had graciously given him the run of the house, Matt had wandered the halls and gardens without catching so much as a glimpse of her. And wandering was not easy. Not when his feet hurt fiercely from the blisters the new boots had made. They still looked splendid, but Matt winced every time he took a step in them. He wondered how he was ever going to manage dancing.

He had hoped to talk to Amalia alone, not only because she had enchanted him, but because her mother, Madame Rodare, had charged him with a mission. He touched his pocket and felt the delicate bulge of the little velvet box. It contained a beautiful ruby ring, a birthday gift from Madame Rodare to her daughter. "Ask her to wear it, Matt, *cheri*," Madame had said in a hushed voice. "Tell her I will watch for her wherever I go—on the street, at the theater, in the market. I will watch to see, *eh bien?* If she is wearing this ring, I will know that she wants to see me. Then, I will somehow find a way to arrange things."

Matt's eyes roamed about the ballroom. It was a far cry from the dances back home where he'd kicked up his heels till the moon was gone. The floor was made of inlaid wood, polished till it shone like water. A thousand candles burned in the elaborate wrought-iron chandeliers, making the ballroom as bright as day. There were four fiddlers instead of one, all playing together. Even

171

so, none of them was a match for old Gambel, the man Matt had heard in Nashville the night he met Carrie. The music was slower, calmer. Somehow he didn't like it as well.

Matt had not asked anyone to dance. The folks here didn't seem as friendly. Besides, his feet hurt too much. He sat on a high-backed chair and let his eyes follow Amalia as she danced, her simple white dress whirling around her. Many of her partners were older men, closer to her father's age than her own. Matt wondered if one of them was her fiance. He saw no one who looked like he would be her obvious choice—young, handsome and attentive. Maybe *Don* Esteban had been bluffing about Amalia's being engaged. Maybe he just wanted to keep Matt away from her.

He watched Amalia turn in the graceful reels and old-fashioned minuets, her little head tilted gracefully, her lace fan hanging by a ribbon from her arm. From time to time, she would look over her shoulder and smile shyly at him. Her black eyes sparkled. Little by little he came to realize that she was dancing for him. Lovely Amalia. She was so beautiful she almost stopped his heart.

Suddenly he couldn't see her any more. His eyes darted about the ballroom, searching for her. Sudden, inexplicable panic tugged at him. Having her out of his sight had suddenly become unbearable.

He was still looking for her when he heard her small, bell-like voice just behind him. "And are you never going to ask me to dance, Matthew Cooper?"

172

She stood at his shoulder, her face flushed, her breasts rising and falling slightly. Matt caught his breath. "I . . . I want to, Amalia, but . . . I can't."

"You can't?" She looked downcast. "But why not?"

Matt glanced helplessly down at his boots. By now, even walking had become excruciating. He would not think of dancing. Not even with Amalia.

She followed his eyes. Then she began to laugh. *"Pobrecito!* You poor thing! You have been walking everywhere in those boots! Those are riding boots, Matthew Cooper; nobody walks in boots like that! Look—look at the men on the dance floor. They're all wearing dancing slippers. If I could lend you a pair of Papa's—" She glanced down at Matt's large feet. "But, no! I see that would not do! *Que lastima!* What a pity! I did want to dance with you."

"Ye could walk with me," Matt said, his heart pounding strangely. "Ye could walk with me in the garden."

Her hand went to her mouth, a dainty, fluttering gesture. "Oh! Papa would not like that." Matt's heart sank, then lifted again as he saw her eyes. They were sparkling with mischief. "Let's do it! See, Papa's over there. He's talking. He won't see us." She laughed softly. "Come on!"

Matt let her lead him out a side door, down a dim hallway, and out into the night. Her hand rested in his like a flower, so delicate that he did not dare tighten his grasp on it.

173

"Here—" she stopped, slightly breathless, beside a bush covered with white flowers. "This is all right. Sit down, Matthew Cooper. I know it hurts you to walk in those boots."

"Would ye call me Matt?" In truth, Matt had forgotten about the boots. He had not felt even a twinge of pain from the moment she'd taken his hand.

"*Si*." She sat down on a bench. The moonlight shone blue on her black hair. Matt had been bursting with a hundred things he wanted to say to her, but now he could put none of them into words. She was so close, and so beautiful.

Amalia, too, was strangely silent. Her hand had slipped out of Matt's and lay in her lap. Both of them felt the overpowering magic that was taking place between them. Both of them were spellbound by it.

Matt fumbled for the velvet box that lay at the bottom of his pocket. "Amalia," he said softly, groping for the right words, "how much do ye remember about your mother?"

Amalia glanced up at him, her eyes wide with surprise. "Matt, do you know my mother?"

"I . . . I met her in town. She found out I was doin' business with your Pa—"

"My Papa won't let me talk about her. He says she's an evil woman. He says she's dead to our family. But I know she's somewhere, here in Natchez."

"Aye. She be here. An' she remembered it's your birthday. She sent ye a present. Told me to give it to ye for her." Matt drew the little velvet-

174

covered box out of his pocket.

"Matt . . . did my mother say she loved me?"

Matt thought for a moment. "Not in them exact words," he replied honestly, "but I could tell she did. She looked kind of sad-like, Amalia. Said she'd like to see ye if ye were willin'."

"I— I don't know. *Por favor*, open the box, Matt. My hands are shaking."

Matt lifted the lid. The moonlight gleamed on the ruby that was set in the delicate little ring. Its color was as dark as blood.

"Oh!" Amalia gasped. "It's beautiful! And . . . my mother wanted me to have it?"

"Aye." Matt studied her face in the moonlight. Her features were perfect, her skin as flawless as a baby's.

"Matt," she said softly, "my father told me she didn't love me. He told me she never wanted to see me again, and that I musn't try to see her, because it would only make her angry. I'd always hoped it wasn't true." She took the ring from the box and put it on her finger. The deep red ruby caught the moonlight. It glowed like dark fire as Amalia held out her hand to study the ring at arm's length. "It's just the right size! I wonder how she knew!"

"Amalia, she's wantin' to see ye," Matt said softly. "She says that if ye want t' see her, ye can wear the ring when ye go out. She'll see it, an' she'll know. Then somehow she'll find a way."

Amalia stared at the ring. Slowly she shook her head. "I'm afraid, Matt. It's been so long. I was only four years old when she went away, but I remember her. She was very tall, and so very beautiful. But I remember how she screamed at my father the night she went away. I— I still remember what she said, what she called him. I loved her, Matt. It hurt me so much." She slipped the ring off her finger and put it gently back in the box.

"Then ye don't want to see her?" Matt asked gently.

Amalia's hands closed around the box. "I want to. But I'm afraid, Matt. I . . . I lost her once. That was hurt enough for all my life." She looked up at Matt with eyes so soft and dark that his heart almost stopped. "But I'll keep the box. Tell my mother that when I find the courage to see her, I will wear the ring."

"Aye . . . I'll tell her," Matt whispered, gazing down at Amalia. He wondered if the girl had any idea what her mother did for a living. Probably not. Amalia probably didn't even know there were such places as the one that Madame Rodare ran. She was so sheltered, so innocent, Maybe she didn't know . . . anything. Matt shuddered with guilt as he remembered the sight of Yvonne on the bed below him, her brown hair spread out on the pillow, her full breasts catching the flickering light of the single candle, her white legs spread wantonly, waiting for him. He remembered the husky, animal sound of her breathing, her lusty little cries as he plunged into her. Matt shuddered again, closed his eyes, opened them, and there stood Amalia, looking up at him.

"Matt," she said softly, "do you know that I have never kissed a man?"

"But your father said you were promised—"

"I hardly know him. He's a friend of my father's. They arranged it all, between the two of them." She shrugged. "My father arranges everything. He says he wants me provided for. But the man—I have never even spoken with him alone. As for kissing—" she laughed nervously. "Family honor means everything to my father. That . . . that's why he made my mother leave, I think. And I also think he is afraid that I will disgrace him as well. An early marriage is his way of seeing that I do not."

Matt's heart ached for her. "Then ye don't love him, the man ye be promised to?"

"Love him?" she whispered bitterly. "How could I love such a man?"

"Amalia—" His hand reached out and brushed her arm. Then, suddenly he drew back, afraid to touch her, afraid of the swift surge of feeling that had warmed his whole body.

"Matt," she whispered. "I . . . I don't want him to be the only man who will ever kiss me. I want to know how it is with someone young . . . someone I want—"

"You're asking me . . . ?" Matt was stunned.

"*Sí.* Yes, Matthew Cooper, I am asking you—" She stretched up on tiptoe, her eyes closed. Her lashes lay like black silk fringe on her white cheeks. Her lips were adoringly puckered.

"Amalia!" he groaned. Then, almost without his consciously willing it, his arms were around her. Her fragrance filled his nostrils as he bent his head and found her lips. He had meant to kiss her

177

gently, but he could not help himself. His mouth came down on hers with a crushing passion. His arms pulled her close against him.

He kissed her again and again, until her lips softened under his, until her own mouth began to give its sweetness to him, until she began to whimper soft little woman-child sounds.

"Amalia . . . " He whispered her name over and over, caught up by the feel of her body in his arms. "Amalia, don't marry him. Don't."

She kissed him back, wildly, half-sobbing. "Matt . . . No, I must . . . No, stop . . . Stop, Matt, I can't." She broke away from him. Her hand clung to his for an instant. Then she had spun out of reach. She was running back toward the ballroom.

"Amalia—" He took a step after her, then realized it was too late. She was gone.

Slowly Matt walked back toward the ballroom. His boots were hurting again, as much from the knowledge that they were out of place as from the blisters. There was no getting around it. He was nothing but a backwoods bumpkin in this city.

But Amalia had wanted him to kiss her. He remembered the sweetness of her upturned face, waiting. His lips were still damp from kissing her. They still felt the warm tingle of her response. "Amalia . . ." He whispered her name. He'd kissed girls before, a good number of them, but never one like her. She was like a flame, this little Amalia, pure but burning. He had felt the welling desire in her. Innocent and sheltered she might be, but on one side she was Spanish—a hot-

178

blooded race if ever there was one—and on the other side of her was Mathilde Rodare. Once Amalia's slumbering nature was awakened she would be a passionate woman. He ached with envy for the unknown man who was destined to arouse that passion. By damn, if he didn't handle her gently, if he didn't awaken the girl with tenderness—Matt clenched his fists. If the bastard proved to be cold and unfeeling, or brutal, or dirty—Damnation! Matt could not stand it. Poor Amalia.

He strode back toward the ballroom, his paining boots forgotten once more. By heaven, he would speak to *Don* Esteban himself. He would plead, beg, threaten if he had to. But a girl like Amalia should never have to marry a man she didn't love, some stranger, old enough to be her own father—Matt swung the door open and stepped inside. The light and music surrounded him. He looked for Amalia. She was not among the dancers. Anxiously his eyes darted about the ballroom until he found her, standing with her father. Evidently *Don* Esteban had missed her. He was speaking sternly, wagging a finger at her. Amalia looked pale. One small hand had crept to her throat.

The dance tune swirled to its ending. *Don* Esteban walked out onto the dance floor, clapping his hands sharply for silence. The crowd parted, the dancers moving into a ring around the floor, buzzing curiously. Something important seemed about to happen.

*Don* Esteban cleared his throat. "My friends

... *amigos mios* ... I have chosen this night, the night of my beloved daughter's sixteenth birthday, to make a most happy announcement. Amalia—" He held out his arm. "Come here, my child." The words were affectionate enough. Their tone was more like what a man would use to call a disobedient dog. "Come, Amalia."

Amalia walked across the floor to him, her face pale, her eyes downcast. She placed a docile hand on his arm.

"My friends," said *Don* Esteban, "It is my pleasure to announce the betrothal of my precious daughter, Amalia Maria Teresa Montoya, to my most esteemed friend, *Don* Andres Cristobal Santana y Galvez."

A murmur swept over the crowd, like the ripple of wind through dry leaves. Not all the sounds were happy. Matt heard—or at least thought he heard—a sour note of disbelief and disapproval. He craned his neck to see the man who stepped forward to take Amalia's hand. The fellow's back was turned at first, but he appeared to be of medium height and build. There was nothing either distinguished or unpleasant about him—until he turned around.

Matt caught his breath as *Don* Andres Santana took Amalia's hand and turned to face the crowd. It was not that he wasn't handsome. Indeed he was, with strong features, dark eyes, slightly graying hair that came to a peak in the middle of his forehead. But there was something in his eyes, in the low line of his brows and the sensuous curl of his upper lip, that made the hair rise on the back of Matt's neck. There was an animal quality about the man. His eyes glided over Amalia's body, and Matt could almost picture him licking his lips. Amalia recoiled slightly from his touch. Her lovely face was pale against her dark hair. No! something in Matt cried out. It wasn't right, Amalia and this lusty old billy goat of a Spaniard. He would do something. He would do something if he had to murder the man to keep him from having her!

As Matt looked across the floor, his eyes met Amalia's, and held until both of them began to tremble and had to look away. He loved her, Matt suddenly realized, the sweet shock of the discovery turning his knees to water. He loved her, and whatever it cost him, he would save her!

# XII

Edward Forny helped his wife down from the wagon. Marie was waiting on the porch, and the two ran to each other across the yard. They opened their arms and embraced, mother and daughter, laughing with pure happiness.

Yes, it had been the right decision, Edward reflected as he watched them. Vincennes, their home for years, was too far from their children now that he and Abby were growing older. Now they could be near Marie and the children, with Henry and Sara's family only a few days' journey away by horse.

He had left the northern branch of Forny & Cooper in the hands of a capable assistant, sold the big stone house, and loaded their possessions on a wagon.

Edward had been a bundle of jumping nerves during the wagon journey from Vincennes to Louisville. He'd remembered only too well the sight of his friends, the Carters, murdered in their cabin; and as far as he knew the killers were still on the loose. This was prime bandit country, and their wagonload of clothes, supplies, and fine furniture would have been a prize for any robbers.

Edward and Abby had not traveled alone, of course. Only a fool would have done that. But even in the company of other wagons and mounted men, his spine had tingled at every unexpected movement of the trees or rustle in the underbrush. One of the men in their company had been south a few months before, down along the Natchez Trace, and had told about finding a murdered traveler on the bank of the Tennessee River. The man's body had been cut open, the entrails removed, and the cavity filled with sand, most of which had washed out, which is why the body had floated and drifted ashore. "It were the Harpe brothers, I tell ye," the man had said, his eyes bulging. "That be the way they work, them two!"

Edward shivered every time he thought of it. Even now that he and Abby had arrived safely in Louisville, he was worried. Not for himself, but for Matt. More and more, he was beginning to regret having sent the boy on such a long journey. He'd be safe enough on the way down, in the company of toughened river men like Mike Fink. But Fink and the others would more than likely find work on a keelboat going back upriver, an arduous trip that took months. That would leave Matt on his own to find his way back to Nashville over the Trace. If the boy had the good sense to listen to what he'd been told, he'd find a group that was going back up the Trace. But Matt was young, and he was impulsive. He just might be naive enough to take on the Trace alone. Young people had a way of believing that the awful things that happened to other people would never happen to them.

*Tonnerre!* Just thinking about it made him break out in a sweat! As soon as Abby was settled, Edward promised himself, he would set out for Nashville. Maybe John Swaney wouldn't mind some company when he took the mail over the Trace. Maybe he could catch Matt in Natchez, or meet him along the way. The idea set his mind at ease, for the time being at least. Matt, he calculated, should have arrived in Natchez, arranged things with Esteban Montoya, and be ready to set out on the last leg of the journey to New Orleans. Edward Forny was not a religious man, but he glanced up at the sky and murmured a little prayer for his grandson's safety.

Marie had dinner waiting for them. The table almost sagged from the bounty of her kitchen, but Edward ate sparingly, as he always did. He had never believed in bloating his body with food, no matter how tasty it might be. With pleasure he glanced across the table at his wife and daughter. They were completely absorbed in each other, laughing, visiting. *Oui*, Edward told himself, he should have brought Abby to Louisville a long time ago.

They were much alike, these two women of his, though little Marie had grown a bit plump. Abby herself was still slender, her hair a dazzling silver that set off her tanned skin and dark eyes. To Edward she had never looked lovelier, this proud, courageous woman who had shared his life for nigh onto forty years. His heart still ached with love when he looked at her. Strong Woman of the Onondaga. Even now, she remembered her days as an Indian captive, and spoke of them to her spellbound grandchildren.

When the meal was nearly finished, there was a knock at the back door. One of the little girls got up to open it.

The young woman who stepped into the room was not a real beauty, but she was pretty enough, with her pert nose and blond curls. She smiled at everyone in the room, flashing her small, well-formed teeth in a day that said she was proud of them. "Oh," she said, "I didn't mean t' interrupt your sup. Just thought I'd drop in for a while. Missus Cooper, I brought ye some blackberries from down by the river. I got time to help ye make some blackberry pies tomorrow if ye'd like." She placed a covered bucket on the cupboard.

"That's right nice of ye, Winifred," Marie said. Did her smile look slightly strained? "I'd like ye to meet Matthew's grandparents, Mr. and Mrs. Forny."

Winifred bobbed her pretty head in acknowledgement. "I'm right pleased t' meet ye. Reckon it's time I got to know Matt's grandfolks, since they's goin' to be mine; too, one of these days!"

Edward and Abby gazed at her, puzzled.

"Oh," she said prettily. "I reckon Matt didn't tell ye afore he left Louisville. Quite a one to keep secrets, that Matt. Now me, on the other hand, I never could keep a secret. Just sort o' bubbles out of me like soapsuds! Can I tell 'em, Missus

Cooper?"

"All right, Winifred," Marie sighed. "You may as well."

Winifred drew herself up tall. "Me an' Matt," she said with a sly grin. "We was sparkin' pretty good afore he left, ye know. What he didn't tell nobody was that he asked me t' marry him the last night. An' I said yes. Matt an' me, we're goin' to get married when he gets back from New Orleans!"

Matt stepped off the gangplank and onto the flatboat again, Slocum trotting at his heels. Once he'd been excited about the final leg of the journey from Natchez to New Orleans. It would be the most fascinating part of the trip, with the Mississippi at its grandest. And New Orleans itself was a city to be dreamed of.

But when Matt looked back toward the bluff, he realized that leaving now was like cutting off his own arm. He was leaving Amalia to the mercy of fate and *Don* Andres Santana. He was leaving, and there was no desire to go.

He had seen her only once since the night of the ball. Her father, though he was pleasant enough in his treatment of Matt, may have suspected there was something between them. For whatever reason, he kept Amalia secluded. Matt had only run into her by chance, in the garden, in the evening.

She'd been standing under a flowering tree, looking at the stars, when he walked up behind her, unable to believe his good luck. For days he had wanted to see her and now, by the sheerest accident (or was it destiny?) here she was.

"Amalia—" he whispered softly. She turned, startled. Then her eyes softened as she recognized him.

"Be still," she breathed the words. "My father—"

"Aye . . . I know." Matt touched her cheek and felt a trace of damp tears. "Amalia, you're crying—"

"Hush. A woman cries many tears in her life, I'm told." She flashed him a bitter little smile in the darkness. "You saw *Don* Andres, my betrothed. Wouldn't you cry if you were in my place, Matthew Cooper?"

"Amalia—" His arms drew her close. He held her gently against his chest, breathing in the fragrance of her hair. "Amalia, don't marry him. Your father can't force you." He looked up at the sky. "Damnation, Amalia, this is America! This is a free country now!"

"Sssh!" She touched his lips, her hand lingering against them. "Out there is America. Here in this house is still Spain. My father can make me do anything he wants. You don't know the power he has."

"Ye could leave. Ye could run away."

"But where would I go?" She met his eyes, and Matt knew that they were both thinking the same thing. Her mother. But that wouldn't do, Matt told himself hastily. A girl like Amalia, in a place like Madame Rodare's. Lord, it would kill the poor girl to find out what kind of a person her mother really was.

"Your mother ain't got a place for you," he said helplessly. "Maybe she could help ye find a place—"

"It wouldn't work." Amalia said. "My father would find me. That's the first place he'd look—with her." She shook her head, her eyes downcast.

Matt lifted her chin with one big, rough hand. He looked into her beautiful, dark eyes. "Amalia," he said softly, "come with me. Come with me back to Louisville. Oh, it ain't like here. But my family's a good family. They'd be glad to have ye there. And I— I'd do everything I could to make ye happy. I'd be good and gentle, and I'd work hard. The business, it'll be mostly mine one day. I'm the oldest of the Forny grandsons. It ain't like we were poor—"

Her eyes widened. "Oh, Matt," she whispered, her voice full of wonder, "Are you asking me to marry you? Is that what you're saying?"

"Aye . . . I reckon I am. I didn't plan it this way, Amalia, but now that I said it, I know I want ye—"

She gave a tiny moan. "Oh, if only I could!"

"But ye can! Listen, Amalia, I'll be back from New Orleans in a few weeks. I can ask your Pa."

"He'll say no. He's already promised me to *Don* Andres."

"Listen, does he want ye to be happy or doesn't he?"

"I can see you don't know Papa. He wants

189

what he thinks is best for me. Matt, *no hay esperanza!* There is no hope, *querido.*"

"Amalia—" He took her shoulders. "Amalia, do ye love me?"

She looked at him for a long time. "*Sí,*" she whispered at last. "I do love you Matt. And I would marry you if I could. Yes."

Matt's heart was pounding as he pulled her tight against him. His mouth came down on hers, firm and sure. He kissed her like a man, not like some hot-headed young fool. He'd asked her to marry him. It was up to him to take care of her now.

A quavering voice floated out from an upstairs window, calling out Amalia's name. "My duenna," Amalia whispered. "She's looking for me. She'll tell my father. Matt—" She gripped his hands.

"Don't worry. We'll find a way." He had pulled her close and kissed her once more, a long, deep, passionate kiss. Then the old woman had called to her once more. Amalia had slipped out of Matt's arms and fled. He had not been able to see her again.

"Wake up, there, Cooper!" Mike Fink's voice grated in his ears and Matt realized he had been daydreaming. "Ye think ol' Mike Fink's goin' t' steer this blasted broadhorn by hisself, eh?"

Matt forced a smile and shook his head. No, Fink wouldn't understand. He picked up girls and discarded them like old stockings. Matt wondered if he'd ever loved even a one of them.

Slocum's tail thunked happily on the deck. The

big yellow mutt was happy to be with his master once more, but from the looks of him he had not suffered during their separation. He had stayed at Madame Rodare's house while Matt was at the Montoya mansion. Madame's girls had made a great pet of him. They'd fed him everything from lamb chops to cream puffs and brushed his shaggy yellow coat till it gleamed. Slocum had never looked so sleek and fat. Slocum leaned against Matt's leg and drooled on his shoe. The soft life is all well and good, his manner clearly said, but it's better to be back in action again.

The other men were back at their posts as well, though Oscar Sutton was nursing a black eye and a well-chewed ear. Kovalenko had kissed a woman and four small children good-bye at the landing. The woman was well along with another child. Her broad, homely face shone with affection for the big Pole. The girl that LeClerc embraced at the foot of the gangplank was prettier and younger, but Matt had the feeling that the little Frenchman wasn't the only riverboat man she'd kissed good-bye. Likely as not, there'd be another one along soon.

Maddox was telling the others about Sutton's fight. "Lor' ye shoulda seed 'im! The other bastard wuz bigger, mind ye, but our Oscar, he were full o' spit an' fire. He stood up on tippytoe like a banty rooster an' he crowed, 'I be the boss o' this whole river an I'll eat any man alive what says different!' Then he tore int' that fat bastard like a weasel into a chicken. He wuz winnin', too, but the bugger got a chaw on his ear. Almost chawed

191

it off, he did, till ol' Oscar here got a hunk o' his nose. Bit the end of it right off, he did, an' spit it out on the barroom floor! The other one, he wuz bleedin' like a pig. He squealed an' squalled an' hollered he'd had enough! Lor' ye shoulda seed it, Mike. Ol' Oscar woulda done ye proud!''

"Aye," Mike Fink muttered, "let's cast off an' get movin'!" Fink was not in the best of moods, Matt reflected. His eyes looked bloodshot, like he'd spent most of the night carousing. And he was anxious to get the trip over with, Matt knew. For a keelboat man like Fink, a flatboat was a step down in the world, almost an embarrassment.

Matt's eyes scanned the landing, his heart still jumping with the insane hope of seeing Amalia there. She would not be there, of course. The riverfront was a rough area, hardly the place for a gently-bred girl like Amalia Montoya. But someone else was there. Madame Rodare waved above the crowd, beckoning to him.

"Just a minute," Matt said to the impatient Mike Fink. "I'll be right back." He made his way back to where she stood, a pink parasol shading her from the sun. In the harsh morning light she looked old and tired, wrinkles showing beneath the rouge and powder that coated her face. Still there were traces in her features of the beauty she had passed on to Amalia.

"You didn't wake me to say good-bye, Matt, *cherie*."

Didn't want to trouble ye." Matt had come by early to get Slocum. The strange little butler had

192

let him in, explaining that Madame was still sleeping.

"One moment, please. I wanted to talk with you. How is my daughter? You have seen her? Does she wear the ring yet?" Madame Rodare's hand gripped Matt's arm.

"Not the last time I saw her," Matt answered. "But it ain't that she don't think kindly of ye. She's afraid. She lost ye once, she says. She's afraid she'll get to lovin' ye and lose ye again. Give her time. She'll come around."

"She is betrothed I hear. To that swine, Andres Santana."

"Ye know him?"

"Know him? *MKon Dieu*, the man is one of my best customers! But the girls, they don't like him. They say he is a beast! A brute! An animal! This man and my little Amalia—*non!* It cannot be. Matt, we must do something!"

"Aye." Matt felt his jaw clench. "I plan to."

Madame Rodare's faded blue eyes searched Matt's face. "You love her? *Ma fille*, my little girl? You love her, eh?"

"Aye," Matt said softly, conscious of the crowd milling around them and of Mike Fink, waiting on the deck of the flatboat with his hands on his hips.

Madame smiled. "*Magnifique*. I thought so. When you did not return to Yvonne—"

"Yvonne, she be a . . . fine girl. Ye tell her I said so. Ain't nothin' against her that I didn't come back—" Matt felt his face reddening in the morning sun.

"You'll be back here, when you're done with New Orleans?" Madame took both his hands and gripped them hard.

"Aye."

"Then we'll talk. We'll do something to save her. You can count on Mathilde Rodare to help, *mon cher*!"

"Aye." Matt released himself from her hands. "I got t' be goin'."

"Come on, Cooper!" Mike Fink bawled out from the deck of the boat. "Come on, if ye don't want t' get left!"

Matt raced for the boat. Fink had already cast off the lines, and it was drifting away from the landing. Matt hesitated a split second, then made a flying leap. He caught the edge of the deck, teetered precariously for an instant, and then fell forward to land in a heap on the planking, safe and dry. Mike Fink guffawed. The onlookers on the landing whooped and cheered. Slocum wagged his big tail and licked Matt's face with a sloppy pink tongue.

The flatboat caught the current of the Mississippi. The people on the landing grew smaller and smaller. Matt watched Mathilde Rodare's waving figure until it was no more than a dot. At least he had one ally, for whatever Madame's friendship was worth. At least there was someone who seemed happy that he wanted to win Amalia. Maybe she'd really loved his grandfather Edward, Matt thought. Maybe that was why Madame Rodare seemed to have a special feeling for him. And maybe that was why she seemed glad about the idea that he loved her daughter.

Matt's eyes left the waterfront and moved up the gray cliffs to the bluff. Somewhere up there Amalia would be waiting for him. Maybe she was watching, even now.

Again Matt thought of *Don* Andres Santana. One fist clenched at his side. "I'll be back for ye, Amalia," he whispered into the wind. "Wait for me. I'll be back for ye!"

# XIII

By the time Matt stepped ashore on the wharf at New Orleans he was totally awestruck. He had thought Natchez the grandest place in the world. It was nothing compared to the sprawling magnificence of New Orleans.

"How d'ye like her, boy?" Maddox glanced up from securing one of the lines. "Queen of the ol' Mississippi, that's what they call 'er up and down the river!"

"Aye," Matt breathed, looking up and down a dock that seemed to stretch for miles. "She be a queen all right." The whole scene was so downright amazing that he kept wanting to rub his eyes. Flatboats, keelboats and barges were tied all along the bank in a solid line, for as far as the eye could see, upstream or down. The river itself bustled with traffic—cargo boats, slim pirogues, rowboats, even towering ocean-going schooners. Matt could do nothing but stare—at the river, at the boats, at the huge stone warehouses that rose beyond the dock.

"Queen o' the Mississippi?" Mike Fink's sardonic chuckle almost made him jump. "Queen, you say, Mister Maddox? Why, you don't do justice t' the lady! New Orleans ain't nothin' but a great big purty painted whore, jest a lyin' out here on the river bank, waitin' for Mike Fink t' please 'er! That's what she be! An' as soon as ye get yer cargo money t' pay us, Mister Cooper, that's jest what ol' Fink here's gonna do! Bed every whore and drain every bottle o' whiskey in New Orleans!" He waved his cap in the air. "Ye hear that, all ye gals out there? Mike Fink's come t' town!"

Matt laughed. He'd grown used to Mike Fink by now. The man was almost like the Mississippi itself—big, dirty, strong, violent, unpredictable in many ways, yet oddly gentle, and not without goodness. "Aye," he said with a smile. "They be a waitin' for ye, Mike. I can almost feel it in the air, like hot breathin'."

"Well, let's be gettin' it done," said LeClerc. "Let's find the cargo man an' get this worm-eaten flatboat sold. Then we can go have our fun!"

"Aye," Matt muttered, realizing that this part was his responsibility, and not quite sure how to go about it. *Don* Esteban had given him the name and address of the man who was to buy the flatboat with its cargo. He had even told them exactly where they were to tie up when they docked (directions that made no sense at all to Matt, but which Mike Fink had understood at once). At the time, many of the details had seemed pointless. Why was *Don* Esteban giving him so many instructions? All he really had to do was find the buyer and turn the cargo over to him. New Orleans couldn't be much harder, not for a real man of the world like he had become.

But now, as Matt stood on the bustling dock, it all made sense to him. New Orleans was so big. A few months ago, when the boundaries of his life had been marked by Louisville, Nashville, Vincennes, he'd not imagined the whole world could be this big! Now, looking out over the brown vastness of a river so huge that even the big ships were no more than dots on its surface, and back the other direction at a city so enormous that he could see no end to it, he began to realize how small the world of his youth had been, and how big the real world was.

Slocum nudged at Matt's hand with his muzzle and whined questioningly. Matt scratched his head. "Aye, boy. Ye be a mite lost, too, I'll wager. Just like me." He took the folded paper out of his pocket and studied the name and address of the buyer *Don* Esteban had found for him. He was just beginning to appreciate the value of the Spaniard's service. To bring a flatboat into New Orleans with no place to tie up and no buyer waiting would have been nigh onto impossible. He gazed at the paper.

Smith and Duchesne, Ltd.
1830 Poydras Street
New Orleans

Lord's mercy, nothing would be easy to find in this place. At least maybe Mike Fink might be able to tell him where Poydras Street was. That would be a beginning.

Matt turned around to look for him, and almost ran into a nattily dressed fellow with an account book under his arm.

"Mister Cooper . . . of Forny & Cooper?" The young man looked Matt up and down, taking in his out-of-fashion clothes.

"Aye." Matt felt a wave of relief wash over him. He wouldn't have to go and find Smith & Duchesne, Ltd. It appeared as they'd just found him. "Be ye Mr. Smith, or Mr. Duchesne?" he asked politely, realizing from the disdainful lift of the fellow's eyebrows that he'd mispronounced the name.

The young man cleared his throat and sort of tittered. "Really, my good fellow. I am neither Mr. Smith nor Mr. Duchesne (Doo-shane, was the way he said it, which was nothing like it looked on paper, Matt thought, though he didn't mention it). If you think either one of them would be running down to the docks every time a flatboat comes in, you're quite mistaken."

"Then, might ye be so kind as t' take me t' one or the other?" Matt said, using the best manners he knew.

The fellow huffed impatiently. "That won't be necessary. You'll be dealing with me. I'm Mr. Smith's assistant, and I've authorization to inspect the cargo and to issue you a bank draft if it is satisfactory."

"Ye mean it's you who'll be payin' me."

"Exactly, my good man. Now if I could see your cargo, please. I haven't got all day, you know. There are four other flatboats in, just this morning."

"Aye." Matt walked back toward the boat, motioning for the man to follow him. The crewmen, well used to such proceedings, were already opening up the cargo area. The young man, who had not even introduced himself by name, walked about as gingerly as a cat, lifting up the pelts, counting them and looking at their condition, squinting at the edges of the millstones to see if they were evenly ground, shaking the whiskey jugs to make sure they were full. He wore a blue satin waistcoat with a ruffled shirt. His coat was a most elegant buff, the matching breeches tight as skin above silk stockings. He moved carefully among the dusty boxes and pelts, taking great care not to get even a speck of dirt on his clothes.

"The count is short on the whisky jugs, Mr. Cooper." He wrinkled his thin nose. "My information says there should be two hundred of them. I count only one hundred eighty-six."

"Aye," Matt said, knowing exactly where most of the whiskey had gone. Mike Fink required it to function at his cantankerous best. It was an investment in the trip. "But the pelts be higher grade than what ye got writ down," Matt said quickly. "That batch there be prime beaver, an' ye have it listed as second grade. I reckon that just about ought t' make up for the lack in the whiskey."

"Not really." The fellow sniffed. "But I have the bank draft already made out and signed by Mister Duchesne and Mister Smith, including the amount. Either I give it to you or I don't, and if it isn't right—"

"Look here, mate," Fink snarled at him. "I been down this river twenty times if I been down it once, an' by hell ain't no cargo ever been turned down on no boat run by Mike Fink! An' by hell, I ain't in no mood to let this be the first time!" He stood with his feet braced wide, hands on hips, and faced the young man, who was a bit taller but nowhere near as powerfully built.

To his credit, the fellow was not intimidated. "I beg your pardon, sir, whoever you are. I have been sent to deal with Mister Cooper, the owner of the boat and cargo, and have no instructions to traffic with the likes of you. Now, if you will please step to one side, I'll be on with my business. And that business is to see that all this cargo is properly accounted for before issuing payment."

The two of them glared at each other. Matt could see a blood vessel throbbing in Fink's neck—a sure sign that his temper was heating up fast. "Come on, Mike, it's all right," he said softly. "We'll settle it fine." The last thing he wanted was trouble, and Mike Fink looked as if he were about to knock this stuffy young dandy over the side. If he did that, they'd never get the cargo sold.

Neither of them would budge. Not, that is, until Slocum came sidling along between the stacked up bundles of pelts. While Matt saw to the cargo inspection, Slocum had been exploring the dock. Evidently he'd found a dead fish, ripened to perfection, and he'd shown his appreciation by rolling in it.

Guided by some unerring, devilish instinct, he headed straight for the foppishly dressed stranger. The smell of the rotten fish preceded him by a good six paces.

"What—?" The fellow wrinkled his nose. "Good Lord, what's that?" He looked down just as Slocum leaned against his legs in his friendliest manner.

"Ugh!" The man jumped away so fast that Slocum almost lost his balance. "Get . . . get that . . . *beast* away from me!"

Slocum sat down, his big yellow tail thumping on the deck.

"C'mon, Slocum, get away from that feller," Matt said, but didn't use the strong voice he generally had to use when he wanted the dog to mind. Slocum stayed where he was.

"Ain't no budgin' him once he makes up his mind," Matt said. "Ye'd best ignore him, friend, and finish your countin' of the cargo as best ye can."

Mike Fink laughed out loud.

The man swallowed hard and opened the account book he had almost dropped when Slocum leaned against his legs. But his heart wasn't in it, Matt could tell. "Very well," he said. "I think Mister Smith and Mister Duchesne will find the cargo satisfactory, in spite of the problem with the whiskey jugs." He backed carefully away from Slocum who was scratching at a flea behind his ear, and pulled a piece of paper out from between the pages. "Your payment, Mister Cooper. The amount agreed upon by you and Mister Montoya, I believe." He handed the paper to Matt.

"But this—this be—" Matt stammered. It wasn't money at all. Only a piece of paper with some numbers and names on it.

Mike Fink nudged him. "It be fine, boy. Ye take the paper to a bank. The bank gives ye the money."

"Oh. Thank ye, Mike. I knowed that," Matt said quickly, though he hadn't really known it at all. There was a lot to be learned in this big world, but by damn he was learning it!

The men were already hauling their personal gear off the flatboat. "The bank ain't far," Fink said. "C'mon. We'll go with ye. That way ye can give us our pay right off."

"Aye." Matt fell into step with him, wondering if the men mistrusted him after all this time, or if they were just anxious to get their money. The bank was indeed not far, and the clerk honored the draft without question. He seemed to know the signatures of Mr. Smith and Mr. Duchesne.

Matt immediately counted out the pay for each of the men. LeClerc was gone almost from the moment his hands closed around the money. Maddox and Sutton went off together, with little more than a wave of good-bye. Kovalenko, at least, stayed long enough to shake hands. "It has been a pleasure to know you," he said softly, in his rather stilted English. "I will remember you always." His hand was huge and warm. Matt felt a sharp little surge of emotion as he returned the handshake. The big Pole had been his first friend on the journey. He had accepted him long before the others did. Now Matt was sorry to see him go. He was on the verge of saying so when Kovalenko turned and walked away.

Now there was no one left but Mike Fink. He was busy stuffing his money into his pocket. At last he looked up. "Well, Matt Cooper, old boy, reckon this be where we part company," he grinned. "Been nice knowin' ye. If ever ye be wantin' to be a right proper riverboat man instead of a trader, ye come see Mike Fink!" Then, with a jaunty nod of his head, he, too was gone.

Matt stood there on the front porch of the bank, feeling very much alone. He had grown close to these crude, brawling men of the river. He had almost grown to love them. Now, simple as that, they were gone. Matt shrugged to hide the small ache that was growing inside him. Maybe that was the way of the river. You were comrades, almost brothers, until the boat tied up in New Orleans. Then you went your separate ways and forgot everything that had happened.

Slocum whined and sniffed Matt's hand. "Don't ye be goin', too, old boy," Matt said softly. He'd have patted the dog, but Slocum still reeked of the nauseating fish smell.

"Come on, boy," he said. "Reckon we be on our own."

The first thing he did was take Slocum back down to the dock and lure him into the river by throwing a stick for him to chase. The water helped some, though Matt knew that the only remedy for a stink like that was either time or his mother's good lye soap. Afterward Slocum clambered back up onto the dock and shook the wetness out of his yellow hide, showering Matt with water. By the time he was dry, much of the fish odor had gone.

"Well, old boy, let's see the town," Matt said. He didn't plan to stay long in New Orleans, no more than a day and a night. That was a shame in a way, Matt realized, because there was enough here to keep him bug-eyed for weeks. But the money, more than he'd ever had on his own, sat like an oppressive lump in his pocket, and responsibility for it sat even heavier on his shoulders. He did not want to run the risk of getting it stolen in this place. Then, too, there was Amalia. Her face had filled his dreams every night since he'd left Natchez. The date had not been set for her wedding with *Don* Andres Santana, but some instinctive sense of urgency pressed upon Matt's mind. Time was short. It might be perilously short. He had to get back to Natchez. He had to fight for her.

Tomorrow morning. That would be a good time to leave. He could find an inn for the night, buy a horse and saddle, and be on his way at dawn. The road between New Orleans and Natchez was well-traveled. There was no reason it shouldn't be safe.

In the meantime, he was alone, and there was nothing to do but see the town. He slung his bundled gear over his back, whistled to Slocum, and set out along the river.

Soon he was swallowed up by the sights, smells and sounds of New Orleans. For hours he wandered aimlessly, staring in awe at the great stone warehouses, with negro slaves scurrying in and out of them like ants. On their strong shoulders they carried bales of cotton, bundles of cane, barrels of molasses, smoked hams, hides and pelts, sides of beef, bolt upon bolt of fine fabrics. He had thought the warehouses of Forny & Cooper were immense. Why, you could take everything his father and grandfather owned and lose it in a corner of one of these great buildings.

The river, too, was a source of wonder. Ships, taller than the tallest tree Matt had ever seen, rocked at anchor, waiting to be loaded with cargo for America's eastern cities. Mostly their sails were furled and tied to the yards, but now and then Matt would catch a glimpse of one leaving or coming up the river, its sails spread like the wings of some enormous white bird, and he would gasp at its beauty. When he thought of the places such a ship might have been, and the places it would be going, he tingled all over with the excitement of it.

When he turned his steps inland, he wound his way through narrow streets, overhung by balconies of lacy iron grillwork, emerging in the surprising openness of little squares and plazas with fountains and benches. The markets were riots of noise, fragrance and color. Matt stared in wonder at the strings of red and green peppers, onions, garlic, the piles of oranges and sweet potatoes, the endless variety of fish, shrimp, chickens, ducks and turkeys. In a little sidewalk restaurant he feasted on a spicy soup of fish, peppers and tomatoes. It was strange, like nothing he'd ever tasted before, but he liked it. The flavor burned pleasantly all the way to his stomach, and lingered on his tongue. The girl who served him had skin like well-creamed coffee, black eyes, and curly black hair. She smiled when she bent over him, giving him a glimpse of the shadowy cleft between her breasts. She even slipped Slocum a piece of chicken that some other diner had left on his plate. The way she looked at him made Matt wonder if she might be willing to offer him more than a meal. But, no, he reminded himself. Amalia was waiting in Natchez, and he had no wish to entangle himself with anyone else, even for one night. He paid for the meal, thanked her, and went on his way.

By nightfall he had found himself lodging in a riverfront inn, one of the few that would let him have Slocum in the room, and he had arranged for a horse, to be picked up the next morning.

He had planned to go to bed right after supper, but when he leaned out of his upstairs window, the sounds of the night seemed to call to him. The street below was gay with lanterns. The sound of singing came from a tavern, punctuated by the ripple of a woman's laughter. The sound of clinking glasses, the comforting babble of friendly voices, and the faint aroma of tobacco smoke floated up to Matt where he stood in the window. The air was rich with the sweetness of flowers that mingled witn the stench of the waterfront to produce a perfume that was almost intoxicating in its richness. Once his lungs were full of it, Matt knew that he would not be able to sleep that night.

With a sigh he locked Slocum into the room to guard the money and went downstairs. He'd have a drink or two, Matt told himself, then maybe he'd be tired enough to go to bed.

If anything, the night was livelier than the day. The streets were teeming with men from the river, strolling, carousing, laughing. Some of them had women on their arms. Dark Creole beauties, colorful as gypsies with their lacy shawls and twinkling gold earrings. Everybody seemed to be having a good time, but Matt only felt lonesome. He needed something—or somebody, if only just to talk to. He found himself thinking of his grandfather Edward, and Slade. Aye, he and Slade, between the two of them, could have torn this town apart! He thought about Amalia, too, and the sense of urgency pressed on him stronger than ever. Something told him that she needed him, soon. Tomorrow . . . the word pounded in his head. Tomorrow he would be on his way back to her.

He wandered into the brightest and noisiest of the taverns and made his way through the jostling crowd to the bar. The man behind the counter poured him a glass of whiskey without his having asked for it, and shoved it toward him as soon as Matt had plunked his money down. Matt sipped it slowly, its taste slightly bitter going down. By the time he'd reached the bottom of the glass, his head felt light, but the loneliness was still there. He even missed the men from the flatboat—tough little LeClerc, Maddox, and brash, brawling Oscar Sutton, big, gentle Kovalenko, and even Mike Fink. There'd been times when they'd gotten on his nerves, times when he'd looked forward to the end of the river journey. But now he felt strangely lost without them.

He was trying to decide whether to have another drink when he felt a touch at his elbow. "Buy me a drink, stranger?" It was a girl, a girl like Yvonne, only with a different face. Her cheeks were rouged, her black gown cut so low that the nipples of her round little breasts almost popped out of it. She was dark—like so many New Orleans women seemed to be—with small, bright eyes and a pretty little heart of a mouth. Her hair tumbled down around her pert face in saucy curls, and the back of it was piled up on her head and interwoven with red ribbon. Her accent was either French, Spanish, or a mixture of both. Matt could not tell.

"Aye . . . Whatever pleasures ye," Matt said, looking down at her and wondering if he'd be able to resist temptation. "Whiskey?"

She shook her head. "Madeira."

The bartender was already pouring the red wine for her, as if he knew it was what she always ordered. She took a sip of the jewel-like liquid. "You come down the river?"

"Aye. Just got in today."

"You come far? Oooh, you are so tall! And such shoulders!" She touched his sleeve. The pressure of her fingertips sent a tingle up his arm.

"Louisville." He knew what she wanted, of course. A man just off the river would have money in his pocket, money to spend on a pretty girl. Matt looked her up and down, from her curly head to little pointed slippers that peeked from beneath the ruffled hem of her skirt. She was pretty. Very pretty. And Matt was tempted for a minute or two. Was she worth it? he asked himself. Was she worth betraying Amalia and risking the money that belonged to Forny & Cooper? No, he decided at last. He would enjoy her conversation while she finished the wine he'd bought her. Then he would go back to the room and try to get some sleep.

A rough hand jerked at his elbow. "Hey, mate, that gal were a-talkin' with me afore ye butted in!" The man who spoke was a stranger, squat and red-headed, with a knife scar down one side of his face. "I tell ye, she was with me!" he snarled, shaking Matt's arm.

"Beggin' your pardon, friend," Matt slowly moved his arm away from the man. One glance at the girl's face told him she had no wish to be with the fellow. "The lady, she be free to go where she chooses."

The red-headed man leaned close to Matt. The sweat gleamed on the long white scar. His breath smelled of whiskey. "Ye give 'er back, mate, or I punch ye right through that there wall!"

"I don't own the lady," Matt said cautiously. "She don't have t' go no place she don't want to, an' I can see she don't want t' go with the likes of ye, so if ye'll just—"

The man's fist caught him squarely on the chin. Matt staggered backward, spilling a glass on the bar. Dazed, he saw the fellow coming at him again. He flung his weight forward and met the bull-mad charge with his head. The impact crunched his neck and made his temples ring, but he kept his hold on the man as the two of them went down, grappling on the floor.

"Fight! Fight!" The cry rang out through the place, and there was an instant stampede to the area around the bar. Men were whooping and cheering. "Aye! A good one there! Five on Red Max!" "Ha! Ten on the young'un" "Kill 'im! Gouge 'is eyes out! Come on, Red Max!"

Matt stumbled to his feet. The whole room was tinged with red, and the man loomed in front of him, a swaying target. Matt swung, and landed a good, solid blow to the side of the man's head. Red Max was as strong as an ox and clearly a seasoned brawler. But he was drunker than Matt, and Matt took good advantage of it. He threw his weight into the blow and saw Red Max stagger, then right himself against the bar. Quickly Matt moved in again, before the redhead could gather himself for another charge. A quick succession of sharp blows caught Red Max's solid gut. Wheezing like a bellows, he began to fold. Matt blinked with amazement. It was over, and it had been so easy— Then the fist of another man caught Matt's jaw. He turned around, swinging, and all at once the entire tavern erupted into a melee of yelling, punching, charging men.

212

Matt's fist crunched into solid flesh and bone. Again and again he hit home, but his adversaries were scoring blows, too. He reeled back from the hammer-blow of two fists against his head. The room spun for an instant, then slowed.

"Need a bit o' help, boy?" He heard the voice close to his ear, deep and rasping. It was Maddox. And with him, as always, was Oscar Sutton. "Let's get 'em!" Maddox bellowed, wading into the crowd at his own voice, whooping like an Indian's.

Somebody behind him swung a chair. One leg of it struck a crushing blow behind the ear. He saw stars, and almost fell, but a pair of strong arms caught him at the last moment. He sank back, letting those arms support him. There was something familiar about their touch—Matt looked up into Kovalenko's homely, grinning face. "Come on," said the big Pole, "This is no place for a boy like you. These men are wild. They get the chance—they kill you! Let's get out of here, eh?"

"Aye," Matt whispered through his teeth. "Ye be right. Let's go." His head was throbbing. His legs felt weak.

The crowd of brawling men was solid between the bar and the door. Kovalenko moved into them, beating a pathway for Matt, who staggered along after him. The going was hard. Kovalenko was a big man, but the crowd was getting ugly. One man reeled into them, blood streaming down his face. Kovalenko grunted as he shoved another pair out of the way. Another man had pulled a knife and was slashing wildly about him.

The girl had climbed up onto the bar. Matt could hear her shrill voice over the sound of the fighting. Was she screaming in fear, or excitement? He would never know.

They were, perhaps, halfway to the door when a knife blow caught the big Pole in the arm. It was a bad cut. Blood came spurting out like a little fountain. Kovalenko's face paled before Matt's eyes. One great hand clutched at his red-soaked sleeve in an effort to stop the bleeding. But the blood kept coming. Matt had never seen so much blood, except maybe when he and his grandfather had buried the Carter family.

Now they were really in trouble. Kovalenko could no longer fight his way through the surging, cursing mob of men. Matt, still dizzy, moved ahead of Kovalenko, but it was all he could do to stand. He was going to topple over any second, he sensed. And with poor Kovalenko bleeding a small river—He stumbled over a man who had rolled against his feet. The door looked a mile away. Matt could feel his own head, throbbing, spinning, growing lighter. The lanterns began to blur. Matt fought for consciousness. If he fell, there'd be no one to help Kovalenko and the big Pole could bleed to death.

It was then that he heard a voice—a loud voice, brassy as the crow of a rooster. "Clear a way, there,' ye bloody bastards! It's Mike Fink tellin' ye! I be man enough t' lick the lot o' ye one-eyed an' one handed! One side, damn ye! One side or I'll blast ye t' kingdom come with one breath.

214

Yeeehaw!" Fink cut a swath through the mob, his fists and feet jabbing viciously. "I'm the son of a hurricane and a lover o' the whole Missis-sippi!"

He was still grinning when he reached Matt and Kovalenko. "Well, I can't leave ye alone for a minute afore you get in trouble! Come on, lads! Follow Mike Fink!" He turned and gave a brutal kick to a staggering riverman with a broken whis-key jug clenched in one fist. "Come on!"

The rest of the crowd parted to clear the way to the door. Matt and Kovalenko stumbled out into the night and collapsed against the outside of the tavern.

"Which one o' ye be hurt the worst?" Fink de-manded.

"Him!" Matt's eyes darted to the big Pole. "Kovalenko's bleedin', Mike. He's bleedin' bad. I'll be all right soon's my head clears." He said it, but he didn't feel it. His skull felt like it was cracked.

Mike Fink leaned over Kovalenko. "Aye, damn it! The bastard musta cut some big vein. Here!" He ripped off the tail of his linsey shirt and wrapped it tight around Kovalenko's arm. The white cloth was rapidly soaked with red blood.

"My room's in the next block," Matt said, fighting the dizziness. "We could get him up there, and then get a doctor!"

"All right. Help me take him! Can ye make it?"

"Aye. I've got to." Matt got his shoulder under

Kovalenko's good arm. "Come on!"

Together the three of them moved up the street, Matt staggering under the big Pole's weight, Fink pressing more cloth on the oozing red cut. They made it to the inn, then up the stairs. Matt heard Slocum barking on the other side of the door. Then the world spun about him and went black.

# XIV

Amalia Montoya stared out the window of her room, her hands twisting her handkerchief. Tomorrow, she told herself. Tomorrow Matt, her Matt, would come and take her away. She had been telling herself the same thing for more than a week, and still that "tomorrow" had not come. Maybe it would never come.

The moon was rising above the bluff. Amalia watched it, a bitter set to her delicate mouth. Maybe she had been foolish to dream, she told herself. Maybe it was only a fantasy. The idea that a young man she had known only a few days would love her enough to save her from the fate to which she had resigned herself since childhood.

The Montoya women did not marry for love. Her father had drilled that fact into her from the time she was old enough to understand. They married for the honor—and the good—of the Montoya family.

Amalia had always known that sooner or later she would be joined in a marriage to a man of her father's own choosing, a man with wealth, influence, and position. She had always known she would have nothing to say about the matter. It was better this way, *Don* Esteban had always assured her. His own sisters had done quite well for themselves, all marrying men of their family's choosing. In fact, the only Montoya marriage that had ended in disaster was the single one entered in passion—*Don* Esteban's own.

Amalia sighed, a melancholy little sound that was almost a sob. Yes, she had always known what would happen, and she had been prepared for it—until she met Matt Cooper. Oh! She stomped her little foot in frustration. If only she hadn't fallen in love. If only she hadn't found out what would be missing in her marriage to *Don* Andres Santana. Matt's kisses had left her shaken, totally unsure now of the life to which she'd so long been accustomed. He was a Yankee. He was poor—not by his own standard, maybe, but his family was not in a class with the Montoyas. His speech and his manners were as raw and unrefined as the walls of the log cabin where he'd probably grown up. He was totally different from anyone she had ever known. And yet something in her responded to him, with a passion she had never felt before. She had never felt anything like this for *Don* Andres.

An unpleasant shiver went up Amalia's spine at the thought of her betrothed. Andres came to the house frequently now, and he was pushing Amalia's father to move the day of their marriage closer and closer. Now he was insisting on next month. He was planning a trip to Spain, he said, and he wanted to take her along with him as his bride. He had made the request at dinner that evening and Amalia's hand had flown to her throat. "Papa, no—you can't let him—" The words had come almost without thought.

*Don* Esteban had glared at his daughter, his eyes glinting with anger. Then he had glanced deliberately back at Andres. "Yes," he had said in a firm voice, "I think that matter might well be arranged. You would enjoy Spain, Amalia. It's a fine place for a honeymoon. I'll speak to the *Padre* tomorrow."

Andres Santana had only looked at Amalia across the table. His eyes were very black, with a disturbing softness about them that spoke, not of kindness, but of sensuality. He licked a drop of oil from his full lower lip. "You'll not be sorry, Amalia," he had said softly.

His eyes had moved up and down her body until she trembled. Why was it, Amalia wondered, that when he looked at her she felt almost as if she had no clothes on? Andres was handsome, or so some girls thought. He had money and fine manners. Why, oh why, hadn't he chosen someone else? He frightened her, those eyes of his— they seemed to be touching her, reaching down into places that no one, not even her maids, had seen. She felt disturbing, fearful shivers radiating up and down through her body. This he could do without even touching her. What would he be like once they were married?

Amalia had choked down the rest of her dinner, excused herself, and fled from the table. She had been in her room ever since, staring out the window in the direction of the Mississippi. "*Ven, mi amore* . . . she whispered, her mind seeing Matt's rugged young face. "Come my love . . . swiftly." Yet, even as she spoke, a strange coldness settled over her heart, and she sensed that he would not come in time— if ever he came at all.

The door creaked softly open behind her. Amalia turned. Andres Santana stood in the long rectangle of light that flooded into the darkened room.

"May I come in, my love?" he asked.

"You may not!" her voice trembled. "This is my bedroom. Please go before I ring for one of the servants."

"The servants have been dismissed for the night." He closed the door behind him. Amalia heard the key turn in the lock. "And your father has gone into town for the evening. We are quite alone, my sweet one."

Amalia felt a strange, cold shiver steal up her spine. He was looking at her, his eyes glittering in the shadows of their sockets. "What do you want?" she asked, her voice slightly unsteady.

"Only to talk with you, *amorcita*." He flowed toward her, stopping on the other side of her bed. "You seem to have . . . this fear of me. This maidenly uncertainty about our marriage. I only wanted to quiet some of those fears, my little dove."

"We can talk in the sitting room," Amalia said quickly.

"Why bother . . . when we are already here." He stood casually, one leg just touching the edge

220

of her lace counterpane. The moonlight gleamed white on the strongly-chiseled planes of his face. His voice was like rough velvet.

"Only a few moments of your time. Alone. That is all I ask of you, Amalia. Come here. It's not easy to talk to you across the room like this." He came around the bed. Amalia felt herself shrinking against the edge of the window, one hand clasping the iron grillwork. The fleeting wish darted through her mind that she could tear the iron barricade loose and jump to the garden below. But she knew that was impossible.

"You're frightened of me . . ." He reached out and captured her hand. "You're trembling like a little bird." He laughed then, a sound that sent a strange shudder through Amalia's body, though she did not understand why. His hand was warm around hers, and slightly moist. She could hear him breathing. That, and the frantic drumming of her heart were the only sounds in the room.

He turned her, so that his dark eyes were looking into hers, the pupils very large in the dim room. She gasped and drew her hand away. "You're frightened . . . It's not at all what you think, *querida*. No . . . marriage to me will be a great pleasure for you once I have taught you—" He caught her wrist again and spun her to him, jerking her against his body. His hands, for an instant, were hard and cruel. Then they softened, gentled as he began to stroke her back, molding her to his lean, sinuous body. His lips nibbled at her hair, at the tips of her ears. Amalia felt her own heart pounding—with fear, yes, but that was

221

not all. Her flesh had begun to tingle beneath her gown, wherever the pressure of his hands passed. Her eyes were huge in the darkness. She wanted to struggle, to cry out, but she could not. She was trapped, hypnotized by the touch of this evil, frightening man.

"*Si. . .*" he murmured, his full, damp lips moving down her neck to her bare shoulder. "Yes, Amalia, love will be sweet between us." His caresses were firmer now, almost rough, as he drew her in against him. Amalia trembled. She could feel the hardness of muscle and bone through her thin gown—and another hardness, a disturbingly hard ridge, almost jabbing her just below the waist. She gasped feebly and tried to pull away, but his arms held her.

"No—" she breathed the word, and then the protest was muffled by his lips. His kiss was nothing like Matt Cooper's (her whirling mind groped for Matt's image, caught at it, clutched it, and then lost it in a flurry of panic). His mouth was hot, almost molten, opening into hers with a thrust of probing, insistent tongue. It frightened her, that tongue. She had not known that men did such things to women. Kissing, yes, her spinning brain tried to reason. But his? It was more like drowning. The horrifying thought passed through her mind that maybe this was the way a baby started.

Amalia's quick, frantic jerk almost freed her from him, but his lunge caught her again. His arm spun her back against him, the force of his weight carrying them both to the bed.

His body pinioned her to the counterpane, pressing her down. She gasped as she felt his hand slide up her leg, seize the top of her pantalets and jerk them down.

He had begun to breathe hard, like a winded stallion. Amalia was struggling now, pinned to her bed by the weight of his body. Her heart exploded with a strange, wild fear as she felt his hand part her thighs. "No—" she gasped. But his mouth caught her words, the lips hot and hard and crushing. She felt his hands on her legs, pulling them apart, anchoring them with his weight while one hand fumbled with his clothes.

Amalia struggled, but feebly now. There was something hypnotic about his weight upon her, and about the way his lips traced a damp path down her throat to the neck of her gown. Then he parted her legs again, and panic seized her. She began to fight him, kicking and gasping. But she was as helpless as a trapped moth. She felt his hands between her legs, touching her in such an unspeakable way that she wanted to die of shame— and then suddenly there was something else, like a huge, blunt finger probing into her. She cried out at the first tearing thrust. Pain radiated through her body, from some central core of her that throbbed and pulsed with it. He was moving on her now, in and out, grunting like a boar. Amalia's whole body felt feverish, alive with the pain of those deep, brutal pushes. The blood was pounding in her head, she cried out, heard him give a deep, heaving gasp, and then he collapsed on top of her, the sweat pouring out of him. Amalia lay beneath him, hurt, sobbing, and bewildered. She only knew that something sweet and pure and delicate was gone from her. Forever.

Matt opened his eyes. The room was dark. He could hear the sound of Kovalenko's heavy snoring in the bunk a few feet away.

He sat up, fighting off the waves of dizziness that still overcame him whenever he tried to rise. In the long run, it seemed that his blow on the head had been more serious than Kovalenko's knife wound. The big Pole was well on his way to mending, and in Mike Fink's absence, had done his best in the role of nurse. "You got a right good crack in your skull, I figure," he told Matt gravely. "I've seen men dizzy like this for weeks with less of a lump than you got. You lie still."

So Matt had tossed in his bunk for days, half-feverish, and aching with frustration to get back to Amalia. Through it all, an unexplained sense of urgency had pricked at him. He had to get back to her, and he had to get back soon. But each time he tried to get out of his bed the dizziness overcame him again. It was lessening, day by day, but it was still a problem.

He glanced over at Kovalenko's hulking form, so large that the big Pole's feet hung off the end of the bunk. His snores filled the room, a comforting sound in a way. But Matt was beyond comforting. He had awakened a moment ago, a sense of pure dread. Something was wrong. Amalia was in danger. She needed him, and he had to go to her.

Matt put his feet on the floor and stood up. That accursed dizziness hit him like a doubled-up fist. He fought it, staggering to the wardrobe where his clothes were kept. When he stumbled over an empty chamber pot, the sound woke Kovalenko. He snorted and sat up.

"And where are you going, eh?" He rubbed his eyes.

Matt clutched the corner of the wardrobe. "I got to get back to Natchez. Now."

Kovalenko yawned. "It's that little Spanish girl, eh? You miss her that much?"

Matt blinked at him through the darkness. He had never told anyone about Amalia.

The big Pole's grin flashed white in the darkness. "You talk in your sleep, boy. But lie down. You aren't going nowhere."

Matt shook his head stubbornly. "Somethin's wrong. I can feel it inside. She needs me. I got to go."

"But hell, boy, you can't ride," Kovalenko swung his legs over onto the floor.

"Never mind that. Somehow I just got to go."

"Then let me go with you," Kovalenko said quickly. "We'll rent a horse and buggy. That way you can rest while I handle the horse. Aye?"

Matt clutched the corner of the wardrobe tighter "Aye," he said, fighting off the dizziness. "Yes, an' thank ye."

"Now, get yourself back to bed," said Kovalenko. "We'll leave first thing come morning!"

Edward Forny watched out of the corner of his eye as his grandson, Slade, drew a bead on a distant squirrel and squeezed the trigger of his new Kentucky rifle. The squirrel dropped silently and landed in the leaves at the foot of the tree. Slade jumped up with a whoop and ran to retrieve it. He had a swift, easy way of moving, Edward reflected, a grace that was almost Indian-like.

Slade came striding back to the log where Edward was waiting for him, swinging the squirrel by its tail. "I keep thinkin' of Matt," he said, as the two of them headed for the road. "I keep wonderin' what he be doin' right now, and wishin' I were a' doin' it with him."

"*Oui,*" Edward mused. "I wonder too." And I worry, he added silently to himself. He had gotten Abby settled with Marie's family in Louisville, and then he had set out for Nashville, some grim sense of urgency driving him all the way. "I keep hoping we'll get word from him," he said.

But Slade clearly had other things on his mind. "Natchez. . ." he murmured, a dreamy quality in his youthful voice. "And New Orleans. Lord, Matt's been all the way down the Mississippi by now, I reckon! What d'ye think he's seen by now?" Slade seized his grandfather's arm. "An' when'll it be my turn to go? Grandpa, I be so tired of Nashville! I keep wantin' to go off on my own—to anyplace I ain't seen yet, an' then farther and farther beyond. I look at the hills an' I figure there be mountains beyond them. Don't

226

reckon they ever stop, an' I don't reckon I'll be happy till I've seen the end of 'em." Slade turned and gave his grandfather a sudden, searching look. "Ye think I be daft, Grandpa? Wantin' things like that? Pa says I can stay in Nashville an' take over the business an' do right well. But I ain't got no stomach for it. There's somethin' out there, Grandpa, an' it just keeps callin' me. One o' these days, I reckon I'll be settin' out t' look for it."

Edward laid a hand on his grandson's lean, hard-muscled shoulders. *Oui*, he was all Forny, this one. "I understand," he said. "I had the same feelings in me as a young man. I have them still, from time to time."

They walked up the tree-shadowed path, and Edward suddenly remembered something else he'd intended to ask Slade.

"*Dites-moi*," he said. "Did Matt mention anything to you about being promised to a girl back in Louisville?"

"Matt?" Slade's blue eyes widened in amazement. "Matt, promised?" He shook his tawny-gold head and chuckled, half in bewilderment. "By damn, if Matt was, he sure didn't say nothin' about it to me! An' he sure didn't act like it, neither. Ye saw him at the party, sparkin' that Carrie— the one with the mole. Hell, if he was promised, he were pretty good at hidin' it!"

"*Oui* . . . I agree with you." Edward said thoughtfully. So much for Winifred back in Louisville. The girl was obviously out to trap Matt and was using every weapon she had. Poor Matt.

"Did ye hear?" Slade said, swinging the dead squirrel, "John Swaney came in off the Trace this mornin'. Says they found another dead body washed up on the bank o' the Tennessee. Lord, why'd anybody want t' do that?

Edward felt himself shudder. "Beasts," he said. "They're nothing but filthy, murdering animals." And the fear clutched at him again, that vague, gripping fear he'd been feeling for days. Matt could be returning, even now, over the Natchez Trace. All of Edward's instincts prickled with fear for him. He would go and talk with John Swaney, he resolved. It could be that the next time the intrepid mail carrier rode south, he would not be alone.

# XV

By the time the wagon neared Natchez, Matt was well enough to share the seat with Kovalenko, and even take his turn at the reins. The dizziness still came and went from time to time, passing over him like a sickening wave, but the few days of fresh air had helped. Now he ached with the anticipation of seeing Amalia again and holding her in his arms.

Over and over, his mind had rehearsed the speech he would make to *Don* Esteban Montoya. He would lay before him the history of the Forny family—their descent from French nobility on his grandfather's side, and from solid Yankee roots on his grandmother's. He would give a good account of the family trading business, especially of its promising future and his own place in it. As the eldest grandson, he would be head of Forny & Cooper one distant day. That should make him a suitable son-in-law for even a rich Spaniard.

True, Amalia had been promised to someone else. But she did not love Andres Santana, and Santana was no proper gentleman. If worse came to worse, Matt had resolved, he would tell *Don*

Esteban what Mathilde Rodare had said about Santana—that he was a frequent customer, and that her girls considered him a beast. The only trouble with that part of the plan was he still hadn't figured a way to explain how *he* had come to know Madame Rodare. *That* was going to be ticklish. Matt shivered as he remembered the wild night he'd spent with Yvonne. He had mixed feelings about that night now. He'd enjoyed. He had learned. He had emerged from it one step closer to manhood. But something, he realized, was gone. He would never have the freshness of that first time to share with Amalia, and for that he was sorry.

Slocum's wet nose nuzzling his hand brought Matt's thoughts back to the present. The big yellow dog lounged in the back of the wagon, on a bed of empty sacks. Beneath those sacks, in a special compartment concealed in the wagon's bottom, lay the money for the cargo and flatboat— gold coins, sewn and sealed into rawhide bags.

"There—" Kovalenko pointed ahead. "Natchez!" Matt peered through the summer haze. In the distance the green-topped bluff rose above the river. "Make you feel better, eh?" The big Pole grinned. "Me too. My wife, she should have made me a papa again by now. Might even be twins! An hour's time and I'll be finding out! And you— Soon you'll be with your little Spanish girl!"

"Aye," Matt muttered wistfully, wishing that his seeing Amalia were as simple as Kovalenko's

230

seeing his wife and family. He would be reporting to *Don* Esteban, of course, but getting past him to Amalia might prove to be a problem. Matt was not yet sure how he was going to accomplish it. He only knew that he would hold her in his arms again, or die in the attempt!

After he'd let Kovalenko off at the crossroads, Matt began to feel a little nervous about the money. He would avoid Natchez-under-the-Hill, he resolved as he turned the horse onto a road that would take him onto the bluff. There was a good-sized inn there, one that catered to wealthy merchants and would likely have an iron safe or a guarded room where he could leave it.

An hour later he had obtained a room, secured the money, bathed, changed his clothes, and left Slocum tied to the wagon in the stable with a hefty bone from the kitchen to gnaw on. He purchased a sturdy horse, with a saddle and bridle, and set out at once for the Montoya house.

It was a shame he'd had no chance to buy some expensive clothes in New Orleans, Matt reflected, glancing down at the familiar brown coat and breeches. He'd fully intended to, but his injury in the tavern fight had prevented that. And now, with Amalia so close, he could not bear to take the time for shopping and tailoring here in Natchez. *Don* Esteban would have to take him as he was.

As Matt rounded the drive that led up to the Montoya house, a wave of dizziness swept over him. He leaned forward, clutching at the saddle for balance, bracing his legs against the stirrup to keep from falling. For a long moment, the trees, the road, the house, and everything around him, spun in a maddening circle. Then little by little the spinning stopped. Matt blinked to clear his vision. He was all right again, he reassured himself, though his mouth was dry, and beads of sweat had formed on his face. He dried them with his handkerchief, then walked the horse up the drive. His heart was pounding. He wanted to give it time to slow down, to give his nerves a chance to stop jumping, but by the time he reached the house he was more agitated than ever. He saw no sign of Amalia, though his eyes had eagerly scanned the upstairs windows as he mounted the front porch. The shriveled little Spanish butler let him in and motioned for him to wait once more in the foyer. Then he disappeared.

With a nervous sigh Matt settled himself on one of the marble benches. His blood felt like cold jelly in his veins, and the nagging fear that had haunted him all the way from New Orleans—the fear that something was terribly wrong.

"I say, Mister Cooper, isn't it? What a pleasure to see you again."

Matt, who had been staring down at his own boots, jumped at the sound of the familiar, reedy voice. He had not realized he was not alone. Rushton, the quaintly ugly artist, sat across the room from him, his gray, powdered wig slightly askew on his bald head.

"Waiting to see *Don* Esteban, I see," Rushton returned Mat's awkwardly murmured greeting. "And how was your trip downriver? Did you find

New Orleans to your liking?"

"Very much, sir," Matt answered politely. "Just stopped by to pay my respects to Mister Montoya and to talk to him about the next shipment my grandpa and the others'll be gettin' ready to send downriver 'bout the time I get back."

"I see." Rushton rubbed his chin. There was a moment of uneasy silence, and Matt felt it might be his turn to say something. "And what be ye doin' here?" he asked, vaguely conscious of the difference between Rushton's educated speech and his own. Strange, he'd never really been aware of it before. Growing up on the frontier as he had, Matt had not met many well-learned folk. Even Andrew Jackson's speech still carried a bit of the backwoods flavor. Somehow the new awareness gave Matt the same sort of uneasy feeling that his out-of-style clothes did.

"Ah, then you haven't heard," said Rushton. "The house is in an uproar. The wedding of young Amalia and Don Andres has suddenly been moved closer. It's to take place in just ten days, and Don Andres wants a portrait of his bride in her wedding gown." He spread his hands and rolled his eyes toward the ceiling. "Try painting a gown that's not even finished! I'll be painting her as she walks down the aisle of the cathedral, I fear!"

Matt felt the blood drain from his face. He fought off the dizziness that had begun to creep up on him again in small, icy waves. "But . . . but—" he stammered helplessly.

233

"I know," Rushton said gently. "It wasn't to be for months. It was Don Andres who kept pressing to have the wedding sooner. A shame. She's so young. I'd have thought she'd needed a little time to get used to the idea—"

"How is she? You been painting her—"

"Very pale. Very quiet. I suspect the poor child isn't happy with the match, but realizes she has no choice." Rushton studied Matt, his head cocked sharply to one side. He had protruding brown eyes, oddly piercing. "You, my young friend—Ah, I might have guessed. You look rather pale yourself. Aye, but that doesn't surprise me. She's a lovely girl, and spirited. If I were your age, I'm not so sure I wouldn't be in love with her myself."

"Tell her—" Matt blurted. "Tell her I'm here. Tell her I'll do everything I can t' save her from it—"

Rushton frowned. "My dear young man, are you asking me to be your go-between? It's quite impossible, you know. If I were caught, the scandal would ruin me. I wouldn't be welcomed by one decent family, and for a man of my profession, that would mean starvation!"

"Aye . . ." Matt admitted. "That it might, sir. But ye be my only hope." He struggled with more words, then slammed his fist on his knee in frustration. It hurt. "No, ye be right, sir. I can't ask ye. But I got t' find a way—"

Matt was interrupted by the butler, who had materialized in the doorway and announced himself with an arrogant little cough. "*Senor*

Rushton, she is ready, *Dona* Amalia. You will come with me, *por favor.*"

Rushton arose without another word and followed the little Spaniard out of the foyer, but he paused in the doorway, and his sharp, almost vulture-like eyes met Matt's for an instant before he looked away.

That look pierced Matt to the quick, but what did it mean? Was it a warning? A sign of disapproval, or of understanding? Would Rushton help him? That look told him everything—and nothing.

Matt was still twisting his hands in a torment of anxiety when *Don* Esteban himself entered. He smiled. "*Senor* Cooper. It went well?"

"The boat and the cargo?" Matt had almost forgotten for the moment why he was supposed to be here. "Aye, it went just the way ye planned it for me," Matt said. "Sold the cargo. Got the money. It's in a strongbox at the inn. All of it."

"*Bueno.*" *Don* Esteban nodded his approval. "That's a safe place for it. But you must be most careful of all riding up the Trace to Nashville. Be very selective of the company you chose." He motioned for Matt to follow him upstairs to his study. "There's a dependable group going up the Trace in a week's time. Eleven men, good shots and excellent reputations, all of them. If you like I could speak to the leader. *Seguramente*, you'd be welcome."

"Thank ye." Matt followed him into the study and took a seat opposite the cultured Spaniard. The desk that separated them seemed as wide as the Mississippi itself.

"I've heard from your grandfather," *Don* Esteban continued, pressing the tips of his outspread fingers together. "He is already arranging for the shipment of another boatload of cargo downriver from Nashville. Will you be taking it, *Senor* Cooper?"

"Don't rightly know," Matt said, shifting in his chair uneasily and wondering how he was going to bring up the subject of Amalia. Lord, if she was planning to be married next week, his proposal had all the chance of a snowball in hell—but he had to try. He had to begin, at least, with the honorable thing. If that didn't work—

"Rushton tells me Amalia's gettin' married in ten days." He blurted out the words.

"*Si.* That is correct, my young friend." *Don* Esteban raised one cautious eyebrow, already sensing trouble. "*Don* Andres Santana has persuaded me that there is no reason to delay the wedding, and Amalia has not argued against it—"

"But—she don't love him!" Matt leaned across the desk. "I know! She told me!"

"She *told* you?" *Don* Esteban's dark eyes narrowed. "Listen, and listen well, my young friend. In the first place, love had nothing to do with the fact of the marriage. I have made an advantageous match for my daughter. She will be taken care of and respected as a fine lady to the end of her days." He scowled, and Matt felt a shiver of dread pass through his body. "In the second place, if you were in a position to have her tell you

236

that, then you have behaved improperly. You have violated my hospitality by making advances to my daughter. And for that I must ask you to leave. As far as I'm concerned, any future business of mine with Forny & Cooper will be done with your grandfather, or not at all. And now, if you'll be so kind, *Senor* Matthew Cooper, I will ring for Juan to show you out." His voice was granite in winter. His eyes glittered as he rose to his feet. Matt met his gaze, but he could not read what was in those eyes. There was anger and pride—and was there pain as well? "You are dismissed, *Senor* Cooper!"

"Beggin' your pardon, sir, but I ain't going." Matt braced his legs for balance as he felt a shudder of the dizziness pass over him. "I ain't going' till I've spoke my piece an' ye've heard me out!"

*Don* Esteban's eyes widened in surprise. "*Muy bien, Senor* Matthew Cooper," he said in a low, tight voice. "But I must ask you to be brief."

Matt felt himself trembling. He had never thought he could stand up to a man like *Don* Esteban Montoya, but he could not just walk out and desert Amalia. "It be me your daughter loves," he said firmly. "An' I love her as well. Where I come from, that's reason enough for a boy and girl to get married. The Fornys be a good family, with prospects, an' we'd be proud to claim a girl like Amalia. I'd take good care of her, sir. She'd never want for nothin'."

*Don* Esteban was not a tall man, but as Matt watched him he seemed to swell, to grow taller by the breadth of a hand. His face was pale with indignation.

"*Senor* Cooper," he said in a tightly controlled voice, "do you have any idea of the ridiculousness of what you're suggesting? Amalia is a *Montoya*, the daughter of one of Natchez's first families. She's had the best of everything—the best home, the best clothing, the best education a young lady could ever expect. And we Montoyas marry our own kind, if we know what's good for us. For *you*, an unschooled backwoodsman, to ask for her hand—*Senor* Cooper, that is a *joke!* I would laugh, but I confess I do not find it funny. And now, if you'll be so kind as to leave, I will bid you *adios.*"

Matt stood his ground. "I was hopin' I wouldn't have t' tell ye this, sir, but I reckon I got to." he shifted his feet and cleared his throat. "Your daughter's intended, sir, he ain't no gentleman. Far from it. If I had a daughter, I wouldn't be for lettin' her marry a man like that."

"That's a serious insinuation, *Senor* Cooper, and I must warn you that *Don* Andres is a man of honor. Be prepared to defend what you say."

There was an ominous note in *Don* Esteban's voice that Matt did not quite understand, but he took another deep breath and stumbled on. "I heard that down under the hill he goes to a—house. An' they say the girls there don't like 'im cause he's—"

"One moment, young man." *Don* Esteban's eyes narrowed sharply. "How is it *you* know what the girls would think, unless—"

"That don't matter," Matt said, feeling the

color creep up into his face in spite of his efforts to control it.

"Never mind," *Don* Esteban snapped impatiently. "In our culture, a man is entitled to his . . . pleasures, and it's no one's business but his own as long as it does not take away from his family responsibilities. But where did you hear this— this rumor, *muchacho?* That much I would like to know."

"I . . . I reckon maybe you can guess that," Matt said quietly, though his heart was drumming.

"*Si* . . . " the Spaniard lowered his eyes. "I can guess. It would be *La Rodare* who told you, the vile creature!"

"And Amalia's mother, sir." Matt felt his heart all but stop. He felt strangely calm all of a sudden, his blood like ice as he waited for *Don* Esteban's reaction.

Amalia's father raised his eyes again. He looked older somehow, and suddenly very tired. "So you know that, too," he said in a hushed, bitter voice. "Well, if you know that, perhaps you can understand how urgent it is that I make a good marriage for Amalia as soon as possible. The girl is headstrong. Already she shows signs of being as stubborn and as rebellious as her mother, and I live in constant fear that the girl may have inherited . . . other traits as well. She needs a strong hand."

"It's love she be needin's, sir," Matt said softly, his fear strangely gone. "An' I got all o' that she'll ever want."

*Don* Esteban went on as if he had not heard him. He seemed to be talking more to himself than to Matt. "You can't know what that *bruja*— that witch put me through. *Dios mio*, I loved her! But she grew bored with me! She began to ridicule me. And the men—the men began to come! Right in my own house! After a while she didn't even try to hide them. I would find their pipe ashes, the tracks of their muddy boots— And she would only laugh at me. I tell, I *had* to throw her out! It was that, or lose my mind! And to have such a creature raising my daughter—" *Don* Esteban's voice shook.

"She be sick, sir," Matt spoke gently. "I think she be . . . dyin'. Aye, she looks it."

*Don* Esteban did not answer for a long time. He only nodded his head slowly. His face looked gray, in the light that slanted through the window of the study. "First Mathilde . . ." he said brokenly. "Now Amalia. The fact that you would have the courage to ask for her hand is reason enough to believe that she encouraged you. *Si*, she is her mother's child, and the sooner she marries Andres Santana the better. You have brought me no surprises, *Senor* Cooper. *Don* Andres is known to be a lusty man, which is precisely why I chose him among Amalia's suitors. Perhaps that very lustfulness will be enough to satisfy her—as I could never satisfy her mother." He drew in his breath and let it out slowly, painfully. "But I have told you too much, quite forgetting that you have violated my trust and the hospitality of my house. Now I ask you to go. Rest assured, if you make any effort to talk with my daughter, I will see to it that Forny & Cooper does no more business on the Mississippi—and that is well within my power. Juan will show you out, *Senor* Cooper." He turned his back on Matt and would not look at him again.

Matt got to his feet slowly. His whole body and spirit cried out for Amalia. Discouragement was a weight that hung like an anvil around his neck. *Don* Esteban had not even considered his honorable request for Amalia's hand. Worse, he had dashed all hope of his even seeing Amalia again. If he so much as tried, *Don* Esteban would see that Forny & Cooper never traded on the Mississippi again. Matt would fail his grandfather, his father, his uncle Henry, and—who could say?—generations of Fornys and Coopers yet to come. But how could he just walk away? How could he leave Amalia to marry a man she claimed to hate?

The little butler had materialized in the doorway of the study and was waiting to usher Matt outside. But as they crossed the foyer, Rushton, the artist, came walking in from the garden. "Women," he was muttering. "Never ready when they say they'll be. I thought Juan told me she was ready to pose. Then she informs me the seamstress is here for another fitting on her gown, and I have to wait. Rubbish! My painting will exist when the gown is dust—ah! Mister Cooper! You're leaving so soon, my young friend?

Matt nodded and forced a twisted smile. He was still in too much of a turmoil to trust his tongue.

"Don't be in such a hurry," Rushton insisted. "You haven't even seen my portrait of the bride. It's drying in the garden. Come on out. I'll show it to you." He turned to the butler and said something in Spanish that seemed to indicate he would show Matt out himself. The little man nodded and scuttled off to his other duties.

Matt found his voice. "Mister Rushton, I don't think I really want t' see—"

"Oh, come, now. It won't take a minute." The artist tugged at Matt's arm. "I'm really quite proud of it. You can't be in that much of a hurry!" He glanced up at Matt, something flashing once more in his prominent eyes. Matt stopped arguing.

The painting sat on an easel beside the fountain. Rushton turned it around so that Matt could see it in a better light. "As you see, it's almost finished except for the gown itself," Rushton said.

Matt stared at the portrait, comparing it with the one Rushton had painted of Amalia just a few weeks earlier, for her sixteenth birthday. The change in her was almost frightening. The Amalia of the wedding portrait was pale and thin, almost a ghost of what she had once been. Her eyes were huge in her small, pinched face. There was a tenseness about her mouth and in the posture of her hands. She had the look of a frightened animal, cornered, ready to bolt.

Matt turned to Rushton. "She . . . she don't look—" Words failed him. He turned back to the portrait and gazed at it once more, something

242

tearing at his heart. Rushton had captured all the tragedy in Amalia's great, dark eyes, all the softness of her childlike mouth. Matt fought back a sudden, wild urge to kiss the painting.

The details of Amalia's wedding gown were not yet painted in. They were only suggested by light and shadow at this point, but the hands, lying crossed in her lap, were completely finished, exquisitely done—

Matt caught his breath. Amalia's hand. Her right hand. He had not noticed it before. She was wearing the ruby ring that her mother had given him for her.

Rushton leaned close to his ear. "May heaven forgive me for this," he whispered, "but she has said that she will see you. Come to the gate in the garden at midnight. She will be there, she says, even if the devil himself tries to stop her."

# XVI

Matt waited outside the iron gate at the rear of Montoya garden. The darkness that cloaked him was silent except for the chirping of crickets in the grass, and the hammering of his own pulse.

Amalia had said she would come. She had said that the devil himself wouldn't stop her. But where was she? Maybe he was early. He gazed up at the waning moon. His horse, tethered a hundred paces off in the trees, nickered softly, the sound carrying in the night. Matt cursed under his breath and prayed that no one would hear. He wondered if the "devil" she'd spoken of could be *Don* Andres Santana.

The house was dark, except for the faint glow of a lantern moving back and forth along the balcony. Matt stepped back into the shadows as the light passed, holding his breath. But the light moved evenly, without a pause. A guard of some kind, perhaps. Or the devil.

"Matt—" The delicate whisper came from just behind him, making him jump. "Matt— *amor mio*—"

"Amalia!" He spun around. She was standing

just on the other side of the wrought iron gate, her hands thrusting between the bars. Matt grasped at the gate, pushing and tugging. It was firmly locked. He reached between the bars and drew her close, the cold shafts of iron hard between them. "Amalia. . ." he whispered the name over and over against her mouth.

"Matt—" Her face was wet and salty with tears. "Matt, *querido*, forgive me. I had to see you just once before—"

"Before what? Lord you can't mean you're really going to marry him—"

"Matt, listen to me. I have no choice. I can't fight them any more. My father . . . Andres . . . I" Her voice broke. She began to sob.

Matt studied her through the bars, the moonlight defining the planes of her tear-stained face. Aye, she had suffered much, his Amalia. What had they done to her? "Never mind," he whispered. "It's all over. I'm here. I'm here, and you be comin' away with me." No, he had not thought it out, but once he had said them, the words sounded right. He knew that the only solution was to take her away from this place where she was so unhappy. "Come with me, Amalia." He said it again, to make the thought more real to him. "Now. Tonight. Come and be my wife. My family— why they'll treat ye just like a queen, I promise!"

"Matt—"

"Ye won't need no more'n the clothes on your back! We'll buy ye a whole passel of new dresses. Just come. I'll get ye over that gate somehow—"

"Matt—" There was agony in her whisper. "Matt, I *can't!* I can't marry you!"

"What? Don't ye love me, Amalia?" He reached between the bars and lifted her chin. Her eyes were black pools of tears.

"No . . . that isn't the reason. But I can't marry you, Matt. I just *can't*, that's all." Her voice had started to quiver again.

"An' why not, if we love each other, you an' me?"

She drew a painful breath, and Matt could feel the hurt in it. "Matt, it— it's too *late!* I can't be a fit wife to you any more. It's too late." She began to sob again.

"What d'ye mean it be too late. Ye mean that son of a—"

"I've been spoiled, Matt. I'm ruined," she said brokenly. "Now I'll never be a proper wife for anybody but—"

"No!" Matt exploded. "Lord no! I'll kill 'im!" He felt the rage boil up inside of him. His hands tightened on the iron bars until he felt as if he could have wrenched the gate out of the wall.

Amalia shook her head. "No . . . no, *amor mio.* You will not. He has killed five men, in duels. With a sword, or with a pistol, he has never been beaten. He would take your life, and then I would truly die."

Matt was still quivering with rage. "An' how many times did he—"

"Only once. He . . . forced me. But it is done. My duenna learned of it— she saw the blood. And she says that I am no longer pure. No man

247

would want me now. Except—" she began to sob again.

"Amalia!" Matt kissed her white hands where they clung to the bars. "No, Amalia . . . that ain't so. I could love ye no matter what he done to ye. An' I do. Come with me now!"

"I can't . . ." she whispered. "I— I want to, Matt. I want to come with you— but my father, and Andres, especially Andres— they'd come after us. They'd never let us go. And they'd kill you." Her hands gripped Matt's. Matt could feel the little ruby ring, biting into his fingers.

"If I could find a way, would ye come?" Matt asked, his mind groping for ideas.

"There's no way," she whispered. "Andres has spies and henchmen everywhere."

"There's got t' be a way—" Matt felt the bite of the stone in the little ruby ring once more. "Your ma— she'd help us, I know. And you're wearin' her ring—"

"*Si*," Amalia whispered. "I put it on after Andres— Somehow it made me feel like there was someone who cared about me." She drew in her breath with a little sob. "I—I'd like to see her, Matt. But my father won't let me out of the house. He keeps me locked up like a prisoner—"

"Does your father know what that bast—what *Don* Andres did to you?" Matt felt his bile rise again at the mention of the detested name.

"No . . . Oh, how could I tell him, Matt? He'd only claim it was my fault. I've never understood it! All my life he's acted as if he expected me to do something bad. And he'd only say that he was right—Oh, Matt, and now I have—"

"Amalia! You ain't done nothin' bad! It were done *to* ye, don't you see? An' you ain't ruined ! Not for me!"

"Matt, I want to see my mother," she said softly.

"Aye," he said. "I'll see what I can do." He wondered what she'd say if she knew how her mother lived.

"*Senor* Rushton can get word to me. He is a kind man. He will help."

Matt reached through the bars of the gate and pulled her close to him again. "I'll find a way," he murmured, his lips close to hers. "I'll find a way to get ye out of here—and ye'll come. Tell me ye'll come!"

She kissed him, her mouth small, soft and wonderfully clinging. "*Si* . . . I will come with you, Matt," she whispered through her tears. "Find a way . . . find a way and I will come."

The lantern was moving again, across the balcony of the house, coming closer. "The watchman," Amalia whispered. "He is an evil man who would make trouble and he has a dog. Go quickly, *querido*, before he sees us." With one last kiss, she was gone. Matt shrank back into the shadows as the watchman passed above him. The man raised the lantern high, casting the light on his own face for the space of a breath. He was a squat fellow, with piggish eyes and a greasy moustache. One powerful fist grasped a heavy chain; at the other end of the chain a huge mastiff strained and growled at the night air.

Had the dog scented him? Matt froze, his heart pounding as the ugly animal swung its big head around, a snarl rumbling low in its throat. It pulled at the chain and growled again, louder this time. Matt clung to the wall outside the gate, not daring to move while the huge, brindled creature snuffed at the air. At last the watchman seemed to grow impatient. He jerked at the chain, muttering something in Spanish, and the dog followed him, back down along the balcony.

Somewhere beyond them, a door closed, and Matt calculated that Amalia had reached her room safely. Only then did he dare let his breath out.

The watchman, with his lantern, was gone now. Matt took to his heels. The horse was waiting in the trees. Matt swung into the saddle and rode slowly back to the inn, lost in thought.


Mathilde Rodare downed a glass of bourbon and poured herself another. It was one of her bad days. The pain was eating at her insides, and she drank to kill it. Still, Matt noticed, her eyes widened with sudden pleasure when he told her that Amalia was wearing the ruby ring.

"Ah!" She put the glass down on the bar. "Tell me, Matt, *Vraiment?* She said she wanted to see me? Could it be so?"

"Aye. She said it." Matt studied the woman, her skin showing ashen beneath the layers of rouge, her blue eyes laced with fine, red veins. How would poor Amalia take to having this kind

250

of mother? "But we got to find a way," he said. "We got to get her out of that house and back to Nashville, so's we can get married."

Madame Rodare looked Matt up and down, squinting a bit in the morning light. "*Oui . . .*" she breathed. "You would make a fine husband for her. My daughter . . . and the grandson of my dear Edouard." Her laugh was not a gentle one. It made Matt nervous. "Don't worry, *mon cher* Matt," she said, showing her teeth. "There are ways! We will find them. Leave it to Mathilde, eh?" She took another sip of the bourbon and made a bitter face as she swallowed it. "I did not leave that house empty handed," she said. "When Esteban banished me, I managed to take a few of the keys. I thought someday they might serve me well. Among them, *mon cher*, is the key to the garden gate."

"Have ye got any friends still workin' in the house?" Matt asked cautiously. "Any of the servants that might help us?"

She shook her head. "Esteban dismissed those who were my friends. Some of them followed me here—ah, but that is another story. None of the swine who work for him now will help us. Juanita, my daughter's duenna—she hates me. She always has. The others are no better. But John Rushton, the painter—you say he is a friend?"

"He'll get a message to her. I think he'd be scared to do more."

"That's enough." Mathilde nodded. "That will help. And we will need a way to get the two of

251

you out of Natchez." She thought for a moment, a shadow of pain crossing her face, then vanishing. "Ah! *Magnifique!* Mike Fink! He is here, with a keelboat crew and they are leaving day after tomorrow! He would take you, *non?*"

"Maybe." Matt tugged at his own ear, a smile dawning on his face. "He be here, ye say. In Natchez? This morning?"

"*Oui.*" Madame's blue eyes rolled toward the ceiling with a glint of mischief. "Upstairs. I would not suggest you disturb him, *cheri.* He has had a long night, your friend Monsieur Fink. He might not be so pleased, *eh bien?*"

"I take it he ain't alone." Matt glanced up at the ceiling himself.

"*Non.* Yvonne this time." Madame shrugged. "She was free. It is her job, *compris?* And you, surely, now that you have found the love of my daughter—" She stopped speaking, her face distorted with a sudden wave of pain. "You will do right by her, eh? You will treat her with honor?"

"Aye," Matt said softly, wondering how Amalia's delicate sensibilities would fare on a keelboat with the likes of Mike Fink. "Could ye do something for me?" he asked. "Would ye have us a parson waitin' somewhere? I don't want to take Amalia on that keelboat less'n she be my wife."

"*Oui.* But of course." Mathilde agreed readily. "But, *mon fils,* be gentle with her, I beg you. Amalia is not like the girls in my house. She is a young lady. For her I am sure it will be the first time. Take what you learned from Yvonne, *cheri,* and use it with *kindness.*"

"Aye, that I will," Matt whispered, tingling at the thought of it. "But it won't be the first time. *Don* Andres Santana seen to that." As soon as he'd said it he wondered why he had. Then, when he saw Mathilde Rodare's face, he began to wish he hadn't said it at all.

Madame's features were twisted with hatred. "That swine!" she whispered in a voice Matt had never heard her use before. "That beast! That rutting pig who comes in here night after night and uses my girls—! That swine forcing himself on a young lady. On my own *daughter!* Just leave Andres Santana to me, *cheri.* Leave him to me!" Mathilde Rodare smiled, a ghastly, death's-head smile that almost made Matt shiver. "Tomorrow night, then you will free my daughter," she said. "Come to me. I will have a priest waiting to say the words over the two of you. And at dawn you will leave on the keelboat. I will speak with Mike Fink myself. Don't worry. He will agree to it." She drained the glass of bourbon, closing her eyes a moment as it burned its way down her throat.

Edward had found John Swaney in the tavern at the inn. The tough little mail carrier listened to his problem, and looked him up and down critically, squinting with his narrow gray eyes.

"Aye," he said at last, "I remember the boy. The one with the big yaller dog. Yer grandson, is he?"

"*Oui.*" Edward took the chair opposite Swaney. "Can I buy you a whiskey?"

"Drank my fill already, thank-ee." Swaney took a wad of Indian tobacco from a pouch around his neck and flipped it expertly into his mouth.

Edward cleared his throat. Swaney was not an easy man to approach. "I'm worried about the boy," he said. "It's not easy to explain, Mr. Swaney, but I have the feeling he's in danger. I'd like to ride with you when you go down the Trace."

"I ride the Trace alone." Swaney worked the tobacco into his cheek. "Allers been that way. Ain't nobody else what can keep the pace an' not slow me down."

"I could," Edward said. "My grandson has a roan filly that runs like a deer. He's already offered to lend her to me."

Swaney chewed his tobacco thoughtfully while his narrow eyes took in Edward's spare, sinewy frame. "Ye ain't a heavy man. An' ye look like ye know how t' take keer o' yerself," he said. "I'll think on it."

Edward felt a bit of the tension go out of him. "How soon do you leave, Mr. Swaney? I could be ready anytime if you're willing to take me along."

"Leavin' in four days. Said I'd think on it." Swaney aimed a thin stream of tobacco out the open doorway. It puddled in the brown dust. He leaned back in his chair and closed his eyes, an evident signal that he had spoken his piece and had no further wish to be disturbed.

"Then *merci*, Mr. Swaney." Edward turned on his chair and stood up. "I will see you in a day or two, *eh bien*? And in the meantime you think on it. That's fair enough." He extended his hand, but Swaney had his eyes closed and did not see it.

Fighting back his impatience, Edward left the inn. He knew Swaney's type, he reassured his own anxious mine. He'd met them before on the frontier—men who belonged to no one but themselves, tough men, stubborn and unyielding. They were hard nuts to crack, but if you could win their respect they could be staunch friends and formidable allies. There was nothing to do but let John Swaney make up his own mind, Edward decided. With Swaney he would have the best possible chance of finding Matt. Without Swaney—a frown passed over Edward's face as he considered the alternatives. He had never been down the Trace. He did not know the trail or the people who lived and traveled along it. The way was full of unexpected dangers and delays. Without Swaney to guide him, Edward concluded, he would not have a good chance of being there when Matt needed him.

And Matt *did* need him. He felt it in his bones, like a midwinter chill, like the fear-instinct of some wild animal that *knows*, even without the sight, scent, or sound of danger, that the danger is there.

# XVII

John Rushton had carried word to Amalia that Matt would be coming for her that night. Now, her small valise packed with necessities, she surveyed her bedroom for the last time. She had grown up here, and every inch of floor, wall and ceiling was as familiar as the palm of her own hand. The whitewashed walls, the dark wooden chest that held her linens, the ornately carved dresser with its mirror and its assortment of pins and brushes, the imposing wardrobe, with most of her beautiful dresses still shut inside. She knew she would have to travel light and fast.

Her canopied bed stood against one wall, the ebony crucifix, made in Spain two centuries earlier, hanging above it. The figure of Christ was carved in ivory, cracked and yellowed with age. The revered figure had looked down upon them the night Andres Santana had violated her body. Even now, Amalia felt her face flush with hot shame at the memory of it. He had been brutal. He had hurt her, humiliated her, and she despised him for it. Yet—the flush deepened in her cheeks—something in her had flickered into life that night. Something had awakened, to surge through her body like a forest fire—and all the while she was hating Santana, she was caught up in the feel of it.

She thought of matt, and the sense of his love crept around her like a protecting cloak. For a moment it blotted out the shame of what Andres Santana had done to her. Matt loved her. Even in her shame he loved her, and he wanted her for his wife. And she knew now—she knew what being Matt's wife would mean, and she shivered with the anticipation of it. Matt, lying beside her, his body young, clean and strong, his lovemaking blotting out the memory of all that had gone before. She wanted him. The intensity of that wanting was almost shameful.

The sound of an owl hooting outside her window brought her quickly back to the urgency of the present. Was it the signal that Matt was outside? Or was it merely an owl—a real owl? Holding her breath, Amalia listened again. Yes, there it was. Three hoots in quick succession. Her heart picked up speed. Yes, he was here, just outside the gate. She snatched up her valise and flitted to the curtained glass doors that opened onto the balcony. A stairway on the outside led from the second floor down to the garden. From there it would be no more than a short sprint to the gate, where Matt would be waiting with the key to her freedom. Amalia hesitated, glanced about the familiar room one last time, then blew out the lamp.

Now she could see through the lace curtain to

the outside. The moon was full—not a good omen for a night when stealth was so important. The moonlight would make it harder for her to steal out of the house—and easier to be caught if she and Matt were discovered and pursued.

The guard—she saw the yellow circle of his lantern, growing larger as he came close. He would cross the balcony, then go down the stairs to circle the garden and the house. Amalia shrank back against the wall as he passed her glass doorway. The light paused. He pressed his face to the glass, as she knew he often did, trying to catch a glimpse of her as she slept. She hated him. He was a vile, greasy fellow with the manners of a pig. Whenever she passed him in the house or on the grounds, his sharp eyes would follow her so closely that they were like fingers, probing the intimate parts of her body.

She could almost hear him breathing through the glass, hear the growl and snuffle of the big mastiff. She held her breath as she waited for him to leave, hoping he would be fooled by the way she had arranged the pillows in her bed. Piggish he might be, but he was not stupid.

The dog growled and sniffed at the door. Grumpily the man tugged on its chain, cursing in Spanish. Then, at long last, he moved past the glass, jerking the animal behind him. Amalia waited until the light was gone. Then, cautiously, she opened the door and slipped through.

The balcony was open, flooded by the dangerous moonlight. She ran the length of it, to the shadow of the stairs, and descended swiftly into the garden below. There, beneath the black shadow of a vine, she stopped to catch her breath. She could hear the sound of crickets and the retreating footsteps of the guard, their dull shuffle growing softer—no, were they growing *louder?* Was he coming back? The frightened drumming of her heart all but drowned out the other sounds. She heard the panting of the mastiff, growing stronger. Yes, he had heard something. He was coming back, coming closer. The tentative hoot of an owl sounded again from outside the gate. Amalia did not dare answer. She pressed herself into the shadows, frozen with terror, as the guard and the dog came closer.

Matt pressed against the gate, the key trembling in his hand. He had glimpsed the dark form of Amalia hurrying along the balcony, but where was she now? She had disappeared in the shadows of the garden. Was she having sudden regrets? Had she changed her mind? He felt a trickle of cold sweat run down his cheek.

The guard had passed with the big mastiff only a moment before. It made sense that Amalia would time her dash for freedom with his going. But she'd had plenty of time to reach the gate. What had gone wrong?

The horse nickered in the shadows, and Matt wished he'd dare tie the beast farther away from the gate. But he knew that once Amalia was with him he would have to get away swiftly. Matt thanked common sense that at least he didn't have Slocum with him. He had left the big yellow dog securely tied in the yard at Madame Rodare's. The gold from the trading venture was there as well. The plan was to take Amalia to her mother's, where they would be well-hidden for the night, then to smuggle her and the gold aboard the keelboat before dawn. Madame had promised to have a priest waiting to perform the marriage. Matt's mouth twisted in an ironic little smile at the thought of it. A wedding in a whorehouse. A wedding night spent in a bed that had been used for other purposes. Aye, he reflected, he wished he could have done better for a girl like Amalia. But things would be all right once he got her safely back to Nashville.

He caught his breath as the circle of lantern light appeared on the balcony once more. The guard had come back, and Amalia was trapped in the garden between the gate and the house.

Matt held his breath as the stout fellow came down the stairs. The mastiff was growling low in its throat, the hairs on the back of its neck bristling in the moonlight. Where was Amalia? Had she vanished? Matt wondered. Then he heard her little yelp of fear as the guard jerked her out from under the gnarled vines.

At first he did not appear to recognize her. Amalia fought like a little wildcat, scratching, struggling, her protests muffled by her own desire not to rouse the house. The mastiff drew back, snarling. Matt fumbled with the key in the iron lock. It fit, but it would not turn. That gate had evidently not been opened for years, the workings

of the lock were rusted shut. He shook and
twisted it frantically, rattling the gate and attract-
ing the mastiff, who began to snarl and lunge at
him through the bars. The guard, too busy with
Amalia to notice Matt, had recognized her by
now, but was showing none of the respect that a
servant should show toward his master's daughter. They were speaking in Spanish, whispering
loudly, both of them. Amalia seemed to be pleading with the lout, offering him money, anything,
if he would only let her go. The guard, on the
other hand, seemed to realize that he had caught
her in a compromising position. He wanted only
one thing from her, his manner clearly said, and
that one thing was not money. He swung Amalia
around against him and buried his thick lips
against the white curve of her neck. She gasped
and struggled, but he was strong. One hand
clasped her waist while the other pulled at the
bodice of her gown, ripping the fragile batiste and
clutching at her half-bare breasts. She gasped
loudly, but did not scream.

Matt was lunging against the gate with all his
might now, but it would not give. The mastiff was
snarling hoarsely. Either it had been trained not
to bark, or perhaps some operation had been performed on its throat to ensure that its masters
would sleep in peace. Its fangs, long, yellowish
daggers, flashed wetly in the moonlight.

It passed through Matt's mind that he could
climb over the gate and get to Amalia. But the
gate was high, and crowned by sharp iron spikes.
The wall itself was even higher, and it was

smooth, clear of any trees or vines where an intruder might gain a foothold. Even if he could get into the garden by climbing, he would never get Amalia out that way. They would both be trapped, inside the yard, at the mercy of the guard and the mastiff.

The horse, sensing the dog's fury, snorted and stamped in the shadow of the trees. It wasn't until then that Matt remembered the rope that was tied to the saddle. It was Madame Rodare who'd given it to him. "You never know, *mon fils*, when you will need a good rope. For scaling a wall, for tying up one who would otherwise chase you. Take it! Good luck!"

He was glad now that he had listened to her advice. Scrambling, he tied one end of the rope to the gate, the other to the horse's saddle. The mortar that held the gate in place was old, Matt could only pray that it would be weak enough to give. If he succeeded in pulling the gate loose, he'd make enough noise to raise the dead, he knew. But there was still a chance he and Amalia could get away in the confusion. Matt gave a final tug on the rope to make sure the knots were secure. Then he mounted the horse and slapped his hand down hard on the animal's rump.

The horse leaped forward. The gate creaked and groaned. There was a rewarding crunch of old mortar giving way. Amalia was still struggling with the guard as Matt backed the horse once more and plunged it forward again.

This time the gate came free. With a screeching crash and a cloud of dust it flew from its anchorings in the wall and clattered noisily to the ground. Matt was off the horse in an instant, running into the shattered hole where the gate had been. The guard stood between Matt and Amalia, his huge, thick-bladed knife drawn and waiting. In the house, lamps had begun to flare at the windows.

"Run, Amalia! Get to the horse!" Matt shouted as he and the burly guard stalked one another across the garden. He caught a glimpse of her out of the corner of his eye, flying toward the opening in the wall. Then he heard the snarl of the mastiff and Amalia's scream as the beast lunged and caught her skirt.

The guard with the knife picked that instant to charge. His momentum struck Matt and knocked him off balance. Matt was unarmed but his quickness saved his life. He rolled to one side.

The flat of the knife glanced off his shoulder, its point jabbing deeply into the earth. But the guard's weight was on him by then, and the man was as strong as a buffalo bull. Matt fought to reach Amalia where she stood with her back against the wall, the huge dog lunging at her again and again. Its fangs had torn her skirt. She had saved her arms and face only by protecting them with her pathetic little valise.

"Run, Amalia!" He gasped again as he wrestled the guard for the knife. His eyes caught only flashing glimpses of her, but he could tell she was frozen with terror. She could not get past the snapping, snarling fury of the mastiff, and the dog was becoming more and more ferocious. One vicious lunge caught Amalia's sleeve and raked her arm. Another ripped a wide gap in her skirt. She was sobbing now, her fear driving the huge beast to near madness. It crouched low, growling. Then it tensed and sprang high for her throat.

Matt heard Amalia's scream at the same instant he heard something else—a snarled challenge as a yellow streak charged through the gate. Slocum flung himself headlong against the mastiff, striking the huge, brindled dog in the side and deflecting the attack on Amalia. The two animals fell to earth at once, slashing, snapping, wrestling and biting.

"Run, Amalia!" Matt sank his doubled-up fist into the guard's belly. "Run!"

This time Amalia did run, away from the battling dogs and the struggling men, away from the house, which was rapidly coming to life. She ran out through the gate opening, to the horse where she stood, hesitant, holding the bridle.

"Get going!" Matt yelled, taking a swinging hammer-blow in the side of the head. "Get on the horse and *git!*"

But Amalia stayed, curse her, there beside the horse. She would not go without Matt, her actions clearly stated. Matt's head rang like the inside of a brass bell. He fought waves of the dizziness that had dogged him since the fight in New Orleans, and he knew that he would never beat this brute. His only hope of saving Amalia and himself lay in making his escape while he still had the strength.

Slocum was not faring well either. The mastiff was a bigger dog, and a trained fighter. Slocum's flanks were streaked with blood where the beast had sunk its fangs, but he fought on, dodging in, darting out, dodging the vicious, steel-trap jaws. He had landed some good bites himself, but the sheer power and endurance of the huge mastiff were winning out. Slocum, too, was weakening. The mastiff would kill him if the fight did not end soon.

The guard had clasped Matt's body, wrestled him to the ground, and was kneeing him in the groin. Matt twisted furiously to one side. With what felt like the last reserves of his strength, he raised his one free arm and brought it hard across the man's nose. He felt the crunching bone and cartilage as he hit home. Blood spurted from the guard's nose, torrents of it. The small pig eyes widened in pain and surprise.

Matt took quick advantage of that surprise. While the man was still stunned, he rolled free and scrambled to his feet. He was dimly aware of a commotion on the balcony above, but he did not even stop to see what it was. He sprinted for the gate pausing only to land a sharp, solid kick against the mastiff's ribs. "C'mon, Slocum!" he gasped.

Slocum was bleeding badly from one ear and he had a long slash on his hind quarter, but this time he had a good grip on the mastiff's foreleg and was crunching bone. "Slocum! Come!" Matt command frantically, but the big yellow dog was caught up in the blood lust of the fight.

"Slocum, come, damn ye!" Matt flailed away at him, but it did no good, and the guard had regained his feet. Matt had no choice. He made for the fence, his eyes burning with tears. If the mastiff didn't finish Slocum off, the guard would. His head was reeling slightly as he plunged through the rubble of the gate to reach Amalia and the horse. In one swift motion that took almost all his remaining strength, he swept her into the saddle and vaulted up behind her.

The voice he heard shouting from the balcony was *Don* Esteban's, calling out frantic orders in Spanish. From somewhere toward the stables, Matt heard the clatter of hoofbeats and the whinny of horses. He did not wait to hear more. He dug his heels into the flanks of the big bay horse. The animal shot forward beneath him. From the garden, a dog yelped in agony. Was it Slocum? Matt bit back the tears. If he and Amalia escaped it would be because the big yellow mutt had given his life to save them.

The horse pounded up the street that led through the main part of upper Natchez. From there they could catch the road that led down the bluff, to safety at Mathilde Rodare's. By dawn they would be on the keelboat, headed up the Mississippi.

Matt glanced ahead, then brought the horse up sharply. Armed men on horseback, half a dozen of them, were clattering out of a side street. They must have come from the Montoya place, with orders to bring Amalia back at any cost.

The horsemen had cut off their escape. There

267

was no way to reach the bluff road now, and Matt realized dimly that there would be no refuge for them, even in Natchez-under-the-Hill. They would be chased, hunted down like rabbits, and dragged from any shelter they could find. They had no place to go.

Matt wheeled the horse and headed it onto a narrow roadway that disappeared some distance off in a darkened wood. He had a slight head start on the horsemen. There was still a chance he could lose them. Frantically he pressed the horse. The dirt flew from its cutting hooves as it pounded down the road. With shouts, the horsemen took up the trail.

They passed into the blackness of the woods, Amalia sobbing with fear. The horse, carrying double, could not hope to outrun the others, Matt knew. He turned off the roadway into the bushes and slipped off the horse's back. Then, muffling its mouth with his hand, he led it deeper and deeper into the woods. Behind a dense clump of bushes he stopped and gently pulled Amalia down beside him. They stood clinging together in terror, their hearts pounding, as the six riders thundered past them and on down the road.

"We've lost them," he whispered reassuringly, partly to Amalia and partly to himself. He could feel her trembling hard beneath her cloak. Her breath came in little sobs. "We can't go back to town," he said. "Your ma's house—that be the first place your pa'd send his men. An' for sure he'll be havin' the landing watched." He stroked her hair, which had come unbound during the chase. "We ain't got nowhere t' go 'ceptin' right where we be, Amalia. An' we ain't got nobody to help us 'ceptin' ourselves. They might come back, those devils o' your fathers. For certain, leastwise, they'll be searchin' this wood come dawn. I be givin' ye one last chance, Amalia. If ye want t' go back home where it's safe, I'll take ye right now."

Amalia was sobbing now, too hard to answer him. But Matt felt her answer in the motion of her head, back and forth against his chest. No, she did not want to go back. He held her tighter.

"We got t' get movin'," he said. "I know ye be tired, but we can't stay here. It's too close to town and too close to the trail. Get ye back on the horse, Amalia. We'll be goin' deeper into these woods, where they can't find us. Come mornin' I'll look about an' see where we be. Come on, now. Back up with ye—" Gently he helped her onto the horse. Then he took the bridle and began to lead the animal quietly through the tangle of trees, vines and bushes.

They kept moving for the better part of two hours, until Matt's own feet began to feel like lead weights, and Amalia had begun to sway with weariness. At last Matt tied the horse to a stump, just in time to catch her as she slid from the saddle.

"Amalia . . ." Matt kissed her softly, his lips brushing tenderly over her small, tired face. She was almost too weary to respond. With great gentleness, he lowered her to a bed of leaves and moss at the foot of a big sycamore. Her body was limp, pliant in his arms. In spite of everything—the terror of their flight, their exhaustion, Matt felt his passion stirring. He was fully ready for her, he realized. And the way she lay there, her lovely head pillowed on the leaves, her great, dark eyes looking up at him in the moonlight, made an ache of longing flow from his heart down into his legs.

"Matt . . ." she whispered.

"Hush, now, love," he said softly, circling her in his arms and fighting down the temptation to tear away her clothes and take her then and there. Aye, he wanted her, more than he'd ever thought he could want any girl, but he loved her as well. If he were to take her now, before they were man and wife, he would be no better than that bastard Andres Santana. He kissed her eyelids. "Go to sleep, love. I'll be here. I'll take care of ye. Close your eyes, now. I'll wake ye when it's morning."

He held her until he felt her head drop sleepily against his shoulder. Then he lay back against the tree, his eyes on the stars, to wait for what dawn would bring.

# XVIII

Sunlight was streaming onto Matt's face. He had slept, in spite of himself, well into morning. Panic seized at him when he remembered last night's danger. He had meant to get well away by dawn. But exhaustion had overcome him as it had Amalia. They had slept like two tired children.

Matt opened his eyes and looked down at her. She lay beside him, still asleep, her slim, frail body warm against his own. Tenderness flooded into him. He raised his head and rolled over to kiss her awake—

Suddenly he became aware that they were not alone. Something else was lying alongside him, something solid, warm and quivering. Matt sat up. Slocum lay stretched out next to his legs, his yellow hide caked with blood. One ear was badly chewed, and flies swarmed along the gash in his flank. But he was breathing deeply and evenly, a sound, healthy sleep.

"Slocum!" Matt let out a low whoop of joy, and the dog opened his eyes. "Slocum! Ye old son of a devil! Slocum!" Matt stroked the great, yellow head. Slocum's tail went wild with joy. His whole body quivered ecstatically as Matt inspected him. The wounds were bloody, but not deep. Only the gash on his flank would need serious tending. And much of the blood in Slocum's coat, especially on his muzzle, did not appear to be his.

Amalia stirred and opened her eyes. She gave a little cry when she saw Slocum. Then she sat up. Gingerly she stroked the massive head. "He saved me, Matt," she whispered.

"Aye." Matt raised her face and kissed her tenderly on the lips. "And now I got to save us all. We got to have vittles and water. Then we'd best find out where we be and where we be goin'." The thought crossed his mind that there still might be a way to catch Mike Fink's keelboat by waiting a few miles upstream—but even that would take some timing and some luck. And, of course, *Don* Esteban's men could be anywhere.

He kissed her again, his heart heavy with a growing awareness of their plight. He had lured this fragile girl from the safety of her home into the hardship and peril of the wilderness. They were alone, unarmed, and except for a few coins in Matt's pocket, without money. He had counted on getting her to Madame Rodare's and so he had not gone to the Montoya house equipped for travel. His fine rifle was at Madame's, as was the gold from the trading venture. He cursed his own lack of foresight. With all the blind faith of his youth, he had not even considered the possibility that something would go wrong.

"Amalia, I got to take ye back," he whispered, stroking her rumpled hair. "I brought ye to this. It was my doin', but I can't put ye through no more. We got no money t'speak of, no vittles, no gun. Not even a knife. An' right now, I ain't got the foggiest notion where we be." He clasped her shoulders and looked into her lovely, dark eyes. "I want ye, Amalia. But I'll not be riskin' your life. If anything happened to ye, I'd want t' die. As soon as I get it figured out where we be, I'll be takin' ye home, or leastwise t' where somebody can find ye—"

He felt her shoulders tense under his hands. Something flashed like a spark in the depths of her eyes. "*Si*, Matthew Cooper," she snapped. "Take me back. Take me back to my father, and to that pig Andres Santana. Take me back to my nice, proper wedding in the cathedral, with all the old families of Natchez there, and watch me *marry* him! Watch him take me to our marriage bed, and . . . and watch me *kill* myself before I submit to him again! I swear to you, Matt, I would rather starve in the woods! Ten times, Matt, I would rather be killed by bandits or eaten by bears! How can you even think of it—?" Her little body was quivering with indignation.

"Amalia—" Matt was altogether bewildered, elated and dismayed by her sudden show of spirit. Lord in heaven, what was he going to do? How was he going to get her to safety?

"Look!" Amalia snatched up her little valise from the ground. She opened the clasp and began to pull things out of it. Matt watched in amazement as she drew out a spare set of under-garments, a cream-colored gown cut in the new way, of a light, airy material that enabled it to fold up to almost nothing. She pulled out brushes and hairpins, ribbons in shades of pink, gold, white and black, a pair of delicate silver filigree earrings. A necklace of amethysts and crystal beads, a small sewing box with thread, needles and scissors, a linen washcloth and towel, and some scented Spanish soap. "Look!" she said, thrusting the seemingly empty valise toward him.

Matt's eyes widened. The bottom of the valise was littered with coins. There were several gold guineas, at least one two-guinea piece, and some American quarter-eagles. There were some Mexican gold pieces as well, and an assortment of small silver coins. Not a fortune to be sure, but enough to buy food or passage—if only he could find a place where they might be for sale. "See," she said, a bit angry still, "we're better off than you think. With this money we can buy what we need."

"Aye." Matt could not help but admire her foresight. It was better than his own. "Supposin' ye get yourself ready for the day, while I scout around. Maybe climb a tree or two t' see what I can see."

"You won't take me back, or signal my father's men—?" Her dark eyes flashed him a swift, guarded glance.

"Amalia—oh, Lord, no!" He took her in his arms and kissed her face from forehead to chin. "No! I must have been daft even to think it! No,

274

love, I'll be right back. An' don't ye fear. Don't ye never fear again! I'll take care of ye!"

While Amalia tended to her needs, Matt shimmied up the tallest pine he could see. Higher and higher he climbed, until the top swayed with his weight. Then he shaded his eyes and looked around.

Natchez lay behind them, just on the horizon. Beyond it lay the Mississippi. But the great river was far away—much, much farther than Matt had hoped. He could only catch glimpses of it, where the morning sun caught the slow-moving water like a mirror that flashed with eye-burning glare. If Mike Fink's keelboat had left on schedule, they had no hope of reaching the river in time to catch him, not even if they rode like demons.

Matt craned his neck to see the other way. The wood stretched as far as he could see, broken here and there by stretches of canebrake and swamp. Wilderness, all of it. Full of snakes, alligators, bear and wildcat, as well as beasts of the two-legged variety that were worse than anything created by the Almighty. And him with no rifle. Matt cursed out loud. Maybe Amalia's gold would pay for a weapon if they were lucky enough to find one for sale. Then they'd have some protection—and he could hunt food for them as well. But that wouldn't mean an end to their troubles. Not by any means. The biggest problem of all lay in finding a safe and sure way through the five hundred miles of wild country that lay between Natchez and Nashville. Matt groaned out loud at the hopelessness of it.

Then, somehow, his eyes began to make out something in the trees. It was a separation, visible only as a faint line from where he perched, but it ran long, straight and true. It was a trail, he realized, his heart leaping, and it led as far as Matt's eyes could see, disappearing over the rolling horizon to the northeast. Matt studied it eagerly, his throat working with excitement. He knew what that trail was now, and the thought of what might lie ahead for himself and Amalia made the skin prickle on the back of his neck. It was the same feeling he'd had when he and Slade had ridden a ways down it from the other end. This, then was the infamous trail, the one he'd heard blessed and cursed by so many tongues. This was the Natchez Trace.

They had used one of Amalia's smaller coins to buy some breakfast and a few provisions from a mean-looking house alongside the Trace. The woman of the place had bitten the coin with her rotting teeth and served up two trenchers of greasy bacon and eggs with boiled hominy. "I ain't runnin' no inn, mind ye," she'd said with a low belch, "but I like the color of yer money."

Matt, always hungry, had eaten his with relish, but Amalia had wrinkled her nose and slipped most of hers under the table to a grateful Slocum.

"Now, ye got t' eat, Amalia, like it or not," Matt had admonished her. "Ye'll be needin' your strength." She had only wrinkled her delicate nose again. "But it's *awful*, Matt! I would be ill if I were to eat such food!" She had nibbled at the hominy, and that was all.

Matt had even tried to buy an ancient musket that hung above the fireplace, or a usable hunting knife, but the woman had refused. "Thet there shootin' piece were my pappy's an' I wouldn't part with it fer nothin'," she said. "Ain't no good nohow. An' I ain't got but one good knife. Take the vittles an' be satisfied with 'em, or git on with ye. Don't make no difference t' me."

So they'd settled for some shriveled-looking smoked ham and a bag of corn dodgers to take along with them. Little else stood between them and starvation.

Perhaps more valuable than the food was the free advice the woman had given them about the Trace. In the dirt outside her cabin she had traced a map, which Matt had swiftly committed to memory. There were, happily, some small settlements, little more than outposts, along the southern end of the trail. There was hope, then, of buying more provisions, a rifle, even another horse. As it cut north, in an almost straight diagonal between Natchez and Nashville, the Trace passed through wilder country. Much of it was little more than a narrow path, edged by woods and tall canebrake where all sorts of dangers could lurk. Matt shuddered, remembering the woman's warnings. His greatest hope in keeping Amalia safe lay in finding some good company for the trip. But he dared not delay at this end of the Trace. *Don* Esteban's men, once they realized that he and Amalia were not in Natchez, would likely guess where they'd gone and would be swiftly on their heels. Matt could only pray that perhaps along the way they could find a few friendly travelers with whom they could band together for protection. In the meantime, they would have to push on alone, as best they could.

They rode up the Trace now, double on the horse, with Amalia sitting behind. Matt shivered with pleasure at the feel of her arms around his waist, the weight of her head and the occasional brush of her breast against his back. They talked from time to time, about the future they would have once they got to Nashville and found a preacher to marry them. Sometimes Amalia sang little songs to him in Spanish, and Matt, just for the fun of it, would sing her some of the bawdy ballads he had learned from Mike Fink. She giggled and protested, but Amalia was having fun, he could tell. This was still a great adventure to her.

"Will we see Indians?" Her hair blew against his ear.

"Aye. Maybe. But they be peaceable. Choctaws at this end of the Trace, and Chickasaws up to the north. Ain't the Indians we have t' worry about, the woman said. Ye can trust the Indians. It be the white men, the renegades. They be worse'n any Indian ever thought of bein'."

"Oh." He felt her shiver behind him, the awareness beginning to dawn on her, perhaps, that they had not come on a picnic after all. Her arms tightened around his waist, and Matt felt a dark sense of lurking danger steal over him, then pass like a cloud.

In one tiny settlement they were able to buy a gun—an antiquated cap and ball dueling pistol that took so long to load and fire that it could not have been much use for any kind of hunting. Still, Matt reasoned, it was better than nothing. It might at least be used to bluff off some enemy. Beyond that—Matt eyed the pistol doubtfully. If he could catch a squirrel or a rabbit maybe he could use the damnable thing for a club.

They had met one sizeable party of twenty— coming south, not going north. "Best you camp here and wait for company," the leader had warned Matt. "Don't be fool enough to take a young girl through that country alone." Matt had considered his advice. Then he had remembered the threat of *Don* Esteban's horsemen, who even now could be hours behind them, and he had pushed on. Surely they did not look wealthy, he and Amalia—but there were other problems. Amalia's own beauty could prove their downfall if they were spotted by some ruffian with a lusty eye. After talking the matter over with her, he bought the ragged clothes off a skinny youth they'd spotted on a cabin porch at the side of the Trace. They should just fit her, he calculated.

Amalia had refused to put them on. "They're *dirty!*" she'd hissed, dangling the shirt, hat and breeches at arm's length from the tips of her fingers. "They've got *bichos* in them! They're crawling!"

Matt inspected the garments closely. Amalia was right. There were tiny white bugs in the seams. And the clothes *did* stink a bit.

"I'll not wear them till they're washed, Matthew Cooper," she said. "I don't care what you say!"

Matt sighed. No, he couldn't blame her. "All right." He took the clothes, hung them on the end of a long stick, and carried them like a banner until that evening, when they came at last to a creek.

"We might as well stop here," Matt said, surveying the spreading trees and surrounding bushes. This would be their first night on the Trace, and he was nervous, but the spot looked well protected. If they lit no fire, no one need even know they were there.

Matt unsaddled the horse while Slocum took long, deep laps of water from the creek. "Give me the clothes," Matt said. "I'll wash 'em for ye."

"I can do it," Amalia said testily. "Go ahead, tend to the horse and the camp. I won't be a piece of helpless baggage on this trip!" She took the stick that held the clothes and stalked on down to the creek, her splendid little head held indignantly high. The bank was muddy. The slick, brown clay had soon coated her dainty slippers and made a sticky, crusted edge around the hem of her gown. She knelt awkwardly at the edge of the creek, splashing water on her skirt as she rubbed her fragrant Spanish soap into the filthy homespun. By the time she'd finished with the breeches her dress was thoroughly splattered with mud, and she had lost one cake of soap. Even the straw hat got a thorough scrubbing. When the clothes were clean, she traipsed over to the bushes and carefully laid them out to dry. By then Matt had spread out a bed of pine needles covered with soft, dry leaves and assembled a rather pitiful supper of the ham and corn dodgers. He could not help grinning as Amalia came up the bank. Poor, wet little rat.

"Ye look t' need a good washin' yourself," he teased.

Amalia only tossed her head, but when a breeze passed by she began to shiver. Matt strode to her side. "Ye'll be catchin' your death! Here, let's get ye out of this—" He began to unfasten her gown from the back, his big fingers fumbling with the delicate buttons. She did not argue, but stood still and trembling as he worked.

"Amalia—" His hands were shaking. He was shaking behind her, and suddenly he was kissing the soft, lovely curve of her neck where the dress had fallen from her shoulders. Matt felt his breath catch in his throat as his arms went around her. He pulled her close to him, his hands moving irresistibly up to her breasts, cupping, curving on them. She moaned softly and melted back against him. Matt felt his pulse pounding in his ears, faster, louder, making the blood race wildly through his veins. As she turned in his arms, he felt that hot, familiar rise, the almost unbearable physical pressure of desire. He crushed her lips with his. Her response was eager, furious, almost desperate. Her slim arms pulling his head down

281

to hers, her body pressing, molding to his, fully wanting the completeness of their love. This was no yellow-haired Winifred Van Cleve, playing games that started and finished according to her own calculations. Amalia wanted him, Matt realized, as much as he wanted her. Her childlike mouth was open, hungry for his kisses, and he gave them, covering her lips, her face, her throat, until their bodies ached for each other.

Amalia's breath came in tiny, gasping sobs now. Her body pressed Matt's, each soft curve molded to him, moving, eager. Matt thought of the bed of leaves he had made, just a few feet away. He lifted her against him and swung her over to it. She clung to him, totally willing.

"Amalia . . ." he whispered, "I love ye . . . I swear it. An' I'll take care of ye, always ye won't ever need t' fear for nothin—" As he kissed her again, his own words caught him like a slap in the face. Aye, here he was, promising to cherish her, honor her, and take care of her. And here he was, ready to tumble her on a bed of leaves with no words said over them. Maybe that was good enough for girls like Elvina or Carrie, or even for Winifred. But he knew that wasn't good enough for Amalia. For her, he wanted a proper wedding. And the first time he took her, he wanted it to be as her husband.

Tensing his will, he forced himself to gentle the kisses he gave her, to move his hands back to her shoulders, lift her face, and gaze into her wide, dark eyes.

"Amalia," he said, his voice a hoarse whisper,

"I promised myself I'd see us wed, an' I mean to stand by that promise like a man. I want ye somethin' powerful, but ye ain't the kind o' girl a man can take advantage of. Ye be . . . somethin' a little better than any girl I ever knew. Ye be a queen to me, Amalia, and I aim to treat ye like one." He pulled her gown back up onto her shoulders and pulled off his own long-tailed shirt. "Now, get over to them bushes, get out of that wet dress, an' put this on. It'll do ye for the night. In the morning the other things ought t' be dry. Go on. Get!"

He turned her gently and nudged her away from him, in the direction of the bushes. She said nothing, but did as he had told her. A few minutes later she emerged with the shirt demurely covering her almost to her knees, lace-edged pantalets emerging below it. She hung her wet gown and petticoat on a bush. Then she went to Matt again and took his hand. Her eyes, black pools in the twilight, gazed into his. *"Te adoro,"* she whispered tenderly. "I love you, Matt Cooper."

He was still aching for her. "Aye," he whispered, "and I love you, too, Amalia." He held her small hands long and tightly, then released them. "Now, love, let's get some vittles in us, an' get some sleep. We can start out again soon as it's light enough t' see our way."

The ham was salty and the corn dodgers were dry. They washed it all down with water from the creek. Only Slocum seemed totally content with the fare. In spite of his wounds, he had limped along behind the horse all day, and the big dog was tired and hungry. He munched down the last corn dodger Amalia tossed him, then stretched out on the ground and closed his eyes with a contented sigh. The horse, a strapping bay whose endurance made up for anything it lacked in the way of beauty, nibbled grass at the edge of the little clearing. Matt put what was left of the ham back into the saddlebag for breakfast. They'd be needing something else by tomorrow night, whether it was to be trapped, shot, or purchased. Somehow he'd have to manage that.

He spread the saddle blanket over the bed of leaves and pine needles. It reeked of horse, but that couldn't be helped. It was all they had. There was nothing but Amalia's cloak to cover them, and the night was cool for midsummer.

"Come on. Time for sleep." He lay down along one edge, leaving plenty of room for her. She came to the blanket with her cloak and lay down on her back, not quite touching him. Matt felt his pulse quicken at her very nearness, but he fought back the warm rising tide of desire. "Good night, love," he whispered, tucking the cloak snugly around her.

She lay still for a moment. "Matt, you'll be cold. You gave me your shirt."

"Aye. But it's all right." Matt lied through his teeth. His bare chest was already getting goose bumps. "I don't feel the cold much," he said.

"No." She raised the side of the cloak that was nearest him. "We can't have you chilled, *querido*. Come close. We will be warmer that way." She opened the cloak wider. *"Ven . . . come . . ."*

284

With a little groan, Matt moved under the cloak beside her. She snuggled against him until she was comfortable, then dropped into sleep, like a tired kitten. Matt lay beside her, awake and aching. Her hair was soft against his cheek, the curves of her body lightly pressing him. Matt swallowed hard. His mouth felt dry. The touch of her against his bare skin was a delicious torment. His loins were hot, hurting almost. Yet Amalia slept peacefully on. She was even more innocent than he'd realized. In spite of what that devil Santana had done to her, she was still a child in her understanding of it. She had no idea what a woman's nearness could do to a man. She did not know that she was tempting him almost beyond endurance.

Matt sighed and shifted his weight slightly. A mosquito buzzed around his face and landed on his cheek. He let it bite him. He had no wish to wake Amalia by swatting. No. Instead he lay there watching the stars move across the sky, his eyes following the forms and patterns of the constellations. Amalia lay beside him, her breath warm and moist against his skin. Matt twitched his toes and cursed his own frustration. By heaven, what he wouldn't give for a preacher—any sort of preacher—to come riding down the Trace. He would give the man a gold coin to say the words over them, and then Amalia would be his. This damned waiting would be over. If not, Matt reflected, they'd have to get all the way to Nashville before they could be wed, and every night alone with her on the Trace would be hell for him. A preacher . . . aye, damn it, any preacher . . . That was the last thought to pass through Matt's head before he finally drifted off to sleep.

# XIX

*Don* Andres Santana would have known about
Amalia's flight a good deal sooner if anyone had
been able to find him the night it happened. Unfortunately, he had been sampling the delights of
one of the newer pleasure houses in Natchez-
under-the-Hill, and though his house servants
had actually looked for him at his usual place—
Madame Rodare's—even they had not known
where he had really gone.

It was noon of the next day before he'd arrived
home, scrubbed and perfumed, but still red-eyed
and surly from the night's dissipation. It was his
butler, nervously wringing his hands, who'd
given him the news. *Don* Andres had answered
the wretch by knocking him halfway across the
parlor. Then he had stormed back out the gate,
swung into the saddle, kicked his horse viciously,
and set out at a gallop for the house of the man
who was to have been his future father-in-law.

"Yes, I've got men out searching for them."
*Don* Esteban had met him in the entryway.
"Where in the name of heaven have you been,
Andres? We could have used you last night—

287

never mind—" *Don* Esteban had frowned reproachfully at him. "A man knows better than to ask. What you do with your time is your own affair as long as it does not become a scandal in the town, and as long as you do not pass some foul disease on to my daughter and my grandchildren. You take precautions, I assume?"

"Yes . . . yes, of course. But Amalia—how did she—?"

"Young Cooper, *naturalmente*. The night guard almost stopped them, but they got away," *Don* Esteban snapped. His eyes were bloodshot and he looked as if he'd been awake all night. "My men have orders not to come back without them. When they're found, Joaquin will see to it that *Senor* Cooper never molests a woman again."

Santana nodded, his blood seething with hatred for that Yankee upstart, Cooper. He had seen the expert knife work of big Joaquin, the chief stablehand—slow, agonizing and precise. Joaquin could make the turning of a man into a eunuch a work of art. And seeing such a punishment dealt to Matt Cooper would be even more delicious than seeing him killed. Still . . . the notion tugged at *Don* Andres's mind. There *was* the question of honor. After all, Amalia was *his* betrothed. It behooved, him, he supposed, to go after Cooper himself, instead of leaving the Yankee to a common lout like Joaquin. Pity, since he hated the rigors of days in the saddle. He much preferred to get his exercise in bed.

Though Amalia was a pretty little bird, *Don* Andres had no illusions about loving her. Actually, he had never really planned to marry at all, but his own fortunes had been so shrunk by gambling and neglect that marriage had become a necessity. He had paid court to little Amalia Montoya because she was an heiress, the only child of one of the wealthiest men in Natchez. His every move had been calculated, studied. The story of Amalia's mother was commonly known in the city. For this reason, none of the truly upper-class Spanish families would consider her as a possible daughter-in-law. *Don* Andres had taken advantage of that fact in pressing his suit. Amalia was fortunate, he had carefully pointed out, in that at least one proper gentleman of good stock was willing to overlook her parentage. It was her beauty and gentleness, he insisted, that had won him in spite of it. And *Don* Esteban Montoya had been impressed, relieved, and willing to accept him.

Even his rather forceful seduction of Amalia had been a deliberate calculation. The girl had been reluctant, he sensed. Worse, he had noticed her attraction to Matthew Cooper that night at the ball. It was the fear of losing her, and her fortune as well, that had led him to Amalia's room that night. He had needed something to bind her to him, to make her feel that she was already his, and it was too late to change her mind. Bedding her had been pleasant enough, though, in truth, virgins bored him. He much preferred women

289

with a combination of experience and imagination. Little Amalia was still so much a child. But in time . . . yes, in time, he would teach her to perform the special tricks that excited him most. They were unusual tricks, some of them. Even the girls in the pleasure houses complained when he demanded them. But Amalia, he was sure, could be persuaded in time . . . or forced.

The voice of *Don* Esteban Montoya brought him back to the reality of the present. None of this—Amalia, the money—would come to pass for him if the girl could not be found and brought back.

"I expect you will be leaving within the hour," *Don* Esteban was saying. "My hounds and horses are at your disposal, *naturalmente*, although, of course, your own are quite equal to mine. My men have already searched the town and inspected every boat that's departed the landing since their disappearance. They found no sign of them. Either they're better hidden than we can imagine, or they've left town by way of the Trace."

"Your own men?"

"They've split up. Half are still searching the waterfront. The rest are riding up the Trace." *Don* Esteban fixed Santana with a penetrating look.

"Then I will search in the town," *Don* Andres said quickly. "For me it would be too late for any hope of catching them on the Trace. But if they are found, bring the boy to me, eh? I wish to deal with him myself!" He turned quickly on his heel and strode from the room. His mind was already plotting what he would do to Matthew Cooper once that Yankee whelp was in his hands. It would not be pleasant, or swift. And Amalia would likely plead for the boy. She would likely do anything . . . anything, if he would only spare Cooper's wretched life. Yes . . . he mused, quickening his stride. The possibilities were becoming interesting. He was feeling better already.

Matt and Amalia had crossed the Pearl River at Grindstone Ford on the third day of their journey. The ferryman had eyed Amalia curiously, and Matt realized that even in the clothes of a ragged boy, her delicate, aristocratic beauty could not be hidden. The man, however, had said nothing unusual to them, and had cheerfully accepted the silver coin which Matt gave him. At a shack on the other side, Matt had bought some bread, some jerky, and some turnips. It was no great feast, but it was food. Even Amalia, who'd have turned her pretty nose up at such common fare two days earlier, was becoming hungry enough to devour whatever could be had.

Slocum's wounds were healing nicely. The big dog trotted cheerfully along beside the horse, panting sloppily, grinning up at Matt and Amalia when they spoke.

"When will we be in Nashville?" Amalia leaned around Matt's shoulder so she could see his face.

"Two, three weeks. Ain't rightly sure, being's I never made the trip afore." Matt grinned at he. He liked the sight of her in boys' clothes. They showed off the lovely proportions of her figure and gave her a pert, childish air that tugged at her heart. She slept in those clothes, which helped matters some, but nights were still torture for Matt, lying beside her, wanting her so badly that he could scarcely sleep for it. He could only pray for the sight of Nashville—or for a traveling preacher.

"That man at the ferry," she was saying. "The way he looked at me—Matt, I think he knew."

"Aye. I been thinkin' the same thing." How could anyone look at her and *not* know? No boy could be that beautiful. He felt her shiver behind him, though the sun was hot.

"Matt, something's going to happen today. I— I can feel it. I can't explain how, but I'm frightened."

"Aye, I feel it, too." Matt said, realizing that he *had* felt it, all morning. A chill of foreboding had stolen into his bones. Even Slocum seemed more quiet than usual. He trotted close to the horse, not even stopping to sniff at rabbit holes or lift his leg on tree trunks beside the trail. Now and again he would stop and glance back over his shoulder, then hurry his pace.

They were passing through bayou country now. The air was hot and damp, and it swam with buzzing, biting mosquitos. Amalia had wrapped herself in her cloak to protect her flesh from them. Matt's face, neck and arms, wherever his skin was exposed, were covered with their itchy bites. Cane rose like walls on either side of them, interspersed with an occasional cypress. It would be a long day's journey, Matt reflected, if they did not pass out of this miserable country before evening, for the idea of sleeping here was unthinkable.

A huge, dead pine tree rose out of the cane. Its needles were long gone, but the bare, gnarled branches were heavily festooned with Spanish moss. "Hold the horse," Matt said suddenly. "I think maybe I'll climb up and have me a look around."

Amalia waited while he made his way through the thick cane to the base of the old tree. Expertly he began to climb, catching the branches and swinging upward through the curtains of gray-green moss. At last, toward the top, he broke clear.

The country around him was flat, most of it canebrake. When Matt looked down, he could see Amalia on the trail, holding the horse and gazing up at him. The tree was tall. She looked tiny on the ground. The Trace cut through the canebrake in a straight, thin line. Matt could see it for perhaps a mile in both directions—forward to the horizon, backward almost all the way to the ferry they'd crossed. He squinted and shaded his eyes. The ferry seemed unusually busy, as if a good number of passengers were being ferried across. Well and good, if it was a company of travelers. Maybe there was a chance he and Amalia could join them.

Matt hitched himself up in the tree in order to see better. Now he could see the passengers leaving the ferry—all of them men, all of them mounted, and traveling at a gallop. A sudden fear clutched at Matt's heart. Long distance travelers would not be pushing ahead at that speed. He was seeing horsemen—horsemen in pursuit of something.

Matt slid most of the way down the trunk in his haste. "Into the cane!" he told Amalia. "Quick. The horse and all!"

The cane was thick as a wall, its leaves razor-edged. They plunged into it, pulling the horse with them. The stalks bent and snapped as they forced their way through, then closed behind them. Already in the distance they could hear the sound of galloping hoofbeats, many of them, coming swiftly closer. Amalia gasped in fear. Slocum growled, the hair standing up in a ridge on the back of his neck.

"Come on!" Matt whispered. "We ain't in far enough!" He dragged the horse after. Amalia put up her hands to protect her face from the sharp leaves. The pounding of hooves came closer. "There—they ought to be goin' past us in a second. Be still." Matt motioned her to stop. He held the horse's head to quiet it. Amalia's hand went to Slocum's collar. Her eyes widened as the horsemen galloped past, scarcely a stone's throw from

294

I learned that early. But Matt, now. Isn't he sweet on the Van Cleve girl?"

"Winifred?" Marie knotted the thread and attacked the loose seam of one of the little girls' dresses. "*She* says he's sweet on her. But I ain't never heard Matt say so."

"She'd like to marry him, I'll wager." Abby's expert fingers flew, plying the needle back and forth.

"Aye. I reckon so. He'd make a good husband, Matt would, once he gets the wildness out of his system."

"I don't think Edward ever really did." Abby lowered her work to her lap, leaned her head against the back of the rocker and smiled bitterly to herself. Aye, Edward had hurt her. He was a man after all, and to make matters worse, he was French. Though he loved her well, and she knew it, there'd been times when he'd given in to temptation. She had forgiven him . . . aye, but the pain still came and went from time to time, like a twinge of rheumatism.

"Remember Mathilde Rodare?" Marie's question broke the comfortable silence like a rock thrown into a pond. "What d'ye suppose ever happened to her?"

"Mathilde Rodare? I'm surprised you'd even mention her name after all these years." Abby's brows had lifted. Mathilde Rodare had been the hardest to forgive. Beautiful, lusty, and poisonous as a toadstool, Mathilde had bewitched Edward when he'd first gone to Vincennes alone.

Then, when Edward had tried to forsake her, Mathilde had turned her venom on his family. Her ultimate revenge had nearly spelled death for Abigail Forny, and ruin for Marie.

Marie glanced down at her mending. "I don't rightly know why I did. But I been thinkin' of her lately, wonderin' what happened to her after she left Vincennes."

"Your father told us she was half out of her mind when she disappeared. Some Indians likely got her, I'd say."

Marie shook her head. "But someone sold her house, some agency that had a right to do it."

"Aye." Abby closed her eyes for a moment, then opened them again. "I don't want to talk about her, Marie. It brings back too much of the old hurt."

Silence was Marie Cooper's only answer as she bent to her work again. Several minutes later, when they did speak, it was about what to fix for supper that night.

# XX

Amalia had not slept indoors for a week now, and she wondered if she would ever be the same. Her skin, in spite of the straw hat, had taken on some color from the sun. Her long hair, she was sure, was permanently tangled. The muscles of her legs, which had been agonizingly stiff from sitting astride the horse, had loosened to the point where she felt almost comfortable in the saddle. And her appetite—that was a source of amazement. She had never done more than nibble at the delicacies that the cook prepared back home in Natchez. Now she found herself wolfing down food that she once wouldn't have considered fit for her father's dogs—rabbit, snared by Matt in the night and butchered with her little sewing scissors, cold ham and stale biscuits, bought along the way at shacks so poor and dirty that they almost made her flesh crawl, greens, berries, fish, roasted on a stick over a tiny campfire. The strange thing was that for all these unappealing foods and for all the hardship of the trail, she had never felt so strong, or slept so well.

But the nights—yes, something bothered her

there. Matt was behaving so strangely. When they lay down together, both of them fully dressed, he held her the way a parent would hold a child, his hands so carefully and discreetly placed. And when she turned to kiss him, her own blood throbbing warmly through her veins, he would sigh, as if he were in some deep pain, and whisper, "Good night. I love ye, Amalia. Now go to sleep."

And what did she really want of him? Amalia asked herself. Did she want him to take her, the way Andres Santana had taken her? Yes—sometimes, at least, she admitted. Especially at night, when he lay close to her, his breathing wonderfully deep. Then she wished with all her might that he would make her his, his love blotting out the thing that Santana had done.

Sometimes she snuggled close to him, fitting the curves of her body to his. Usually he would sigh deeply, even moan, and then she would know he was not really asleep. But she still did not understand him. He seemed so tormented, so unsettled by her nearness. And she could not understand why—unless he had decided that he no longer loved her.

She lay awake beside him now, staring at the sky and enjoying the warmth that radiated softly from Matt's slumbering body. It was their first night of real rest in several days. That morning, as they hid in the woods, her father's men had ridden past them along the Trace, going south, back to Natchez. They had given up, or so it appeared, at least. Matt and Amalia had ridden in the open for the rest of the day, breathing easy for a change. But now there were other worries.

They had passed the Choctaw Agency the previous day, and had circled the place rather than go in and buy much-needed supplies. *Don* Esteban's riders had still been ahead of them at the time, and they'd been fearful of walking into a trap, or exposing themselves to the eyes of men who would tell what they had seen—for a price. Now that danger, at least, was past. But the next outpost, Doak's Stand, was at least three days ride up the Trace, and their food was gone. They would have to depend upon whatever they could catch, trap, or forage.

Worse, perhaps, this was open country, the haunt of renegades and bandits. Every snap and rustle in the underbrush set their nerves to tingling with wariness. Even Slocum was more alert, sniffing, growling at each unfamiliar sound.

"Amalia . . ." Matt stirred beside her. "You awake?"

"*Si.*" She snuggled close to him, edging her small buttocks into the hollow made by the curve of his legs and body so they lay like two spoons. "Will it be morning soon?" she asked.

"Aye. Time we be getting up, I reckon."

"But it's still night." She snuggled closer and felt the reward of his arm slipping gently around her. A feeling of warm excitement began to creep through her body. She felt her own breathing quicken.

"It'll be dawn afore we know it. Time to get movin' " He pulled her tighter against him, his lips brushing the back of her neck. Something stirred against the curve of her, something warm and hard and alive.

"Matt—" she turned in his arms and he crushed her to him. His kisses fell hungrily on her lips, her eyelids, her throat. One hand fumbled at the neck of her homespun shirt. In her eagerness, she helped him with the buttons, and in turn with the top of her lacy camisole, until her firm, young breasts lay bare in the starlight. Matt's breath came hard as he touched them, stroked them, kissed them. Amalia's heart was pounding now. She wanted him with her whole body—all of him. "Matt . . ." She quivered with desire, clinging to him, wanting to touch him in exciting, new ways.

"Amalia, love—" She felt him tense, then shudder convulsively before he drew back to kiss her, gently this time. "You be as temptin' to me as cold spring water to a man that's dyin' of thirst. But this ain't the time and place for us." He shook his head as he buttoned her shirt again. "Ye be nigh onto drivin' me wild, Amalia, but I want to have ye' proper, with a preacher to say the words. I want ye for my wife, Amalia, an' I don't want to do ye no wrong."

He moved away from her. Amalia lay back on the blanket and closed her eyes while she waited for the trembling to go away. Yes, Matt was right, and he was a good man. She ought to thank the Blessed Virgin that he cared for her enough to re-strain himself. Still, there was that ache inside her that would not go away—that painful knowl-edge that another man had possessed her, and

Matt Cooper had not.

"It's time we were gettin' up, anyway," Matt stretched, rolled to the edge of the blanket, and eased himself to his feet. Amalia lay there, not wanting to face the morning yet. The darkness had begun to gray slightly in the east.

"I'm hungry," she said, and it was true. Now that her passions were calming, Amalia was aware of a gnawing emptiness in her stomach.

"Aye." Matt was seated on a log, pulling on his boots. "An' we ate the last of the vittles last night. Sorry, love, but we'll have to start out empty. Maybe along the way we'll come across a stream with some fish in it, or a good patch o' berries."

Amalia groaned. She did not want fish or berries. She wanted fresh bread and bacon. She wanted eggs and hot Spanish chocolate.

"Come on," Matt said. "We may as well get movin' afore the heat comes on."

Amalia sat up and rubbed her eyes. How she would have loved a warm bath, scented with oil of roses. Slocum, who had curled himself at their feet, opened one eye, then the other. Stretching one leg at a time he stood up, yawned hugely, shook himself, and wagged his tail. The big yellow dog's wound from the fight with the mastiff were no more than scabs beneath his fur now, and he was fully his old self.

Matt saddled the horse while Amalia went to the bushes, brushed the worst of the tangles from her long, black hair, and pinned it up beneath the straw hat. By then, Matt had mounted the horse. He swung her up behind him, and they moved out of the trees, back onto the Trace itself.

"Maybe we'll meet someone," Amalia mused hopefully. "Maybe someone will be having breakfast and will share it with us, or at least be willing to sell us some food."

"Aye," Matt said, and she could tell from the tone of his voice that he was angry at himself for failing to provide for her. "That we might."

They kept the horse to a walk, so as not to tire it so early in the day. The sky grew pale, like a gray pearl, and the first faint, pink rays of dawn began to show over the horizon. Matt and Amalia said little. They were hungry, both of them, and their minds were filled with the pain of desire that had almost overcome them both that morning. Only Slocum was full of life, darting off into the brush after squirrels, to reappear up the Trace moments later, panting, grinning, and drooling.

They had been riding for an hour, perhaps, when Amalia smelled the bacon and coffee. At first she thought her mind might be playing tricks on her, because she was so ravenously hungry. Then, as the tantalizing fragrance grew stronger, she knew she could not be mistaken.

"Aye, I smell it, too," Matt said. "Sure do smell good, too. It's comin' from somewhere off the Trace over past them trees, I reckon."

"Well, hurry!" Amalia urged him. "Surely they'd share with us, if we offered them money."

"Aye. And maybe just to be friendly," Matt said, nudging the horse's flanks with the toes of his boots.

They followed the beckoning aroma, up the

Trace, into the trees. Slocum stayed close behind the horse now. The big dog had grown strangely quiet, and once Amalia thought she heard him growl, but she paid little attention. The thought of food, real, delicious food, drove all thought of caution out of her mind.

They had gone perhaps two hundred yards off the Trace when they broke into a small clearing. Two horses, bony and tired-looking, were tied at its edge, and a shelter of sticks and boughs had been built a short distance from a glowing campfire.

Two men were crouched by the fire, their backs to Matt and Amalia. They were cooking their breakfast, in a big iron skillet over the coals— fresh bacon, popping, sizzling so enticingly that Matt and Amalia were almost hypnotized by it. A charred coffeepot sat at the fire's edge, steaming invitingly.

The men themselves were wearing dark suits, and both appeared to be dark-haired. One was a hulking figure, tall and broad shouldered. The other was small, wiry, compact. When Slocum growled they both turned around.

Their swarthy faces reflected surprise at first. Then the big man smiled crookedly and beckoned Matt and Amalia toward the fire.

"Welcome, friends," he said. "Come ye closer. Don't be afraid. We won't harm ye, not men o' the cloth like we be. Ye look a mite hungry, ye do. Come sit a spell. Have some vittles."

"Thank ye." Matt halted the horse at the edge of the clearing, slipped down from the saddle,

305

and then helped Amalia dismount.

Trying not to show their hunger more than was polite, they walked toward the campfire. Slocum, usually a friendly animal, sat down beside the horse, the hair on his neck bristling.

Matt reached out and caught Amalia's hand. "Look," he whispered. "Look at them, Amalia. Our luck's with us today. See the way those two be dressed—they ain't just ordinary men. They be preachers!"

# XXI

The bigger of the two preachers stood up. He was taller by a finger's breadth than Matt, and a good deal heavier. "Sit yourselves, boys," he said in a deep, jovial voice. "We got plenty, an' both of ye look half starved. Roberts be my name, Reverend Micah Roberts. This here be my brother, Reverend Wiley Roberts. Both of us got the call and took to preachin' nigh onto a year ago."

Matt introduced himself, and cautiously presented Amalia as his "cousin," Joseph. "Joe, here, he don't talk much. Reckon he's a bit shy around strangers, even preachers." There was little else he could say. The moment Amalia opened her mouth, her small, soft, girlish voice would betray her, if the delicate structure of her face and body had not betrayed her already. But then again, the men were preachers, not rogues. Maybe it would do no harm if they knew her secret.

"Have some coffee. The bacon be just 'bout cooked, an we got johnny-cake to go with it." The smaller of the two preachers spoke in an oddly wheezing voice. He had a jutting jaw and narrow, black eyes, and was probably the better looking of the two—not that either of them was a prize, Matt reflected. But preachers! Two of them! Matt's mind was already racing. Aye, when he got a little better acquainted with them, he could ask one of them to perform the ceremony that would make Amalia his wife. His heart hammered with anticipation.

"Thank ye kindly," he said. "We can pay ye for it—"

"Pay? Wouldn't think of it!" the bigger man boomed. "Sit ye down! Ye look like two starvin' lambs, ye do. It's a good thing ye happened onto us, and not onto some o' the likes as had been seen 'round here lately."

"Aye," added the other man. "Why we heerd talk back at the agency that the Harpe brothers be about in these parts. Tain't safe for two purty young'uns like you to be travelin' alone. Here—" He motioned to a seat on a fallen tree not far from the fire. Matt and Amalia came closer and sat down, Amalia keeping close to him, her eyes downcast. The bacon sizzled away in the iron skillet, its aroma so tantalizing that it almost made Matt's head swim.

The smaller man leaned toward them, squinting slightly. "An' what might two young'uns like you be doing out hyar in—" He suddenly stopped speaking and leaned closer, his eyes narrowing on Amalia. He studied her carefully for a moment before his face broke into a gap-toothed grin. "Well, I'll be! Praise the Lord, it's a little gal!''

the big preacher's eyes opened wide. He stared at Amalia, then let out a loud guffaw. "Well! I'll be a blue-eyed bullfrog! We asked ye what ye be a'doin out here alone by yerselfs. Reckon we got our answer. What be it, eh, lad? Ye be takin' this little 'un away from 'er pa? Two lovebirds flyin' away together!'' He laughed again. "Well, ye don't need t' worry none. We won't hurt ye. We be men o' the cloth, an' right honorable men at that!''

"Aw, stop yer jawin', Brother Micah!'' The smaller preacher spat into the coals, creating a brief hiss. "These young'uns is hungry! Let's git 'em something t' eat!'' He used a rag to lift the skillet off the coals and handed Matt and Amalia each a greasy-looking fork to spear it on. Then he tossed them each a hunk of fresh johnnycake to sop up the bacon grease. Amalia took a bit of it, closed her eyes and chewed hungrily.

"Ye'll have t' share a cup. We travel light.'' The big preacher handed Matt a tin cup filled with steaming coffee. It was hot and good. He passed it to Amalia. She gulped it, half-scalding her tongue in the process.

"Careful.'' Matt grinned as her eyes reddened. The bacon and hoecake were the best thing he'd tasted in a week, and he was beginning to feel alive again, strong and cheerful. The two preachers gathered around the skillet with their own forks, spearing the bacon, chewing with their mouths open and talking at the same time.

"We travel mostly the back trails," said the little preacher, stuffing his mouth with hoe-cake. "There be folk what don't get t' hear the word o' the Lord but once, twice a year. They always be ready to hear a good preachin' an' to give two men o' the cloth a meal an' a bed. It's not such a bad life."

"But don't ye have families?" Matt asked politely.

"Aye," said the big preacher. "We got wives an young'uns. Jist left 'em yesterdy, up the Trace. They be strong women, all three o' em. They can take care of theirselves."

Matt was to recall later that there was something odd about what the big man had said. Three women, not two. But now he paid it little mind. He had heard wrong, that was all. Or maybe the preachers had a sister or mother there, along with the wives.

Amalia helped herself to another piece of bacon. She had not spoken except to murmur a word of thanks for the food. Matt studied her delicate profile as she ate. Would she consent to marrying him here on the Trace, with one of these strange, unkempt preachers to say the words over them? Or would she insist on waiting for a proper wedding in Nashville? He thought of the night that lay beyond the day. This could be their wedding night if she was willing. Just the idea of it made his pulse race.

They finished the meal, and the two preachers wiped their mouths on the sleeves of their black suits. Their white collars were grimy with sweat. Matt couldn't help wondering what kind of sermon these two would preach, but no matter. They were preachers, and preachers could marry people.

"Ye headin' up or down the Trace?" the big preacher asked Matt.

"Up. Got an uncle in Nashville, and folks of my own in Louisville. We run a tradin' business—Forny & Cooper, they call it. That be my name, Matthew Cooper."

The big man nodded and ran his fingers through his frizzy-looking black hair. "Up the Trace? But ye got t' be careful, boy. That be dangerous travelin' fer a couple o' young uns like you. There be Injuns about, and bandits. Why, I heerd tell the Harpe brothers were spotted less'n two days north o'right here where ye be standin'."

"The Harpes? You ever see 'em?"

"Us?" The small preacher shook his head. "Ain't nobody what sees the Harpes an' lives to tell 'bout it. They be terrible men, I heerd tell, though. Kings o' the Trace, that's what they be."

"Aye," the big man put in. "They don't trouble with us, mind you, cause we be simple preacher folk. But young'uns like you, a wearin' good clothes, an' a girl what's purty to look at—I'd be a'watchin' my step if I were ye."

"Aye." Matt frowned thoughtfully. "Too bad ye can't travel with us. But if ye left your families up the Trace just yesterday that must mean ye be headed down south, t'ward Natchez."

"Oh, we wander here an' there. Don't make much difference t' us, long as we can find folks t' preach to. Now, we'd be pleasured to go along with ye for a spell, back as far as our families, leastwise, if ye don't mind a little preachin' along the way." He ran a finger under the edge of his dirty, white preacher's collar.

"That'd be right kindly of ye," Matt said, genuinely relieved. They were odd chaps, these two preachers, but they seemed harmless enough, and even the appearance of a larger group might be enough to scare off the marauders that lurked ahead along the Trace.

Amalia had gone back toward the horse to feed Slocum. Matt leaned confidentially toward the two preachers. "Mind ye, I ain't asked her yet, but if the lady be willin'—the two of ye bein' preachers—would one of ye be willin' t' marry us?"

"Marry the two of ye?" The big minister's face broke into a grin that showed slivers of bacon between his teeth. "Why, sure! We'd be happy to, wouldn't we, brother?"

"Aye. That we would."

"I'd be much obliged," Matt said, trying to keep the excitment out of his voice. "I'll speak to her. I got a feelin' she'd be willin'."

The short preacher nodded his bushy, dark head vigorously. "Wait. I just got an idee. T'wouldn't be much of a weddin' out here in the woods. Our womenfolk back up the Trace, they ain't seen a real weddin' since they had their own. It'd pleasure em' t' no end if we brought ye home with us and had the weddin' there! Why they could help the bride git ready, they could cook up some vittles, make a real party of it. What d'ye think o' that, Brother Micah?"

The big preacher's eyes lit up. "Why that'd sure be a right fine idea if your young friend is willin'. What d'ye say to that, Master Cooper?"

Matt thought about the idea for a moment. It did sound like the right thing to do, providing it was all right with Amalia, of course. It would be better than having their wedding out here in the woods, with nothing but the two of them and this odd pair of wild-haired, wild-eyed preachers. There'd be women to help Amalia dress and arrange her hair. There'd even be a wedding feast of sorts, maybe. And it might be a welcome event for the lonely frontier women who certainly didn't get much socializing. "I—I'll ask her," he said, and walked over to where Amalia was standing by the horse. He was surprised to find himself trembling.

"Amalia, love," he said softly, "they said they could marry us—"

"Matt—" She turned to him, her eyes large and luminous. "Matt, we could be married today!"

"Then ye'd be willin—?"

313

"Willing! Oh, Matt, *querido mio*—" Her arms went around him, and she hugged him so hard that her small feet left the ground. "But I want to wear the dress I brought with me, and take a bath, and brush my hair. Oh, Matt, I at least want to *look* like a bride! I do not want to be married looking like some *picaro* boy!"

"Aye. That's part of what I wanted to ask ye. They say it'd pleasure their womenfolk t' have the wedding at their place, up the Trace. They want to take us there. What d'ye think?"

Amalia seemed to hesitate for a moment, her lovely face pensive. "*Ay*," she said. "Why must things get complicated so fast. Yes, I would like a nice wedding, Matt, but I have no wish to take a long time with it. I want to finish this journey and get to your uncle's family in Nashville as soon as we can."

Matt shrugged. "Well, then, I'll just tell 'em—"

"No—" She put a hand on his arm. "No, they've been kind to us. Those poor wives of theirs must not have easy lives. If it would give them pleasure—"

"Then ye'll do it?"

"*Si.*" Her smile melted Matt's heart. "If they want to help us have a nice wedding, how can we refuse them?"

In a half hour's time the two preachers had gathered up their gear, loaded it onto their two spavined horses, and were headed back up the Trace, Matt and Amalia following behind them on the bay. Slocum hung in close, almost under the horse's legs, his tail down instead of high and banner-like. He had not come in close to the fire that morning, not even to eat, which was not like him at all. He had wolfed down the tidbits Amalia had saved him from breakfast, but Slocum was definitely not himself this morning.

"Wonder if he might be ailin'?" Matt voiced his worries out loud.

"He was fine when we got up." Amalia's arms tightened around Matt's waist. "Maybe he got into something—" She glanced down at Slocum and made a little dove-like sound. The big dog glanced up at her. His tail quivered but did not really wag. "I'll watch him," she said. "*No te preocupas, querido.* Don't worry."

They rode on through the sun-dappled morning, Matt whistling softly to himself. From time to time one of the two preachers would glance back over his shoulder and grin, but no one said a good deal. The morning was unusually quiet, except for the occasional caw-cawing of crows. What was it about crows? Matt tried to remember why the sound struck a note of coldness and dread in him, and for the life of him he could not.

The day passed into afternoon. They lunched on cold hoecake and water, which at least filled their stomachs and then pushed on again. "It still be a fur piece up the trail, but we'll be there afore dark if we don't dilly-dally here on the Trace," the small preacher said, spitting out a blade of grass that he'd been

315

chewing on. "Our women folk, they'll be right glad t' see these young'uns, won't they, Brother Micah?"

"Aye, they'll be right tickled. Don't get out much, not since they all got young'uns o' their own. But don't ye worry none 'bout vittles. We got plenty o' those, an' they allers put a good spread on the table. Why my Susan, now, she be the best cook in these parts, an' it pleasures her nigh t' death t' have company t' show it off fer."

"That's right kind of ye," Matt answered, feeling the tightness of Amalia's arms around him. It was comforting, her closeness, her warmth, and Matt wondered again why, on such a glorious day, he would feel he *needed* comforting. There was an uneasiness in the air. The day was too quiet. Even Slocum was grim. The occasional jests and shouts of the two preachers seemed out of place, too loud and disturbing in this silent, vast, muggy wilderness. He squeezed Amalia's hand where it rested at his belt. Then he brushed the apprehension aside, quickened the pace of the horse, and moved forward.

John Swaney was not exactly a talkative traveling companion, Edward reflected as he gazed up the trail at the bobbing back and shoulders of the tough little mail carrier. They had been pounding the Trace since the night before, and Swaney had not spoken more than

316

three or four sentences all the way.

They had left Nashville at eight o'clock in the evening, and ridden steadily through the darkness. At midnight they had crossed the Harpeth River and passed the clearing and cabin of one Tom Davis—their last touch with civilization before the blackness of the wilderness closed around them. By morning they had reached Gordon's Ferry on the Duck River, 51 miles south of Nashville, where they stopped just long enough to feed the horses, munch a few cold biscuits, and go to the bushes. Then they were off again.

Swaney traveled light. In addition to the small pouch of letters and dispatches, he carried a half bushel of corn for his horse, a little food for himself, one thin blanket, and a tin trumpet. The horse he rode was as tough and wiry as Swaney himself, and as sure-footed as a goat.

From Gordon's Ferry it would be eighty miles to the crossing of the Tennessee, where they would spend the night. "Got t' cover it afore night. Otherwise the Injuns what live on t' other side an' run the ferry won't git out o'bed an' bring us 'cross."

So they had gone thundering down the Trace at a speed that Edward swore was enough to exhaust a man and kill the stoutest horse. But amazingly, Swaney's homely mount had forged tirelessly on, and Fanny, the fleet little roan that Slade had lent his grandfather for the trip, had held up almost as well. Edward found himself breathing his thanks for her youthful strength and swiftness.

Every ten miles or so they stopped, dismounted, and rested the horses by walking for a time. Then it was back to the saddle again, flying down the Trace. Swaney had an amazing sense of how much strain a horse could stand, and he never pushed the mounts beyond that point. He was a kind man, and wise in the ways of the wilderness. Edward's respect for him had grown by the hour.

Twilight was coming on now. Edward felt every day of his sixty-four years, and his stomach roared with hunger. Swaney had said they had to reach the ferry by nightfall. Surely it couldn't be much farther. He had thought himself used to rigorous travel—for he could paddle a canoe from dawn till dark without tiring. But now he ached in every bone and muscle. He would be agonizingly stiff tomorrow morning, Edward reflected, and John Swaney, he knew, would give him no pity.

Fanny's red flanks were flecked with foam. Edward patted her damp neck. The filly had done good service this day, but even she was tiring. Edward sighed and leaned forward in the saddle to ease the bruising pressure on his buttocks. He was river man, not a blasted jockey, Edward told himself. And what he wouldn't give to be in a canoe!

Half an hour later they sighted a thin column of smoke rising above the trees in the distance. Swaney said nothing, but Edward guessed, to his great relief, that they must be getting near the ferry. A few minutes more, and he could smell the aroma of corn roasting over the coals of fire.

The trail had widened a bit. Swaney slowed his mount and allowed Edward to catch up with him. "There be an old Chickasaw chief what runs the ferry," Swaney said. "James Colbert be his name, and he's a funny one. His pa was a Scot, they say. Good man. Ye'll see."

They came out of the trees and onto the bank of the Tennessee. Edward had traveled the lower reaches of the river before, but this wild section was unfamiliar to him. The current was swift and treacherous here—that much he knew. Even the most nimble canoe would be in danger on this river.

The ferry was rigged to ropes and pulleys that spanned the river. It stood, empty and waiting, a single Chickasaw Indian watching it. There was little sign of civilization on this, the near side of the river, but looking across, Edward could see a cluster of log cabins that somehow had about them the look of an Indian village.

Swaney blew a blast on his tin trumpet that aroused a flurry of action on the other side of the river. Soon he and Edward had led their horses onto the flat, wooden ferry and were being pulled across the current of the Tennessee. They bumped against the grassy bank on the other side and came ashore.

James Colbert himself was waiting to greet

them. He was an old man, his body gone to fat, his eyes, small and bright, peering out from above his plump cheeks. A curious mixture of Indian and white, he wore long braids, a shapeless felt hat, and a soiled brown Yankee suit that looked as if it had once been expensive. His feet were clad in beaded moccasins. He was altogether a dilapidated figure. Yet, Edward reflected, there was an elusive majesty about the old man, as if he were some aging king dressed in a beggar's garb. He shook hands with Edward and clapped Swaney on the back. Then he ushered them into a large building that looked like a cross between a log cabin and a longhouse.

"This be where we'll sup an' sleep," Swaney explained to Edward. "Food ain't much but it be the best ye'll get afore we come t' Natchez, so eat hearty."

An Indian woman flaunting a gaudy Paris hat brought them their supper. Colbert's wife, Swaney said. Edward could not help smiling at the sight of her. With the hat, in which she clearly took great pride, Mrs. Colbert wore a dumpy buckskin dress and no shoes. She plunked down two trenchers and two mugs filled with coffee, which was cold. The meal was not so bad. And Edward was ravenous. He ate all of it.

By the time they'd finished, it was dark outside. "Best we git ourselves t' sleep," Swaney said. "We'll be startin' out agin afore daylight."

*"Oui."* Edward glanced dubiously around the long hall, which was filled with Indians, perhaps fifty of them. Some were eating, some smoking or arguing, some already stretched out on the floor, wrapped in their blankets.

"Come on," said Swaney. "Ain't no other place t' sleep 'ceptin' outside, and the skeeters is fearsome at night. Mrs. Colbert, she don't allow no white men t' sleep inside her own house, so's we got t' sleep here, jist like everybody else."

Edward shrugged his acceptance, gathered up his bedroll, and found a quiet place along the wall. No one seemed inclined to bother him. The Indians ignored him as he rolled up in his blanket, made a pillow of his own arms, and closed his eyes.

It was noisy in the long building, as well as being smoky, smelly and crowded, but Edward was exhausted. *Ouf,* I am getting too old for this, he thought as he turned over, trying to get comfortable. My own warm, soft bed back in Louisville, and my Abby's arms—that's what I want right now. The devil with this trip! His bones and muscles were aching from the long ride, and he knew he would be agonizingly stiff by morning. But he had come. His anxiety over Matt had brought him on this fool's errand, and there was nothing to do but make the best of things.

His mind had begun to drift. Light and darkness formed shapes that floated in and out of his consciousness. Matt. His face. The tall,

321

young body that was flesh of his flesh. Matt
. . . in danger. Edward moaned softly in his
sleep. Even in dreams he sensed it. Something
was wrong. His grandson was in grave peril.

He was an old man now, Edward's flowing
sleep-thoughts reminded him. What could he
do? How could he help Matt even if he did arrive in time? He moaned again, his head swimming with weariness. He only knew that he had
to find Matt. He had to—

# XXII

They had left the main path of the Trace an hour past. Matt was beginning to get nervous about it when they came at last to a small clearing in the tangled, swampy wood. A single, two-storied cabin stood there, a thin finger of smoke pointing upward from its crude chimney.

It was large enough, that cabin, but it was a rude place, hastily built and poorly kept. The yard was cluttered with the bones and hides of deer. A few scrawny chickens pecked at the ground around the cabin, but aside from them and the smoke, Matt could see no sign of life.

Then the big preacher gave a long, low whistle that ended in a series of yips, like the call of a fox. Slowly, cautiously, the cabin door began to open. The barrel of a rifle was the first thing to emerge, then a hand, with one finger resting on the trigger.

"Ease up, Susan," the big preacher called out. "Brought ye all some visitors. Some right purty young'uns what wants t' git married!"

The door opened a bit more, little by little,

until the tall, rangy figure of a woman emerged. She looked to be about thirty, with a grim, lantern-jawed face, narrow eyes of a pale, washed-out blue, a jutting nose and a little slit of a mouth. She was dressed in buckskins, like a man, and she held the rifle like she knew how to use it.

"My Susan. The pride o' the Trace." The big preacher grinned. "Susan can outrun, outshoot an' outlove any woman in these parts!" He swung off his horse. "Susan, these two purty young'uns be wantin' t' git married, so, us bein' preachers an' all, we brung 'em here for the weddin'."

Susan gave a jerky nod of her head and leaned the rifle against the side of the porch. Her expression did not change.

"Where be Sally an' Betsey?" The little preacher talked. "Git 'em out here so's they can meet our guests!"

Susan opened the door and stuck her head back inside. In a moment, two other women appeared, both of them younger than the grim Susan. The taller of the two was the better looking. Her coloring and something of her bone structure were similar to Susan's though they were more delicate and in better balance. Matt guessed that they might be sisters. "Howdy. Betsey Roberts is the name," she said with a playful glance in Matt's direction. She was wearing buckskins, too, and they showed off her buxom figure to good advantage. She seemed to know she was on display, for she turned slightly to Matt's view, showing off the profile of her full breasts. Then she looked at him over her shoulder and gave him a bold, undisguised wink.

The third woman was dark, with hair that hung down in straggles around a plain, plump face. She was wearing a shapeless cotton dress, and she carried a baby on her left hip. Her expression was as sullen and disinterested as a toad's.

"My woman, Sally," said the smaller preacher. "An' that be my young'un. They all got young'uns, all three o' the gals. All had 'em 'bout the same time. Purtiest babies ye ever laid eyes on." He raised his voice. "What ye all standin' there gawpin' for? These two, they's tired an' hungry! Git some vittles on the table an' some beds rigged up. We got guests for the night, an' then tomorrow we'll give 'em a right proper weddin'! One they'll not be forgettin' fer a long time t' come!" He gave a most un-preacher-like whoop and winked at his wife.

"Hope ye don't mind waitin' till tomorrow for the weddin'." The big preacher grinned at Matt and Amalia, his teeth yellow in the twilight. "Wouldn't be fair t' do it tonight, with the womenfolk too tuckered out t' do things up proper, now, would it?"

"No, I reckon not." Matt glanced at Amalia. He had hoped to make her his bride before nightfall, but what the man had said made sense. They'd come all this way for a wedding. It was too late to get things ready tonight. He and Amalia would sleep apart—But, Matt vowed, this would be the last time. Tomorrow night they would share the same bed, as man and wife.

Susan, the tall woman, spoke for the first time. "Reckon it be all right for ye t' come in, then," she said. "Ain't got nothin' fancy for sup. Jest venison stew. But it's hot an' it's ready."

The stew *was* good, the best thing Matt and Amalia had eaten since they'd left Natchez. They wolfed it down with all the vigor of their healthy, young appetites.

The three women sat across from them at the long, puncheon-slab table. Susan, who had done most of the cooking, eyed them with sullen suspicion, saying little beyond, "Pass the salt." Dark-haired Sally, the most timid of the three, kept her eyes on her trencher, taking big mouthfuls of stew and chewing intently. Only Betsey, who had indeed turned out to be Susan's younger sister, was animated. She had seated herself directly across the table from Matt, and every few seconds he would feel the deliberate brush of a knee or foot. More often than not, he would keep his eyes on his food, but when he did look up, her saucy face would be laughing at him. At such times, Matt would feel a warm redness creeping up into his cheeks. Betsey was not a bad looking girl, even though she laughed with her mouth full. Her hair was as tawny and tousled as a catamount's, and her features, though far from pretty, had a tough, impish quality about them that was easy enough to like. She had small, sharp, bright eyes, like a magpie's, and a long, thrusting jaw that was like her sister Susan's. On Susan, however, it was homely, while it was almost attractive on the lively Betsey. Matt was still trying to fit her exactly into this strange family. Three babies, all of them nearly the same age, lay fussing on one corner in the rumpled bed. One of them, he knew, was Betsey's. Yet there was no sign of her husband on the place, whoever he might be. Maybe she was a widow, he speculated. Or maybe he was off trading or trapping somewhere. Finally he decided to ask.

He cleared his throat. "Not meanin' t' be nosy, Ma'am," he said politely, "but where might your husband be? I didn't see no sign of him. Might he be a travelin' man?"

"A travelin' man?" Betsey threw back her head and guffawed loudly. "Ye hear that? My husband a travelin' man! Ain't that a rich one?" She gulped down the bite of stew she had just taken. "Sweetie," she said, addressing Matt, "It's me what does the travelin'!" She laughed again, and both preachers joined in, the little one almost choking on a chunk of turnip. Matt shrugged. Maybe she'd run off from her husband, then, and moved in with her sister's family. That, at least, made some sense. If that was the case, then it was personal, he decided, and it would be prying to ask her any more about it.

They finished, and the women brushed off Amalia's offer to help with the cleaning. Matt sopped up the gravy on his trencher with some leftover johnnycake and took it outside to Slocum. He found the big dog still crouched next to where they'd tied the horse. His tail thumped noisily on the ground when Matt came close, and he gulped down the bread and gravy, but when Matt tried to call him back to the porch, he would not come. He hung back, growling softly, low in his throat. "Come on, Slocum. Come on up t' the cabin, boy, so's ye can sleep on the porch. They said it'd be all right." He tugged at Slocum's collar, but the stubborn mutt dropped to his stomach and would not budge. Slow Come. He was aptly named, all right, Matt told himself as he walked back to the cabin. Still it wasn't like him, hanging back like that. Maybe he was really ailing.

When the supper table was cleared away, the big preacher glanced around the cabin. He yawned, without covering his mouth. "Reckon it be time fer bed," he announced. "Friend Matthew, there ain't much sleepin' space in here. But it's a right mellow night, an' there be lots o' nice, soft shavin's in the woodshed, if'n ye don't mind." He shifted his dark eyes to Matt.

"Not at all," Matt said quickly. "I'll be comfortable anywhere."

"An' yer young gal, now. Ain't no place t' put 'er ceptin' in the bunk with Betsey an' the baby."

Amalia's eyes widened and her nostrils flared slightly. It was plain to see she had never slept in a bed with anyone else. "I—I can sleep in the woodshed, too," she declared. "Please," she added more softly.

"A lady? An' sharin' the shed with her intended the night afore the weddin'? Wouldn't hear o' it!" The words exploded out of the little preacher. "Ye be sleepin' in the cabin, like is fittin' fer a young gal. An' Betsey, she won' mind none, will ye, Betsey?"

Betsey shook her tawny hair. "I reckon not," she said indifferently.

"Matt—" Amalia put a hand on his arm. It was all too clear she did not want to sleep with Betsey.

"Now, Amalia," Matt soothed her. He was used to frontier hospitality. There wasn't a good deal of room in cabins like this one, and guests had to be put wherever they'd fit. "Won't hurt ye for one night," he said softly. "They's preacher folk, after all, an' they might think we're uppity an' that we ain't grateful fer their havin' the weddin'. Just one night, Amalia."

She sighed. "All right, Matt. It's just that I'm not used to it."

"Hope the baby won't bother ye none," Betsey said with a slow grin. "He don't cry much, but he do wet the bed now an' again."

Amalia's eyes widened again, and she shot Matt a final, pleading glance, but she said nothing. Tonight wouldn't be easy for her, but at least it was safer than sleeping in the open on the Trace. Anything could happen out there.

Betsey had plopped down in the rocker, uncovered one full brown-nippled breast, and started to nurse her baby. Matt squirmed uncomfortably. He remembered his mother feeding his little sisters that way, but she had always covered herself with a blanket or shawl. Betsey had no such modesty. She seemed to be enjoying Matt's obvious discomfort.

"I'll be gettin' my bed ready," he said awkwardly, and made his way out the door, avoiding Amalia's stricken eyes. No, he told himself, it wouldn't do for her to sleep in the shed with him. With their wedding so close, the temptation to rush the wedding night would be too much.

In the shed, he smoothed out the shavings and spread the saddle blanket. Then he lay down and closed his eyes. Tomorrow seemed like a long, long time away. As he was drifting off to sleep he heard the shavings rustle. Slocum, whining softly, nuzzled his hand and curled up in the curve of his legs. "Good boy." Matt patted the big, yellow head. "Good boy." Then, slowly, he fell asleep.

*Don* Esteban Montoya pounded on the door of the most infamous brothel in Natchez. The little butler, his eyes popping led him into Madam Rodare's private sitting room.

"It was kind of you to come calling during business hours, Esteban," she said, her voice dripping sarcasm. "Would you care to go out into the *salon* and make a selection."

No, she had not changed. Don Esteban gritted his teeth. "I came at night, Mathilde, because you do not keep the same hours as respectable people. You sleep during the day."

"*Oui.* The night has many creatures, and Mathilde is one of them." She studied him from under under her painted eyelids. She looked old, he thought, and ill. Yet the allure was still there, in the languorous intensity of her gaze, in the sinuous movements of her heavily ringed hands, in the throaty voice. He had loved this woman, and she had hurt him to the depths of his soul.

She stretched like a lazy cat. "So, you still have not found them, eh, Esteban?"

"My riders came back empty handed," he answered bitterly. Amalia was gone, vanished, and he was frantic. "I cannot help believing

331

you had a hand in this, Mathilde."

"I?" Her hand fluttered to her breast in mock outrage. Then she laughed. "*Mais oui!* Of course I did. But I only gave suggestions and lent a key. I'll confess, Esteban, I planned to give them refuge here until dawn of the next day. Then they were going away on one of *Monsieur* Fink's keelboats. I even had a priest waiting here to marry them—don't look so shocked, Esteban. I am more concerned with Amalia's honor than you are. At least I would not put her at the mercy of a beast like Andres Santana!" Mathilde's silver bracelets jingled as she spread her hands. "But they did not come. As God is my witness, Esteban, I have not seen them. I can only guess that your horsemen cut them off, and they had to find another hiding place."

"*Pero . . . donde?* Where? My men rode a hundred miles up the Trace. Amalia and her wretched swain could not have kept ahead of them. I still think you know something, Mathilde. Something you are not telling me!"

She laughed then, a bitter laugh that seemed to tear at her throat. To kill the pain she drained a glass of cognac that sat on a little table beside her. "I am sorry, Esteban, but I know nothing. I wish I did. I wish I could tantalize you with my secret! I wish I could dangle it before your eyes and make you squirm. But, alas, I know nothing. I only know that the young man who has taken her,

Matthew Cooper, has the heart of a lion! I like him, Esteban! He'll be ten times the husband to her that Santana could ever be!"

"He's a *campesino*! A peasant!"

"He's a fine boy!" she smiled like a sly cat. "But I'm glad you do not have the good sense to like him, Esteban. I had calculated you wouldn't. That, *mon amour*, is part of my revenge on you for throwing me out of your house, *eh bien?* You hoped to keep Amalia free from scandal. You hoped to make a fancy marriage for her. Oh—it didn't matter to you that the man was a brutal, slathering beast! No, as long as he had an honorable name to give her. That was all you cared about! The quality of the man does not matter to you—. You would marry your daughter to a rutting wild boar, as long as its mother was a Galvez! Ah, but Mathilde has changed your plans for you! How sweet!"

Don Esteban was growing angry. She had always had the power to do this to him. No matter that under most circumstances he was a man of utmost gentleness and restraint. Mathilde had this maddening ability to drive him to rage. "You used her, then," he said, masking his anger with icy calm. "You used her more cruelly than I did, because you used her as your tool for vengeance against me."

Again Mathilde laughed. *Madre de Dios*, why did she always have to laugh at him? She had even laughed at him the night he'd caught her with a lover in their own bed and had thrown her out into the night.

"Ah, Esteban, you stupid Spanish donkey! Amalia will be happy with that boy! He will care for her! He will protect her with his life! *Regardez moi!* Andres Santana is a piece of dog offal! Matthew Cooper is a *man!* Like his grandfather, Edouard Fornay!"

Don Esteban quivered with rage. Yes, she was playing him, the way a *torero* plays a bull before the kill. He knew it, and he was helpless in her hands.

"*Bruja!*" he hissed at her. "Witch! He was one of them, wasn't he? One of your lovers?"

"*Oui.* Before your time. *Mon Dieu,* what a man! I would have *killed* to have him, Esteban! If it had not been for his wife—" She shook her head, coughed, and poured herself a few drops of cognac from a crystal decanter. "Never have I known such a man, Esteban. He was the *best!* And you—you should get down on your knees and thank your precious Spanish saints that Amalia has run off with his grandson! And while you are there—on your knees—pray that they are safe, and that they have found some preacher to marry them!"

*Don* Esteban Montoya stared at the woman who had once been his wife—and was still his wife under the law of the Holy Mother Church, but under no other. Yes, she had won, for whatever the victory was worth. Amalia was gone from him. Run off to God knows where with the grandson of one of her mother's old lovers! His hopes of bringing the girl up as a lady and marrying her into a good family were gone. He had tried, but Amalia's stormy Rodare blood had boiled up in her, and she had gone.

Mathilde was laughing. Why did she always laugh? *Don* Esteban felt the rage boiling up into his chest. He felt his head bursting with it. He raised his hand, wanting to strike her, but he could not do it. All the frustration, all the rage, all the love, all the hate he felt for this woman exploded out of him in one loud cry of anguish. Then he turned from her and strode out of the room.

Matt was awakened by the sound of rustling wood chips. He opened his eyes, only half awake, still blinking in the moonlight that shone in through the open side of the woodshed. What had made that sound? It was an animal, he decided, closing his eyes again. A wood rat most likely, or a hunting weasel. It was nothing to be concerned about. Even Slocum had not stirred. Matt took a deep breath and tried to go back to sleep. Tomorrow would never come, if he did not sleep, and tomorrow would be the happiest day of his life.

Only moments later, he became aware that a shadow had fallen across his face and was blocking out the moonlight. He could hear the sounds of a woman's low breathing close to his face.

"Amalia . . ." he murmured. Maybe she had sneaked out of the cabin to spend the rest of the night with him. Lord, what did she think she was doing? He wasn't made of stone! "Amalia, get back in the cabin . . ."

"Hush, now!" The voice was not Amalia's. Matt's eyes shot open. The figure bending over him was only a silhouette, but he recognized the tousled mane that was Betsey's hair. "Hush now, purty boy! Ye don't need t' say a word. Just leave things t' Betsey here!" She giggled softly. Matt could see her better now, the moonlight making patterns on her face and outlining her buxom figure. "Your intended, she be sleepin' like a baby. Skinny little thing—not much woman there for a big'un like ye be." She cocked her head and tittered. "I'll wager ye be big all over. What d'ye say we find out?"

She had been bending over him, but now she stood up, full height, her body outlined in the wide opening of the shed. She was wearing a ragged muslin nightgown that would have been shapeless on most women—but on Betsey the fabric had a way of clinging to her breasts and her full, round haunches that was downright disturbing. The night had cooled, but Matt found himself breaking out in a sweat.

"What ye gonna do with this, eh?" One of Betsey's hands tugged at a knot. Then the entire nightgown dropped in a circle around her ankles. Betsey stood naked against the moon, its blue light gleaming on the curves of her milk-swollen breasts, and full, rounded hips. Matt sucked in his breath. She was nothing but trouble, this woman. A man would be a fool to take her. But she looked like a fully-spread banquet standing there in the pale light, hair tousled, arms behind her head to raise the line of her breasts. In spite of himself, Matt felt the hot rising of his own body. Lord, no, he thought. Not with Amalia twenty paces away in the cabin.

Betsey stepped out of the circle of her nightgown and moved toward him, a determined smile on her face. "Come on, big'un," she whispered. "Let's see what kind of a man ye be, eh?"

She leaned toward him, her hair falling down around her face, her breasts hanging in enticing globes, like twin oriole nests, swinging slightly. Matt could hear her breathing, deep and husky. His nostrils were filled with the woman-smell of her body. His loins throbbed. No—his reason protested. No! It was pure foolhardiness. And it wouldn't be fair to Amalia either. But his body was ready. His head was spinning, throwing reason all out of kilter.

She was moving closer, slowly, letting the moonlight flicker on her body, giving the sight of her time to drive him wild. Aye, she knew how to play a man, this one. Not too fast and not too slow—Betsey took another step toward Matt. Then—suddenly there was a growl and a yelp. Slocum had been slumbering so soundly he hadn't paid any mind to her, but Betsey had stepped right on him. In a flash he was up, growling, his fangs bared.

"Oh!" Betsey sprang backward, clutching at her breasts. "Oh, law, what is it?"

Slocum, not fully awake himself, growled. Betsey picked up her nightgown with the toes of one foot, and slowly raised it up to where she could get it with her hand. "There, boy . . . easy, boy . . ."

Matt could only watch the little drama. He didn't know if he should try to quiet Slocum, let the big fellow have his way and scare her off, or burst out laughing.

"Call him off!" Betsey panted. "Ye didn't tell me ye slept with no wild animal!" She jerked the nightgown up in front of her and began to back out of the shed, Slocum still growling at her. At last, when she thought she'd achieved enough distance, she turned and ran back toward the cabin. Her white buttocks flashed in the moonlight. Then Matt saw her no more.

"Slocum!" Matt rumpled the dog's ears. "Dumb dog. Didn't wake up till she stepped right on ye!" he cursed. "What if she'd a been some varmint or robber, or one o' the Harpe brothers, eh?" Limp with relief now that it

338

was over, he began to chuckle, then to guffaw, then to roar. It was funny, the way Betsey had yelped and backed off. He hugged Slocum and laughed himself to sleep. But one last thought sobered him. He remembered his last glimpse of her face in the moonlight. She'd been embarrassed, angry. Aye, she'd let herself be made a fool of, and she didn't like it, Matt told himself. He'd have to be careful till he could marry Amalia and get out of this place. A woman like Betsey was nothing but trouble, especially when she thought she'd been scorned.

Matt shivered and snuggled closer to Slocum. He knew women like Betsey. They could be sweet one minute, spiteful and vicious the next. He would have to watch out for her—and so would Amalia.

# XXIII

The morning was gone before the women pronounced everything ready for Matt and Amalia's wedding. Susan had roasted a wild turkey, boiled up some turnips, and made corn fritters, sizzled to a golden brown in hog fat. The stone-faced Sally had lent herself with at least a half-hearted enthusiasm to helping Amalia bathe, dress, and do her hair. Betsey had disappeared in the early morning hours, leaving her baby for the other women to mind, and Matt had thought she was peeved about last night. But when she returned before midday, her apron spilling wild flowers, he decided he'd misjudged her. Betsey had nursed her infant, and then set to work decorating the house and porch with clumps of beebalm, mallow, and wild aster. She hummed as she worked, flashing Matt a mischievous grin whenever he came near her. Undoubtedly she was up to something, he decided, watching as she put together a clever bower for the ceremony. But how could he think badly of the woman when she seemed so enthusiastic about making an occasion of the wedding?

"Ain't had so much fun in years!" she declared,

standing back to admire her own handiwork. "What's a weddin' without flowers?"

"And did ye have flowers at your own?" Matt asked with polite interest. It had been a long morning, and he'd not had much to occupy his own time except watching the preparations of the womenfolk.

"Weddin'? Mine?" She'd looked at him, the expression in her light blue eyes half incredulous, half amused. Then she'd thrown back her head and laughed uproariously, like a man, and had said no more about the matter. Betsey was a strange woman, Matt decided, and he'd gone off and left her to her work. The next thing he knew, she'd be bringing up last night, and he wanted to leave that be.

The two preachers had spent most of the morning sitting on the front steps, whittling and chewing Indian tobacco. They'd argued about who was to perform the ceremony, and finally agreed on a compromise. The little preacher would give a short sermon from the Good Book. Then the big preacher would perform the marriage. Matt had not been asked for his opinion. If he had, he would have said that they'd manage just fine without the sermon, thank you. Amalia might not appreciate it anyway, her being a Catholic. Instead Matt had simply kept his peace and hoped the little preacher's sermon wouldn't prove to be a long one.

After a morning that had seemed an eternity in length, Susan strode out onto the porch and announced that everything was ready. "The bride be dressed," she declared, "an' the vittles be ready. We can have the weddin' afore we eat!"

Matt took his place on the porch, under the bower that Betsey had made. He wished that at least he could have changed his clothes for the wedding, but he'd fled Natchez with nothing but the clothes on his back. He'd washed himself as best he could, scrubbed his face, ears and neck, shaved with a razor borrowed from one of the preachers and slicked back his hair. That was the best he could do.

The two preachers moved into place beside him, and the women, holding their babies, sat down together on a split-log bench at one end of the porch. A flutter of movement behind the half-open doorway told Matt that Amalia was there, waiting to come out.

The big preacher cleared his throat. "There bein' no music, we may as well start the weddin'. Ye can come out now, little lady."

Slowly the door opened. Amalia, her eyes lowered, stepped out into the sunlight. Matt felt his throat tighten. For as long as he had known her, he had thought Amalia was the most beautiful girl he had ever seen. Today she took his breath away.

She was wearing the gown that had been tucked away in her little valise. It was a rich cream in color, the fabric so light that it nearly floated in the air around her. Matt had heard his grandfather talk about silk—a material spun in China from the cocoons of a special moth, and carried halfway around the world in tall ships. Silk, he decided.

That airy wisp of a dress could be nothing else. The bodice was cut low, showing Amalia's lovely throat. It clung to her breasts, then flared out softly just below them, in graceful lines, without hoops or stiffened petticoats. Her long, black hair must have taken Sally half the morning to arrange. It was pulled up to the crown of her head, then twined with dozens of tiny, white wild flowers, so delicate that they almost formed a veil. Yes, the little preacher's wife had done herself proud, and her smug expression told Matt that Sally knew it. His heart warmed to these three strange, rough women, each of whom had given a measure of herself to making their wedding a nice occasion. They were funny folk, this family of preachers, but they were good-hearted. Matt couldn't fault them that.

Amalia floated toward Matt, looking so radiantly lovely that his heart wanted to burst. He reached out and took her hand. Aye, it was a perfect day for a wedding; a perfect place. Even these odd, wild people seemed perfect at this moment. He drew her to his side and stood expectantly, his hand clasping hers.

The little preacher stepped forward. "First, my sermon!" he announced, and he drew a well-thumbed Bible from his coat. He cleared his throat and stood holding the book and looking oddly foolish, as if, now that it was his turn, he had forgotten what to say. At last he opened the Bible, almost randomly, squinted at the page, and began to read it painstakingly aloud.

"While the king sitteth at his table, my spike-nard sendeth forth the smell thereof. A bundle of myrrh is my well-beloved unto me; he shall lie all night betwixt my breasts . . . My beloved is unto me as a cluster of camphire in the vineyards of Engedi . . ."

He continued on for the entire eight chapters, stumbling over some words, mispronouncing others, sometimes muttering as if to himself, sometimes almost shouting out the passages. When he had finished the verse about the heart upon the mountain of spices he stopped, uttered a booming "Amen," and looked around the assembled group, grinning from ear to ear. He was evidently much pleased with himself.

"Amen!" his wife Sally intoned piously, and the others echoed the response. Matt joined in rather sheepishly. The day was hot with the midday sun blazing down, and he was glad the little preacher had finished. Amalia, he noticed, remained silent. Her small hand trembled in his.

Now it was the big preacher's turn. He brushed a cobweb off his black sleeve, drew himself up to his full height, and began.

"Now, Lord, we don't hold much with formal words in these parts. If these two purty young'uns want t' be man an' wife, why there ain't no power what can stop 'em, now. So I say to ye, little lady, d'ye take this boy t' be your lawfully wedded husbin'?"

Amalia's whisper was as soft as a breath in the silent afternoon. "*Sí.* I do."

"And you, young man, d'ye take this little gal t' be your lawfully wedded wife?"

"I do," Matt answered firmly, though he was shaking inside. It seemed awesome to him that a few words from this unkempt backwoods preacher could change him into a husband and change Amalia into a wife.

"Well, then, it be done. I now pronounce ye man and wife!"

"Well, don't just stand there! Kiss 'er!" the little preacher put in quickly.

Matt took Amalia in his arms. Their kiss was a bit self-conscious, as he had never kissed her in front of other people. But when he released her and looked down into her face he saw that there were tears in her dark eyes. "Amalia, I love ye," he whispered. "I'll always take care of ye—"

In answer her eyelashes lowered, then lifted again. The look she gave him was one of complete love and trust. Matt felt something swell and burst in his heart.

Susan stood up. "Well, with that over, let's get the vittles on the table an' be done with it."

Sally got up to go and help her, leaving Betsey sitting alone on the bench. She was nursing her baby again, the little smacking noises of the infant's mouth loud in the afternoon stillness. Betsey threw back her head so that her loose hair tumbled down her back. Her mouth opened in a wet-lipped smile, and she laughed, an impish, wicked sound. Deliberately, she popped the nipple out of the baby's mouth, giving Matt an ample view as she

346

slowly tucked her breast back into her blouse. Her eyes were as bold and sharp as a crow's. She lifted the baby against her shoulder, stood up slowly, and walked ahead of Matt and Amalia, into the cabin.

The meal was a hearty one, but neither Matt nor Amalia had much appetite for it. They sat together, along one side of the table, the center of everyone's attention. Damnation! Matt thought. Just when all he really wanted to do was be alone with her, they had to spend their time in this crowded cabin, eating a meal that had been prepared in their honor. The day was hot, and the cabin was stuffy. Flies buzzed about the table, and Susan was constantly shooing them off the food. The two preachers sat on either side of Matt and Amalia. They ate with their fingers, and Matt found himself wondering how long it had been since either of them had washed or changed his linens. In this close, hot, cabin, the stink of their unwashed bodies almost made his nose curl. What he wanted was Amalia, alone somewhere in the freshness of the forest, on a soft blanket thrown over a bed of pine needles. Amalia. His.

She glanced up at him, her plate almost untouched. Her hand crept into his under the table. Aye, she wanted the same thing. As soon as it could be done without offending these rough preacher folk, he would take her away from this place.

When the meal was done, the big preacher wiped his mouth on his sleeve and called for a jug. Susan got one out of the cupboard, a big one, stoppered with a corn cob. He raised it on the crook of his arm, took a long, deep swallow, and let out a wild whoop. "Yee-haw! Now we can git t' the fun!" He took another deep swig of the jug and passed it to Matt. "Now, none o' that, boy! Ye wouldn't be refusin' our hospitality by not drinkin' with us, would ye now?"

He pressed the jug on Matt who, to please him, took a small sip from the dirty opening. The homemade whiskey was hot as fire. It burned all the way down to his stomach. "Any for the lady?" the big preacher asked. "Now I know this ain't a lady's drink, mind ye, but my Susan has a sip now an' agin!"

Amalia shook her head and he took the jug back again without trying to push it on her. Then the little preacher snatched it out of his hands and took one great, noisy gulp.

"Ahhh!" He smacked his lips and belched. Then he passed the jug to Betsey. She snatched it out of his hands, opened her full, red mouth, and poured an amber stream of it into her throat. Matt blinked as Betsey swallowed it and tossed the jug to her sister. Susan tilted back her head, closed her eyes, and took a long swallow. Sally took a few short swigs and then went back to minding her baby, but Susan and Betsey each sucked at the mouth of the jug once more before they tossed it back to the men. The preachers in turn each drank deeply once more, but Matt, when the jug was passed to him, tipped it high and only pretended to drink. He didn't want to be drunk for his wedding night. And he didn't want to offend a gentle girl like Amalia. Besides, he told himself, his father and mother wouldn't have approved, and he still owed them some respect, even though he was a married man now, about to start his own family.

Amalia touched his arm. "Matt—it's so warm in here. Couldn't we go outside?" She looked pale.

"Aye." Matt mumbled a few polite words to his hosts, stood up, and helped her off the log bench. "My wife's feelin' faint," he apologized, and was greeted with titters from the women. "If ye'll excuse us, we'll step out for a breath of air."

Amalia clung to his arm as they walked out onto the porch. Both of them gulped at muggy outdoor air. At least it was clean air out here. He slipped an arm around her shoulders and held her quietly against him. "Matt," she said after a time, "I don't like it here. I know they've been kind to us. And I know they're preachers—but I'm afraid. There's something . . . something savage about them." She looked up at him, her eyes huge in her delicate face. "Matt, let's go. Now. I don't want to spend another night here. They're getting drunk, and they're getting . . . *pues* . . . strange!"

Matt glanced out to the edge of the clearing where the horse was tethered, munching grass. Slocum lay in the puddle of shade made by its body. Even with so much food around, the big dog had not ventured near the house.

"All right," he said softly. "What about your things?"

Amalia swallowed. "They're in Susan's bedroom. I'll sneak in and get them, and we can be out of here. The way those people are drinking, they might not even see us go."

"I'll get the saddle. It'd be in the woodshed," Matt said. Aye, she was right. These were strange people, preachers or not, and now that he and Amalia were married it might be best to be out of here.

Amalia had been gone for only a minute and Matt was on his way to the woodshed when he heard the sound of raised voices.

"Leavin' li'l lady? Why that won't do. Fun jest started, an' we ain't had no dancin' yet!" It was the big preacher, his voice a whiskey-tinged growl.

"Lawse, Micah, we ain't got no music!" The little preacher whined.

"Well, sing somethin' then! I'm gonna have me a dance with the bride!" He came out onto the porch, swinging Amalia by the hand, her eyes were wide and frightened.

In three long strides, Matt was on the porch. "Beggin' your pardon, but I ain't danced with her myself. She bein' my wife, it's only fittin' that I ought t' have the first dance." He caught Amalia about the waist and snatched her away from the big preacher. The little preacher had begun to whistle, a tuneless sound, but the clapping of his hands along with it at least made a rhythm. Matt danced Amalia once around the porch conscious of the strain in the air. He stopped in front of the big preacher. "Ye been right kind to us. But it's time we were headin' on up the Trace. We'd like to

350

make a few miles afore dark."

The big preacher's bushy eyebrows lifted. "Why, ye cain't go yet. Fun's jest beginnin'! An' ye cain't spend your weddin' night on the Trace. Lord's mercy, ye could be stabbed in your sleep by some o' the riff raff what's out there!" His eyes narrowed as he leaned closer to Matt. "Why the Harpe brothers was seen in these parts jest a few days ago. We cain't turn ye loose with dark jest a few hours off. Ye can have Susan's an' my room for the night—that is—" He gave Matt a wink. "That is if ye need t' be alone."

Matt glanced down at Amalia. She shot him a pleading look. No, she didn't want to spend another night in that cabin, not even in a separate bedroom, and neither did he. Not with so many smells and sounds, and so many curious eyes and ears. "We'll stay, thank ye," he said quickly, "But only if ye'll let us make up a bed in the woodshed. It was right comfortable for me last night. Besides, Amalia was too hot in the cabin."

"Oh, *si!* It would please me!" Amalia put in quickly.

"Then, with that settled, let's git back t' the dancin'!" He grabbed Amalia around the waist and began to spin around the porch with her while the little preacher whistled and clapped. Amalia endured it, her face taut with anxiety.

Betsey grabbed Matt. "Come on, sweetie! Let's you an' me show 'em!" She seized his wrist and clapped his hand onto her waist. She was a strong dancer, full of bounce and life, her head thrown back, her hips bobbing with the rhythm of the clapping. If she'd been a regular girl, Matt told himself, and if this had been a regular dance, he might have enjoyed dancing with her. But the whole afternoon had taken on the face of some strange dream—the whiskey-swigging preachers, and their women, the heat, the flies, the food, the thin whistling and sharp clapping of the small preacher.

The makeshift music stopped now, and the whistler stepped out onto the floor. "I want t' dance with her!" he declared. "Your turn t' whistle." He took Amalia's hands. His brother leaned against a support pole of the porch and began not to whistle, but to sing, something that sounded like an Indian war chant. He had a powerful voice, and he sang it punctuated with little yelps and grunts that sounded so Indian they almost made Matt's scalp tingle.

"We lived with the Injuns for a spell. Bunch o' Cherokees, they were. Stayed with 'em nigh onto two years. Picked up a few o' their ways, I reckon. My brother, now, he's a right good singer. Knows all the Injun songs!" The little preacher stopped dancing with Amalia long enough to explain. "Good man with a tomahawk, too." Something glittered in the depths of his small, black eyes, and Matt felt a swift chill pass down his back. Aye, he had to get Amalia out of here. Tonight, as soon as the place was quiet, they'd go. They were queer ducks, these preachers. Maybe even dangerous. It might not be wise to provoke them, he told himself.

"I'd like to claim my wife if ye'd be so kind," he said politely but firmly, taking Amalia's hand. "She's had a long day and she's tuckered out." He bowed informally to Betsey, who he'd left standing at the edge of the makeshift dance floor. "We'll just sit an' rest ourselves," he said. "Ye can show us your dancin'."

The little preacher whooped like a Cherokee and grabbed Betsy's two hands. He began to swing her around and around, faster and faster, until they both were dizzy and weak with hilarity. Amalia's hand clung to Matt's. "Don't worry, I won't let ye go," he whispered. "Soon's as it's dark and they all bed down, we'll be leavin' this place."

Amalia gazed up at him frightened but trusting. You'll protect me, I know, her eyes seemed to say, and Matt felt his heart swell.

The merriment lasted till dusk. By then the two preachers and the three women were soundly drunk. Good, Matt told himself. They'd at least sleep soundly.

His heart drummed as he smoothed the wood chips and spread the blanket over them for himself and Amalia. No, it wasn't much of a bed for their wedding night. But at least they'd be alone, out in the fresh air. He had even tied Slocum up near the horse, in the shelter of some bushes. They'd rest for a while, he'd decided. Then when it was very late and everyone in the house was asleep, he and Amalia would make their escape. It was a funny thought—escaping from their hosts. But he had come to think of it as an escape. He had to get the girl out of this place, and soon. Something about the way the big preacher had looked at her, something else about the way the little preacher had held her when they danced, bothered him. Preacher folk or not, there was something very odd about these people.

A lamp was still burning in the house. "Come on, love." Matt made room for Amalia beside him on the blanket. She had changed her clothes in the darkness of the shed and was wearing the ragged shirt and breeches again. She lay down beside him, soft and warm and trusting as a child.

"Amalia—" He kissed her gently, slowly, again and again. She whimpered like a small animal. Her arms crept around his neck.

"Matt—"

"Yes, love?" He knew that she was thinking. It hadn't been much of a wedding for her. Not even a priest of her own faith to say the words over them.

"Do you think we're really married?"

"What?" He had been pleasantly drowsy, but her words shocked him into total wakefulness.

"Those men. Just because they say they're preachers—"

Aye, he knew what she meant. He had been dodging the truth all afternoon. Those wild brothers acted like no preachers he had ever met in his life. "We got no way of knowin' that," he said, still not wanting to face it. He had been wanting her all day, and now she lay beside him, so near that he could feel the curves of her body through his clothes. "We took our vows, Amalia," he said. "An' we meant 'em, didn't we?"

"*Sí*," she murmured, her breath warm against his neck where his shirt collar opened. "But Matt—"

"On the frontier, when a boy an' girl want to get married an' there ain't no preacher or judge t' be had, they just say their own words. Then whenever a preacher comes by, he marries 'em legal an' proper. Ain't no sin in that, Amalia." His hand traced its way down her slim back, tingling at the warmth of her skin through the thin shirt. She sighed her pleasure.

"I know ye'd have wanted a priest t' marry us," Matt went on, conscious of the blood surging through his body. Aye, she had him going now. "Who's t' give any man the right t' make two people man and wife? Whether that big preacher got the right or not, we still said the words, you an' me." He leaned over and kissed her mouth, gently at first, then with a passion that grew in its intensity until he wanted to devour her with kisses.

"Matt—" She had caught his fire. Her arms went around his neck, pulling him down to her. Her fingers wound in his hair. Her lips opened eagerly, and her whole body began to quiver with desire.

No, there was no stopping it. Not now. Matt's hands unfastened her shirt and breeches, to find the silken warmth of her flesh. His own clothes— they were gone, somehow, almost without his being aware of having taken them off. He kissed her

355

face, her throat, her small, perfect breasts, until she moaned with pleasure. Her hands moved up and down his bare back. He felt her skin, warm and bare against his own. Then, in the next moment he became part of her, the joining as natural as if their bodies had been fashioned purposely for each other. She gave one soft, little cry. Then the madness took them both, catching them up in its wild, overpowering sweetness. No, it was nothing like it had been with Yvonne. This time there was love. This time there was commitment. This time it was more wonderful than anything Matt had ever experienced.

When it was over they lay in each other's arms, limp with happiness. "We be man and wife, Amalia," Matt whispered against the damp tangle of her hair. "Ain't nothin' that'll ever change it now."

"No," she murmured, her voice trembling. "Nothing. *Nada, mi amor.*" She sighed and snuggled closer to him. He ran one hand along the curve of her hip.

"The lights are out in the house, love. Let's make sure they all be asleep. Then we'll take the horse an' get out of here."

"*Si* . . . yes, I'm frightened of them Matt. I don't know why, but there's something wild about them."

"When we get t' Nashville, we can be married again if it'll make ye feel better, maybe even by a priest."

"Yes. That would make me happy. Come on. Let's go."

356

"Best we wait a spell," Matt cautioned. "Give 'em time t' get to sleep for sure. Then we'll go." He pulled her into the half-circle of his body again. They lay there in the darkness, enjoying each other's nearness. Amalia closed her eyes. Her black hair was spread like a net over Matt's arm and shoulder. He kissed one fragrant lock of it. Aye, but he was happy. For all the worry, all the anger of getting himself and Amalia over what was left of the Trace, he had never been so happy in his entire life.

His mind began to wander. He remembered the dance in Nashville, the one where he'd sparked Carrie Buchanan. Carrie was a toad compared to Amalia, but what a night it had been. He remembered Andrew and Rachel Jackson. He remembered how Slocum had hidden under the table and popped his head out to steal corn dodgers. And he remembered, at last, John Swaney. Maybe Swaney'd be riding down the Trace right now. Maybe they'd meet him.

Matt yawned and shifted his arm under Amalia's head. A breeze had sprung up, cooling their sweat-dampened bodies. Something was bothering him, in the back of his mind. Something he couldn't quite bring into focus. Was it something about John Swaney . . . something Swaney had said? What was it? Two men, one big, one little . . .

He sat bolt upright, spilling Amalia's head onto the blanket. "We got t' get out of here," he said, trying unsuccessfully to keep the fear out of his

357

voice. "Get dressed, Amalia. And don't make any noise."

She got up quietly and began to pull her clothes back on. Matt did the same, his heart drumming in his ears. They'd played a game, those two so-called preachers with their dirty suits and their strange, wild womenfolk. Aye, he knew now where they'd gotten those preacher garbs. More than likely they'd murdered for them.

"Hurry, Amalia," he whispered.

"I'm ready," she said softly. "Matt, what is it?"

"It's all right," he said, not wanting to frighten her any more than he had to. "Come on."

He gathered up the blanket while Amalia twisted her hair up and tucked it under the old hat. The cabin was quiet, with no light coming through the chinks in the log walls. Matt could only pray that everyone inside had passed into drunken slumber.

They stole across the clearing to where the horse was tied. Slocum sprang up from under the bush, growling softly. Then when he recognized his master, his tail began to wag.

Matt had saddled the horse and was just tightening the cinch when the dog growled again, a loud, sudden sound.

"Hush, now, boy. What is it?" Matt strained his ears, but he could hear only the crickets in the underbrush.

Slocum growled again, snarling and showing his long fangs. Amalia clutched at Matt's arm as two men stepped out of the shadows. It was the big preacher and the little preacher, only this time they didn't look much like preachers any more. They were wearing greasy buckskins. The little man carried a rifle. The big preacher carried a heavy, flat-bladed ax.

"An' where might ye be goin'?" the big man spoke up. "We told ye, it ain't safe out on the Trace after dark. 'Sides, we wanted t' send ye off proper like after breakfast."

Matt couldn't answer. His chest was too tight with panic. The little preacher knew it, too. He was grinning, enjoying the fear.

"Brother Micah," he said. "Something tells me these young'uns figgered somethin' out fer themselves. Seems they think they's too good fer us. Maybe it'd impress 'em some if'n we told 'em our real names." He glanced at his tall companion.

"Aye. Go ahead, then." The big preacher smiled. He had long, yellow teeth that gave him a wolfish look. In the moonlight he looked like the devil incarnate. How, Matt wondered, could he have ever been fool enough to believe these two were preachers? How, unless he'd wanted so badly to believe it?

"Wiley Harpe's the name," said the little preacher. "An' this be brother, Micah Harpe." He grinned. "Reckon ye've heard of us."

# XXIV

Slocum snarled again, then lunged for the smaller of the two outlaws. But Little Harpe had dealt with dogs before. One boot shot out and caught Slocum with a crushing kick in the ribs. The dog yelped and rolled backward.

"Run, Amalia!" Matt tried to take advantage of the confusion. He seized her arm and broke past the two men. But Little Harpe's swift foot came into play again, tripping him deftly. As he fell, Big Harpe grabbed Amalia's wrist with a hand that was as big as a bear paw and strong as an iron vise.

Little Harpe's rifle jabbed Matt in the neck. "Stand up," the outlaw ordered. "Don't be as stupid as that ugly hound." Slocum was cowering in the grass, his black lips pulled back in a snarl. The kick had clearly hurt him, maybe broken a rib or two. Big Harpe, still holding Amalia with one hand, glared down at the dog, lifted the huge ax, and let it fall.

"No!" Matt shouted. But it was Amalia who twisted her body enough to swing around and collide with Big Harpe's arm. Slocum jumped to one side. The ax, which would have hit him, except for Amalia, buried its head in the ground. Big Harpe cursed and wrenched out the ax. "Git, Slocum!" Matt shouted. "Git out o' here!"

Big Harpe was raising the ax again. Slocum shot Matt one desperate, loving look. Then, for once, he obeyed. He streaked for the trees and disappeared. Matt heard the sound of thrashing bushes. Then the noise died into silence.

Little Harpe jabbed Matt hard with the rifle. "I got ye covered," he said. "Now, little gal, hand us over that bag. Let's see what ye got." When Amalia clutched at her valise, he snatched it away from her. "We had our fun with ye young'uns. Our womenfolk ain't had such a good time since last summer. But the funnin's over now. Give us what ye got, an' then we'll be thinkin' on what t' do with ye." He opened the valise and dumped its contents onto the ground. The moonlight glittered on the amethyst earrings and on what was left of the coins.

"Not bad . . ." Little Harpe muttered. Then he picked up something that had rolled into the grass. It was a ruby ring, the one Amalia had received from her mother.

"No! Not that!" Amalia protested. "You can't take that!"

Big Harpe raised one hand and brought it slanting downward across Amalia's face with a resounding slap. The muzzle of Little Harpe's rifle stopped Matt when he lunged to help her. "We'll be takin' what we want," the big man growled. "An' we don't take no orders from no high falutin' gal!"

The blow had staggered Amalia, and stung her. She stumbled backward, regained her balance, and stood glaring at Big Harpe. Her cheek was fiery red where he had slapped her. Matt strained against the muzzle of Little Harpe's rifle. He remembered the sight of the Carter family back on the Cumberland. He remembered the stories he'd heard—bodies disemboweled and filled with sand so they'd sink in the river. Cruel, senseless, bloody murders. These men were maniacs, wild beasts who killed for the lust of it. Whatever it cost him, Matt swore, he had to save Amalia.

"Ye got anything else?" Big Harpe had taken the valise from his brother, inspected its inner seams and linings, and thrown it disgustedly on the ground. "The two of ye ain't much of a prize, I'll tell ye that! Well, at least we'll have a good time figgerin' out what t' do with ye—eh, brother?"

Little Harpe jammed the barrel of the rifle hard against Matt's ribs. "Aye. Right pretty li'l gal ye got there, boy. Reckon she'd make sweet lovin'. How would ye like to watch while we both have a turn at 'er, eh? Then we'll cut out yer gizzard!"

Matt lunged for him, knocking the rifle aside, but Big Harpe was quicker. The flat of the ax blade caught Matt in the side of the head, knocking him down. He lay sprawled on the ground, his ears ringing, his eyes seeing little explosions of light.

But the blow, at least, knocked some sense into him. No, he told his spinning mind. He could never hope to outfight these two monsters. They were wise to every trick, and they killed at whim. If he and Amalia were to live, Matt told himself, he would have to use his wits.

"Listen t' me," he said, getting up slowly to keep them from jumping him again. "Amalia an' me, we ain't got much with us, but ye'd be fools t' kill us. Amalia's pa, he's one of the richest men in Natchez—*Don* Esteban Montoya. Maybe ye know the name. An' my family, they have a tradin' business on the rivers. Forny and Cooper. Maybe ye've heard o' them, too. Our families, they'd pay a good sum t' get us back safe. Ye could go off an' live like kings somewhere."

Big Harpe scratched his head and spat in the dirt. "Don't traffic much with the Spanish. Never heard o' no Montoya. But I heard o' Forny an' Cooper, all right. Up on the Ohio, an' up Nashville way."

"I heerd o' Montoya in Natchez." Little Harpe had the rifle on Matt once more. "But we ain't never done no kidnappin' for ransom. Too damned risky, I say. Let's have our fun with these two an' be done with it!"

The women had come out of the house by now. Betsey took the amethyst necklace from Big Harpe and held it up. The purple stones sparkled in the moonlight.

"Ain't never seen nothin' so purty in my life!" she said. "I want this 'un. An' neither of ye ain't gonna get nothin' from me fer a long time less'n I get it!" She pinched Big Harpe's cheek, then waltzed over and tweaked Little Harpe's ear, her lips twitching seductively. Then she looked at Matt and giggled. So that was it. Susan was Big Harpe's woman. Sally was Little Harpe's woman. And Betsey belonged to both of them. Or maybe both men belonged to Betsey, Matt thought, as he watched her fasten the necklace around her tawny throat. "How does it look?" she asked her sister Susan. Susan, shapeless as a board under her flannel nightgown, only stared sullenly at her.

Amalia stood beside Big Harpe, one of his huge hands gripping both her wrists. She had been silent since he'd struck her, but now she raised her head and spoke. "I have plenty of those things at home," she said, looking at Susan and Betsey. "I have enough to deck all three of you out like queens. In a box I have a set of combs inlaid with tigereye that would be beautiful in your hair, Susan. And there are ruby earbobs that hang all the way to my shoulders. And emeralds, Sally. They'd be just your color. If only I had them here, I'd give you all of them." She tossed her head, flinging her hair out of her eyes. "I've got gowns, too," she said. "Belgian lace and Chinese silk. Velvet from France, and a cape trimmed with Russian sable. What a pity I didn't bring them." She glanced at the faces of the three women. "My father would send them to you, anywhere you like, if I were released safely."

She looked at the two Harpe brothers, her defiant spirit blazing in her eyes. "And Matt's family trades in guns and whiskey," she said. "In powder and lead . . . in blankets and saddles and new leather boots. Oh, you'd be fools to kill us now, when our families could make you rich!"

Susan grunted, unimpressed. "Foolishness, all o' it! Damned fol de rol! An' she be lyin' t' boot, most likely. Even if she ain't, we ain't never held nobody for ransom. We done had our fun, Micah. Kill 'em, get rid of the bodies, an' be done with it!"

But Betsey fingered the necklace where it lay around her throat. Her eyes were wistful. Sally, too, was gazing at it. Her hand reached out to touch one of the stones.

Betsey tossed her hair. "What be the harm in thinkin' it over? We can tie 'em up good an' tight. Tomorrow's soon 'nough to decide what t' do with 'em."

"Guns an' whiskey . . ." Big Harpe licked his lips. "That don't sound too bad. Might be worth thinkin' on, all right."

"Risky, if'n ye ask me," said Little Harpe. "But I reckon it won't hurt t' think on it. Let's git the rawhide, then, an' tie 'em up in the cabin." He stared at Matt. Wildness showed in his eyes. "If'n ye know who we be, ye know what we can do t' ye, an' to the lady" he said. "No tricks, now." He poked Matt's ribs with the gun muzzle again.

Matt and Amalia were marched into the cabin. Their hands and feet were bound with rawhide thongs. Then their arms were raised above their heads, the rawhide looped over metal hooks that were imbedded in the support poles of the cabin—Matt in one corner, Amalia in another. The tears came to Matt's eyes when he looked at her. He was uncomfortable enough himself, but her own small feet barely reached the floor. She had to stand on tiptoe to ease the wrenching strain on her arm sockets. "Let her down, at least," he pleaded with Big Harpe. "Leastwise tie her so she'll not hurt. What can she do?" But the big outlaw only turned away and spat into the fireplace.

"Gag 'em," he said. "Then, let's get some sleep."

Matt fought his rawhide bonds as Little Harpe approached Amalia, stuffed a dirty kitchen rag in her mouth, and jerked a handkerchief tight around the lower part of her face. Little Harpe's hand slid deliberately up under her shirt and fondled her breasts. She thrashed and moaned helplessly behind her gag.

"Why you dirty—" Matt's own words were interrupted by Big Harpe, stuffing a greasy hunk of cloth into his mouth and tying it shut. He was helpless as a trussed-up pig waiting to be slaughtered—and so was Amalia.

Sally Harpe glared at her husband. "Now, that's enough Wiley," she said waspishly. Little Harpe took his hand out of Amalia's shirt, but his eyes were wild with lust. Sally edged him toward the bedroom. "Betsey, she be one thing," Matt heard her say. ""But this'un, she ain't family. So no foolin' around with her, y' hear me?"

Little Harpe's answer was lost somewhere in

the recesses of the bedroom. Big Harpe blew out the lamp and followed Susan up into the loft overhead. Betsey's bed was in the main room of the cabin, over in one corner. In the darkness, Matt could hear the sound of her nursing her baby. Then, for a time, all was quiet, except for the sound of Amalia's painful breathing in the darkness.

Matt's head ached, and the taste of the greasy rag was nauseating in his mouth. He wondered what had happened to Slocum. Maybe with luck the dog would make it all the way back to the main path of the Trace. Maybe someone would find him.

But Matt's main concern was for Amalia. He had brought her to this, with his eagerness to see them married. By this time tomorrow night they'd both likely be dead. And who'd even dare to say what kind of pain and horror they'd be put through before that happened? Aye, it would have been kinder in a way if the Harpes had killed both of them outside tonight.

Matt blinked to clear his head. His ears were still ringing from Big Harpe's ax blow, and he was feeling a touch of the dizziness that had plagued him on and off since New Orleans. He could hear Amalia in the other corner of the cabin, her breath coming in little gasping sobs. He had to save her. That above all. And this time it was up to him. There would be no Kovalenko or Mike Fink to come to his rescue. He had nothing to depend on but his own strength, his own resources. Somehow, he would have to find a way to save her.

Edward Forny leaned forward in the saddle as his horse leaped a stream, his body one with the little roan's flowing movement. "Good girl, Fanny." He patted the filly's neck and silently thanked Slade again for the loan of her.

John Swaney galloped ahead along the moonlit trail, a tough, taciturn figure on his bony little horse. After a week on the Trace, Edward stood in awe of the man. Swaney knew every pebble on the trail, every log, every Indian encampment for miles around. So respected was he that even outlaws left him alone. He meddled in no one's business, and expected no meddling in his, which was nothing more or less than the safe passage of mail and dispatches down the Trace.

They had kept up an astounding pace, covering an average of fifty miles a day, sometimes more. When they slept, they slept in the open now, rifles loaded and ready for trouble. This country was pure wilderness, with no white settlers for a hundred miles in either direction.

"The Injuns in these parts is fine folks," Swaney had told Edward in one of his rare talkative moments. "Choctaws and Chickasaws. Ain't no better. Never hurt nobody. Why, the worst words in the whole Chickasaw language is 'skena' and 'pulla'. Bad, an' mean. They cain't say nothin worse. Don't even know how. Nay, it be the white men 'long this part o' the Trace what gives human beings a bad name!"

Edward had half-expected to find outlaws popping out from behind every tree, but they'd seen none. The nights had been quiet, the days long and arduous. They'd passed the points called French Camp Pigeon Roost, and Doak's Stand, which were little more than watering places. Now they were within 150 miles of Natchez—three days at Swaney's trail pounding pace. In one way it would be a relief to have the journey over with. But Edward had found no sign of Matt, and the few white travelers they'd met had not seen the boy. Edward had strongly expected to meet him somewhere along the Trace. It was high time for Matt to be headed back home. What had happened to him?

Swaney pulled up his horse before a weathered lean-to. "We'll be holin' up here till morning," he said, dismounting. "Git yourself some rest."

They fed the horses and lay down under the shelter. Edward slapped at a buzzing mosquito, pulled the blanket up to his shoulders, and closed his eyes. *Peste!* Why couldn't he sleep? Visions of Matt kept swimming through his head. Matt, in trouble, in danger, maybe dead somewhere along the Trace. *Mon Dieu,* it could be they had even passed his grave, or his body, somewhere along the way. Restless, he turned over and adjusted the blanket again. Another vision swept through his mind—the Carter cabin on the Cumberland; the blood; the flies; the butchered bodies he and Matt had buried. There were men out there somewhere who would do a thing like that—monsters in human form. And he had not found Matt.

Swaney had already fallen asleep, but Edward lay awake, staring for hours into the night.

Something was stirring in the cabin. Matt could see nothing in the darkness, except the patterns on the floor where the moonlight came through the chinks in the logs. At first there had been no sound except Amalia's soft, labored breathing from the other corner. But now he heard something else, and was conscious of movement near him.

"Say, purty boy—" It was Betsey's voice, whispering a few inches from his ear. "Are ye awake?"

Silly question. Matt moaned softly behind the gag.

"Aye, an' I forgot ye couldn't talk." She reached up and untied the kerchief, then pulled the rag out of Matt's mouth. Matt moved his tongue, trying to spit out the awful, greasy dryness in his mouth.

"Thank ye," he whispered, wondering if maybe she had a good heart after all. "Now if ye could do the same for Amalia over there—"

"For *her?*" Betsey laughed. "Why I wouldn't do nothin' for her. She can rot, sweetie. But I wanted t' talk to ye. Talk, an' a few other things . . ." She sidled up close to Matt, and he felt the warm press of her body against his. Matt's hands were tied high above his head, but even through his clothes he could tell she was naked. She stretched on tiptoe, and her lips found his. Her

371

mouth was warm, wet and open, her tongue darting in and out like a snake's. Something began to turn in Matt's mind. Aye, if he had one chance to save himself and Amalia, it could well be Betsey. He let himself respond just a little, enough to tantalize her. She moaned. Her hands slid up and around his neck.

"Cut me loose an' I'll kiss ye proper," he said, wondering if Amalia could hear him across the room. Somehow he hoped she would understand.

Betsey giggled. "Cut ye loose? Why, Big Harpe'd have my hide for that! 'Sides, ye ain't doin' such a bad job o' kissin' as it is!" She pressed her mouth onto his, nibbling at his lower lip and making little hungry noises. Her mouth moved down to his neck; her hands unbuttoned his shirt till it fell open to the waist. "There . . . how's that?" Her arms slid around him, and she pressed her bare breasts against his chest. Slowly, sinuously, she began to twitch and wiggle, rubbing his body with hers. Incredibly, in spite of his fear and his agonizing discomfort, Matt felt his blood began to stir.

"Damn it, woman, cut me loose," he muttered, letting himself respond to her frantic, nibbling kisses. "Cut me loose and let's do it right!"

"No—" she murmured against his mouth. Her hands snaked downward to his waist and began to undo the buttons on his breeches. "Aye, ye be jist as much a man as I thought ye'd be! Look at ye!"

Matt hung there, in an agony of discomfort, while Betsey admired his manhood, inspecting, exclaiming. It was a wonder to him that there was anything there for her to admire. But there was. Nature played strange games.

Betsey was breathing hard now. She kissed Matt, straining upward against him, clearly wanting one thing and one thing only. "I got t' have ye," she moaned. "Cuss it, I jist got t' have ye."

"Then cut me loose."

She shook her head again. "I could pull a bench over—but somebody'd hear. Wiley an' Sally, they be jist in the next room, and Sally's got ears like a fox!" She flung her arms around Matt's neck, pulling herself upward. The strain of her added weight on his arms and hands was excruciating.

"No—" he gasped. Betsey let go and dropped back to the dirt floor. "Damn it, cut me down!" Matt said.

Betsey was silent for a moment, weighing things, perhaps. "Ye'll get away," she said peevishly.

"Maybe, would it matter?"

Betsey glanced toward the opposite corner of the cabin where Amalia was tied. "What 'bout her?"

"D'ye think I'd go off an' leave her here?" Matt said truthfully.

Betsey was silent again. "No," she said at last. "I ain't that big a fool. I want ye, purty boy. But ye'd git away, both o' ye. An Big Harpe, he'd skin me alive!" She shuddered. "I ain't just funnin' bout that neither! I saw him do it once to a woman what crossed him!" She kissed Matt, lingeringly, her hands moving up and down the length of his body.

"Come with us," Matt whispered. "Ye don't have t' stay with him."

"If I could have ye, purty boy, I might jist do that." she looked over in Amalia's direction again. "But I know better."

She buttoned up Matt's shirt and breeches again. Then she kissed him one more time and moved away. Matt heard the boards creak as she got into bed. Her baby began to whimper, then to suck and smack as she put it to her breast.

After a few minutes, there was no more sound in the cabin.

# XXV

It was getting light now. Pale gray light was beginning to filter through the chinks in the cabin walls. Matt could make out Amalia's small form in the distant corner, and see the bed where Betsey still slept.

His arms were numb, and his mouth tasted like rancid grease, even though the gag was gone. How much worse it must be for Amalia, he thought, fragile as she was. She would have been in terrible pain all night, unless—The thought almost made Matt's heart stop. Maybe the ordeal had been too much for her. He strained his eyes to see her in the dim light. "Amalia!" he whispered, as loudly as he dared.

In answer, she moved. Her head rolled back and forth. Her body stained at the rawhide bonds, and that was all. He thought of her in his arms less than twelve hours ago, sweet, warm and willing. He thought of her exquisite body, and he ached for her.

"Don't be afraid, Amalia," he whispered across the stillness. "I'll find a way t' save ye." He saw her head move again. She could do nothing else.

Matt strained at the hook. It was firmly imbedded in the wood, as he knew it was from having tried most of the night to loosen it. And it was too high for him to stretch up and lift his hands off. He had tried that, too.

Someone was stirring in the bedroom. Little Harpe came out, yawning and scratching the dark stubble on his chin. He was wearing nothing but a dirty-looking breechclout that covered no more than the bare necessities and showed a body that was spare, hard, and nicked with knife scars. It was an ugly body, pot-bellied in spite of its leanness, and bandy-legged. "Mornin' little gal." He walked over to where Amalia was tied and removed her gag. "How'd you sleep, eh?" He plastered a wet kiss on her mouth. Amalia wrenched her head away. "*Cabron!*" she hissed. "You dirty old he-goat!"

He snaked his hand up her shirt and laughed while she writhed with indignation. "From the first look I took at ye, gal, I knowed ye was too purty t' be a boy!" He had begun to undo the fastening of her breeches, but just then Sally came wandering out of the bedroom, her baby over her shoulder.

"Wiley, what did I tell ye?" she snapped. Little Harpe withdrew his hand and sauntered back into the bedroom. By the time he came out a few minutes later, Betsey was awake, and Big Harpe, with Susan, had come downstairs.

Big Harpe cleared his throat and spat into the fireplace. "I done some thinkin'," he announced, and the others turned to listen. "These two young'uns might have rich families, an' we might could get rich by holdin' 'em for ransom. But we ain't never done that afore. We got prices on our heads, all o' us, even the womenfolk. Seems t' me it'd be too risky t' try it. Me, I'd rather be poor an' alive than rich an' hung."

376

The others gazed at him and nodded slowly. Matt felt his heart sink. Their best chance for survival had just flown away.

"If we be all agreed," Big Harpe growled, "let's take these two young'uns out in the yard an' finish 'em off, eh? Can't afford t' have 'em live an' tell tales."

Little Harpe tugged at his brother's arm. "Listen, Micah, I want my chance with the little bride afore we take care o' her."

"Be damn fast about it," Big Harpe growled. "Haul 'er down an' take 'er in the bedroom in there."

Little Harpe advanced toward Amalia with a grin on his face.

"Devil! Ye damn, dirty devil!" Matt thrashed against the hook that held his arms fast.

Little Harpe laughed. "Now, ye had a taste o' her last night, an' I know it, boy, even if ye wasn't really married. Only fittin' that I should get a sample this mornin'." He reached for Amalia to lift her arms off the hook, but Sally stopped him.

"I told ye, Wiley Harpe, I don't want none o' that foolin' with her!"

"Aww—ye don't mind none when it's with Betsey," Little Harpe whined.

"That's different. Betsey's family. She's one of us. I won't stand for it, Wiley Harpe. Touch that'un an' ye'll be sorry!"

Little Harpe glared at his wife, but he hung back. Sally evidently had some power in the family.

"So what ye gonna do with us? Matt spoke up boldly. "Best ye tell us so we can be ready."

Big Harpe picked his front teeth with his thumbnail. "Ain't rightly decided. We could jist blow your heads off—but that'd be fast, an' not too sportin'. There be the ax. I do purty good work, now, with that ax. There's hangin', too. But I never liked hangin' much. Too much bother."

"Got an idea," Matt said, trying to keep the fear out of his voice. "Ain't as quick as some things, but it'd be more sportin'."

"What'd that be?" Big Harpe raised one bushy black eyebrow.

"Ye could hunt for us," Matt said. "Turn us loose. Together or apart. Don't matter which. Give us a minute's head start, an' then ye come lookin' for us. All o' ye could hunt for us, even the women-folk. The one what finds us could haul us back here, or do whatever they want—" Here Matt glanced over at Betsey and gave her a deliberate wink. Aye, if that didn't put the thought in her mind, nothing would. And with any kind of luck Little Harpe would go along with the plan for a similar reason.

"Sounds like a fool idea t' me," said Big Harpe.

Little Harpe looked Amalia up and down. "Oh, I don't know, Micah. Sounds like fun. Almost as ex-citin' as the weddin' was. I say let's do it!"

"Aye, let's do it," Betsey chimed in, her bold magpie eyes meeting Matt's over Little Harpe's shoulder. "If somebody'd offer t' watch the ba-bies—" She glanced at Susan, but Susan shook her head.

"Ain't had no good shootin' practice for a month. Reckon I'd like t' go along on it." Susan gazed sternly at Sally. "Ye ain't never been much o' a one fer huntin'. S'pose ye watch 'em."

Sally shrugged her shoulders, settling the matter.

378

"Damn foolishness," growled Big Harpe. "What if they get away?"

"Hell, they won't get away. Not from us," Little Harpe grinned, leering at Amalia. Matt could almost see the little outlaw's mind working, thinking of ways to trap her in the woods.

"But don't turn 'em loose together," said Betsey. "More sportin' t' turn 'em loose apart." She gave Matt a lewd wink. Aye, thought Matt, the gamble was working. At least he and Amalia would have a chance to escape instead of being slaughtered there in the yard.

After a quick breakfast of cold turkey and biscuits, washed down with chicory coffee, the Harpes led their captives back out into the yard. Amalia had sobbed with sudden pain when her arms were lowered, but now she was silent, gazing at Matt with huge, fear-filled eyes.

"It's our only chance, Amalia," he whispered to her. "Whatever happens, run. Get away from here. Don't wait for me, an' don't look back!"

Silently she nodded, and he could only pray that she understood. To wait for him could be fatal, for Matt's one aim would be to see that she got away, if he had to take on the whole Harpe family with his bare hands. Matt swallowed hard as he gazed at her, love swelling his heart. He did not expect to live through this ordeal. But if somehow Amalia could get away, that was all that mattered to him.

"We'll let the gal go first," Big Harpe announced. "We count t' twenty an' we come after 'em." He grinned at his brother and the two women. Susan and Betsey were dressed in buckskins like the men, and were armed with long Kentucky rifles. They carried the guns like they knew how to use them.

"Good hunting!" laughed Big Harpe. Then he reached down with his knife and slashed the rawhide thongs that bound Amalia's ankles. Her hands would remain tied. "Run, Amalia!" Matt shouted as Susan began to count.

Amalia ran. At first she was wobbly, but as the circulation returned to her legs, she picked up speed and streaked for the trees. Little Harpe grinned as he watched her go. "I know which way I'm goin,'" he said. Unlike the women, he carried no gun, only a thick bladed knife stuck in his belt. Big Harpe had his ax, newly sharpened.

" . . . Eighteen, nineteen, twenty!" Susan finished counting. Big Harpe cut Matt's legs free and shoved him off at an angle to the direction Amalia had gone. Matt sprinted for the trees. As soon as he was out of sight he changed directions, heading so that, he hoped, his path would cut Amalia off from their pursuers.

He could no longer hear Susan counting, but he could tell by the blood-curdling whoops that she must have reached fifty. Matt dodged his way through the underbrush, hindered by his bound hands. He could not tell where Amalia had gone, but he could already hear the crashing in the brush as the Harpes took up the chase. Some distance off to his left, he could hear a thrashing in the willows. That would be Betsey, most likely. She would have followed the first direction he'd taken, Matt told himself. But then again maybe it was Big Harpe, or Susan. They could have gone either way.

One thing was sure. The swift, rustling footsteps coming toward him now, following Amalia's trail, had to be Little Harpe. He had wanted only one thing: to get Amalia alone. Matt hesitated a moment, calculating the precise direction of the sound. Then he moved toward it, creeping cautiously through the bushes. He held his breath. The rustling was very close now. A figure came into sight through the thick growth. Only it wasn't Little Harpe. It was Susan, her rifle balanced loosely on her shoulder.

Matt cursed his bound hands. If they were free, there might be a chance of overcoming Susan and getting the rifle. But the thongs were so tight they almost cut into his wrists, and there was no time.

Whatever he did, he would have to act fast. Susan, in a way, was the most dangerous of the four pursuers. The brothers, armed with knife and ax, would at least have to kill at close range. And Betsey, if nothing else, might be affected by her desire for Matt.

Matt glanced swiftly around him. Some dead limbs lay on the ground nearby, one of them close to the right size for a club. With his bound hands he seized it, and at the same time picked up a small rock. Then slowly, silently as he could, he began to inch toward Susan.

When he had come as close as he dared, Matt put the club down, positioned the rock in his fingers, and tossed it as well as he could, into the trees on the other side of her. Susan, alert and rangy as a coonhound, turned in the direction of the noise and raised her rifle.

Matt picked that instant to strike. Leaping up behind her, he brought the club down on the back of her head. Susan gasped and crumpled, dropping

381

the rifle. She lay on the fallen leaves, unconscious, but breathing evenly. There was a small skinning knife in her belt, the kind used on squirrels and rabbits. With some awkwardness, Matt managed to get it out, brace it between his feet, and begin rubbing the rawhide thong against the blade. Now that he had a rifle, it was essential that he get his hands free.

A movement in the bushes froze him where he sat. He was about to roll for cover when Amalia stepped into sight. "Matt!" She ran to him.

"What ye doin' here, Amalia?" he rasped. "I told ye to run! Here—wait!" His own hands came free at that moment. He took the knife and sliced her bonds. Take this—" He thrust the small knife into her hands. "But run! Run, Amalia! Don't look back!" He shoved her away from him. She gave him a stricken look and sprinted off into the trees like a doe.

Matt pulled Susan's unconscious body under a thick bush. Off to his right, he could hear someone else coming, moving fast. He ducked behind a sycamore, and a moment or two later he sighted the hulking form and kinky, dark hair of Big Harpe.

The tall outlaw was striding through the trees in the direction Amalia had taken. The ax swung in balance from one great, hairy hand. He was moving, covering ground fast. At that rate, he'd overtake her in a minute. Curse it, Matt thought, why had she waited for him? Amalia should have gone while she had the chance. Narrowing his eyes, he leveled the rifle at Big Harpe's head. Matt had never killed a man before, but if there was one on the face of the earth that ought to be killed, by damn, it was Big Harpe. His finger tightened on the trigger.

Then something happened, one of those small quirks of fate that can never be explained. At the instant Matt fired, Big Harpe stumbled in a badger hole. The rifle ball grazed his hair, that was all. Big Harpe whirled like a wild animal at the shot, lifted his ax, and made straight for Matt.

There was no time to reload, and little time to run. Big Harpe came like a charging bull, the ax swinging. Matt darted and dodged, but the bushes hemmed him in, and the hulking outlaw was only a few steps behind him, roaring his anger. Matt sprinted frantically behind a tree and tripped over a root, dropping the gun. He fell sprawling, and before he could scramble to his feet, Big Harpe was there, the ax blade swinging downward.

Matt rolled clear of the first blow, and was almost on his feet by the time Big Harpe got the ax up again. But the brambles were thick here. They tore at his clothes and his flesh, holding him. Big Harpe grinned as he raised the ax. This time he would not miss.

Then something hit him from behind, throwing the big outlaw off balance. It was Betsey, scratching and clawing like a wildcat. "He's mine!" she hissed. "I was jist about t' grab him myself!"

"Aye, an' I know what ye'd have grabbed him for!" Big Harpe snarled, raising his hand to slap her.

By the time the blow landed, Matt was gone, running at full speed, heedless of the tearing brambles. He made no effort to be quiet or to hide his trail. If he could lead them away from Amalia's path, that was all that mattered. He could hear them behind him, still arguing, still shouting and swearing at each other. They weren't coming fast, at least. Most likely, Matt thought, they were too busy fighting. Like a streak of jagged lightning he ran away from them. He had a chance! Lord, maybe he was going to do it. The sound of Betsey and Big Harpe arguing was getting farther and farther behind. Matt was just beginning to wonder where Amalia had gone to when he heard a scream, loud and close by.

It was Amalia.

Just after dawn, Edward and John Swaney had passed a group of fifteen men, some of them with families, riding up the Trace. Edward had asked anxiously, and the answer he got was disturbing. No one in the party had seen any sign of Matt.

Edward had ridden on for the past hour, his skin almost crawling with anxiety. After forty years in the wilderness, he was a man who trusted his instincts—and those instincts told him something was terribly wrong. Even the roan seemed nervous, snorting, stamping, resisting the bit. The air itself was oppressive. Hot, damp, and heavy, it hung about him. Even the leaves on the trees seemed to droop. The thick trees and bushes on either side of the Trace had a threatening look about them.

Swaney was whistling, a thing he rarely did. The song had no tune to it. It was nothing but breath and rhythm. Edward was beginning to wish Swaney would stop when he heard a noise in the brambles at the side of the trail.

"What's that?" he asked out loud.

"Don't hear nothin'." Swaney said. "Ye be right

jumpy today."

"*Non*. I heard something, Listen, there it is again—" Edward strained his ears. Yes, there it was again, a low, plaintive whine, like an injured animal might make.

"Come on," said Swaney.

"Go on if you have to. I'll catch up. Just give me a—" Edward's words died in his throat as a massive, ugly yellow head thrust its way out of the brambles. Tired, dirty, and covered with burrs, Slocum limped out onto the Trace.

Edward was out of the saddle at once kneeling in the dirt beside the dog. Slocum's tail thumped wildly on the ground. He licked Edward's hands and face, whining anxiously.

"There, old boy," Edward soothed the dog, though his own heart was pounding with dread. "What is it, eh? Where's Matt? Where's your master?"

Slocum whined, licked Edward's hand again, and chewed on burr that had imbedded itself in his flank. Edward sighed. He had heard tales of heroic dogs bringing aid to their injured or endangered masters. Slocum, it seemed, was not one of those dogs.

Swaney gazed down from his saddle. "There be an off-trail up ahead. Not much more'n a squirrel path, but I know it. Goes t' this ol' homestead that some squatter built an' give up on a few years back. Cabin's still standin', or so they say. T' ain't far. Dog coulda come from there."

Edward sprang back into the saddle. "*Allons-y!* Let's go!"

Swaney had already shot out ahead of him. He

dug his heels into the roan's flanks and followed at a gallop. Slocum, forgetting his injuries, streaked after them.

Matt followed the sound of Amalia's screams. It had to be Little Harpe who had her, and they weren't far away. He ran through the trees, all caution flung aside. Amalia screamed again. Aye, there she was, in the small clearing. He had her on the ground, her breeches ripped open. With one arm and the weight of his body, he was holding her down. His free hand fumbled with the fastenings of his trousers.

"Hush up, gal," he was saying. "I'm gonna give it to ye like no man ever give it to ye afore!"

Matt's charge knocked him off her and sent them both rolling across the clearing. Little Harpe went for his knife, jerking it out of his belt. The wide blade flashed in the sunlight as it jabbed downward. Matt twisted to one side, and it grazed his neck, leaving a thin, red line.

Little Harpe grunted as Matt grabbed his wrist. Matt was strong, but the outlaw knew all the tricks. His knee shot up into Matt's groin with smashing force. Matt gasped and doubled up with pain. Helpless for that instant, he lay on the ground. Little Harpe knelt above him, grinning in triumph. His eyes were wild with blood-lust. He raised the knife high, to give it thrust for the fatal blow. Just then something came singing through the air like a wasp. The small skinning knife struck Little Harpe in the shoulder and buried itself to the hilt in his flesh. He turned and saw Amalia standing there, a few yards way lowering her arm. That was all the time Matt needed. In a flash he was up. His fist crashed into Little Harpe's jaw, sending the outlaw tumbling backward. Little Harpe yowled as he landed on the handle of the small knife, wrenching the blade inside his shoulder. He rolled on the ground yelping with pain.

"Come on! I hear the others!" Matt grabbed Little Harpe's knife with one hand and Amalia's arm with the other. He would not let her out of his sight again, he vowed. But now they could only run. The crashing in the bushes had to be Big Harpe, and maybe Betsey as well.

Amalia had lost her shoes, and her feet were tender. She gasped with pain as she ran over thorns and rocks. Looking back over his shoulder, Matt could see Big Harpe striding after them, the huge ax ready. He pulled Amalia after him, but on her bleeding, bruised feet she could not run fast enough. At last he thrust the knife into his belt and swept her into his arms like a child. She clung to him as he ran, zigzagging, dodging, trying desperately to lose their relentless pursuer. Big Harpe was not fast, but he came on steadily, never slacking his pace. Matt was getting tired. His arms ached with Amalia's weight. Aye, it was only a matter of time before Big Harpe caught up with them. And when he did, they would have no chance against him. Even the broad-bladed knife was a pitiful weapon compared to that monster of an ax.

Matt's legs had begun to ache. His rib cage throbbed from the effort of breathing. His head was beginning to swim with the old dizziness. It was getting worse. The trees were beginning to blur before his eyes. The sunlight was forming yellow ripples in the air, like reflections on water. Amalia was slipping from his arms. He could not hold on. He could not even stand up—

The last thing he remembered hearing, before the whole world went black, was the bark of a dog.

# XXVI

Matt opened his eyes. Slocum was licking his face, whimpering with joy. No, he was dreaming. His grandfather stood over him, and Amalia sat holding his hand.

"Am I . . . am I alive?" he asked shakily.

"*Oui, mon fils,*" Edward Forney grinned. "You found us just in time."

" . . . Big Harpe?" Matt asked. "What has happened to that monster?"

"He got away. When he saw that there were two of us, both with rifles, he turned and ran. We fired at him, but we could not hit him through the trees. A pity. That one I'd like to have killed."

Matt squeezed Amalia's hand. "An' where'd ye learn to throw a knife like that? Ain't never seen nothin' like it!"

Amalia smiled, her eyes sparkling. "Oh, when a girl is not allowed the freedom of the streets, she finds many ways to . . . amuse herself, *no*? Embroidery gets boring after a while."

"Grandpa, this is Amalia—" Matt glanced from one to the other.

"*Oui.* I know. We have already had time to become friends while we tended you." Edward touched Amalia's shoulder.

389

"Amalia and me, we—"

"Yes, I know. She has told me." Edward gazed at his grandson, and Matt thought he saw something in his grandfather's eyes that had not been there before. Edward Forny was looking at him not as a man looks at a boy, but as one man looks at another, as his equal. "We passed a company going up the Trace earlier this morning. It's not too late to catch up with them. One of the men, I chanced to learn, is a preacher—a real one, an ordained minister from Boston. It's up to you."

"What think ye?" Matt gazed up at Amalia. Her glowing eyes told him all he wanted to know.

"And then what?" Edward asked him. "Home to Nashville and Louisville with your bride, eh? Or do you want to go back to Natchez and resolve this mess?"

Matt sat up and rubbed his head. His dizziness was gone. And, he realized, his grandfather was not telling him what to do. No, Edward was *asking* him. It was a big decision, a life and death matter, Matt reminded himself. So many things hung in the balance of it—his own future, Amalia's happiness, even the destiny of Forny & Cooper. And he, Matthew Cooper, was being asked to decide what to do. Aye, maybe this was what it really meant to be a man. It wasn't like coming out the winner in a brawl, holding down your whiskey, or bedding a woman. This was the real test of manhood—making a decision, sticking to it, and living with the consequences.

Matt was silent for a long moment. Danger waited back in Natchez, as well as painful problems and inevitable, angry confrontations. But the future prosperity of Forny & Cooper lay on the Mississippi—and that prosperity depended heavily on the friendship and good will of *Don* Esteban Montoya—Amalia's father. Matt took a deep breath. "First the preacher," he said.

390

"We'll do this right, Amalia and me. Then—back to Natchez."

Andres Santana sat alone at his usual table in the *salon* of Madame Rodare's establishment, sipping a brandy and nursing his hatred. Everything had been going his way until Matthew Cooper'd come along.

As the son of one of Natchez's oldest families, Santana had been able to maintain a fair reputation and prominent social standing. His credit had been good anywhere, and to crown it all, he had won the hand of Montoya's daughter. But since Amalia's elopement everything had gone sour for him.

Who had spread the stories? Santana could not be sure, but little by little it had become common knowledge in Natchez that he had ravished Amalia before their wedding date. It was also a joking matter these days that Santana had been less than swift in running to avenge the Montoya honor, to say nothing of his own, when she had disappeared.

He drained the glass and filled it again. Everywhere he went, he seemed to hear the whispers, the snickers. Invitations to balls and parties had fallen off to a trickle. Store clerks turned their backs on him. No one bought him drinks any more.

He strongly suspected who had started the rumors. Madame Rodare, as Amalia's mother, had both the reason to dislike him and the means of spreading the tales. He had meant to go to her, to confront her with his anger. It wasn't right, after all, that she would turn on such an old and faithful customer. But he had not been allowed to see her. Madame's illness, it seemed, had taken a sudden turn for the worse. Mathilde Rodare, it was whispered in the town, was dying.

Santana took another swallow of brandy, fighting the temptation to crush the crystal glass in his fist. It had been less than an hour since he'd heard the accursed story in the market. That young bastard, Cooper, was back in town. Cooper and his grandfather, a Frenchman named Forny, had gone straight to *Don* Esteban, where they had remained, closeted in *Don* Esteban's library, for the biggest part of a day.

Santana's hand shook with rage as he drained the glass. He simply could not understand it. The night of Amalia's disappearance, *Don* Esteban had been so furious with young Cooper that he'd ordered his guards to castrate the boy on sight. What kind of spell-caster was this Edward Forny? What kind of silver-tongued magician could work such wonders? *Don* Esteban had emerged from the long conference, summoned his business associates, and announced a new, long-term partnership with the trading company, Forny & Cooper. Then—Santana ground his teeth in frustration—*Don* Esteban had formally presented young Matthew Cooper as his son-in-law. *Madre de Dios*, it was more than a man could stand!

He stared down at the damask tablecloth, his blood sizzling with rage. Somehow, he vowed, someday, he would find a way to kill Matt Cooper. Then he would claim Amalia for his own, and all would be saved—his honor, his fortune, everything!

He turned his head slightly as the *salon* door opened. Madame's ugly little butler ushered in three figures. Santana sat up, his fingers gripping the edge of the table. The first of the trio was Matt Cooper, elegant in a new suit of clothes. The second was a small figure, completely covered by a long, hooded cloak. Yes, it had to be Amalia. The third was an older man, lithe, muscular, vigorous. Edward Forny, Santana concluded. It could not be anyone else. The three of them crossed the room and disappeared through the door that led to Madame Rodare's private chambers.

Dizzy with hatred, Santana watched them. Then, when they had gone, he shoved the brandy aside and began to make his plans.

Matt felt Amalia trembling beside him. "It's been so long, Matt," she whispered. "And nobody told me she was so ill. I'm frightened."

"Ain't nothin' to be frightened of." Matt slipped an arm around her shoulder. "She's your ma, and she loves ye. Remember that. It'll mean a lot to her, your comin' like this. I know how much she wanted to see ye, Amalia."

Matt glanced at his grandfather's silent profile as they walked together down the long hallway toward Mathilde Rodare's room. Where was Edward's mind now? He had once made love to this woman. For twenty years he had not set eyes on her. Now she was dying. What would Edward be feeling? Matt wondered as the butler opened the door ahead of them.

The room they entered was dim in the twilight. A single candle flickered on the nightstand beside the bed. It was an opulent room, the windows curtained in blue velvet, and a thick, gold rug on the floor. The bed itself was white, a ruffled canopy suspended from its four tall posters.

Mathilde Rodare had been a stately woman in her prime, a statuesque, ripe-bodied goddess. Now she looked strangely lost in the big bed, a shrunken doll, her head propped up by pillows.

"*Mama . . . ?*" Amalia's hood had fallen back. Timidly she approached the bed.

"Amalia—" Mathilde held out her hand. Her voice was hoarse, her breathing labored from the fluid that filled her lungs. "Let me look at you," she whispered as the fingers clasped. "Ah . . . *tres belle* . . . You are a beautiful woman, my daughter. A beautiful wife,

393

now." She smiled feebly at Matt, who stood just behind his bride. "She is yours now, *mon fils*. Care for her . . . love her." Mathilde's eyes closed for a moment as a wave of pain passed over her. Her eyes lay in pools of shadow. Her cheeks were hollow, the bones prominent, like a skull's. Without make-up she looked old, and very frail.

"Aye," Matt whispered, the tears filling his eyes. "I'll take care of her. Always."

Mathilde's blue eyes, bright with fever, darted about the room. "Edouard . . . ? Edouard, mon amor, is it really you? Or have I already died and gone to heaven? Come closer!"

Edward walked to the side of her bed. For the space of a few long breaths they looked into each other's eyes.

"I wronged you, Edouard," she whispered. "I was so cruel, and you almost killed me for it. I have never forgotten . . . but I always loved you. I—I never really found another man like you."

"*Oui.*" Edward patted her hand. "I have long since forgiven you, Mathilde. We could not be enemies forever, could we, *ma belle?* Neither of us is capable of it."

"Thank you," she breathed. "Oh, *merci*, Edouard . . . *merci.*" Her eyes closed. Her breath bubbled in and out.

The little butler, devoted as a dog, glided forward. "If you will be so kind. Madame must not tire herself—"

"Yes. Yes, of course," Edward murmured, and the three of them allowed themselves to be led out of the room.

They crossed the bustling *salon* in silence, each of them lost in his own thoughts. They had almost reached the door leading to the entry when a voice boomed out behind them.

"Matthew Cooper! You son of a devil, stand and fight!"

Matt turned around. Andres Santana had stood up and stepped away from his table. "Woman-stealer!" Santana rasped. "Dog! I challenge you! Fight me like a man!"

"I accept," Matt answered calmly, though he knew Santana's reputation as the best swordsman and pistol shot in Natchez. Santana, Matt knew, had killed men in duels.

"My challenge," Santana said icily. "Your choice of time, place and weapons. That is the rule, in case you don't know it, you Yankee bumpkin. You *campesino!*"

Matt thought swiftly. "Then I choose bare fists. And I choose here, and now!"

Santana glared at him scornfully. "Bare fists? The sword and pistol are the weapons of a gentleman, *Senor* Cooper."

"Then, by hell, I ain't no gentleman! I be ready t' kill ye for what ye did to Amalia, you bastard. So if ye be a man, fight me now!" He turned to Edward. "Take Amalia back to her father's house, Grandpa."

"*Oui.* As you wish." Edward gazed at his grandson, pride and worry meeting in his eyes. "Watch him, Matt. I know the kind. He'll be a tricky one, and he won't fight fair."

"Matt—" Amalia reached out and clasped his hand. "Be careful—" Then she shook her head. "No, *amor mio.* It isn't worth it. Come with us. Don't fight him."

Matt lifted her hand and pressed it to his cheek. "Best get it over with. Go with Grandpa, now."

He watched her leave, then turned back to the raging Santana. A crowd was already gathering to watch the excitement. "Move the tables back," he said. "We'll have it out here and now."

395

An open space was quickly cleared. "Fists! Peasants fight with their fists!" Santana, protesting, peeled off his coat.

Matt laid his own coat on the back of a chair. Santana was already crouching low, moving closer. Matt darted in fast, taking advantage of the surprise to land a blow that grazed Santana's chin and landed with a crunch on his shoulder. Santana reeled, then swung a wild punch, just missing Matt's chin. Matt moved like lightning. Punching sharply upward, he planted his fist hard at the base of Santana's rib cage. The blow had hurt. Santana grunted. His face reddened with fury. His foot shot up to kick Matt in the groin, but when Matt sidestepped, he missed.

Matt was getting confident now. He'd licked tougher men than Santana. "Come on," he taunted his enemy. "Show me what a man ye be, Santana! Show me what kind of man would spoil his own bride afore the weddin'! Show me what ye be made of!"

Santana swung a wild punch that glanced off Matt's chest. He was still reeling from the blow to his ribs. This wasn't even sporting. "I'm going to put ye to bed!" Matt said. "Ain't much fun, fightin' a drunk."

The crowd that watched had begun to jeer Santana. "*Cobarde!*" "*Mujer!*" they taunted.

"Finish the *borracho!*" someone shouted at Matt.

"Aye," Matt answered calmly. "That's just what I'm about to do."

He caught Santana with three swift, hard jabs to the jaw, and the Spaniard went down, crumpling, like a burning hunk of paper. The crowd cheered.

Winded, beaten and humiliated, Santana glared up at Matt. His hair was mussed, his shirt was lightly flecked with blood, and his jaw was beginning to swell, but Matt had not really done much physical damage.

"I'd beat ye some more," Matt said, contempt filling his eyes and voice. "But ye ain't worth the trouble, Santana." Then he turned and walked away. He knew that he'd hurt Andres Santana worse than if he'd pounded him to a bloody pulp. He had shattered Santana's pride and vanity, and the man would hate him for it. Well, that couldn't be helped, Matt told himself. He'd had enough. Now he only want to join his bride at her father's house.

"Cooper!" Santana spat out the name. "Turn around! Look at me!" Matt turned. Santana's eyes were blazing pure hatred. "Look at me and remember me each time you make love to your wife! Remember that I had her first!" He smiled, his lips pulling back over his teeth like a dog's. "And it wasn't all force. No, she *liked* it, Cooper. I could tell. She wriggled and moaned like a regular little *puta!* Remember that! Remember it every time you make love to her!"

Matt glared at him. The man was cringing like a dog, one hand reaching for something in the top of his boot. He probably wanted Matt to come at him again so he could pull a knife, or try some other trick.

Matt shook his head. "Ye ain't even worth spittin' on, Santana," he said. Then he turned and walked away. The crowd hooted its approval. Aye, Matt reflected, he had put Santana in his place right properly. The son of a devil would never be able to show his face in Natchez again without shame.

Suddenly the jeers of the crowd turned to gasps. Matt, who'd been headed for the door, spun around to see that Andres Santana had risen to his knees. His right arm was flung back; his hand held a long, sharp dagger.

As Santana's arm came forward to hurl the knife, a shot rang out in the room. The Spaniard reeled from the blow of a lead ball. Blood spurted from his neck. The knife clattered harmlessly onto the floor as he fell.

The crowd stared at him as he writhed in the growing pool of blood, shuddered, twitched, and lay still.

Matt looked up. Mathilde Rodare stood in the doorway, a smoking pistol in her hand. Pale as a ghost, she leaned against the door frame and smiled—a ghastly, death's head smile.

"My wedding present to you, *mon fils*. To you, and to Amalia, from a loving mother." Then she collapsed on the floor in a heap of while silk and lace.

The autumn air was deliciously crisp after the heavy heat of summer. Edward inhaled deeply, taking full pleasure. It was a good time for a man to be alive.

Matt and Amalia rode beside him, their eyes and hands meeting from time to time between their two mounts. Once more they were going up the Trace toward Nashville—but this time they were not alone. A company of fifteen men, mostly traders, rode with them. There would be no danger on this journey; only joy. Even Slocum, frisking along behind the horses, had caught their high spirits.

"I heard some news this morning," Edward said, wondering how the two of them would receive it. "Big Harpe is dead. Killed a week ago, up the Trace. It was a man name Steigal who did it, they say. When the Harpes killed his wife and baby, he got up a posse and hunted them down. They shot Big Harpe, wounded him in the spine. And they rounded up the women, too."

"What about Little Harpe?" Matt asked.

"He got away," Edward answered. "Folks think he may have headed West. But nobody expects to see him around these parts again."

Amalia touched Edward's arm. "But you said Big Harpe was dead. If he was only wounded—"

"*Oui*, that is so. But he died . . . later." No,

Edward reflected, he couldn't tell her the truth. Matt had told him only the day before that she was with child. A woman in Amalia's delicate condition should not hear such things. Later he would tell what had really happened. While Big Harpe lay dying, Steigal had taken a butcher knife and hacked off the outlaw's head.

"Let us talk of pleasant things, *eh bien?*" he said. "Let us talk of home, my children. As soon as you arrive in Louisville, we must think of building a house for you. And we must talk with your father, Matt, about your future with the trading company there."

Matt was silent for a moment. "Beggin' your pardon, Grandpa, but I already done some thinkin' on that. If we aim to set up Forny & Cooper on the Mississippi, we'll be needin' somebody to work with Amalia's pa in Natchez. I been thinkin' that somebody could be me. Amalia could be near her pa that way. He'll be lonesome without her . . . and Amalia, I think, would be more at home there."

Slowly Edward nodded. The boy was right. Forny & Cooper did need a representative on the Mississippi, and Matt knew the river better than anyone else in the family. As for Amalia—Edward gazed fondly at his granddaughter-in-law. Amalie was a joy to him. Nothing would have delighted him more than to be surrounded by her, by Matt, and by their children as he grew old. But no, Edward understood. Amalia was bred to the gentle climate and cultured life of Natchez. She would probably never feel at ease in a frontier town like Louisville, Worse—and the thought saddened him—Amalia might never adjust to living around two women who still despised the memory of her mother. They were good women, Abby and Marie, but old hurts died slowly. They would try to accept her, of course. They would try to be kind to her. But each time they looked at Amalia, they would remember Mathilde Rodare—and Amalia would know it.

Mathilde was gone now, her body laid to rest in a grave beneath a magnolia tree in the Montoya plot. Edward allowed his mind to linger on her for a moment, remembering her beauty, her gaiety, her lusty, animal appetites. Then he buried her memory as well. Abby would be waiting for him at home.

"*Vraiment*, you are right, Matt," he said. "It is an excellent idea. I take it then that you and Amalia plan only a visit to Louisville, then?"

"Aye. We'll be heading back down the Trace before cold weather sets in." Matt reached over and squeezed his wife's hand.

Edward smiled as he watched them together. They were a perfect match, these two, like himself and Abby, like Henry and Sara, like Marie and Ned.

A disconcerting thought crossed his mind. Winifred Van Cleve, Matt's yellow-haired sweetheart, would be waiting in Louisville. Poor Winifred, she'd be madder than a wet cat when she found out that Matt was married. But that was Matt's problem, Edward reminded herself. Matt could handle it, he had no doubt of that now. Matt could handle almost anything. He had grown up. The dynasty was in good hands.